BLUE'S BAYOU

CreateSpace ISBN: 1-4663-4081-9

www.bluespikepublishing.com

Printed in the United States of America

To the members of
The Alexander Hamilton Post 448
of the American Legion,
and all the gay men and women
who have served our country.

OTHER BOOKS FROM DAVID LENNON

The Quarter Boys

Echoes

Second Chance

Reckoning
(Available April 2012)

Fierce
(Available April 2013...or sooner)

Author's Notes

I don't always know exactly what a book is about before I start writing. I usually have the mystery mapped out (at least partially), and some of the characters in mind, but it's only after I'm well into it that I start to understand the connective tissue that ties everything together. In *The Quarter Boys*, that tissue was the search for identity. In *Echoes*, it was the reverberations of past events. And in *Second Chance*, it was dealing with transitions. I don't know if anyone else even picks up on these themes, but for me, they're critical. They help guide me.

Blue's Bayou was different, because for the first time I understood what the story was about before I started writing. I'd already had the plot rolling around in my head for months, but a few weeks before I started writing, I got an email from my friend Paul Saltzman. He'd just finished reading *The Quarter Boys*, and wrote, "I'd be interested in meeting Michel as a younger, more conflicted gay man." That idea suddenly unlocked the overall theme that had been lurking in my subconscious. The book is essentially about family: both the families we're given as children (and how they shape us,) and the families we choose as adults. So thank you, Paul. I hope you won't be disappointed.

Speaking of family, we have a dog named Blue. And in this book, I introduce a dog named Blue...who just happens to have warm brown eyes, big ears, spots, and a white star on her chest...just like the Blue who's lying upside down on the chair behind me right now.

I had a number of reasons for basing the fictional Blue on the real one:

1) Although our Blue is from Puerto Rico, she appears to be part Catahoula Leopard Dog, and Catahoulas are the Louisiana State Dog, so that worked.

2) We spend almost all day, every day together, so I know her pretty well.

3) The book is set in a fictional bayou town on the edge of the Atchafalaya Swamp Basin, and *Blue's Bayou* has a catchy (some might even say musical) ring to it.

4) She's my dog, so of course I think she's the most amazing dog ever and deserves to be a star.

That said, I want to make it clear that, although I've blurred the line between fiction and reality by including Blue, Michel is *not* a fictionalized version of me. We may share some traits and experiences (which I won't enumerate), but he's not me...and his childhood was *nothing* like mine. I'm also taller, and a much better dancer.

My thanks to the following sites for information on the culture, wildlife, and history of the Atchafalaya Basin: frenchcreoles.com, eatel.net, covebear.com, audubon.org, lsm.crt.state.la.us, louisiana.gov, lwrri.lsu.edu, basinkeeper.org, and landrystuff.com, and to wikipedia.com and wlt.org for information on land trusts.

Finally, thanks to Esme McTighe, Vion DeCew, Bob Mitchell, my family, and Brian for all your support, encouragement, and other stuff. And, of course, thanks to Blue for allowing me to immortalize her in fiction.

D.L.

BLUE'S BAYOU

A Novel

DAVID LENNON

Chapter 1

Verle Doucette knew he was being stalked. Though he hadn't seen anything moving in almost ten minutes, he could hear the occasional snap of a twig or stirring of leaves through the dense cypress and tupelo forest on his right. The creature was keeping its distance, but always staying abreast of him.

He could see a clearing up ahead in the moonlight and stopped. He knew that was where it would strike, once he was in the open. He closed his eyes and listened. There was a faint rustling just ahead on his right, much closer than before. He took a deep breath and began moving slowly forward again, his senses fully alert.

As he reached the edge of the clearing he stopped again, his eyes searching the tangle of vegetation along the right perimeter. He couldn't see anything moving. He cocked his head and listened. He couldn't hear anything except the steady buzzing of mosquitos and chirping of grasshoppers. He realized he was just going to have to trust his instincts.

He paused another second to ready himself, then jumped into the clearing, landing in a sumo wrestler's crouch in the muddy water, facing to the right.

"Ha," he yelled, ready for the creature to bound out of the darkness at him.

Nothing happened. He slowly straightened up and stared curiously into the forest. A mosquito hovered close to his nose and he absently swatted it away with his left hand.

Suddenly he heard a low growl behind him. He carefully

turned and saw the dog, its head and chest close to the water and its hind quarters raised, ready to pounce. Before Verle could react, the dog lunged forward and jumped up, its muddy front paws hitting him hard in the chest and causing him to stagger back a foot. Then the dog's face moved closer and its long tongue shot out and began to bathe his face.

Verle began to laugh.

"Okay, you got me," he said. "You're the best hunter in the whole wide swamp, Blue."

The dog continued enthusiastically licking his face for another few seconds, her long, bushy tail furiously brushing the surface of the water as Verle rubbed the thick damp scruff of her neck. Then suddenly she stopped and dropped her front legs silently into the dark water. Her nose began to pulsate quickly as she stared into the blackness farther up the trail. Then she bounded away.

"Wait," Verle called, as he saw the dog disappear into the night.

Despite the fact that Blue had lived almost her entire life in the Atchafalaya Basin and was naturally cautious, Verle still worried about her. Though she'd proven herself more than capable of handling herself with the smaller predators that lived in the swamps and bayous, at forty-five pounds she was no match for the Florida Panthers and Louisiana Black Bears that were occasionally spotted there.

Verle unshouldered his shotgun and started after her, his heavy rubber boots slogging through the muddy water. Up ahead he heard Blue begin to bark, and broke into an ungainly run.

"Come here, girl," he called, trying to sound authoritative despite his anxiety and the immediate raggedness of his breathing. "Come on back."

In response, the urgency of the dog's barking increased. Verle stopped for a moment and concentrated. He knew too well that the still, thick waters of the swamp could play tricks with sound. He turned to his left and began running again.

Twenty yards ahead a thick curtain of Spanish moss hung from the branches of a massive live oak, its lowest tendrils nearly touching the water. Blue's barking was clearer and sharper now.

Verle quickened his pace, despite the stabbing pain that had begun along the lower right side of his rib cage.

"I'm coming, girl," he managed to call through heavy, labored breathing.

As he reached the moss he ducked below it, then froze, still in a crouching position. Fifteen feet away, a nude woman lay on a moss-covered hummock at the base of a tree. Blue stood beside her, now silently staring at him.

Verle slowly straightened up and took a few hesitant steps. He could hear his heart beating quickly and loudly in his ears.

"Hello?" he said reflexively, although he already knew the woman wouldn't respond. If Blue's barking hadn't stirred her, his own timid greeting certainly wouldn't.

He stopped again, suddenly unsure that he wasn't dreaming. He'd seen this woman before, lying in that exact position: on her back with her pelvis and legs twisted toward him, her right arm out to her side with the hand resting just above the water, and her left arm draped languidly over her eyes and forehead. It was all so familiar.

Then he remembered where he had seen her before. It was in a painting called "Repos" by Wojciech Gerson that he'd seen at the National Museum in Warsaw many years ago.

"Okay," he said, taking a calming breath. "I'm not losing my mind."

Blue stared at him quizzically.

"It's all right, girl," he said reassuringly as he waded forward.

As he reached the hummock he scratched Blue behind her right ear for a moment, then placed the back of his right hand

3

against the side of the woman's neck. Her skin was cool and damp. Verle slowly withdrew his hand and searched the shadows around them. He couldn't see anyone else.

"I'm sorry," he said to the woman's body.

He stood staring at her for a few minutes as he considered what to do. He knew that if the woman had been killed, he should leave her there and hike the mile back to his truck to radio the police so that they could investigate the scene, but he also knew that before very long the inhabitants of the swamp would find her and there might be nothing left to investigate. Though the alligators had all moved into deeper water for the winter, there were still plenty of carnivores left who would welcome a free meal.

"Looks like we're going to have to carry her out of here," he said to Blue. "But I want you to stay close by me. You can't go running off, okay?"

Blue tilted her head and began to wag her tail. Then she began trotting farther into the woods to their right.

"No, not that way," Verle called.

Blue stopped and cocked her head at him.

"This way," Verle said, pointing to his left.

Blue hesitated for a moment, then came back and started in the direction he'd indicated.

"Good girl," Verle said.

*****

Verle was slick with perspiration and his heart was thumping wildly in his chest. He'd kept his focus by counting the number of mosquitos who had bitten him over the last forty-five minutes.

He'd had to stop four times to rest, and each time the exertion of lifting the woman back onto his shoulders had become more difficult. He hoped he could make it back to the road without having to stop again because he wasn't sure he could manage it again.

In the distance he thought he saw a brief flash of light through the trees. He stared at the spot and waited. The light flashed again.

"Hey! Over here!" he called out. "I need some help."

The light turned in his direction and began to move closer.

Verle let out a deep sigh and dropped to his knees. He lowered his right shoulder and gently laid the woman on the mossy ground.

"It's going to be okay," he said in a hoarse whisper.

The light was moving quickly toward them now. Verle could see it bouncing up and down through the trees.

"Right here," he called out.

Suddenly the fur on Blue's back rose into a pointed tuft and her tail lifted into the air. She let out a deep, low growl.

"It's okay, girl," Verle said. "They're going to help us."

Then the light was on Verle's face, momentarily blinding him. He moved his right hand in front of his eyes to shield them and looked between the fingers. He could just make out the shape of a man wearing a wide, flat-brimmed hat. The man had a pistol pointed at him.

"Don't move!" the man called out.

"Okay, officer," Verle replied quickly, his weariness suddenly gone as adrenaline coursed through his body.

"Now I want you to slowly take that shotgun off your shoulder and place it on the ground in front of you," the State Trooper said.

From the tone of his voice, Verle could tell that he was both young and nervous. Blue emitted another growl.

"Lie down," Verle said tersely.

Out of the corner of his eye he could see the dog settle next to the woman's body.

Verle reached over his right shoulder with his left hand and grabbed the muzzle of the shotgun, then slowly slid the strap off his shoulder and brought the rifle out in front of his body. He lowered it until the butt was resting on the ground, then gently laid it down. Then he straightened up and clasped his hands behind his head.

"Okay," he said in a calming voice. "Now just do me a favor and lower your gun. My dog is very protective of me and I don't want either of you getting hurt."

Chapter 2

"I'd say it's a toss-up," Michel Doucette said as he and his partner Sassy Jones walked into their office. "I wouldn't kick either of them out of bed."

"Me neither," Sassy replied, "but I'd still have to go with Connery. What about you, Chance?"

Chance LeDuc was seated at Sassy's desk, staring at them with a tight-lipped frown.

"What about *what*?" he asked curtly.

"Who would you rather sleep with? Sean Connery or Daniel Craig?" Michel replied.

"Where the fuck have you been?" Chance asked angrily, fixing Michel with a hard stare.

"Wow, looks like there's a new sheriff in town," Sassy said, holding her hands up with mock defensiveness.

It had been three weeks since she and Michel had hired Chance to manage the office of their fledgling private investigation business.

"It's not funny," Chance replied, his tone almost hurt.

"We went to the movies," Michel said. "Is that okay with you? We *are* the bosses, after all."

"No, not when I've been trying to call you for the last hour," Chance replied.

"Oh," Michel replied, slightly chastened. "We turned our phones off when we went in the theater. Guess we forgot to check them when we came out."

Chance just stared at him in response.

"So what's so important?" Michel asked with a shrug.

"Do you have a cousin named Verle Doucette?" Chance asked, his tone suddenly shifting to concern.

"Yeah, why? Did he call?"

"No," Chance replied, then hesitated for a second. "He's in jail."

"Jail?" Michel repeated, surprised. "For what?"

"I don't know," Chance replied. "I got a call from a Sheriff Turner in Bayou Proche, wherever that is. He said he found your number at your cousin's house and thought you ought to know. He said he was going to be out of the office most of the day, but you could call him after 3 PM. Here's his number."

He handed Michel the slip of paper, then added, "He sounded pretty serious."

Michel stared at the paper blankly for a moment, then shook his head.

"Well, it can't be too serious," he said. "Verle's one of the nicest, most gentle people I've ever known."

"So who's this cousin Verle?" Sassy asked with a look of both concern and curiosity.

Michel stared at the paper for another second, then looked up at her.

"Remember a week or two ago you were joking that you were sure I had some rich relatives stashed away somewhere?"

Sassy nodded.

"Well, that would be Verle," Michel replied.

"You have a rich cousin named *Verle?*" Sassy replied skeptically. "No disrespect given that the man's in jail, but that sounds like a hillbilly name if I ever heard one."

"His real name is Verdell Earle," Michel replied, "but everyone's always just called him Verle."

"Oh, that's much less redneck," Sassy replied with a smirk. "So how come I've never heard you talk about him before?"

"I kind of forgot about him," Michel replied guiltily.

"You forgot?" Sassy asked. "How do you forget about someone? Especially when you don't seem to have too many relatives."

"Actually he's the last on the Doucette side," Michel replied. He stared down at the floor for a moment.

"I don't know," he said finally. "I don't have an excuse."

"So I take it you're not close," Sassy said.

"Not anymore," Michel replied thoughtfully. "Not that we had a falling out or anything. But over the years we just kind of lost contact. He sent me a note when my mother died, though I'm still not sure how he found out, but other than that we haven't seen one another or spoken in about ten year."

He stared back at the floor again, lost in thought for a few moments.

"Even though my father left before I was born," he said finally, "my mom thought it was important for me to stay connected with his family, so every summer starting when I was four or five, she'd take me up to Baton Rouge for a week to stay with his brother's family."

"That was very generous of her, given the circumstances," Sassy said.

"Yeah, it was," Michel agreed. "I loved going up there. They lived on a farm a few miles outside the city. It was so different from being back home."

"What were they like?" Sassy asked, fascinated to get a glimpse into a part of Michel's past she'd never known about.

"Nice people," Michel replied. "Hard working. Simple. It was like something out of a movie. Or at least that's the way it seemed to me at the time. I'm sure they had their problems, but there was a lot of love in the house."

He smiled to himself at the memory.

"During the day my Uncle Lee would work the farm, and my Aunt Betty was usually busy with cooking and cleaning and stuff, so I'd hang out with Verle," he continued, seeming to

9

warm to the subject. "He was great. Even though he was twenty years older than me, I never got the feeling that he felt it was an imposition to spend time with me, and he never talked down to me. It wasn't that we did anything extraordinary. It was just stuff like fishing and hiking and swimming, but Verle always made everything fun. It was like he could still see the world through the eyes of a kid and knew how to make everything a little more special. I always wished he was my big brother."

He was silent for a minute, lost in his memories.

"But then my aunt passed away when I was twelve," he said, "and Verle went out to Berkeley to go to grad school, so I stopped going up. I didn't see Verle again until my uncle's funeral when I was a senior in high school, and then just once after that when he came to visit me about ten years ago."

"So what was he like then?" Sassy asked.

"Pretty much a hippie," Michel replied. "I mean, I guess in some ways he always was. He was always kind of a free spirit and believed in being connected to the land and all that, but that last time he had the long hair and a full beard and mustache and he was wearing a tie-dyed shirt...which was actually a little weird considering it was 1996...but he was still the same Verle inside."

"A rich hippie named Verdell Earle," Sassy said, as much to herself as Michel. "And he lives in Bayou Proche? That's up near Des Ourses Swamp in the Basin. How did that happen?"

"That's actually the end of a story," Michel replied.

"Okay, so what's the beginning?" Sassy asked.

"Yeah, you're actually talking about something interesting for once," Chance chimed in.

"Don't you have any work to do?" Michel asked with pointed sarcasm.

"Gee," Chance replied with equal sarcasm, "maybe I would if you guys spent more time looking for clients and less going to the movies."

Michel just stared at him with a deadpan expression for a few seconds, then turned back to Sassy.

"Okay," he said, as he settled onto the edge of Sassy's desk with his back to Chance. "My father's people originally settled up near Baton Rouge in the late 1700s. They were traders and later bankers. Then around 1880, my great grandfather started a logging company in the upper Atchafalaya."

"Ah, raping and pillaging the land of my people," Sassy said, referring to her Atakapa Indian ancestors who had been living in the Atchafalaya Basin for centuries before the first European settlers arrived.

"Well, yeah," Michel admitted with embarrassment. "But I'm sure their best friends were Indian."

"Uh huh," Sassy replied. "That's what they all say. Anyway..."

She gestured for Michel to continue.

"When my grandfather took over the business in the 1920s, it was dying," Michel said. "All the good cypress had been forested, we'd just come out of the war, there was a lot of uncertainty, et cetera. But he was pretty shrewd..."

"Obviously that gene didn't get passed down," Chance chimed in.

"Hush," Sassy said sharply, swatting her right hand toward him from across the room. "I've been waiting for years to hear this story."

Chance wilted back against his chair.

"So anyway," Michel continued, "my grandfather decided that he could make more money without the risk by leasing the mineral rights on his land to gas and oil companies."

"How much land are we talking about?" Sassy asked.

"About 10,000 acres at that point," Michel replied.

"At *that* point?" Sassy replied with surprise. "And *now*?"

"I'm getting there," Michel assured her. "Turned out his timing was perfect. When the Depression hit, the farming and logging industries tanked, but he had guaranteed leases and the oil companies were still making enough money to pay him. Then he used that money to buy more land since everyone else needed the cash."

"Your grandfather was a carpetbagger?" Sassy asked with a shocked laugh.

"Essentially," Michel replied guiltily.

"Wow," Sassy replied, shaking her head. "I think you owe some people."

"Well, maybe I would if my father hadn't been my father," Michel replied.

"How's that?" Sassy asked, her curiosity piqued.

"When my grandfather died in '52, he left the company to Uncle Lee and my father because my grandmother had already passed away. Uncle Lee was in his early twenties then and my dad was seventeen."

Sassy nodded.

"But my father didn't have any interest in it," Michel continued. "Apparently, the only reason he'd stuck around as long as he had was because my grandfather was still supporting him. But once my grandfather was gone, my father decided it was time to cash in his inheritance and take off. So he asked Uncle Lee to buy his share of the company and left."

"For where?" Sassy asked.

"Around the world and eventually to New Orleans, where he met my mother," Michel replied.

"Did your mother tell you all this?" Sassy asked.

Michel shook his head.

"No, she never talked about him. I asked her about him a few times, and all she'd say was that 'he had his charms,' and Uncle Lee wouldn't talk about him either. But when Verle came to visit me the last time, he told me the story."

"Did he tell you what your father was like?" Sassy asked.

"Yeah," Michel said. "My father used to visit them every so

often while Verle was growing up, so Verle knew him. He said my father was sort of a larger-than-life character. His nickname was Black Jack Doucette."

"Black Jack Doucette?" Sassy said. "Sounds like a dangerous man."

Michel smiled.

"Verle said he was very handsome, very charming, full of stories about big game hunting in Africa and gambling in Monte Carlo and all the beautiful women he'd met. I guess he was a real man's man, you know?"

"I guess that gene didn't get passed along either," Chance interjected.

This time Sassy and Michel both silenced him with harsh looks.

"So did Verle tell you anything about how your parents met?" Sassy asked.

"Not really," Michel replied. "He said my father just showed up with my mother one day, said they'd met in New Orleans, that they'd gotten married, and that she was pregnant. They stayed for a week, then went back to New Orleans. Eight months later my mother called and said my father had left and I'd been born."

"That's quite a story," Sassy said. "Did Verle tell you where your father was?"

Michel shook his head.

"I didn't ask," he said matter-of-factly.

"You were never curious?" Sassy asked with surprise.

"Of course I was curious, but I figured that anyone who would leave his wife with a baby on the way probably wasn't worth having as a father."

"Amen," Chance said behind him. "I guess we have something in common, after all. We both had asshole fathers from rich families. But at least yours didn't stick around to shit all over you."

Michel turned to look at him. His initial impulse had been to chide Chance for trying to get into a game of one-upsmanship about who had the worst father, but he could read the genuine hurt in Chance's eyes.

"I suppose you're right," he said instead.

"Okay," Sassy said, "so let's get back to how Verle ended up in Bayou Proche."

Michel turned back to her.

"Let's see," he said, trying to remember where'd left off. "So Uncle Lee ran the company after my father left. He really wasn't that interested in it either, but it was a steady income so he held onto the land and kept renewing the leases. But he pretty much devoted himself to running his farm, even though he had more than enough money to retire."

"Yeah, blah, blah, blah,," Sassy said impatiently. "What about Verle?"

Michel gave her a mock annoyed look that she ignored.

"As I said earlier," he said, "Verle left to go to grad school at Berkeley, but when he came back he started to show an interest in the business. He'd always spent a lot of time in the Basin, and he studied forestry as an undergraduate, so I guess it didn't seem that surprising to anyone. He convinced my uncle that their property could be viable for sustainable timber again if they managed it correctly, and even talked him into buying some more land."

"How much more?" Sassy asked.

"All told, they had about 50,000 acres," Michel replied.

"That's almost a tenth of the whole Atchafalaya Basin," Sassy replied, shocked. "That's a lot of timber."

Michel nodded.

"Yeah, but Verle never actually planned to start up the logging operation again. He had something else in mind."

"Which was...?" Sassy prompted.

"To turn the whole area into a nature preserve," Michel

replied. "When he came to visit me the last time, he told me that it had always been his dream."

"So he's a tree hugger?" Chance asked with obvious distaste.

"Yeah," Michel agreed. "When Uncle Lee died, Verle inherited everything. He stopped renewing the leases and moved to Bayou Proche so he could keep a closer eye on things. Then he started campaigning to have the land put under federal protection."

"Did he succeed?" Sassy asked.

"I don't know," Michel replied with a shrug. "I doubt it, unless he got it done before Bush took office."

He fished a cigarette out of the pack in his jacket pocket and lit it.

"So how come you never told me any of this before?" Sassy asked.

Michel took a long drag and exhaled it slowly.

"Ancient history, and not really even my history" he said without conviction.

"But Verle was obviously very important to you when you were a kid," Sassy replied.

"Yeah," Michel replied with a faint nod. "I don't know. It's hard to explain. It's sort of like it was part of my life for a while, but then it wasn't. I guess I just sort of put it in a little box and left it there."

"*It?*" Sassy replied. "Don't you mean *him?*"

"Well, I mean that whole period of being connected with my father's family," Michel said. "When I think about my life, I think about being with my mother and living in New Orleans. My aunt and uncle, Verle, the farm...all that was just something I got to visit for a week every summer. And then when I left I'd try to forget it until the next year."

"Why would you try to forget it?" Chance asked. "If I'd been able to escape like that I'd never have wanted to forget it."

Michel turned to face him.

15

"It was different for you," he said sympathetically. "It's not like my life was bad. There was nothing wrong with it. My mother loved me very much. It was just that sometimes..."

He trailed off for a moment and looked down at the desk. Then he looked back into Chance's eyes.

"Sometimes I was lonely. But when I was at the farm, I didn't feel that way. Then when I left, it always hurt for a while, so I tried to not think about it. It was just...easier that way. You know?"

Chance felt his throat tighten and took a quick breath.

"Yeah," he managed, then quickly looked away.

Michel turned back to Sassy and took another drag on his cigarette. His expression was wistful.

"You know, Michel," Sassy said carefully, "it's never too late to reconnect. I mean family is family, and Verle's really the only family you have left."

Michel nodded as he stubbed his cigarette out in the ashtray next to him.

"How a long a drive is it to Bayou Proche?" he asked.

"Less than two hours," Sassy replied. "You going?"

"Yeah," Michel replied. "I'm sure the whole jail thing is just something stupid. I doubt I'll be any help. But it would be nice to see Verle again."

Chapter 3

Michel put out his last cigarette and checked his watch again. It was 3:21 PM. He'd been parked in front of the squat, red-brick Bayou Proche police station for almost an hour, and now he was thirsty.

"If there's one thing I can't stand, it's a tardy sheriff," he muttered to himself.

He stared up the narrow main street. The entire downtown area was only five blocks long, and was lined on both sides by medium-sized oleander trees. All of the buildings were brick, though some had been painted white. Directly opposite the police station was a diner, but it was closed. Next to that was a hardware store, and then a theater with a blank marquee. The whole town looked as though it had been placed into a time capsule sometime in the 1950s and left there.

Suddenly a movement caught Michel's eye. An old woman had emerged from a corner building one block up on the right, and was slowly walking toward the far end of the town. She was the first person he'd seen in all the time he'd been sitting there. Michel noticed she was carrying a brown-paper bag.

Bingo, he thought. He opened the car door and stepped out into the sun. It was slightly cooler than it had been when he'd arrived, but the humidity was still oppressively thick. He moved into the shade along the sidewalk and walked up the block.

The bell above the door sounded weakly as he entered the store. An old man behind the counter looked up from his newspaper for a few seconds, then went back to reading.

Michel looked around. The store was cramped but neat, and blessedly cool. It had a small section with fresh produce near the door, but the shelves were packed with canned and boxed dry goods. Michel spotted a faded yellow cooler emblazoned with a red Royal Crown Cola logo in the back corner and walked to it.

Not much of a selection, he thought as he surveyed the rows of Coke, 7Up, and Orange Crush cans through the glass. He opened the door, grabbed a Coke and walked up to the counter.

The old man put down his newspaper and shuffled slowly toward the counter.

"That going to be it?" he asked without much interest.

"And a pack of American Spirits," Michel replied. "The yellow ones."

The man stared at Michel as though he'd just spoken in a foreign language.

"Cigarettes," Michel clarified.

"I've got Marlboros, Winstons, Camels, and Kools," the old man replied flatly.

"Okay, a pack of Camel Lights," Michel replied.

"I said I've got Marlboros, Winstons, Camels and Kools," the old man replied, narrowing his eyes at Michel. "I didn't say anything about Lights."

Wow, I guess when you're the only game in town you don't need charm, Michel thought.

"Camels, then," he said.

"You got it," the old man replied as he reached up and pulled a pack from the overhead rack. He tossed it on the scarred linoleum counter.

"That'll be $5.00," he said.

"That's cheap," Michel said with mild surprise as he counted out five one dollar bills.

"We don't charge for ambience around here," the old man replied dryly. "We throw that in for free."

He chuckled to himself as he took the money and placed it in the cash register. Then he slammed the drawer shut, shuffled to his stool and buried his nose back in his newspaper.

Michel stared at him for a moment, then walked out. He stood in front of the store and unwrapped the cigarettes, then pulled one out and lit it, inhaling deeply.

Ugh, that's awful, he thought as he exhaled. How can anyone smoke these things? He made a face but took another drag anyway. The idea of going back into the store and buying a pack of something different didn't appeal to him.

He looked up the street toward the police station and saw a white cruiser pulling up in front.

"Thank God," he said aloud, tossing the cigarette into the gutter along the sidewalk.

He hurried up the block as a black man in a tan police uniform got out of the car. The man looked to be in his mid-50s. He was tall and solidly built, with close cropped black hair shot through with flecks of gray, and a thick black mustache.

As Michel approached, the man watched him without expression.

"Sheriff Turner?" Michel asked when he was fifteen feet away.

"Yeah," Turner replied, eyeing Michel suspiciously. "What can I do for you?"

Michel took a few steps closer and held out his right hand.

"I'm Michel Doucette," he said. "Verle's cousin."

Turner's gaze warmed immediately.

"I'm sorry," he said as he stepped forward and firmly grasped Michel's hand. "Pleased to meet you, Mr. Doucette. Russell Turner. I thought you were another damned reporter."

"A reporter?" Michel asked, surprised and suddenly uneasy. "Why are there reporters here?"

"Let's step inside," Turner replied, as he took a look up and down the main street.

He walked to the door, quickly unlocked it, and ushered Michel inside.

"I didn't expect you to show up in person," he said as soon as he'd closed the door, "but I'm glad you did."

"Why? What's Verle been arrested for?" Michel asked.

"Murder," Turner replied.

"Murder?" Michel repeated with disbelief. "There's got to be some mistake."

"I agree," Turner replied. "I've known Verle for a long time, and I don't think he has a violent bone in his body."

"But you're still holding him," Michel said, a hint of challenge in his voice.

Turner shook his head.

"The Staties have him in Baton Rouge. He was arrested outside my jurisdiction. I tried to get him released to me, but so far no go."

Michel frowned with both worry and disappointment.

"What happened?" he asked.

"Why don't we sit down," Turner said.

He walked to his desk and indicated a chair for Michel.

"The Staties got a call that there was a car off the side of one of the roads that cuts through the Des Ourses," he said as he settled in behind his desk. "A trooper went out to investigate but couldn't find anyone. About a mile farther on, he found Verle's truck parked. He was checking around when he heard someone yelling. He found Verle with the woman's body. She'd been strangled."

"Who was the woman?" Michel asked. "Was she local?"

"No," Turner replied. "She was from down around your way. Name of Dolores Hagen according to the registration found in the car. Thirty-four years old. Had several arrests and one conviction for prostitution."

"Have you talked to Verle?" Michel asked.

Turner nodded.

"He said he found her in the swamp and was afraid to leave her there because of the animals that would be drawn by her scent, so he carried her back to the road."

"Did he tell that to the Staties?"

"Yeah," Turner replied. "And just between us, the captain there is inclined to believe him, but until they finish their investigation, Verle is the only suspect they've got."

Michel nodded thoughtfully.

"I'm sure it'll be okay," Turner said with a reassuring smile. "Verle's been very cooperative. He showed the Staties where he found the body and gave them permission to search his house without a warrant. In fact, that's where I've been. Just keeping an eye on things to make sure it was all done according to procedure and that they didn't mess the place up too badly."

"I appreciate that," Michel said.

"No problem," Turner replied.

"So did they find anything?"

"Nothing I saw," Turner replied, "but they took his computer so they can search the hard drive to see if Verle had any contact with Hagen. I'm sure you know how thorough the Staties are."

Michel gave Turner a quizzical look.

"Oh, I know you were a cop," Turner replied with a low chuckle. "It was one of the first things your cousin told me when we met."

Michel noticed that Turner had used the past tense.

"So you also know I've been off the force for a while now?" he asked.

"Yeah, Verle told me that, too," Turner replied.

"He did?" Michel asked with surprise. "How would he know that? And how did you know to call my office? We've only been in business for a few weeks."

"Apparently Verle's been keeping tabs on you," Turner replied with a shrug. "I found your number in his address book.

He'd crossed out an old work number and written in the new one."

Michel felt a confusing mixture of surprise and unease that Verle had been watching him so closely from a distance. He pushed the feeling away.

"How far is it to the State Police station?" he asked.

"'Bout a half hour," Turner replied.

He looked at Michel for a moment, then checked his watch.

"Technically, visiting hours are over," he said matter-of-factly, "but I imagine they might be willing to bend the rules a little for me. But it'll have to be quick. I need to get home for dinner with my son."

"That would be great, if you don't mind," Michel replied.

Turner shook is head.

"Then you can join us for dinner," he said.

"I really don't want to impose," Michel protested weakly.

"We'll be happy for the company," Turner replied. "Besides, the diner's only open for breakfast and lunch, and if I know Verle, you're not going to find much worth eating at his place."

Michel smiled and nodded.

"I'd appreciate that."

"Besides, it'll give you a chance to get to know Blue," Turner said as stood up behind his desk.

"Blue?" Michel asked. "Is that your son?"

Turner gave Michel a wide, amused grin.

"No, my boy is Corey. Blue is Verle's dog."

Chapter 4

Michel had been waiting alone in the stark visitation room for almost ten minutes when the door suddenly opened and Verle walked in, followed closely by a young, stone-faced state trooper. Verle was wearing an orange jumpsuit. His wrists and ankles were shackled.

"Michel!" Verle exclaimed with unrestrained joy when he saw Michel standing in the middle of the room.

Although he was at least 40 pounds heavier than he'd been the last time they'd seen one another, and his long hair and beard were now mostly gray, he still looked the same to Michel. He still had the same twinkle in his bright blue eyes, and his smile was still warm and easy.

"They didn't tell me you were here," Verle said, taking a few awkward steps forward.

He turned to the trooper who had taken up a sentry position by the door.

"Is it okay if I hug my cousin?" he asked.

The trooper nodded without changing expression.

"Excuse the cuffs," Verle said, as he shuffled toward Michel and tried to place his hands around Michel's waist.

He could only manage to rest them on the front of Michel's hips. Michel wrapped his arms around Verle's thick shoulders and hugged him tightly. He felt an unexpected surge of happiness.

"Let me take a look at you," Verle said after a few moments.

Michel reluctantly let Verle go and took a few steps back.

"As handsome as ever," Verle said as he looked Michel up and down. "And how do I look?"

He turned from side to side, comically imitating a model at the end of a catwalk, then smiled.

"I have to say you've looked better," Michel replied, suddenly noticing how tired Verle's eyes actually looked.

"Must be the orange," Verle joked. "Not my color."

"Perhaps," Michel agreed. "You want to sit down?"

Verle nodded.

"Not so easy walking around in these things."

He slumped into a straight-backed wood chair with a weary groan. Michel pulled up another chair and sat facing him a few feet away.

"So how are you doing?" Michel asked.

Verle shrugged.

"I have a cell to myself and they feed me," he replied. "All in all, not so bad."

"You know that's not what I meant," Michel gently chided. "What about emotionally?"

"I know I'm innocent, so I'm not too worried," Verle replied, though the anxiousness in his eyes suggested otherwise. "It'll just be a matter of time before I can go home."

"Well, I'm going to stick around until that happens," Michel said.

Verle looked at him with surprise.

"You don't need to do that," he protested, though he was obviously pleased. "I'm sure you have more important things to do back in New Orleans. You have a business to run now."

Michel sat back in his chair and fixed Verle with a curious look.

"How do you know that?" he asked.

Verle's face reddened slightly.

"What? I can't keep an eye on my only cousin?" he asked.

"Of course you can," Michel replied quickly, as he realized

that his tone had been more accusatory than he'd intended. "But how did you find out about my business? And that mom had died?"

"I get the Times-Picayune," Verle replied.

Michel gave him a skeptical look.

"Verle, I don't think the Times-Picayune ran an article about my little private investigation business," he said.

Verle lowered his eyes and smiled crookedly, like a child caught with his hand in the cookie jar.

"Okay," he said. "I have a friend in New Orleans who told me."

"A friend?" Michel asked. "Who?"

"His name is Severin," Verle replied.

"Severin Marchand?" Michel asked with surprise.

A few weeks earlier, Severin Marchand had hired Sassy and Michel to find out who had destroyed the costume he'd been working on for the Bourbon Street Awards during Mardi Gras. Michel had discovered that Marchand had faked the crime in a successful attempt to garner sympathy.

"I don't know his last name," Verle replied. "His screen name and email are SeverinIV."

"So you've never met him?" Michel asked.

"No," Verle replied, shaking his head.

Michel leaned back in his chair and frowned.

"What's wrong?" Verle asked.

"Maybe nothing," Michel replied absently.

He stared at the floor for a few seconds, then lifted his gaze back to Verle.

"How did you two start communicating?" he asked.

Verle gave him a worried look.

"He's a member of one of the conservation groups I belong to," Verle replied. "I was in one of the chat rooms, and he asked if I was related to you."

"How long ago was this?"

"About six months ago," Verle replied. "Maybe a little longer."

"And you've stayed in touch ever since?" Michel asked, trying not to sound too much like he was conducting an interrogation.

Verle nodded.

"Yeah, every few weeks or so he'd send me an email," he replied. "About a month ago he told me that you and your partner from the police were opening your business."

"Did he ever say anything else about me?" Michel asked.

"Like what?" Verle replied.

Michel considered what to say, wondering whether Marchand had ever said anything about his sexuality. He decided to let it drop for now.

"Nothing," he said, shaking his head. "It's just kind of an odd coincidence that you know one another. He was actually our first client."

"Maybe because we're friends he decided to hire you," Verle offered.

"Maybe," Michel agreed, though the whole situation made him very uncomfortable.

"I'm sorry if I did something wrong," Verle said, looking at Michel with pleading eyes.

"You didn't do anything wrong," Michel replied. "But if you wanted to know what was going on with me, why didn't you just call?"

Verle dropped his eyes for a moment and lightly bit his lower lip. "I didn't want to impose," he said finally.

"Impose?" Michel asked incredulously. "Why would you think that?"

"The last time we saw one another, I got the sense that maybe you didn't want me there," Verle replied.

There was no recrimination in his tone. He was simply stating a fact.

Michel started to protest, then stopped himself. He realized that Verle was partially right. His twenty-something self *had* been embarrassed by his hippie cousin. Verle had wanted to take Michel to one of the best restaurants in the Quarter, but Michel had insisted they go to an out-of-the-way dive on the outskirts of the Marigny. He felt a surge of shame as he realized how callous he'd been.

"Verle, I'm so sorry," he said. "It wasn't that I didn't want to see you. It was that…"

He faltered for a moment, not wanting to hurt Verle's feelings, then realized that Verle had already been hurt far worse believing what he did.

"It was that I was embarrassed to be seen with you," he said. "It was about me. My own insecurities. I'm sorry."

Verle stared at him with wounded eyes for a moment, then the spark returned to them and he began to chuckle.

"I suppose I can't blame you," he said. "Sometimes I'm embarrassed to be seen with myself. Why do you think I live out in the middle of nowhere?"

Michel smiled and shook his head.

"No, it was stupid," he said. "I should never have been embarrassed. You're one of the best people I've ever known. I should have been proud to introduce you around."

Verle smiled in return.

"Gentlemen, time is up," the trooper interrupted.

Michel stood and watched as Verle struggled up out of his chair. For a second it looked like Verle was going to lose his balance and Michel reached out to steady him.

"Are you okay?" he asked, studying Verle closely.

"Oh, yeah," Verle replied. "Just a little tired. Carrying that poor woman out of the swamp was hard work. I thought I might have to leave her behind a few times."

"Well try to get some rest," Michel replied. "I'll be back in the morning."

Verle turned to the trooper.

"One more hug?" he asked.

The trooper nodded impatiently.

Verle and Michel embraced again, and Verle gave Michel a kiss on the cheek.

"I appreciate your coming, Michel," he said. "It means the world to me."

Michel swallowed hard as he felt tears forming in the corners of his eyes.

"I'm sorry it took me so long," he said.

Chapter 5

Michel was sitting on the sofa in Russell Turner's small but comfortable living room, watching the dog who was watching him from the doorway, while Turner prepared dinner in the kitchen. Michel tilted his head to the right and the dog mirrored the movement, tilting its head to the left. Michel straightened his head and the dog did the same. Michel smiled and the dog backed away a few steps into the hallway.

Turner appeared in the doorway carrying two bottles of Dixie Beer. He handed one to Michel, then sat in a well-worn easy chair by the fireplace. Blue followed him into the room, then stood beside the chair so that Turner could scratch her rear haunches. She continued to watch Michel quizzically.

She had the face and body of a small shepherd, but with proportionally larger ears, a higher, narrower waist, and longer, bushier tail, like that of a wolf. Her straight fur was short around her face and on her legs, but longer on her torso. It was flecked with tan, black, and gray, creating the overall impression of a brownish gray, and she was spotted with irregular black patches. On the center of her chest was a tufted white patch. Her eyes were a soft brown and very expressive.

"So what kind of dog is she exactly?" Michel asked.

"Most likely a mix of shepherd and Catahoula," Turner replied.

Michel knew that Catahoula was a parish in Louisiana, but he'd never heard the word used to refer to a breed of dog.

"What's a Catahoula?" he asked.

29

Turner gave him a curious look.

"You've never heard of your own state dog?"

"I didn't realize we had one," Michel replied with a shrug.

"We have since about the late 1980s," Turner replied. "Before that, people just called them Catahoula Curs or Catahoula Hog Dogs, but then somebody got the idea of changing the name to Catahoula Leopard Dog and making it the state dog."

"So what are they?"

"I've heard a few different stories," Turner replied, "but the most common is that they're a mix of mastiff, greyhound, beauceron, and red wolf. The Spanish and French explorers brought the dogs with them, and then the local Indians bred them with the wolves to create herding and hunting dogs. Usually they're larger than this one and have blue or cracked glass eyes and floppy ears, but those spots and the star on the chest are unmistakable."

"She looks pretty wild," Michel said. "Is she tame?"

"Depends on what you mean by tame," Turner replied. "She's pretty independent, and you wouldn't want to be a raccoon around her, but she's sweet with people so long as they don't threaten Verle or someone she likes."

At that moment the dog walked over to Michel and sniffed his right hand. Then she began pushing her long nose under his fingers.

"Looks like she likes you," Turner said.

Michel began to scratch the top of the dog's head. He noticed a long scar just behind her left ear, extending a few inches down onto her neck.

"How'd she get the scar?" he asked.

"Got into a fight with a bobcat," Turner replied.

"A bobcat?" Michel replied. "I'm surprised she wasn't killed."

"She can be pretty ferocious," Turner replied, "and she's

strong and quick. I've heard that a pack of three or four Catahoulas can take down an eight-hundred-pound wild boar."

"Wow," Michel said, looking back at the dog.

Suddenly she sat and opened her mouth. Her long tongue dropped out the left side and she began panting. Michel could swear that she was actually smiling.

"Hi Blue," he said. "Pleased to meet you."

The dog suddenly lifted her right paw. Michel looked at Turner quizzically.

"It's one of her few tricks," Turner said. "Go on and shake it."

Michel reached down and shook the dog's paw. All at once she seemed to lose interest in him. She stood up and walked to the far corner of the room, where she settled down and closed her eyes.

"Like I said, she's pretty independent," Turner said with a laugh. "Verle's always sworn that the only reason she sticks around is because she's convinced he's helpless without her."

Suddenly the front door opened. A tall teenaged boy wearing earphones walked in and started for the kitchen.

"Corey!" Turner called.

The boy's head jerked toward the living room and he pulled off the earphones.

"Oh, hey dad," he said with a goofy smile as he stepped into the doorway.

Michel noticed that he was considerably lighter than his father, but the family resemblance was obvious.

"Come on in here and say hello to our guest," Turner said. "This is Mr. Doucette. He's Verle's cousin."

The boy crossed the room as Michel stood.

"Pleased to meet you, Mr. Doucette," Corey said in a soft, shy voice. "I'm really sorry about Verle being in jail."

"Thank you," Michel replied. "And you can call me Michel."

"No, you can call him Mr. Doucette," Turner interjected.

Corey gave a tolerant smile that suggested he was used to his father's corrections.

"Dinner's almost ready," Turner said, "so go wash up. And put on a decent shirt."

Corey looked down at the yellow and purple Lakers jersey he was wearing over a white t-shirt. It hung halfway down his thighs.

"What wrong with this?" he asked, though his tone suggested he knew the battle was already lost.

Michel realized it was probably just a reflex, the need to question parents common to most teenagers.

Turner just stared unyieldingly at his son.

"But this how everyone dresses," Corey said, not yet ready to give up.

"Well they're not my children so that's none of my concern," Turner replied, his voice suddenly much sharper. "And don't think I don't know your drawers are hanging halfway down your behind under that shirt either. So pull them up and put on a damn belt."

Corey continued to meet his father's gaze for a few seconds, then lowered his eyes.

"Yes, sir," he said sullenly, then turned and walked down the hall.

"I'm sorry about that, Michel," Turner said after the boy's footsteps had faded. "Sometimes I don't know what gets into his head. Why would anyone want to walk around looking like a fool?"

"No problem," Michel replied with a small chuckle. "My mother would have said the same thing to me. I guess it's just the eternal struggle between parents and children when the children get to that point where they want to express their individuality...by dressing like everybody else."

Turner laughed.

"I suppose you're right," he said. "I'm sure my parents felt the same way when I started parading around in platform shoes and bell bottoms with my big old afro."

"You have any pictures of that?" Michel asked, sharing the laughter.

"Not that you'll ever see," Turner replied, shaking his head. "So, you have any kids?"

"No," Michel replied, then paused for a second. "Actually I'm gay."

Turner studied Michel for a moment.

"Well, I can't say as I'm an expert on the subject, but unless I'm missing something, seems like gay people can have kids just the same as everyone else. I hear you don't even need to do the do these days. It can all be done with needles and such."

"So I've heard." Michel replied with a smile. "But honestly, I don't think I'm cut out to be a parent."

"Well, you never know," Turner replied. "You might just surprise yourself. I sure did."

"How so?" Michel asked.

"Well, I was thirty-three when I met Thesalee," Turner replied. "My whole life up until that point was the job, and I figured that was all it was ever going to be. I was in it for life."

"I know how that goes," Michel said.

"But when I met her, that all started to change," Turner continued. "Suddenly I could see the possibility for more."

Michel smiled, thinking back to how he'd felt when he first met Joel, his on-again-off-again boyfriend, almost eighteen months earlier.

"But I still wasn't sold on the idea of having kids," Turner said. "I mean, when you're a cop you see the worst in people every day. You see all the horrible things they're capable of doing. It's tough to imagine bringing a child into that world, you know what I mean?"

Michel nodded, though he found it hard to believe that

33

Turner had seen much that was so terrible in a place like Bayou Proche.

"But Thesalee kept at me," Turner continued with a chuckle. "And finally she got pregnant. That's when we moved down here, because she was afraid I was going to get killed and she'd be left raising the baby on her own."

"So you're not originally from here?" Michel asked.

"No, Thesalee grew up here," Turner replied. "I'm from Detroit. We were only supposed to be here temporarily until we found a place in Baton Rouge or closer to New Orleans, but then this job opened up and they offered it to me."

"So where's Thesalee now?" Michel asked.

From the way Turner had spoken about her, he expected her to walk through the door at any moment.

Turner was silent for a moment.

"She died when Corey was three," he said finally.

From the tone of his voice, Michel knew that Turner had said all he was going to say on the subject.

"I'm sorry," Michel said.

Turner nodded almost imperceptibly.

"But having Corey was the best thing that ever happened to me," he said, his voice brightening. "Despite the challenges, being a father has been the most satisfying experience in my life. And I think I've done a pretty good job at it. Of course, Corey might say different, but I think he turned out pretty well."

Michel smiled. "I agree. He seems like a great kid."

Turner sighed and leaned forward in his chair.

"So what do you say we have some dinner?" he asked.

*****

Throughout dinner Corey had peppered Michel with questions about life in New Orleans. It was clear that the idea of living in a big city fascinated him.

"I have a feeling that as soon as he graduates high school, Bayou Proche is going to have one less resident," Michel said as he dried a plate.

Corey had gone up to his room to do his homework while Michel and Turner did the dishes.

"I suspect you're right," Turner replied, placing another dish in the drainer. "That's okay. We've all got to make our own lives at some point."

His voice conveyed both pride and resignation.

"So how long have you known Verle?" Michel asked.

"Since he moved here," Turner replied. "Must be eleven or twelve years now."

"Are you friends?" Michel asked.

"Yeah. I'd say I'm as close to Verle as anyone. Not that that's saying much."

"What do you mean?"

Turner placed the last dish in the drainer and shut off the faucet. He turned to face Michel.

"Your cousin isn't exactly well loved around here," he said. "People have a tendency to avoid him."

Michel looked at him with disbelief.

"But Verle's one of the sweetest people I've ever met," he said.

"That he is," Turner agreed, "but that's not how other people see it."

"Why's that?" Michel asked, suddenly feeling very protective of his cousin.

"Most of the folks around here worked for the lumber companies and Gulf Coast Oil," Turner replied. "When Verle stopped renewing the leases, a lot of them lost their jobs."

Michel felt his growing indignation suddenly wither.

"I can imagine that wasn't very popular," he said.

"To say the least," Turner replied.

"Did Verle try to explain why he did it?"

"Oh, yeah," Turner replied. "But people just didn't understand it. I wouldn't say they're ignorant, but certainly myopic. They figure that people have been logging and drilling these parts for decades and it's all been fine, so why change things now? All they could see was that Verle was taking food off their tables."

"I guess I can't blame them," Michel said, though he felt slightly guilty, as if he were betraying Verle.

"No, you can't," Turner agreed. "But what most of them don't realize is that Verle has been keeping this town afloat for years. It was dying before he shut down his land. They just didn't recognize it. You were downtown. How many people did you see?"

"One," Michel said.

Turner nodded.

"The only places doing any business now are the diner, the funeral parlor, and the gin joint out on Bayou Road. The rest are able to stay open because folks own the buildings and frankly they have nothing better to do all day, but this whole town will be gone before too long. The old folks are dying and the young folks are moving away."

Michel felt a stab of sadness. It wasn't for the people exactly, but more for a way of life that would be lost.

"What did you mean that Verle's been keeping the town afloat?" he asked.

"There's no money coming in," Turner replied. "There's barely enough coming in through taxes to pay my salary. So Verle created a trust to fund everything else."

"And people don't realize that?" Michel asked with surprise.

Turner shook his head.

"Verle didn't want them to know. The only folks who know are me and Porter DeCew, the head of the town council, who also happens to be Verle's lawyer."

36

Michel wondered how the town's people would feel about Verle if they knew about his generosity. He let the thought go.

"So are you Verle's *only* friend?" he asked.

"No, he's close with Porter and Porter's son, Terry," Turner replied. "And then, of course, there's Ruby."

"Who's Ruby?"

"I suspect you'll meet her soon," Turner replied with a chuckle. "She's the only person around here less popular than Verle, but in her case there's good reason."

"Why's that?"

"Ruby's the town crazy," Turner replied. "People see her coming and they go the other way fast. She's been known to cuss people out for nothing and even spit on them on occasion."

"She sounds charming," Michel replied. "I'm surprised she hasn't been run out of town."

"She has been," Turner said. "She lives in a cabin out on Verle's property, about a mile from his place."

"Did she grow up here?" Michel asked.

"No," Turner replied. "She's from Bayou Chene. Wandered up here about ten years ago. Verle kind of adopted her. He's got a calming effect on her. She's only allowed in places in town if Verle's with her. Otherwise they call me."

"You must love that," Michel said.

"Oh yeah," Turner replied. "Ruby doesn't like me at all. She's tried to bite me more times than I can count. I think the only creatures on this earth she likes are Verle and Blue."

Blue lifted her head for a few seconds from her place under the kitchen table, then settled back down.

"So is she schizophrenic?" Michel asked.

"I dont think so," Turner replied. "I just think she has a hard time being around people. Sort of like a feral dog. But I think she's smart, too. Sometimes I wonder how much of it is real and how much is an act so people don't bother her."

Michel nodded thoughtfully. He was intrigued by the idea

of meeting Ruby, but hoped that Verle would be with him when it happened. Suddenly he realized that the light outside the kitchen window was fading and checked his watch.

"I probably ought to get going," he said. "I still haven't found a place to stay yet. Are there any hotels in town?"

"There is a rooming house," Turner replied with a definite lack of enthusiasm, "but why don't you stay at Verle's?"

"Verle's?" Michel replied doubtfully.

"It's not what you're imagining," Turner said with a laugh.

"Oh, and what am I imagining?" Michel replied.

"A plywood shack with a mattress on the floor?"

"Well, I wasn't actually picturing a floor," Michel replied.

Turner laughed.

"No, Verle's got himself a pretty nice place. I think you'll be pleasantly surprised."

"But I don't have a key," Michel said.

"A key?" Turner replied. "Verle never locks the place."

"Okay," Michel replied with a shrug. "How do I get there?"

Turner drew him a simple map, then walked Michel to the door. When she heard the door open, Blue came bounding into the room, wagging her tail. She walked up to Michel and stood beside him.

"Looks like Blue's going with you," Turner said.

"I'm not sure that's such a good idea," Michel replied hesitantly. "I don't know how to take care of a dog."

"Don't worry, she'll take care of you," Turner said. "Just make sure she has food and water in her bowls. The food's in the pantry. Beyond that, there's nothing else to do. She'll let you know when she needs to go out and do her business."

Michel gave Turner a doubtful look, then looked down at Blue.

"Do you want to go with me?" he asked.

The dog's tail began to wag more vigorously, then she ran out through the open doorway.

"Call me if you have any problems," Turner said. "My number's on the map. Otherwise I'll see you in the morning. We can meet at the diner around eight for breakfast, then head up to see Verle."

"Sounds good," Michel replied. "And thanks for dinner."

"No problem," Turner replied. "Have a good night."

Michel walked out to his car. Blue was already standing next to it, watching him. Michel opened the rear door and motioned for her to jump in. She simply stared at him.

"Go on," Michel coaxed.

Blue sat in response and looked at the driver's door.

"You've got to be kidding," Michel said as he closed the rear door.

He opened the driver's door and Blue immediately stood and jumped in. She crossed into the passenger seat and sat down, then looked at Michel with her mouth open and her tongue hanging to the side. Michel shook his head and climbed in.

"Okay, but no drooling on the upholstery," he said as he started the engine.

Chapter 6

Twenty minutes later, Michel pulled to a stop in front of Verle's house. Turner had been right: he was pleasantly surprised. Instead of the rundown shack he'd been expecting, he found an oversized, contemporary log cabin on a high stone foundation. Across the entire front of the house was a deep covered porch. In the fading light, Michel could see a pair of rocking chairs at one end and a hammock at the other.

He opened the car door and stepped out onto the dirt drive. Blue followed him and immediately walked a few feet away, squatted and peed.

"Good girl," Michel said, happy that she hadn't decided to relieve herself in his car.

Blue looked up at him for a moment, then cocked her head toward the left corner of the house. Her tail began to wag, and then she disappeared around the side of the house.

"Wait," Michel called, unsure what to do.

He started to follow her, then wondered if he should go back to the car and get his pistol from the trunk. Then he heard a woman's voice.

"Blue!"

The voice sounded joyful and almost girlish.

Michel walked to the corner of the house and stopped. A woman was squatting on the ground, rubbing the scruff of Blue's neck. She was dressed in heavy green rubber boots, faded blue overalls, and a red t-shirt. Her face was covered by her long, stringy gray hair.

"I was worried about you, girl," the woman said, then leaned forward and kissed the end of Blue's noise.

"Hi," Michel said.

The woman jumped to her feet with surprising quickness, and suddenly a shotgun was aimed directly at Michel's chest.

"Who're you?" the woman asked in a heavy Cajun accent.

Her face was flat, with small narrowed eyes and a tight angry mouth.

"I'm Verle's cousin, Michel," Michel replied quickly, holding his hands up in front of him.

"The policeman?" the woman asked, tilting her head and eyeing him suspiciously.

"Well, I used to be," Michel replied.

The woman immediately lowered the barrel of the gun.

"If you'd said you still was, I'da shot you cuz I'd know you was lying," the woman said.

She took a few steps forward and aggressively thrust out her right hand.

"I'm Ruby," she said.

Michel took her hand. It was dry and callused, and her grip was frighteningly strong.

"Nice to meet you, Ruby," Michel replied.

For a moment, a small smile flashed across Ruby's face and transformed it. Michel imagined that she'd been quite pretty in her younger days. Then the smile was gone and Ruby's expression was closed again.

"So you come up to get Verle out of jail?" she asked.

"I hope so," Michel replied.

"Good, cuz I don't trust that Sheriff Turner or that Porter DeCew," she said.

"Why not?" Michel asked.

"Because if no one's in jail Turner'll be out of a job," Ruby replied, "and that crooked lawyer just wants to get his hands on Verle's land."

"I don't know," Michel said. "Sheriff Turner seems like a pretty good guy. I think he genuinely cares about Verle."

Ruby studied him carefully for a few seconds, then nodded thoughtfully as though she'd just discovered that Michel was an expert on character assessment.

"Okay," she said, "but I still don't trust Porter DeCew or his sissy boy."

"Why's that?" Michel asked, wondering what Ruby meant by "sissy boy," but letting it go for the moment.

"Because they're lawyers," Ruby replied, then opened her mouth wide and let out a harsh bark of a laugh.

Michel noticed that her teeth were surprisingly intact.

"What did you mean about him wanting to get his hands on Verle's land?" he asked.

"Him and Verle have all the land in a trust," Ruby replied. "If Verle's gone, then DeCew can sell it to the oil company and get rich."

"Are you sure about that?" Michel asked, his police instincts kicking in.

"Sure," Ruby replied with certainty. "You ask Verle yourself. He'll tell you."

Michel nodded, having already decided that he would.

"So what do you think of the place?" Ruby asked suddenly.

"I don't know," Michel replied. "We just got here. I haven't even been inside yet."

"Well, I'll show y'around," Ruby said, then walked past him without waiting for his agreement.

"It's good you brought Blue with you," Ruby said over her shoulder. "Jail's no place for a dog."

"Actually she was at Sheriff Turner's house," Michel replied.

Ruby stopped and turned to face him.

"Same thing," she said, then let out another harsh laugh.

She slapped Michel on the shoulder, then turned and continued toward the stairs to the front porch.

*****

"So that's it," Ruby said as they returned to the large, open living room. "Except that there used to be a computer over there."

She pointed at a desk near the back wall.

"The sheriff told me the state police took it," Michel replied.

"What for?" Ruby asked. "Was the woman hit with a computer?"

The question struck Michel as too simple-minded to be genuine. He remembered what Turner had said about Ruby's craziness possibly being an act and decided to toy with her a bit.

"Well, as a matter of fact she was," he said.

Ruby cocked her head and stared at him for a full five seconds, then unleashed another laugh.

"Nah, you're funning with me," she said, wagging the index finger of her right hand at him.

"How can you be sure?" Michel asked playfully.

"Because there's no extension cords long enough to reach out into the swamp," Ruby replied, nodding her head with certainty.

There was a crazy sort of logic to the answer, but again Michel wondered about its sincerity. He decided he would be careful around Ruby.

"Well, I best be going," Ruby said suddenly.

She walked to the door and picked up her shotgun, then turned back to Michel.

"You say hi to Verle for me, okay?" she said.

"Sure," Michel replied.

Ruby nodded and blinked her eyes.

"And if you need anything I'm through the swamp that way," she said, waving her hand toward the back of the house.

"There's a path, but Blue knows the way, too. Probably best if you bring her with you if you come so you don't get eaten by the gators."

Then she turned and walked out.

"I'll be sure to do that," Michel said to the empty doorway.

Chapter 7

Michel picked up the two ceramic bowls from the floor just outside the kitchen and carried them to the sink. He rinsed them and filled one with water and the other with dry food from a bag in the pantry.

"There," he said as he placed them back on the floor. "I'm already getting the hang of this uncle thing."

Blue looked at him for a moment, then walked to the bowls and began loudly lapping at the water.

Michel checked his watch. It was a little after 9 PM. He picked up his jacket from the chair where he'd tossed it and took out his cell phone and the pack of Camels.

"I've got to make a call, okay?" he said to Blue.

She continued drinking without acknowledging him.

He stepped out onto the front porch and took a deep breath. The night air was comfortably warm and dry. He searched the trees and bushes surrounding the front yard for a minute, then settled into one of the rockers. Blue walked out onto the porch and sprawled out by his feet.

Michel flipped open his phone and hit the speed dial.

"How's Verle?" Sassy answered after the first ring.

"He's doing okay," Michel replied.

"So what was he in for?"

"Murder," Michel replied around a cigarette.

"Seriously?" Sassy asked.

"Mmm hmmm," Michel replied as he flicked the lighter and took a drag.

Blue looked up at him, then stood and walked to the far end of the porch to lie down again.

"You don't sound too concerned about it," Sassy said.

"I'm not," Michel replied. "The state police got a call about a car off the road. A trooper went to investigate, didn't find anything, but he found Verle's truck about a mile away. While he was there, Verle came walking out of the swamp carrying the victim's body. He said he found her and brought her out so she wouldn't be eaten."

"Did he know the victim?"

"He says no. The Staties are checking his computer to see if he had any contact with her," Michel replied. "She was from Metairie. Had a few busts for prostitution."

He looked at the cigarette and grimaced. It tasted like sawdust that had been collected from the bottom of a hamster cage. He decided he'd have to try a different brand tomorrow.

"Did you have a chance to see to him?" Sassy asked.

"Yeah, briefly. The sheriff took me to visit him this afternoon," Michel replied. "He's being held up in Baton Rouge. The crime was in state jurisdiction."

"And how did it go?" Sassy prodded.

Michel paused for a moment to consider.

"It was nice," he said finally. "It was like no time had passed. And we had a chance to talk about things. About *us*."

"Good," Sassy replied with genuine enthusiasm.

"Yeah," Michel agreed, smiling. "I'll fill you in on the details when I see you."

He dropped the cigarette onto the porch and carefully put it out with his right foot.

"One weird thing, though," he added.

"What?"

"I was wondering how the sheriff knew to call the office. He said Verle had the number in his address book. So I asked Verle about it. He said he's been chatting with someone in New

Orleans for about six months. A guy from one of his nature groups. They met in a chat room and the guy asked if he was related to me."

"That's odd," Sassy replied.

"It gets even odder," Michel replied. "The guy's screen name is SeverinIV."

"Severin Marchand?" Sassy asked incredulously.

"Seems likely," Michel replied. "I mean how many Severins are there in New Orleans, especially who know who I am?"

"That *is* odd," Sassy replied. "What do you think that's about?"

"I don't know," Michel replied, "but it's kind of creepy. It's like he was stalking me. I remember the first time I went to his house, he asked me why we'd never met before. Makes me wonder if he hired us just so he *could* meet me."

"You think he has a crush on you?" Sassy asked.

"Well, if he did, I'm sure he got over it when I called him 'an ignorant, petty, frightened old queen'." Michel replied with a laugh.

"You and your silver tongue," Sassy said, laughing, too. "You want me to check it out?"

"No," Michel replied casually. "I'll ask him the next time I see him."

"Okay," Sassy replied. "So when are they letting Verle out?"

"I don't know," Michel replied. "I suppose as soon as they're convinced he's innocent."

"Wait a second, you didn't bail him out?" Sassy asked, her tone suddenly concerned.

"No, he hasn't even had a hearing yet. Why?"

"Because $10,000 is missing from our bank account."

"What? Did you ask Chance about it?" Michel asked.

"He's the one who noticed it," Sassy replied. "He was paying bills online and noticed that the balance had dropped $10,000 since two days ago. We figured you'd used it for bail."

"Fuck," Michel replied.

"Well don't worry about it," Sassy said quickly in a reassuring tone. "I'm sure it was just a mistake. We'll take care of it. You just focus on helping Verle."

Michel nodded to himself.

"Yeah, I will," he said. "Thanks. I'll give you a call tomorrow and let you know what's going on."

"Okay," Sassy replied. "Oh, and I almost forgot. Chance talked to Joel today. He's coming back this weekend. I figured you'd want to know."

Michel stared out into the darkness for a moment. Before Joel had gone to Mississippi to help out while his grandfather recovered from a heart attack, he'd told Michel that he was willing to give their relationship another try, and that when he returned he wanted to know if Michel was willing, too. Michel knew he still wasn't sure.

"Okay, thanks for telling me," he said. "Good night."

He stood up and stretched.

"What do you say, Blue? Time for bed?" he asked.

He turned and looked across the porch. Blue was on her side with her legs stretched out toward him. Suddenly she rolled onto her back, her hind legs splayed open and her front paws curled in above her chest like the arms of a T-Rex. She looked at him expectantly and brushed the porch with her long tail.

Michel let out a short laugh.

"Okay, I get it," he said, walking toward her. "A few minutes of belly rubs and *then* bed."

Chapter 8

Michel got into town at 7:50 AM. Ruby had shown up at Verle's just after 6 AM while he was sitting on the front porch in his boxer shorts, drinking coffee and trying to enjoy another cigarette. She didn't seem to take any notice of his lack of clothing and had offered to take Blue for the day. He'd gratefully accepted, not wanting to leave the dog alone at the house, and worried about keeping her in the car while he ate breakfast and visited Verle.

He parked in front of the police station. Turner's car wasn't there yet, so he decided to walk up the block to see if the market was open. Through the window he could see the old man already perched on his stool reading the paper.

"Another pack of Camels?" the old man asked as soon as Michel walked up to the counter.

"No," Michel replied, "Something else."

"Good, because that was the last pack," the old man said.

"Really?" Michel replied. "Guess that must be the popular brand around here."

The old man shook his head.

"Nope, you're the only one who smokes 'em. That pack's been waiting for someone to buy it for at least two years. But I've still got..."

He looked up and peered over his glasses, counting each pack with the bony index finger of his right hand.

"...two packs of Marlboros, three Winstons and one Kool."

Michel gave him a disbelieving look.

"Wait a second," he said. "Those Camels were two years old?"

The old man nodded.

"Are they all two years old?" Michel asked.

"More or less," the old man replied. "I think the Kools are a little older."

No wonder they tasted like shit, Michel thought.

"So no one in town smokes?" Michel asked.

"Oh sure, lots of 'em smoke, but they don't buy 'em here," the old man replied. "They get 'em at the gas station out on the highway or at the Gator's Belly."

"What's the Gator's Belly?" Michel asked.

"It's the local roadhouse," the old man replied with sudden impatience. "So you buying or what?"

Michel nodded. He really didn't want another stale pack of cigarettes but felt obligated.

"Yeah, I'll try the Marlboros," he said.

"You got it," the old man replied.

He pulled down the pack and tossed it on the counter.

"Four dollars."

Michel handed him a ten and picked up the cigarettes.

"So you're Verle's cousin, are you?" the old man asked as he counted out the change.

"Uh yeah," Michel replied, surprised. "How'd you know?"

"Pretty small town in case you hadn't noticed," the old man replied with a hint of sarcasm. "Stranger shows up and everyone notices. Word gets around fast."

"I guess so," Michel replied.

He suddenly felt a little uncomfortable. He took the bills and quickly stuffed them in his pocket.

"Well, thanks," he said, then started toward the door.

"Tell him I said hello," the old man said.

Michel stopped and looked at him, wondering whether he was being sincere.

"Verle's all right," the old man said as though reading his thoughts. "Can't say as I understand why he'd want to give away all that land when he can make good money on it, but he's always treated me well, so…"

Michel nodded. He appreciated the old man's directness and perspective.

"So who should I tell him said hello?" he asked.

"Cyrus," the old man replied, then shuffled back to his stool.

*****

Michel could feel eyes on him as he walked back down the block toward the police station. He looked to his right and saw at least a dozen faces turned toward him through the plate glass windows of the diner. He was about to cross the street to wait for Russell Turner in the relative privacy under the marquee of the movie theater, when Turner's car came around the corner. It was moving fast and Michel felt suddenly apprehensive.

The car pulled to an abrupt halt next to Michel and Turner jumped out. His expression was grave.

"What's wrong?" Michel asked, his adrenaline surging.

Turner walked around the front of the car. Michel felt as though a bullet were moving toward him in slow motion, yet he was helpless to move out of its path.

"Verle's dead," Turner replied gently.

He put his left hand on Michel's right shoulder.

"I'm sorry, Michel."

Michel felt numb. His mind was buzzing from the adrenaline, but his body felt completely slack.

"How?" he managed to ask.

"They think it was a heart attack," Turner replied.

"A heart attack? But he was only fifty-three years old."

Turner nodded.

"He was complaining that he didn't feel right this morning, so they called an ambulance," he said. "Before it arrived, Verle collapsed. They rushed him to the hospital, but he didn't make it."

Michel stared at the ground. Suddenly he thought of Blue and felt his throat tighten. He looked at Turner and took a deep breath.

"I want to see him," he said.

Chapter 9

Verle lay on a steel table with a white sheet covering him from the chest down. Michel stared down into his face. The tension and fatigue that he'd seen there the afternoon before were gone. Verle looked truly at peace.

"I'm sorry," Michel said quietly. "I never meant to hurt you."

Although he'd always believed that once people died they were simply gone, the thought that Verle's soul might be hovering nearby listening gave him some comfort.

He leaned down and kissed Verle on the forehead. Verle's skin hadn't yet grown cold.

"I promise I'll take care of Blue," he said, then started to cry.

*****

By the time he stepped into the hallway a few minutes later, Michel had achieved a state of emotional detachment. It was a familiar feeling: a coping mechanism he'd developed while working homicide that allowed him to focus on his work until the investigation was complete. He'd used that same mechanism in the days immediately following his mother's death, going about the business of making arrangements with business-like efficiency while postponing grief. Since then he'd found it more and more difficult to set his emotions aside, but now he was feeling composed and focused.

Turner was waiting for him with a trooper in formal dress uniform. The trooper's face was handsome and unlined, but his iron-gray flattop suggested he was at least a decade older than he appeared. By his steady gaze and rigid bearing, Michel guessed that he'd been in the military.

"Michel, this is Captain Lewdet," Turner said.

Lewdet extended his hand crisply.

"I'm sorry for your loss, Mr. Doucette," Lewdet said.

"Thank you," Michel replied, shaking Lewdet's hand. "Can you tell me what happened?"

Lewdet nodded.

"The trooper on duty brought your cousin breakfast at 0-six-hundred hours. Your cousin indicated that he was nauseated and experiencing pain in his chest. The trooper noted that he was also sweating profusely and immediately called for an ambulance. While they were waiting, your cousin suffered an apparent heart attack."

"How long did it take for the ambulance to get there?" Michel asked.

"Six minutes," Lewdet replied with certainty. "The trooper administered CPR until it arrived."

"Was he trained?" Michel asked.

"Yes, sir," Lewdet replied. "All of our detention facility personnel are certified in CPR."

"And Verle was still alive when the ambulance arrived?" Michel asked.

"He flatlined on the way here," Lewdet replied with a nod. "The EMTs attempted to revive him but were unsuccessful."

Lewdet's tone was professional but not without compassion. Michel decided he liked him.

"Did the doctor say anything about what might have caused the heart attack?" he asked.

Lewdet tilted his head slightly and looked at Michel curiously.

"Are you a cop, Mr. Doucette?" he asked.

"I *was*," Michel replied. "NOPD homicide division. Why?"

Lewdet gave him a small smile.

"I can tell," he said.

Michel realized he'd been asking questions as though he were conducting an interrogation.

"I'm sorry," he said. "Force of habit."

"No problem," Lewdet replied. "It's understandable given the circumstances. The doctor thinks it was probably a combination of stress and the exertion from carrying the woman out of the swamp."

"But that was almost thirty-six hours ago," Michel replied.

Lewdet nodded.

"Apparently it's not uncommon for there to be a delayed reaction for people with heart problems."

"Heart problems?" Michel replied with surprise.

"According to his medical records, your cousin had a bypass two years ago," Lewdet replied.

"Did you know about that?" Michel asked, looking at Turner.

Turner didn't respond for a few seconds. He was staring at the floor, lost in thought. Finally he seemed to realize Michel was talking to him and jerked his eyes up.

"Huh?"

"Did you know about Verle's bypass?" Michel asked.

"Yeah," Turner replied, nodding distractedly.

"He was also on several medications," Lewdet continued.

"Was he taking them in jail?" Michel asked.

"He told the arresting officer about them, so we sent someone by the house to pick them up," Lewdet replied.

Michel nodded. Everything seemed in order: what Lewdet had said made sense, and everything had been handled by the book. Still, he couldn't help but feel that something wasn't right.

"Well, thank you, Captain," he said. "I appreciate your time."

*****

Michel unwrapped the pack of Marlboros and lit one. He took a stale drag and stared out the window at the passing trees as Russell Turner drove them back to Bayou Proche.

"I'd like to have an autopsy done," he said.

"An autopsy?" Turner asked. "Why?"

"Verle was accused of murder and two days later he's dead," Michel replied.

"So what are you saying? You think he may have been killed?" Turner asked, looking at Michel skeptically.

Michel shrugged.

"Something about it just doesn't feel right. Verle goes out for a walk in the swamp and just happens to find a body, then as he's bringing it back to his truck a state trooper just happens to be there, and then Verle just happens to have a heart attack. It all just seems sort of...convenient. I mean that swamp is huge. What are the odds of him happening across the body?"

"He had Blue with him," Turner replied. "She's the one who found the body. If she hadn't been there, Verle probably *wouldn't* have found it."

"But she *was* with him, and if someone were trying to set Verle up, they would have known that he'd have Blue with him."

"I don't know, Michel," Turner replied, shaking his head. "That really feels like a stretch."

He looked back at the road.

"And even if he was set up, how could someone kill him once he was in jail? You think they paid a trooper to poison him?"

"No," Michel replied, "but it would have been easy enough to switch his medication at the house."

"Seems like a lot of trouble to go through," Turner replied. "If someone wanted to kill Verle, it would have been easy enough to just shoot him in the swamp and leave him there.

Within a week or two there wouldn't even have been any bones left."

"But someone would have noticed he was missing," Michel replied. "You would have investigated. You might have found his body. This way it's all tied up nice and neat."

Turner looked at Michel, but Michel continued to stare out the window.

"But what's the motive?" Turner asked with a hint of frustration.

"To get Verle's land," Michel replied.

His tone suggested that the truth of the statement was immutable.

"You've been talking to Ruby," Turner said.

Michel turned to look at him with mild surprise.

"Yeah, how'd you know?"

"Because Ruby's had it out for Porter DeCew since day one," Turner replied. "She's convinced that he's been trying to rob Verle blind."

"Isn't it possible?" Michel asked.

Turner shook his head.

"Porter doesn't need Verle's money. He had a big practice in Baton Rouge for years. Worked for a lot of the oil companies. He made plenty and I suspect he still has his first nickel."

"The oil companies?" Michel replied. "You mean the same oil companies that have been trying to get Verle's land?"

"Hold on," Turner said. "I see where you're going, but you're wrong. The whole reason that Porter got involved with the wildlife trust is *because* of his dealings with the oil companies. He was on the other side of the table trying to sue Verle for years, but eventually he saw enough that he didn't like and decided to change sides."

"Or maybe he's a Trojan horse," Michel replied.

"No offense, Michel," Turner said carefully, "but I think you're clutching at straws. I understand that you want to clear

Verle's name, but don't you think it's possible that you're seeing conspiracies because you need to see them?"

"No offense, Russ," Michel snapped back, "but I think you might be a little out of your depth on this one."

Even as he said it, he regretted it. Turner had been nothing but kind to him.

"No offense, Michel," Turner replied tersely, "but I think your concern for your cousin might be coming a little late."

Michel felt like he'd been sucker-punched. He glared at Turner, but Turner returned his gaze coolly.

"Yeah, I know that you and Verle hadn't spoken for ten years," Turner said. "He never told me the details, but given the way he talked about you, I'm guessing it was your choice."

Michel was silent for a moment. He could feel his anger slowly ebbing away and sadness taking its place.

"I'm sorry," he said finally. "I was out of line. That was a shitty thing to say. I'm just feeling...I don't know...angry, I guess."

"Angry at who?" Turner asked pointedly.

Michel considered it for a moment.

"Myself, I guess," he said finally. "You just said it. For ten years I've had nothing to do with Verle. It was like he didn't exist. And now he's gone and it's too late to do anything about it. I can't help feeling that if I'd reached out to him, this whole thing wouldn't have happened. I know it's not logical, but that's how I feel."

Turner was silent for almost a minute, his eyes fixed on the road.

"I understand," he said finally.

His voice was subdued, almost mournful. Michel noticed his hands tighten on the steering wheel.

"I was supposed to be there when Thesalee died," he said. "She was sick and wanted me to take her to the hospital, but I had a meeting with the town council, so she left Corey with a neighbor and went alone. On her way back from Baton Rouge, a semi crossed over the median and hit the car."

"I'm sorry," Michel said.

"For years I beat myself up over it. I felt like if I'd been there I could have done something. I could have swerved to avoid the truck, or I might have been driving a little faster or a little slower and the car wouldn't have been in that place when the truck crossed over."

"Or it might have happened the exact same way and Corey would have lost both of you," Michel offered.

"Exactly," Turner replied. "And this same thing might have happened with Verle even if you'd called him every day and visited him once a month. The only difference is that you wouldn't feel so guilty now. But if you think you can wash away whatever guilt you're feeling by proving he was innocent, then you're wrong. That's just something you'll have to come to grips with on your own."

"You're right," Michel replied after a thoughtful pause, "but I still feel like it's something I have to do. I need to find out the truth. For Verle *and* Dolores Hagen."

"That's police business," Turner said.

Something in his tone caught Michel's ear. It had almost sounded like a warning.

"What aren't you telling me?" Michel asked.

Turner looked at Michel for a moment, then back at the road. He seemed to be mulling something over.

"Look Michel," he said, "I didn't want to say anything right now because I wanted to give you a chance to grieve first, but Lewdet told me they found emails on Verle's computer."

"Between Verle and Hagen?" Michel asked with disbelief.

Turner nodded.

"Saying what?" Michel asked.

"I don't want to go into the details," Turner replied. "It was pretty graphic. But it looks like he found her online and made arrangements for her to come here for sex."

"When?" Michel asked, though he already knew the answer.

"The night before last," Turner replied solemnly.

"There's got to be some mistake," Michel replied immediately. "Or someone planted the emails."

Turner sighed.

"I hope so," he said. "But I think it's best to leave things to the state police now."

"Why?" Michel asked, sensing there was more that Turner hadn't told him.

"I'm just saying that maybe it's best not to stir things up," Turner replied. "The victim apparently didn't have any close family, so no one's going to be pressing for justice for her. Lewdet is prepared to release a statement saying that Verle was a suspect but that the investigation is inconclusive at this point. The press will lose interest in a week and the whole thing can just go away. With Verle gone, there's not going to be a trial, and without a trial, Verle will still be presumed innocent according to the law."

"Since when do people form their opinions according to the law?" Michel asked sarcastically. "As far as everyone's going to be concerned, Verle was arrested for murder and just happened to die before he could go to trial. They're going to assume he was guilty. I can't let that happen. Verle deserves better than that."

Turner suddenly turned the wheel hard to the right and slammed on the brakes. The car skidded to a stop by the side of the road, spewing gravel into the bushes.

"You know what?" he said, banging his hands on the steering wheel. "You just need to shut the fuck up."

Michel gave him a startled look.

"Excuse me?"

"When you asked me yesterday if Verle and I were friends, I lied," Turner said angrily. "Verle was my best friend."

"Why didn't you tell me?" Michel asked helplessly.

"Because I don't know you, Michel," Turner replied more calmy. "Verle always said good things about you, but all I know is that you didn't talk to him for ten years. So I'm grieving for my best friend and you're carrying on some bullshit about conspiracies and doing justice for Verle and it's just starting to piss me off. Excuse me, but Verle was a memory for you. He was real for me."

They sat in tense silence for a few moments.

"I'm sorry," Michel said finally.

"No," Turner replied wearily. "I'm just hurting. I didn't mean to take it out on you. I know your heart's in the right place. It's just...hard right now."

He rubbed his eyes with the heels of his hands for a few seconds, then looked at Michel. His expression was resigned.

"Besides, what if you're wrong?" he asked.

"What do you mean?" Michel asked.

"What if Verle really did kill Dolores Hagen? Right now, people will believe what they want. You push this thing and it turns out Verle was guilty, that's not going away. People will always think of him as a killer. Are you willing to risk that?"

Michel slumped back against the seat as the enormity of what Turner said hit him. He realized that his need to ease his own guilt was so great that he'd failed to consider the possible consequences.

"Maybe you're right," he said, as much to himself as Turner. "Maybe I should just let it go."

Chapter 10

After Turner dropped him in town, Michel had driven slowly back to Verle's house. He felt as though he'd been caught up in a tornado. Twenty-four hours earlier, he'd been sitting in a movie theater with Sassy. He'd been in his own world, living his own life that didn't include a cousin he hadn't thought of for more than a few seconds in years. Now that seemed like so long ago. Now he was in Verle's world, and Verle was dead.

He tried to focus on the practical matters at hand. Unlike sorrow and guilt, those were things he could control, at least to some extent. Verle's funeral had to be arranged and possibly his estate settled. He realized that it was going to be much more difficult since he didn't even know Verle or what Verle would have wanted. He hoped that Verle had named Russell Turner or Porter DeCew as his executor.

He pulled to a stop in front of the house and got out, then looked around, half-expecting Blue to be waiting for him. He felt a small pang of disappointment that she wasn't.

He went into the house and searched through the dresser in Verle's bedroom until he found a pair of jeans and a black t-shirt that looked like they'd come closest to fitting him, then changed and went back to the living room. Several pairs of boots and sneakers were neatly lined up by the front door. He grabbed a pair of well-worn tan construction boots and laced them on, hoping they'd be adequate for his journey.

He knew that one task lay immediately ahead of him: telling Ruby that Verle was gone. During his years on the force, he'd never had to inform next of kin about deaths. It was a duty usually handled by uniformed officers or the police chaplain. He thought about how Turner had told him. It had been simple and direct. There'd been no preamble, no "I'm sorry but I have bad news," or "Michel, I have something to tell you." Turner had gotten immediately to the point. That approach felt right, and like one he could comfortably manage. Still, he was filled with anxiety, though he wasn't sure if it was because of the grim duty, his uncertainty about how Ruby would react, or the fact that he had to walk through the swamp alone first to get to her house. He decided it was probably a combination of them all.

He went out to his car and unlocked the trunk. He pulled out his holster and clipped it on his belt, then took his Smith & Wesson M&P out of its locked case, inserted a magazine in the grip, and placed it in the holster. Then he walked around the back of the house.

In the far right corner of the yard was a break in the dense underbrush. He walked to it and started up the path.

*****

He'd been walking for almost fifteen minutes when he saw a roof about a hundred yards through the trees to his right. A bend in the path ahead seemed to lead to it. Somewhere to his left, he heard a rustling noise and stopped. He scanned the tall, dense ferns that covered the ground deep into the forest.

Ten yards away, a small cluster danced for a moment, then was still. He watched carefully, his heart beating faster. Then the ferns shook again, this time more violently. He pulled his pistol and racked the slide, wondering whether the .45 caliber rounds would be enough to stop a charging alligator.

He levelled the gun, bracing his right arm with his left, and closed his left eye. He shifted his arms down a few inches and to the left until the gun's sights were centered on the moving

63

ferns, then took a slow deep breath. He could feel a trickle of sweat rolling down the center of his back.

Suddenly something broke out of the ferns. Michel's finger tightened reflexively on the trigger but he stopped himself from firing. A large gray and black bird with a long neck and dangling legs flew up to the branches of a nearby oak. Michel could see the legs of a frogs protruding from its spiked bill.

He exhaled and let out a nervous laugh.

"That was almost your last supper," he said, flicking the safety on the gun.

He turned back toward the path and jumped. Blue was standing at the bend watching him.

"Shit, don't you know better than to sneak up on a twitchy guy with a gun?" he asked.

He took a step toward her and her ears went back. She backed away two steps.

"Hey, it's just me," Michel said in a reassuring voice.

Blue let out a low growl. Michel looked at her warily, then realized she was looking at his gun. He slowly placed it back in his holster.

"I'm sorry, girl," he said, crouching down. "Come here."

Blue took a few tentative steps forward, then her ears came up and her tail began to wag. She came to him, cantering like a pony, and pushed her head into his stomach. He rubbed the soft fur of her neck and thought his heart might break.

*****

As he approached the yard of the small cabin, Michel remembered the shotgun Ruby had been carrying the night before. He guessed that she always kept it handy in case any trespassers came her way.

"Ruby!" he called from the edge of the yard. "It's Michel Doucette!"

A moment later Ruby poked her head out of the open door of the cabin. In the daylight, Michel could see her more clearly. With her weathered skin and hard-bitten expression, she reminded him of the migrant workers photographed by Walker Evans and Dorothea Lange during the Depression. Her pale blue eyes also had the same steely resolve.

"Expecting trouble?" she asked, as she stepped into the bare but tidy dirt yard.

Michel noticed that she was wearing the same clothes from before, but was barefoot.

"Huh?" he asked distractedly.

Ruby nodded at his holster and Michel gave an embarrassed smile.

"Well, you did tell me to look out for the gators if I came out here," he said.

"I was just funning with you," Ruby replied with a dry chuckle. "The gators are all out toward the bayou right now. They won't be back this way until we get the spring rain. So what's wrong?"

Michel was startled by the abruptness of the question. He wondered if she'd been able to read the trouble in his face.

"Verle's dead," he replied.

Ruby pursed her lips and looked down at the ground for a few moments.

"That's what I figured," she replied resignedly. "The dog's been acting funny since about seven this morning. I knew something had happened."

Michel looked down at Blue. She looked back at him and he swore he saw sorrow in her eyes.

"So what happened?" Ruby asked.

"It looks like a heart attack," Michel replied. "Probably from the stress of carrying the woman out of the swamp."

Ruby nodded. "I guess it was bound to happen sooner or later what with his bad heart. I kept telling him not to go swamping by himself but he wouldn't listen. Said if he was meant to die out there, he was meant to die out there."

They were both silent for a minute, then Ruby scratched her head and nodded emphatically as though she'd just come to a decision or accepted a truth.

"So I guess this means you won't be sticking around much longer," she said.

To Michel's surprise, she sounded slightly sad. He wondered if the thought of being alone was so intolerable that she would even consider spending time with a stranger preferable. His initial take on Ruby had been that she spent time with others only by choice, not out of need. Perhaps he'd been wrong.

"I won't be leaving until the state police figure out who really killed Dolores Hagen," he said.

He decided there was nothing to be gained by telling her about the emails found on Verle's computer for now.

"And you don't think it was Verle?" Ruby asked.

Michel was caught off-guard by the question.

"No. Why, do you?" he asked.

"No," Ruby replied, "but I just wanted to make sure *you* didn't."

"I may not have been close with Verle for a long time," Michel replied slowly, responding to the challenge he thought he'd heard in her voice, "but I know he wouldn't kill someone."

"Good," Ruby replied. "So you going to be staying at the house?"

"Yeah," Michel replied. "Seems as good a place as any."

"Better than most," Ruby said. "Besides, I think that'll be good for the dog."

"Yeah, I imagine so," Michel replied.

Ruby studied the ground for a moment, then looked up at Michel with a worried expression.

"You gonna take her with you when you leave?" she asked.

Suddenly Michel understood the previous sadness in Ruby's voice. It wasn't his leaving she was worried about.

"I hadn't thought about it yet," he replied honestly. "Everything's happened so fast."

"Well, if you want to leave her with me...while you're doing whatever you're doing...feel free," Ruby said. "She's always welcome here."

"I appreciate that," Michel replied, "and I will."

"Good enough," Ruby said.

"There's something else you might be able to help me with, too," Michel said.

"What's that?" Ruby replied.

She seemed to brighten at the thought that her help might be needed.

"I have to make arrangements," Michel said. "Do you know what Verle would have wanted?"

He thought that perhaps Verle would want to be cremated and his ashes spread in the swamp.

"I imagine he'd want to be buried alongside his folks," Ruby replied. "Seems he was close with them from what he said."

Michel nodded, knowing it was true.

"Did he go to church?" he asked.

"I imagine he must have at least once," Ruby replied.

Michel wondered again if she was being purposefully obtuse or just overly literal-minded.

"I mean did he belong to any particular church?" he clarified.

"I don't remember him going nowhere on Sunday mornings," Ruby replied.

Something about the way she said it suggested that she and Verle would naturally have been together on Sunday mornings. A thought suddenly occurred to Michel.

"Ruby," he said, choosing his words carefully, "were you and Verle...more than friends?"

Ruby looked at him without comprehension for a moment, then her small eyes grew wide and her mouth opened slightly. Michel thought he detected a hint of a blush on her cheeks.

"Oh, gosh no," she replied quickly. "We weren't intimate, if that's what you're asking."

Michel smiled to himself at her word choice. It sounded so quaint and delicate.

"I'm sorry," he said. "I didn't mean to pry. I was just wondering..."

"Well you can stop that," Ruby interrupted with a sudden force that suggested Michel's interest had crossed the line into prurience.

"I'm sorry," Michel said again, this time defensively.

Ruby studied him for a moment, then nodded, though warning clouds remained in her eyes. Michel decided it would be a good time to leave.

"So'd they find anything on Verle's computer?" Ruby asked suddenly with a casualness that suggested the previous few seconds hadn't happened.

Michel felt himself blink involuntarily. Ruby's quicksilver mood shift had already unsettled him, and now her abrupt, unexpected question had blindsided him. He realized she would have made a very effective interrogator. He also realized that he had already betrayed the answer on his face.

"I'm afraid so," he said. "He and Dolores Hagen had exchanged emails. They'd arranged to meet the night she was killed."

Ruby looked at him with wounded eyes.

"He didn't say nothing to me about it," she said.

Her lower lip pushed forward into an exaggerated pout and she stared at the ground. Michel wasn't sure what to do or say.

"But you said you don't think he did it," Ruby said suddenly, looking up at Michel.

Her expression was a mixture of desperation and hope.

"No," Michel agreed. "I don't."

"You planning to prove it?" Ruby asked.

"I don't know," Michel replied with a shrug.

"Why not?"

"I'm not sure what I can do," Michel replied. "I'm not a cop anymore. The best way to prove that Verle was innocent would be to prove that someone else killed Hagen, but without access to evidence and forensic resources that's almost impossible."

He let out a weary sigh and shook his head.

"Russ Turner thinks I should just leave it alone. He said the state police are willing to release a statement saying that Verle had been arrested but the investigation was inconclusive. Turner thinks I should just accept that and let the whole thing blow over."

He'd expected Ruby to unleash a torrent of invective directed at Turner, but to his surprise she simply nodded.

"Even a broke clock's right twice a day," she said. "I suppose the sooner it's left be, the sooner people will stop talking and forget about it."

It was a completely reasonable sentiment, but Michel was surprised.

"You'd be okay with that?" he asked. "People thinking that Verle killed Dolores Hagen?"

Ruby seemed to consider it thoughtfully for a few seconds.

"I don't know as it matters much to Verle what people think now," she said. "Not sure that it ever did. Only thing that matters now is what God thinks, and if Verle didn't do it, God already knows that."

Michel didn't know how to respond. Faith was something beyond his comfort zone. He'd seen too many horrible things happen to good people to believe that a God was watching and keeping score. He'd spent his entire adult life seeking justice in this life because he lacked faith that rewards and punishment would be doled out in an afterlife.

"Of course, if you don't believe in such things, I suppose you have to do what you feel is right," Ruby said, as though reading his thoughts.

Michel decided that Ruby might be eccentric, but she was shrewd.

"Yeah, I suppose so," he replied.

Chapter 11

"Hey, it's me," Michel said.

He was sitting on the front porch of Verle's house. Blue had taken up her position at the far end as soon as he'd lit his cigarette.

"Yeah, I know. I know how to use Caller ID," Sassy replied. "So how's Verle doing?"

"He's dead," Michel replied. "He had a heart attack."

"Oh Michel, I'm so sorry," Sassy replied. "How are you doing?"

Michel felt his throat constrict slightly. He'd always found Sassy's concern for him deeply touching. He took a sip of the Jack Daniels he'd found in the kitchen.

"I'm okay," he said finally. "I just need some advice."

"I'm all ears," Sassy replied.

Michel filled her in on the details surrounding Verle's death, and his subsequent conversations with Turner and Ruby.

"So I'm not sure what to do," he finished. "Part of me feels like I need to see this through and find out who really killed Dolores Hagen, and part of me just wants to cut and run."

"Which part is winning?" Sassy asked.

"Honestly, I'm not sure," Michel replied. "I understand that I might make things worse if I push for an investigation, but after being a cop, it's hard to just let it go."

"Not to mention the guilt factor," Sassy replied, not unkindly.

"Yeah, that, too," Michel admitted.

They were both quiet for a moment. Michel took another sip of Jack Daniels and finished his cigarette. He dropped it into his makeshift beer can ashtray.

"So are you asking me for advice or permission?" Sassy asked finally.

Michel smiled. Sassy always had a knack for reading him and cutting through his bullshit.

"Permission?" he replied in a small, hopeful voice.

He could hear Sassy laugh appreciatively.

"Well, I'm afraid all I can give you is advice," she said. "Look, I get the whole need for justice thing. Been there, done that, and have the scars to prove it. And I get the guilt thing. But right now it seems like you're trying to connect dots that really have no connection. And I get that, too. You said it yourself: Verle was like a big brother to you, and now you want to protect his memory. But unless you find out that Verle left all his land to an oil company, it doesn't sound like there's really anything going on, in which case I don't see an upside to you getting involved. Seems the thing most likely to come out of it is everyone thinking there's another crazy Doucette. Besides, we both know the state police are going to keep investigating anyway. If it wasn't Verle, it'll come out. And if it was..."

She didn't need to complete the thought.

"As far as permission goes," she said, "I'm afraid you're going to have to give that to yourself, but it sounds like the two people closest to Verle would be okay with it if you just let it be."

Michel nodded to himself. Everything Sassy had said made perfect sense.

"Thanks," he said sincerely.

"No problem," Sassy replied. "Do you want me to come up there?"

"No. Thank you," Michel replied. "I appreciate it, but I'll be okay."

"You sure?"

"Yeah. Hopefully we can have the funeral in the next few days, then I can head home."

"Okay, but let me know if you change your mind," Sassy said. "I could visit my cousin Pearl while I was in the area."

"You have a cousin named Pearl?" Michel asked.

"Yeah, Pearl Cousins," Sassy replied matter-of-factly. "She's on my mother's side. She lives in Opelousas."

There was a pause as Michel felt a giggling fit coming on and tried to suppress it.

"So wait," he said after a few seconds. "You have a cousin named Pearl Cousins? In Opelousas?"

"Yes, I have a cousin named Pearl Cousins in Opelousas," Sassy replied patiently "Is there a problem with that?"

"No, not at all," Michel replied, barely able to hold back the laughter now. "It's just funny that...you never mentioned it."

Then he burst into loud, helpless laughter. It felt good. He realized that it really didn't have much to do with Sassy's cousin. It was just a release from the emotional stress of the day.

"I'm sorry," he managed, though he could barely breathe.

He continued laughing hard for almost a minute, then finally managed to bring it under control.

"Are you done?" Sassy asked with mock indignation.

"Yeah, I think so," Michel replied, wiping the tears from his eyes with the right sleeve of his t-shirt.

"Good," Sassy said. "Because I have just two words for you: Cousin Verle."

Then they both began to laugh uncontrollably. Each time one's laughter would begin to subside, the other would snort and it would start up again. Finally, after a full minute, Michel knew he had to hang up. His stomach hurt and Blue had skittered into the house to get away from him.

"Sas, I have to go," he said, his breathing ragged from the exertion. "I can't take anymore."

"Me neither," Sassy replied with a loud theatrical sigh.

Michel waited a few seconds until they'd both had a chance to catch their breath.

"Thanks again, Sas," he said, his tone suddenly serious.

"You're welcome, partner," Sassy replied. "Try to get some sleep. I'll talk to you tomorrow."

Chapter 12

Michel sat on the porch and smoked another cigarette, making a mental note to find a gas station the next day to buy a pack that hadn't already had a birthday, then went inside. Blue was lying on the floor next to the couch. She lifted her head for a moment to look at him, then lowered it and closed her eyes. She seemed much less energetic than she had the day before.

Michel looked around the living room. Despite the fact that Verle's appearance had always been somewhat unkempt, he'd obviously inherited his mother's love of neatness and order. Even the magazines on the low table in front of the couch were stacked perfectly.

Despite the neatness, though, the room felt comfortable and welcoming. The floor, walls, and ceiling were all a warm reddish-orange wood. Michel guessed it was cedar, either reclaimed or milled from deadfall that Verle had found in the swamp. The couch and two chairs were well-stuffed and covered in cheery red fabric, and were arranged around a large, colorful, patterned rug. Above the stone fireplace that dominated the left wall was a rough-hewn mantle holding neatly arranged black-framed photos, and above that a large painting in tones of orange and yellow.

Michel walked over and studied it. There was no signature, but the bright colors, rough geometric shapes, and cloud-like texture were distinctly Rothko-esque.

"That must have cost a pretty penny," he murmured.

He looked down at the photos. They were arranged

chronologically: his aunt and uncle on a picnic, looking like fresh-faced teenagers; then leaving the church on their wedding day; then beaming as they held a newborn who was undoubtedly Verle; then in front of the farm, with Verle in a carriage. The last few were from their later years, with the final being just his uncle looking very much the way he had the last time Michel had seem him. Michel smiled wistfully, then walked to the back of the room.

He began perusing the titles of the books that filled the shelves lining the whole wall. They were mostly biographies and nature books, with a few volumes of poetry here and there.

"I don't suppose there's a TV hidden somewhere?" he asked, turning to look at Blue.

She let out a slow groan that sounded like a tired cow mooing.

He continued down the shelves, moving to his right. At the far end were two photos in simple silver frames, resting in front of three thick leather-bound volumes with no printing on their spines.

Michel picked up the first photo. It was of him, sitting on the back of a pony. He was dressed in jeans and a blue-and-white-checked shirt, and wearing a straw cowboy hat. He looked to be no more than five or six. He was smiling from ear-to-ear while Verle stood beside him holding the reins.

"The littlest member of the Village People," Michel said, then placed the picture back on the shelf exactly as it had been.

He picked up the other photo. It was of his mother and a man standing arm-in-arm in front of the farmhouse. They were both smiling, and the man had his right hand resting on the small mound of his mother's belly.

Michel looked closely at the man's face. It was like looking at a photo of himself, but with longer, slicked-back hair.

"Hi Dad," he said. "So finally we meet."

He stared at the photo, waiting to feel some kind of reaction to seeing his father's face for the first time, but nothing came. It was like looking at a photo of a stranger.

He placed it on the shelf below where it had been and pulled one of the leather-bound volumes off the higher shelf. He flipped it open. Under a yellowing plastic film was a large photo of an infant wearing a blue-knit cap. It had been inscribed along the bottom border in his mother's familiar looping handwriting: "Jean-Michel Doucette, Jr., February 13, 1973, 7 lbs., 13 oz."

Michel stared at it dumbly for a moment, then let out a hard, short laugh. It had been so long since he'd seen or heard his full name that he'd almost forgotten it. For as long as he could remember, he'd always been just Michel. In fact, he hadn't even learned his full name until he'd seen it on his birth certificate when he was applying for his driver's permit.

He'd asked his mother about it then and she'd told him that he'd been named after his father, though his father had been called John as a boy, then had adopted the more rakish Jack as a teenager. His mother had said that she'd decided to call him Michel because Jean-Michel or John would have been painful reminders of his father.

When he'd turned eighteen, Michel had legally changed his name. His full name had been a needless connection to his father that he no longer wanted. He'd never told anyone his birth name—not even Sassy—and now that his mother and Verle were gone, he was the only one who still knew it.

He flipped the page and saw another dozen baby photos. They were all dated, with his age noted in his mother's script. He continued through the book. It was a document of the first twelve years of his life: holidays, birthday parties, school photos, report cards, visits to the farm. In most of the photos he was alone, though in a few there were other children he no longer remembered.

He replaced the album on the shelf, grabbed the others, and carried them to the couch.

*****

He was halfway through the second album when he noticed hot breath pulsing against the left side of his face. He turned and saw Blue sitting on the cushion next to him. He hadn't even felt her climbing onto the couch.

"Are you supposed to be up here?" he asked skeptically.

Blue just looked at him with her tongue hanging out.

"Well, I suppose it's your couch now," he said.

Blue immediately lay down and Michel returned his attention to the album. He turned the page and saw a picture of himself in his high school track uniform. Although he'd always been on the lean side, he was surprised by how much thinner he'd been then.

"It's amazing I could walk on those skinny legs, never mind run," he said.

He felt Blue's nose pushing its way under his elbow and lifted his arm. She put her head in his lap.

"Look," Michel said, tapping the page. "That's me."

Blue lifted her head, then poked the page with her nose, leaving a wet spot on the plastic directly over Michel's face.

"Yeah, I was pretty hot then, huh?"

Blue dropped her head and closed her eyes, and Michel began absently scratching around her ears.

He turned the page. On the left was his high school graduation photo. He was wearing an oversized gray jacket with padded shoulders, a black shirt, and thin red tie. His hair was short on the sides but long in the back, and his bangs nearly covered his eyes.

"Mind you, I'd just gotten back from touring with Duran Duran," he said, shaking his head at his five-years-too-late fashion faux pas.

Under the protective sleeve on the right was a folded piece of paper. Michel took it out and opened it up. It was a letter.

Dear Verle,

Here's Michel's graduation photo that I promised you. I have to admit, it's a look I hope he'll outgrow soon.

He received his acceptance letter to the police academy yesterday. I still wish he'd go to college first so he could keep his options open, but once he gets something in his head, it's hard to change his mind. Who knows? Maybe it will be good for him. Maybe he'll make some friends.

Michel smiled to himself. Ultimately he had chosen to defer enrollment at the academy to get a Bachelor's Degree in criminology at LSU. At the time, he'd told his mother that he was heeding her advice, but the reality was that he knew a degree would help when he went up for his detective's shield.

He continued reading.

I've been thinking about what you said, and perhaps you're right, that he's just at that point where he regrets not having a father, but it's hard. He seems more withdrawn and distant every day, and I feel like I'm intruding if I ask him about anything. I worry that he's lonely.

But I'm sure he'll be okay. He's very strong and self-reliant. Maybe too much so. I imagine he'll be very successful some day. I just hope that he'll be happy.

Thank you again for your generosity. It means so much to me that your father, and now you, have continued to treat me as family.

Love,
Vera

Michel sat back and took a sip of Jack Daniels. He felt slightly dazed. While the photos had made it obvious that his mother had stayed in touch with his father's family over the years, the letter indicated that it had been a tight connection.

The tone of the letter was familiar, and it seemed to be part of an ongoing conversation between his mother and Verle.

He laid the letter on the coffee table and turned to the next page. On the left was a photo of him in his dress uniform, shaking hands with the superintendent of police as he received his diploma from the academy. On the right was another letter. Michel took it out and began reading:

Dear Verle,

Enclosed, please find a photo of Michel at his graduation. I must say he looks very handsome in his uniform, though I'm still worried about him being a policeman. I just wish he'd chosen a less dangerous career. But he seems excited to start working.

Despite your advice, I spoke with Lady Chanel yesterday. She was hesitant to say anything at first, but finally admitted that she has seen Michel on a few occasions leaving gay bars outside the French Quarter.

I want to tell him it's okay, but as usual I feel like I'd be intruding. I hope that at some point he'll be comfortable enough to tell me himself. I just feel like this secret is keeping us apart. He's a wonderful son in most ways, but there's a distance between us.

I look forward to speaking with you soon.
Love,
Vera

Now Michel felt dizzy. Emotions were hitting him so hard and fast that he could barely identify them.

"Sorry, girl," he said to Blue, "but I really need a cigarette."

*****

Five minutes later he sat back on the couch, a full glass of

Jack Daniels in his right hand. He picked up the album and began thumbing through it again.

The next few pages contained newspaper clippings, with his name highlighted in yellow. They were minor mentions in arrest reports, hardly indicative of a rising career, and certainly not worth saving. He turned to the last page. A light green card with an illustration of a white daisy was inserted under the sleeve. Michel slid it out and opened it.

Dear Verle

Happy birthday. I wish you much happiness in the coming year and always.

I'm sorry I haven't called in a while, but I have some wonderful news. Michel has been promoted to detective in the homicide division. Apparently it's quite an accomplishment for someone his age. I'm very proud of him, and also relieved.

He has a partner. Her name is Alexandra Jones, though Michel says she goes by Sassy. It sounds like the name of a character from one of those Pam Grier movies in the 1970s to me, but I would never say so to Michel. He seems quite impressed by her. In fact, if I didn't know better, I'd say he has a crush on her. Perhaps over time they'll even become friends. That would be nice.

Again, I apologize for being out of touch. Your news about Jack was quite a shock and I've been sort of lost in my own world since. I keep wondering whether I should say anything to Michel. I promise to call soon.

Love,
Vera

Michel took a long sip of Jack and re-read the last paragraph twice. The first two letters had put him on an emotional roller coaster. Now he felt as though that roller coaster had flown off the tracks and he was plummeting toward the ground.

He closed the card and placed it next to the letters, then picked up the third album. The pages were all empty, as though waiting for the rest of his life to unfold. He closed it and put it on the table with the others.

"Fuck," he said loudly.

Blue looked up at him with alarm from her resting spot just inside the front door.

"Sorry," Michel said. "I'm just feeling a little overwhelmed at the moment."

He looked at his watch, then picked up his cell phone and dialed Sassy. She answered after the second ring.

"What's wrong?"

"Nothing," Michel replied. "Did I wake you?"

"No, I'm just lying here watching another damn show about Nostradamus," Sassy replied. "It's a wonder he never predicted he'd be the star of the History Channel. What's up?"

Michel hesitated, suddenly unsure where to begin.

"I need to read you some things," he said finally.

Chapter 13

There was a long silence after he finished reading the final letter before Sassy spoke.

"Well, I can certainly see why those hit on all your issues."

"I don't *have* any issues," Michel shot back testily.

"And *who* did you think you were calling?" Sassy retorted with a dry laugh.

"Okay, fine. I have some issues," Michel replied.

"That's a start," Sassy said. "So talk to me. What are you feeling?"

There was a pause.

"I don't know...I guess...erghhh!" Michel growled with frustration.

"Okay, you're going to have to use your words," Sassy replied patiently. "Let's break it down and take them one by one."

Michel took a deep breath to clear his head.

"I'm pissed," he said.

"Okay, that's probably the easy one," Sassy said, "but go ahead. Why?"

"I feel like she invaded my privacy," Michel replied.

"What?" Sassy replied.

"She asked Chanel about me. She told Verle I was gay. And who knows what else she said to him?" Michel replied.

"Come on, Michel," Sassy chided. "Can you blame her? She was your mother and she was worried about you. She needed to talk to someone. Next?"

Michel took a quick sip of his drink. He knew Sassy was right, but still it bothered him to have his feelings dismissed so quickly. He decided to let it go for the moment.

"And I'm embarrassed," he said.

"Why?"

"Because I always thought I was doing a such good job of hiding how I was feeling," Michel replied. "Yeah, I was lonely in high school, but I didn't think *she* knew that."

"Not to mention about you being gay," Sassy said.

"That, too," Michel replied. "God, when I think about it. For years I filtered everything I told her because I was afraid I might give it away, and now I find out she already knew for over ten years. I just feel so stupid."

"I get that," Sassy replied sympathetically. "Anything else?"

"I can't believe my own mother thought I was guarded and secretive," Michel said incredulously, more venting than responding to the question.

"But you *were*," Sassy replied with a hint of exasperation.

"Well, yeah," Michel replied sheepishly, "but still."

He suddenly realized how foolish he sounded and wished he'd taken more time to think through what he was feeling before talking with Sassy.

"So why do you think that was?" Sassy asked. "I mean aside from being afraid she'd find out you were gay."

Michel thought about it for a moment.

"Probably because *she* was guarded and secretive," he replied finally. "I mean, I never really knew much about her either. I didn't know what she did all day while I was at school. I didn't know how she supported us. I didn't know anything about my father or her friends. It was like there was her life when she was physically with me, and then the rest was a mystery. I guess I just figured that was the way I was supposed to be, too."

They were both silent for a few moments, then Michel sighed deeply.

"It's just sad," he said. "I spent so much time pretending to be the perfect son, and all I was really doing was pushing her away."

"That's one interpretation," Sassy replied.

"Meaning what?" Michel asked.

"You just said it yourself. She kept you at a distance, too."

"But she was responding to my behavior," Michel said.

"That's not what *I* heard," Sassy replied. "I heard how you were responding to her behavior, following her lead. But nothing that suggests she kept her distance because of anything you did."

"But she said she felt like she was intruding if she asked me about anything," Michel replied, feeling a surprising need to defend his mother.

"That's true," Sassy replied, "but I don't *think* she said, 'Well if Michel is going to be all secretive, then I am, too.' Sounds like she did that on her own, and she did it first."

"Maybe," Michel replied grudgingly.

Sassy hesitated for a moment. She realized that she was heading into potentially sensitive territory and didn't want Michel to feel that she was attacking his mother.

"Let me ask you something," she said carefully. "What was she like with you?"

Michel suddenly felt very uncomfortable.

"What do you mean?" he asked, stalling.

"Well, was she affectionate? Was she warm?"

Michel considered how to answer. His mother had never been particularly affectionate nor warm, but neither had she been cold. She had been reserved. To say that, though, felt like a betrayal. He knew mothers weren't supposed to be reserved with their own children.

"I don't know," he said, a little too casually. "Like a mother, I guess. Why?"

Sassy knew he was being evasive. She suspected she'd tried

85

to push him someplace he wasn't ready to go. At least not with her.

"It doesn't really matter," she said, backtracking. "I'm just saying that you need keep in mind that the letters were from her perspective. That doesn't mean that was the whole reality. A lot of times people lament situations but fail to see their own role in creating them. I don't mean this as a criticism, but maybe your mother was more comfortable keeping some distance from people. Even you."

"But what about her letters to Verle?" Michel asked. "She didn't seem to have a problem opening up to him."

His tone was curious rather than contradictory, and Sassy relaxed a little.

"That may have been a comfortable enough distance," she replied. "I mean, really, how well did she know Verle? She met him once that you know of. He was essentially a stranger, and sometimes people find it easier to be open with strangers. Look at the shit that people do and say on the internet."

Michel tried to step outside of himself and view his mother objectively. He thought about her funeral. A lot of people had come, and they'd all told him what a wonderful woman she'd been, but none of them had had any personal memories to share. No one had seemed to actually know her well. He wondered now if any of them had even considered her a friend. Certainly no one had called to find out how he was doing in the weeks that followed, as a friend might.

"Maybe you're right," he said. "But why didn't I realize that before?"

"Because it's natural to idealize our parents," Sassy replied kindly. "We don't want to admit they're human."

Michel nodded to himself and took a sip of his drink. He knew that was only half true, but it was good enough for the moment.

"So what about the part about your father?" Sassy asked.

"You mean what do I think it meant, or what am I feeling about it?" Michel asked.

"Either or both," Sassy replied.

"I assume it means he's dead, and I don't feel anything about it," Michel replied simply.

The first part was true, but the second part was a lie. He didn't know what he was feeling, but it was powerful.

"Am I still closed and guarded?" he asked suddenly, wanting to move on quickly.

Sassy knew he had been disingenuous about his father, but decided to let it go.

"Not anymore," she said. "At least not very often. But in the beginning, it was tough getting to know you. It took you a while to open up. I think you've gotten better since your mother passed, though you might want to ask Joel about that."

"No wonder Verle didn't feel he could reach out to me," Michel said, shaking his head. "He kept a distance because he thought that's what I wanted. That's the picture my mother painted."

"Sounds like it wasn't that far from reality," Sassy said.

"No, I suppose not," Michel admitted. "And when he came to visit me the last time, I just reinforced the idea."

They were silent for a few moments.

"Okay, doctor, so how much do I owe you?" Michel asked finally.

His tone was much brighter, though Sassy suspected he just wanted to get off the phone.

"No charge," she replied, "but when I'm ready to explore my personal demons again, you better be there."

"You have *more* personal demons?" Michel asked. "I thought you'd already exorcised them all."

"We *always* have more," Sassy replied mordantly.

"I suppose that's true," Michel replied.

Sassy suddenly let out a small, almost girlish laugh.

"What?" Michel asked.

"Nothing," Sassy replied with teasing innocence.

Michel knew from her tone that she wanted him to keep pressing.

"*What?*" he asked.

There was a momentary pause.

"So you were impressed with me when we first met, eh?" Sassy asked.

Michel laughed.

"Maybe a little."

"Who wouldn't be?" Sassy replied breezily.

"But I got over it," Michel replied. "And I *never* had a crush on you."

"Of course, you did," Sassy replied dismissively. "Everyone does."

They were both quiet for a few seconds, content to bask in their friendship.

"By the way," Michel said finally, "did Chance have any luck tracking down the missing money?"

"He still hasn't figured out what happened," Sassy replied, "but the money's back in the account."

"That's odd," Michel replied. "So it was just an error?"

"The bank swears there were no payments in or out," Sassy replied. "They're still looking into it."

"And you're sure Chance didn't just make a mistake when he was looking at the balance?" Michel asked.

"Michel, when it comes to money I don't think Chance makes any mistakes," Sassy replied flatly.

Michel nodded to himself.

"Okay, well let me know if you find out anything."

"You got it. Good night."

Michel hung up and drained his drink. He walked to the bookshelf and picked up the photo of his parents. Sassy had been right. Of course he'd idealized his mother on some level.

That was natural. But he'd also been only too aware that she was human.

He studied her face carefully. Even though she was smiling, her eyes still held their familiar sadness. Growing up, he'd always assumed it had started when his father left, but now he could see that she'd had it even then, when she was newly married and pregnant, with a life of possibilities in front of her. It seemed to be something she'd always carried with her.

So much of his early childhood had been spent trying to make his mother happy, not in the traditional sense of a child trying to please a parent, but rather trying to make her feel actual joy. Even then he'd recognized her sadness and tried to take it away. Eventually he'd given up and settled for trying not to make her unhappy.

He wondered why, if he'd been sensitive enough as a child to recognize her sadness, it had taken Sassy to help him realize that his mother hadn't really been close with anyone. Perhaps he'd just been too caught up in his own head to notice.

"Wow, talk about egocentric," he said aloud. "My mom is only distant with *me*!"

He realized that "distant" didn't seem quite right. "Distant" suggested moroseness, maybe even a haunted quality. It conjured an image of someone who floated around the periphery of life, but was never engaged by it. That hadn't been his mother.

His mother had been engaged. She'd been energetic. She'd interacted regularly with their neighbors and the merchants around the Marigny. She went to church. She read voraciously. She was aware of what was happening around her and in the world. He imagined that most people viewed her as a pleasant, intelligent woman.

She simply never formed close relationships with anyone, and with him she'd always been emotionally restrained. Not that he'd ever doubted her love or devotion, but she'd never made him feel the warmth he'd felt from his Uncle Lee, Aunt Betty, and Verle. He'd often thought that perhaps she'd been worried that if she were too affectionate, he'd grow up weak. In a perverse logic, maybe she'd seen emotional remoteness as a way to compensate for the lack of a father's influence.

He placed the photo back in its original place and walked over to Blue. He lay on the floor facing her and began rubbing her offered belly.

"Did you ever meet my father?" he asked.

Blue let out another of her bovine groans.

"I'm not sure whether to take that as a yes or a no," Michel replied.

He stared into Blue's soft brown eyes.

"You miss your daddy, don't you?" he asked. "I guess we're both orphans now, though I'm not sure I miss mine."

Even as he said it, he knew it wasn't true. He wasn't sure what he felt about Black Jack's death, but he knew he missed his father, just as he'd always missed him.

"It's kind of complicated," he said with a sigh, as though Blue had asked him a question. "It's sort of like I've always had two fathers. There was Black Jack Doucette, the shit bag who married my mother, got her pregnant, and left, then there was my 'real father,' the one who would have stayed around and been a dad if he could have. That's the one I miss. Not that he ever existed except in my head."

The man in the photo was a stranger, just a face that looked like his own. His "real father" was entirely familiar. He'd always been a part of Michel's life. Like his visits to the farm, though, his "real father" was something he'd tried not to think about too much because it hurt.

He'd always been ambivalent about meeting the real Black Jack. Part of him was curious to see the man whose blood he carried, and part of him wanted the chance to ask why Black Jack had left, and whether he'd ever thought about him. But a larger part of him hated Black Jack. He knew that if they ever were to meet, the resentment and anger he'd been harboring his entire life might be unleashed. As a teenager he'd fantasized about that moment many times.

Still, in his more vulnerable moments, he'd found himself hoping from time to time that one day he'd meet Black Jack, and find that Black Jack and his "real father" were the same man, and that there'd been a reason Black Jack couldn't stay that would allow him to forgive his father. Now that hope was gone.

"You know, your daddy didn't leave because he wanted to," he said quietly. "He couldn't help it. He loved you very much."

He thought about what he'd said, and wondered whether he'd been trying to comfort Blue or himself.

"Did that make you feel any better?" he asked. "Yeah, me neither."

Chapter 14

Michel woke just after six the next morning and walked Blue to Ruby's house to leave her for a few hours. Then he showered and headed into town in hopes of meeting up with Russell Turner for breakfast. He parked in front of the theater, then crossed the street to the corner market. He noticed that Turner's car was already parked in front of the police station.

Cyrus was standing at the counter waiting for him when he walked in the store.

"I'm sorry about Verle," he said immediately.

"Thank you," Michel replied.

"It's just not right a man dying in jail like that before he has a chance to prove his innocence," Cyrus said, shaking his head sadly.

"No, it's not," Michel agreed.

He decided to leave it at that.

"So another pack of Marlboros?" Cyrus asked.

"I think I'll try the Winstons this time," Michel replied.

"You got it," Cyrus replied.

He went through the now-familiar routine of pulling down the pack and tossing it on the counter.

"You know, I could maybe order in some those American Spirits if you think you'll be sticking around for awhile," he said as he counted out Michel's change.

"I appreciate that," Michel replied, "but I'll probably only be here another few days. Just until the funeral."

The old man frowned slightly.

"Well that's too bad," he said. "I hate to lose a good customer."

Michel searched his face to see if he was being facetious and decided he wasn't. He felt slightly guilty that he hadn't been buying more.

"Well, I'm sure I'll see you tomorrow," he said.

"I imagine so," Cyrus said, then shuffled to his stool.

Michel stepped outside and crossed back to his car so that he could approach the diner from the same side of the street. He'd felt like the central attraction in a freak show the way the customers had stared at him the day before.

He opened the door of the diner and stepped inside. The room quieted noticeably and he could feel eyes on him. He tried to ignore them and scanned the room for Turner. He spotted him in the back corner booth, engaged in what appeared to be a serious conversation with another man whose back was to Michel.

Michel quickly crossed the room. As he approached the booth, Turner looked up.

"Michel," he said with surprise. "How are you doing?"

"Fine, thanks," Michel replied. "You?"

"Okay, I suppose, given the circumstances," Turner replied as he half stood and shook Michel's hand.

He sat and gestured toward the man on the opposite side of the booth.

"This is Terry DeCew. Porter's son."

"Nice to meet you," Michel said, extending his hand. "Michel Doucette."

"Same," Terry replied. "I'm so sorry about Verle. He was a good man."

Michel understood immediately why Ruby had referred to Terry as Porter DeCew's "sissy boy." He was thin and pale, with large blue eyes and sandy blond hair. Michel guessed that they were probably around the same age, but Terry had the soft

93

features of a child. He imagined that Terry had been picked on a lot in school.

"Thank you," Michel said. "I'm sorry. I didn't mean to interrupt you."

"That's okay," Terry replied. "I was just waiting for my takeout order. It should be ready by now."

He slid out of the booth and gestured for Michel to take his place.

"Are you sure?" Michel asked.

"Yeah, I need to get into the office," Terry replied.

His voice was as soft as his features.

"It was nice to meet you," he said. "I'll call you later, Russ."

He crossed the crowded room to the cash register while Michel took his place in the booth. A waitress carrying a white cup and glass coffee pot appeared immediately. Her black name plate was engraved DARLENE.

"Coffee, hon?" she asked.

"Sure," Michel replied, amused that she'd called him "hon" despite the fact that he was at least ten years her senior. It was the sort of expression that only waitresses and receptionists seemed to use anymore.

Michel noted that she was still pretty around the edges, but had the tired eyes of someone who had already lived a hard life.

"Oh oh, here comes trouble," Turner said, nodding toward the window.

Darlene turned her head to look and Michel twisted in his seat to follow her gaze.

A scruffily-bearded young man in mirrored sunglasses was standing in front of the plate glass window, smoothing his tousled brown hair. He was dressed in loose jeans and a worn green t-shirt, and looked like he'd just rolled out of bed after a heavy night of drinking. The slow deliberate way that he ran his fingers through his hair suggested that he was only too aware that he was being watched.

Michel recognized the type immediately. He'd arrested hundreds of them before joining the homicide division: loud and full of overcompensating bravado, pathologically in need of attention, and the first to cry like a bitch when they got caught.

"At least he's not my trouble anymore," Darlene said, shaking her head wearily. "You eating?"

Michel turned back and smiled at her.

"Yeah, scrambled eggs, bacon, and home fries," he replied.

"White or wheat?" she asked.

"White, please," Michel replied.

"You got it, hon," Darlene said, then sauntered back to the counter.

Michel heard the bell above the door tinkle, then a loud voice.

"Hey, Terry, how's the wife?"

He looked over his shoulder. The man in the green t-shirt was standing just inside the door, blocking Terry from leaving. He had a lewd smile on his face.

Terry took a half step to his right, but the man moved to block him again. Then he broke into a sadistic laugh and pushed past Terry. As he walked up to an empty stool at the counter, he looked around the room in a predatory way, as though searching for another victim. Michel noticed that everyone else in the room was making a point of avoiding eye contact with him.

"What was that about?" Michel asked, turning back to Turner.

"I don't know," Turner replied. "It's been going on for a while. If I didn't know better, I'd say that Donny had slept with Terry's wife, but I *know* that didn't happen. She wouldn't touch Donny with a ten-foot pole, even if she weren't married."

Michel nodded. He'd definitely sensed that the interaction had something to do with sex, though he doubted that it had anything to do with Terry's wife.

"Terry's married?" he asked.

"That surprise you?" Turner replied.

"Honestly, yeah a little."

"You figured maybe he played for your team?"

Michel shrugged.

"Who knows?" Turner replied. "Could be."

"So who's this Donny?" Michel asked, looking toward the counter.

Donny was swinging his knees from side to side on his stool, fidgeting like a kid who'd had too much sugar. Suddenly he spun around and faced the booth. He seemed to be staring directly at Michel through his sunglasses. Then he cracked a crooked smile and spun back toward the counter. Michel felt oddly violated. The smile had felt like a cross between a promise and a threat.

"Donny Heath," Turner said, oblivious to the interaction. "Born and raised here. He was a big football hero in high school, and hasn't done a damn thing since."

Michel was still distracted by what had happened. It took him a few seconds to realize Turner had spoken to him.

"Huh?" he said, turning back to Turner. "Oh, sounds like another curdled former superstar."

"That's a good way of putting it," Turner agreed. "I honestly thought he'd leave and go to college, but for some reason he decided to stick around. Maybe he was afraid of being a small fish in a bigger pond. Kind of a shame."

"Why's that?" Michel asked, honestly curious.

"Because he's a smart kid," Turner replied. "If he'd had an ounce of ambition, I think he really could have made something of himself. But he just seems content to sponge off other people."

"Like Darlene?" Michel asked.

Turner nodded.

"They were together on and off for a few years. King and

queen of the senior prom. He kept cheating on her, she kept dumping his ass. Then he'd wear her down and she'd take him back. She finally called it quits when she got pregnant. Guess she decided she could only take care of one child."

Michel nodded.

"So what does he do?"

"He worked in the supply yard at Gulf Coast Oil," Turner said. "Supposedly injured himself on the job about eight months ago and he's been on paid disability ever since. Seems like he's fine to me."

"Isn't that kind of unusual?" Michel asked. "I'd imagine a company like Gulf Coast would do whatever they could to keep from paying. You'd think they'd have a team of doctors down here checking him out."

"You'd think," Turner replied, shaking his head, "but Donny's like that. Somehow shit never seems to stick to him."

"He ever been arrested?" Michel asked.

"A few times," Turner replied, "but like I said, nothing ever sticks. He turns on the charm and flashes a smile and gets off with a slap on the wrist."

Michel looked toward the counter. Darlene was standing in front of Donny. Despite her earlier assertion, the smile on her face suggested she might take him back at any moment.

"What kind of stuff?" he asked, looking back at Turner.

"Drunk and disorderly, mostly," Turner replied. "He likes to pick fights when he's had a few. I brought him in for questioning a few times on some vandalism, but someone always swore he was with them at the time."

"Sounds like you've got yourself a regular Peyton Place here," Michel replied with a smile.

"I suppose even the smallest towns have something going on if you look hard enough," Turner replied.

Michel decided that he'd have to look harder. The interaction between Donny and Terry intrigued him.

"So have you given any more thought to what we were talking about yesterday?" Turner asked suddenly.

"Yeah," Michel said nodding. "I think you were right. There's nothing to be gained by pushing for an investigation."

It was a lie, but he still didn't know how well he could trust Turner. While he'd decided not to press the state police, he planned to do some investigating on his own.

"So does that mean no autopsy?" Turner asked.

Michel shook his head.

"Well, then I hope you don't mind, but I contacted the cemetery where your aunt and uncle are buried," Turner said. "They said Verle already had a plot there next to his folks. They could do the burial as soon as tomorrow if you'd like."

Michel thought about it. There was no reason to put it off.

"What about a memorial service?" he asked.

"Under the circumstances, I don't know if that's the best idea," Turner replied gently. "Besides, Verle didn't belong to any church."

"Okay," Michel replied. "I'll let Ruby know. If you wouldn't mind telling anyone else you think might want to be there, I'd appreciate it."

Chapter 15

Michel stood beside Russell Turner on one side of the grave. Terry DeCew, a woman Michel assumed was his wife, and an older man who was undoubtedly his father stood on the other side. There were no other mourners.

To Michel's surprise, Ruby had chosen not to come, saying that she needed to stay behind to watch after Blue. Michel suspected the truth was that she was uncomfortable sharing her grief, particularly with Turner and the DeCews. Though she'd remained outwardly stoic, Michel knew that Verle's death had to have hit her hard.

Although he'd already become surprisingly attached to Blue, he'd decided that it would probably be best for both her and Ruby if she stayed behind with Ruby when he returned to New Orleans. Blue had grown up in the swamp. She would undoubtedly find it hard to adjust to life in the city and in a house with only a small walled yard. And Ruby seemed very attached to Blue. Perhaps being with Blue was a way for her to hold onto Verle. It felt like the right decision, though he knew he would miss Blue.

The simple walnut casket was lowered into the ground, and after a respectful pause the DeCews began slowly walking to their car. Michel noticed that both Terry and his wife were holding onto Porter DeCew's arms to steady him.

"I'll be there in a minute," Michel said to Turner.

Turner nodded and followed the others.

Michel walked to the other side of the grave and stood in

front of the headstones of his aunt and uncle. He'd never visited a cemetery to pay respects before and wasn't sure what to do. He assumed most people prayed, but prayer wasn't in his repertoire.

"I miss you," he said instead. "And I'm sorry I wasn't there for Verle."

As he walked back toward the cars, he realized that he found it oddly easy to express exactly what he was feeling to people who weren't there. I guess I am my mother's son, he thought.

Turner and the DeCews had taken refuge from the midday sun in the shade of a large oak near the cars.

"Michel, this is my wife, Carolyn," Terry said as Michel joined them.

Michel could imagine Carolyn DeCew being cast as the small-town spinster librarian in a movie. She was tall and gaunt, with a narrow face, thin lips, large staring eyes, and mousy brown hair pulled back into a tight bun. The only thing missing was a pair of thick-framed glasses. The severity of her features was complemented by her Amish-inspired black ensemble. Michel guessed she was a few years older than Terry, perhaps in her mid-forties.

"I'm very sorry for your loss," she said.

Though it was a stock sentiment, her tone sounded heartfelt, and her smile seemed genuinely sympathetic.

"Thank you," Michel replied.

"And this is my father, Porter DeCew," Terry said.

"It's nice to finally meet you, Mr. Doucette," DeCew said in a surprisingly deep and rich voice. "I've heard a lot about you over the years. I'm just sorry it had to be under these circumstances."

Again it was a stock sentiment delivered sincerely.

Despite his difficulty walking, DeCew seemed quite robust. His handshake was firm and his posture was unusually straight for a man his age. Like his son, he had large blue eyes, soft features, and thinning hair. Unlike Terry, however, Porter

DeCew exuded an air of confident masculinity. While Michel felt like a little kid in the oversized suit he'd borrowed from Verle's closet, and Turner and Terry both looked uncomfortable in their suits, Porter DeCew seemed completely at ease. He had the grave expression and formal bearing of a man born to wear dark suits. Michel could easily imagine him navigating the cutthroat waters of corporate law.

"I hate to bring up business right now," DeCew said, "but as you probably know, I was Verle's attorney as well as his friend."

Michel nodded.

"He also named me as the executor of his estate, so I'll need to meet with you before you leave town."

Although it was still early in the day, Michel already felt surprisingly tired.

"Would tomorrow morning be all right?" he asked.

"Certainly," DeCew replied. "Ten o'clock?"

"That would be fine," Michel replied.

*****

"So what's with DeCew?" Michel asked as he and Turner drove back to town.

"What do you mean?" Turner asked.

"I noticed that Terry and his wife had to help him walk to the car," Michel replied.

"He had a stroke about a year ago," Turner replied. "Pretty bad one. For a while it looked like he wasn't going to make it, but now he's almost back to the way he was before. He still has trouble walking some days, but his speech and motor skills are pretty much back to normal."

"That's amazing," Michel said.

"He's a tough old bird," Turner replied with a nod. "I wouldn't want to get on his bad side."

"I got that sense," Michel replied. "So how long ago did he switch sides and hook up with Verle?"

"Has to be at least ten or twelve years now," Turner replied.

"How'd that happen?" Michel asked.

"Verle and Terry were already friends," Turner replied. "They met through the Audubon Society when Terry was working as a lobbyist."

"So he and his father were working on opposite sides?" Michel asked.

"Yeah, and from what Terry's told me, Porter wasn't too happy about it," Turner replied. "He'd always expected that Terry would join his firm after law school, and when Terry decided he wanted to work for Audubon instead, they had a bad falling out. Didn't talk for a few years."

"So what changed?"

"Like I told you before, Porter finally saw enough that he realized he was working for the bad guys," Turner replied.

"Just like that?" Michel asked skeptically.

"Well, I suspect that when his wife died it probably made him rethink some things," Turner replied. "Reevaluate his priorities."

Michel knew that Turner was speaking from experience.

"And that's when he hooked up with Verle?" he asked.

"Yeah, Porter and Terry mended fences and Porter moved down here a few months later. Then a while after that, they created a conservation trust."

It all sounded logical, though a little too good to be true to Michel. He decided he'd have to ask Porter DeCew more about it when they met.

A hundred yards ahead, the sign for the Gator's Belly came into view. Michel had noticed it on the way to the cemetery.

"All right with you if we stop in for a drink?" he asked.

"It's kind of early," Turner replied, "And I'm not sure the sheriff ought to be seen in a bar in the middle of a work day."

"Come on, just one," Michel cajoled. "Besides, I need to get some cigarettes. And no one's going to recognize you without your uniform, anyway."

"Why's that?" Turner asked.

If he'd been with Sassy, Michel would have made a joke about all black folks looking alike, but he didn't know Turner well enough to risk it.

"Because I barely recognize you," he replied weakly.

Turner relented with a sigh.

"Okay, but just one."

Michel slowed the car as he approached the sign, then turned right onto a narrow dirt and gravel road that cut through the trees.

"There must be a lot of accidents on here," he said.

"Not really," Turner replied distractedly. "Must be that whole thing about God watching out for drunks and fools, because there are plenty of both at the Gator."

Michel noticed that Turner's mood suddenly seemed more subdued, and wondered if they should skip the drink and just head back to town.

"Are you okay?" he asked.

"Yeah, just a little tired," Turner replied. "The last few days have been tough."

Michel nodded sympathetically.

"If you just want to head back to town, that's fine," he said. "I can get cigarettes someplace else."

"Naw, that's okay," Turner replied. "We're here now. You might as well see Bayou Proche's finest watering hole."

There was a break in the dense foliage to the left, and Michel slowed the car. Through the trees he could see a dilapidated shingle building with a porch and a sagging roof. The entire front wall of the building was painted bright red, while the vertical supports for the porch roof were white.

"It doesn't look very big," he said.

"Just wait," Turner replied.

After another fifty feet, the road turned sharply left and the trees ended. They pulled into a gravel lot that could easily hold a hundred cars. Michel stopped the car.

"Wow," he said.

"Yeah, it's really something, isn't it?" Turner replied, shaking his head.

What had appeared through the trees to be a single small building was actually two buildings, connected at the back wall of the small building.

The main building was a large, windowless cinder block rectangle. The only break in the facade was a door in the center. At the right end of the building was a stepped cinder block wall. It started at the height of the main building, then got progressively lower as it curved forward until it was the height of a single cinder block. The building and the wall were painted dark green.

On the far left was the shingle building. It was at a forty-five-degree angle to the entrance of the parking lot so that the red front and white supports were visible. The shingled side had been painted the same green as the main building and its one window had been painted black.

Michel squinted his eyes and laughed. It looked like a giant Lego® alligator in a pool of gray water, its mouth open toward the road.

"Someone put a lot of thought into that," he said.

"Too much," Turner replied sardonically.

"How long has it been here?" Michel asked.

"Almost 300 years in one incarnation or another," Turner replied. "The original one was just a shanty on the bayou about a quarter mile back. That got washed away in the early 1800s. They built the new one a few years later, then kept adding onto it. About thirty years ago, they tore down everything except the original entrance and built that cinder block monster."

"You have to admit it's kind of witty," Michel replied.

"I suppose," Turner agreed grudgingly.

Despite the fact that it just past 1 PM, there were a dozen cars and trucks parked in the lot. Michel eased the car forward and parked in the shade in front of the curved wall.

"Into the belly of the beast," he said.

Chapter 16

The interior of the Gator's Belly followed through on the motif established by the exterior. The walls, ceiling, and carpet were all blood red. It was surprisingly clean, though the cool air was heavy with the smell of fried food and stale beer.

Michel and Turner walked through the cluster of empty tables and chairs just inside the door and took two empty stools in the center of the long bar along the back wall. Two old men who were eating boiled crawfish from red plastic baskets at the far right end looked up at them for a moment, then went back to their meals.

Michel nodded at the red velvet curtain that spanned the entire width of the room behind the men.

"What's back there?" he asked.

"Dance floor," Turner replied. "They've got a little stage, too. Gets pretty hopping on Friday and Saturday nights."

"I'll bet," Michel replied sarcastically.

"Son of a whore!" a voice yelled to their left, followed by an explosion of derisive laughter.

Michel and Turner turned to look. A large man with a thick beard and mustache was bent over the edge of a pool table with a look of frustration on his face. A younger man stood nearby, chalking his pool cue and smirking. Michel realized it was Donny Heath. Three other men sat at the side of the bar, their backs to Michel and Turner, watching the play.

"Fucking table's warped," the bearded man said as he stood up and banged the butt of his cue on the floor.

106

Michel guessed he was about 6' 4" and at least 300 lbs.

"Your fucking shot was warped," one of the men at the bar called back to more laughter."

"So what can I get you gents?" a voice said nearby.

Michel turned back to the bar. A tightly built man with a long gray ponytail and a full, black horseshoe mustache was standing in front of them. He was wearing a red t-shirt with the sleeves ripped off and "God Bless America...and Nowhere Else" emblazoned on the front in blue and white letters. His expression was friendly, but Michel got the sense that he wasn't someone to be messed with.

"A Jack on the rocks," he replied.

"And you?" the bartender asked, looking at Turner.

"Just a Dixie, Chappy," Turner replied.

The bartender stared at him curiously for a few seconds, then broke into an embarrassed smile. Michel knew it had been a long time since the man had been able to eat corn on the cob.

"Shit, I'm sorry, Sheriff," the bartender said. "I didn't recognize you there for a minute. It's not Sunday is it?"

He looked down at Turner's suit.

"No," Turner replied. "We just buried Verle Doucette."

The bartender tilted his head and gave a puzzled look.

"That's funny," he said. "I would have thought..."

"Thanks, Chappy," Turner interrupted pointedly.

Chappy looked momentarily hurt, but then nodded and walked to the cooler.

"See, I told you," Michel said with a self-satisfied smile.

"What?" Turner replied.

"He didn't recognize you," Michel replied.

"Oh yeah," Turner replied weakly.

There was a loud "Whoo hoo!" from the pool table. Michel turned and saw Donny Heath holding his pool cue over his head victoriously.

"Rack 'em up, bitch!" he crowed.

As the big man began dejectedly racking the balls on the table, Donny grabbed the two five dollar bills from the side rail and sauntered up to the side of the bar to exchange high fives with the other men.

"Give me another, Chappy," he called.

He drained the remainder of his beer, then looked around in his predatory way. His eyes settled on Michel. For a moment his expression didn't change. He just looked Michel up and down slowly. Then he smiled. It was a taunting smile, as though he knew a secret about Michel. Michel had the same feeling of being violated that he'd experienced at the diner, and quickly looked away.

Chappy put their drinks on the bar and took the ten dollar bill Michel had laid down, then moved away to get Donny's beer. Michel watched out of the corner of his eye until Donny had walked back to the pool table, then turned to Turner. He suddenly wanted to leave.

"All right, who's my next victim?" Donny's voice cut through the room. "Black Jack, I think you're up."

Michel's head spun to the left and he felt his mouth go dry. Donny was watching him, looking exceedingly pleased with himself. Then one of the men who'd been seated at the bar stood up and sauntered toward the pool table. Unlike the calculated saunter of Donny, however, his was the uneven, rolling gait of a man with a bad back and stiff joints.

"Easy money," the man said. "Easy money."

Michel felt a hand close on his right forearm and turned to see Turner studying him closely.

"Did Donny say 'Black Jack'?" Michel asked, though he already knew the answer.

Turner nodded gravely.

"That's my father?" Michel asked, then turned to watch the man again.

Black Jack was turned so that he was three-quarters facing

Michel. He had the same black-slicked back hair that he'd had in the photo at Verle's house, though now the color looked like cheap shoe polish. His craggy granite face and wary expression made it clear that he'd traveled a lot of road in the years since the photo had been taken, most of it hard.

"Why didn't you tell me?" Michel asked, looking back at Turner in bewilderment.

"I was hoping you wouldn't find out," Turner replied.

"Why?"

"Because Verle was paying Black Jack to stay away from you," Turner replied. "I figured I owed it to him."

"He was paying him?" Michel replied numbly.

He remembered the third letter from his mother. It wasn't his father's death she'd questioned telling him about. It was his father's reappearance.

He started to turn away on his stool, but Turner held onto his arm.

"You don't want to go over there," Turner said quietly.

"Yeah, I really do," Michel replied in a tight voice, as he yanked his arm away.

He stood up and walked toward the pool table. Donny saw him coming and took an overly dramatic step back. The other men noticed and turned to see what was happening. Black Jack was intently chalking his cue, apparently oblivious.

Michel felt as though he were in a dream. Each step seemed agonizingly slow, while his thoughts raced. Though he'd fantasized about meeting his father thousands of times and had imagined all of the things he'd say, now that it was really happening, he was drawing a blank. Finally he was standing directly in front of his father.

"Are you Black Jack Doucette?" he asked.

Black Jack looked up and stared at him for a few seconds, then nodded.

"I'm Michel Doucette," Michel said.

He watched for a reaction, but didn't see any.

"I know who you are," Black Jack replied. "Everyone in town knows who you are."

Then he made a sweeping gesture around the group of men.

"Boys," he said, "this is my son, Michel."

"Michel?" Michel heard a voice behind him say. "Is that like a boy named Sue?"

All of the other men laughed, though Black Jack just smiled and kept his steady gaze on Michel.

"The boy's mother called him that," he said. "After I left."

"Are you sure he's your son?" Donny asked. "He sure doesn't look like you. In fact, he seems a little sissy, if you ask me."

He gave Michel a challenging smile, but Michel didn't look at him.

"You better watch your mouth," Black Jack said without any menace in his voice. "He's a fancy homo-cide detective from N'Awlins. He might arrest your ass."

The exaggerated pronunciation clearly seemed intended as mockery. All of the men laughed again.

"Nice suit," the man closest to Michel's left said. "Did your mom buy you that?"

Again all the men laughed, and Michel realized the situation was out of his control. While he felt certain that one-on-one he could have intimidated any of the men—save perhaps for his father—he knew he lacked the authority and quiet menace to intimidate the whole group, particularly in his oversized suit. Still, he was too angry to back away now, regardless of the consequences.

He turned his head sharply and looked at the man who had spoken. It was the same man who'd just lost to Donny.

"Was I talking to you, fat ass?" Michel asked.

The man blinked at him, then drew himself up a little taller. He towered over Michel.

"What did you call me?" he asked.

"What, are you fat and deaf, too?" Michel replied as he turned to face the man squarely.

The man's hard expression faltered for a second.

"If you weren't Black Jack's son, I'd kick your ass," he said.

It was clear that Michel had taken him off-guard and he was trying to salvage his dignity.

"Don't back down on my account, Bubba," Black Jack said. "I'm kind of curious to see what my boy's got."

Michel turned his head and looked at his father. Black Jack was smiling maliciously.

"Then why don't you find out for yourself...*Dad*," Michel replied.

The smile was gone from Black Jack's face in an instant and he took a step toward Michel.

Suddenly there was a loud bang from the bar and Black Jack froze.

"You boys want to fight, you take it outside," Chappy said, lifting the baseball bat he'd slammed down.

"Or better yet, everyone just calm the fuck down," Turner said, as he pushed into the center of the group and stood next to Michel.

He gave Michel a pointed look, then stared down all of the other men.

"We going to have a problem, Jack?" he asked, locking eyes with Black Jack.

There was no doubt that Turner had the necessary authority to take control of the situation. Black Jack stared back at him for a moment, then put his hands up and shook his head innocently.

"Of course not, Sheriff," he said. "We were just having a little family reunion."

"Well, the reunion's over," Turner replied with finality.

There was a moment of awkward silence, then Black Jack looked at Donny.

"We going to play pool, or what?" he asked irritably, as though Donny had been delaying the game.

"Yeah, sure," Donny stammered.

"Then finish racking the damn balls," Black Jack replied.

His tone seemed intended to convey that while he'd been willing to defer to Turner momentarily, he was still in charge.

"Let's go," Turner said quietly as the other men drifted back to their drinking and pool.

He turned and started toward the door. Michel stood there for a few seconds longer, then followed. He felt oddly emasculated.

"You want your change?" Chappy called to him.

"Keep it," Michel replied.

*****

They were both silent for a moment when they got in the car, then Michel banged his palms on the steering wheel.

"Fuck!" he exclaimed with frustration.

"I'm sorry," Turner said. "I should have told you about Black Jack."

"It's not that," Michel replied. "I forgot to get cigarettes."

Turner stared at him with disbelief for a moment, then began to laugh.

"Really?" he said. "After what just happened, that's your biggest concern?"

"No, but after what happened I really need a cigarette, and these moldy Winstons aren't going to do the trick," Michel replied.

He took one out of the pack and lit it anyway.

"You want to talk about it?" Turner asked.

Michel shrugged.

"What's there to talk about? My father is as big of an asshole as I always thought he'd be. Maybe bigger."

Turner nodded.

"Still, you have to have some feelings about seeing him," he said. "That must have been quite a shock."

"Yeah, thanks for that," Michel replied dryly, then took another drag on his cigarette and made a sour face. "You know, you could have warned me,"

"I know. Like I said, I'm sorry," Turner replied. "I was hoping he'd still be sleeping off last night. It's early to be drinking, even for Jack."

"But this is a pretty small town," Michel replied. "You had to know there was a good chance I'd run into him or that someone would say something."

"Not really," Turner replied. "Jack pretty much stays away from town, and most people around here mind their own business. Except for Donny, obviously. I figured you'd only be here for a few days so you'd probably never have to know."

Michel thought about it for a moment.

"So was Verle really paying him to stay away from me?" he asked.

"More or less," Turner replied. "Verle never talked to me about it, but I heard rumors. Jack likes to talk."

"What did you hear?"

"Jack came looking for Verle about six years ago when he'd run out of money. Verle refused to give him anything, but Jack found Verle's address book and threatened to pay you a visit. Verle agreed to give Jack a place to stay and enough money to live on if Jack would promise to stay away from you."

Michel stared out the front window for a moment, lost in thought.

"It just didn't go the way I'd always imagined," he said finally.

"How's that?"

"I figured either he'd be an asshole and I'd finally have the chance to tell him off, or he'd be a great guy and I'd be able to forgive him," Michel replied. "I certainly didn't imagine him mocking me and trying to goad me into a fight with one of his buddies."

"No, I wouldn't imagine you would have," Turner replied with a gentle smile.

They sat in thoughtful silence for a few seconds, then Michel sighed and started the car.

"You know, I'm a big boy," he said. "I could have taken care of myself."

"And I'm the sheriff," Turner replied. "Keeping peace is part of my job. It wasn't a slight against your masculinity. Anyone can see you're a real scrapper."

"Fuck you," Michel replied with a laugh.

He backed the car out of the parking space and headed toward the road.

"Truth is, the last time I got into a fight an 80-year-old man kicked my ass," he said.

"When was that?" Turner asked with amusement.

"A few weeks ago," Michel replied.

"Seriously?"

Michel nodded.

"What happened?"

"The guy had a gun on me," Michel replied. "I managed to disarm him, but when I headbutted him it was like hitting a rock. He was an ex-boxer. It didn't even faze him."

"Why did you headbutt him?" Turner asked. "Is that what they teach you at the New Orleans Police Academy? Why didn't you hit him in the throat or the solar plexus?"

"I don't know," Michel replied as he pulled onto the road. "It seemed like a good idea at the time."

Chapter 17

When Michel got back to Verle's cabin, there was a note on the front door.

Blue must have been missing you because she came back here twice. The second time I just put her inside. — Ruby

Michel smiled. It made him feel wanted that Blue had been looking for him. He opened the door and walked in.

"Where are you, Blue?" he called.

Blue's head appeared around the side of the couch. Her ears were back and she stared at him with what looked like uncertainty. Michel smiled and knelt down.

"Come here, girl," he said enthusiastically.

Blue took a few shy steps forward, then her tail began beating quickly from side to side and her whole body seemed to vibrate with energy.

"Come on," Michel urged.

Blue made a little leap, then pranced coltishly across the room and buried her head in Michel's lap.

"What a good girl you are," Michel said as he scratched the sides of her face. "Did you miss me today? Huh?"

Blue lifted her head and gave his nose a quick lick.

"Thank you, that was sweet," Michel said. "I missed you, too."

Blue danced back a few steps, stretched, then shook her whole body.

"Shaking off the love?" Michel asked as he stood up. "Yeah, you wouldn't want too much love, would you?"

Blue just stared at him in response.

"Okay, I need to call your Aunt Sassy," Michel said. "You want to go outside?"

Blue ran to the open door and out onto the porch. Michel took off his jacket and tie and followed her. He took his now-customary seat and Blue settled down next to him.

"Hey," he said when Sassy answered the phone.

"Hey yourself," Sassy replied. "How was the funeral?"

"It was a funeral," Michel replied unenthusiastically.

"Was there a big turnout?" Sassy asked.

"Six more and we could have fielded a football team," Michel replied.

He took out a cigarette and lit it. Blue immediately jumped up and ran to the other end of the porch.

"I'm sorry, honey," Michel said. "Come on back. I'll put it out. See."

He dropped the cigarette into the beer can ashtray, but Blue just stared at him for a moment, then lay down under the hammock.

"What are you talking about, and who are you calling 'honey'?" Sassy asked.

"Sorry," Michel replied. "I was talking to Blue, Verle's dog. She doesn't like when I smoke."

"You have a dog now?" Sassy asked excitedly.

"For the moment," Michel replied. "I think I'm going to leave her with Verle's friend Ruby when I come home."

"You should keep her," Sassy replied.

"Me?" Michel replied with a laugh. "I don't know anything about taking care of a dog."

"You'll learn," Sassy replied. "You're not totally inept."

"Thanks," Michel replied dryly.

"So what kind is she?" Sassy asked.

116

"Shepherd and Catahoula," Michel replied.

"Oh, she must be adorable," Sassy replied.

"You know what a Catahoula is?" Michel asked, surprised.

"Of course I know," Sassy replied with feigned indignity. "It's our state dog. Why, didn't you know?"

"Of course I knew," Michel lied. "I just never took you for a dog person."

"Oh, we always had dogs when I was growing up," Sassy replied. "Usually just mutts, but my father had three Catahoulas for a while. Used to take them boar hunting."

Blue lifted her head for a half-hearted attempt to eat a fly that was buzzing around her ears.

"She is pretty adorable," Michel said.

Blue gave up on the fly and dropped her head to the porch.

"Aren't you, sweetheart?" Michel asked in a high-pitched, cooing voice. "Aren't you the most adorable dog in the whole world?"

Blue lifted her head to look at him, wagged her tail twice, then dropped her head again and let out a deep sigh.

"Okay, now you're going too far," Sassy said flatly. "Once you start talking baby talk, that's too far."

"Whatever," Michel replied.

He decided to light another cigarette since Blue didn't seem inclined to come back over to him any time soon.

"So are you okay?" Sassy asked after a pause.

"I wish," Michel replied. "You'll never guess who I met today."

"Charo?"

"What?"

"You said I'd never guess, so I tried to think of the most unlikely person to be in Bayou Proche," Sassy replied.

"No, not Charo," Michel replied. "My father."

"Holy shit!" Sassy exclaimed. "He's alive?"

"Sure seemed that way," Michel replied sardonically.

"So how did it go? What was he like?" Sassy asked eagerly.

"Let's put it this way," Michel replied. "If I ever have to see him again, I hope he's lying in a coffin."

"That bad?"

"Oh yeah."

Michel recounted what had happened.

"I'm sorry," Sassy said sympathetically when he'd finished.

"It's okay," Michel replied. "At least now I know for sure that I'm happy he left."

"Was there ever a doubt?" Sassy asked.

"Sometimes," Michel admitted.

He thought about saying more, but decided to leave it at that. He felt too drained to start revealing his secret fantasies about his "real father."

"So what now?" Sassy asked, sensing the conversation about Michel's father was over for now.

"I'm meeting with Verle's lawyer tomorrow morning," Michel replied. "Verle named him executor of his estate."

"That sounds like fun," Sassy replied sarcastically.

"Yeah. Really looking forward to it," Michel replied. "But at least it'll give me a chance to find out what happens to all Verle's land now that he's gone."

"I take it that means you haven't entirely given up on the idea that someone set Verle up," Sassy said.

"Not entirely," Michel admitted. "I don't think he was killed. I think that was natural. But I still can't believe that Verle would kill anyone, and if he didn't, then that means someone planted the emails on his computer."

"Or he really was in touch with the woman, someone found out about it and didn't like it, and killed her," Sassy said.

Michel suddenly sat up straighter.

"Someone jealous?" he said, as much to himself as Sassy.

"Or someone who didn't like the idea of him hooking up with a prostitute," Sassy replied.

Michel knew that the list of suspects in either scenario was extremely narrow: Russ Turner, Terry DeCew, Porter DeCew, and Ruby. He couldn't think of anyone else who might have a stake in Verle's personal life.

He thought about it for a moment. He couldn't imagine any circumstance under which Turner would commit murder, and the DeCews' interest in Verle seemed primarily professional. Of the four, Ruby seemed the most likely suspect. Michel remembered how she'd reacted when he'd asked her if she'd had an intimate relationship with Verle. He wondered if she and Verle really had been in a relationship at some point, or if Ruby had secretly longed for one.

"Thanks, Sas," he said. "I'll check into that."

"No problem," Sassy replied. "Any more word from the state police?"

"None that I know of," Michel replied. "I'll have to check with Russ tomorrow."

"Russ?" Sassy asked.

"Sheriff Turner," Michel clarified.

"Oh, so now you're on a first-name basis?" Sassy asked.

"What, are you jealous?" Michel teased. "Afraid you've been replaced?"

"Oh please, I could never be replaced," Sassy replied with a carefree laugh.

"No, that's true," Michel said seriously. "You couldn't be."

Chapter 18

The old courthouse was located at the north end of the main street, on the opposite side of a small park from the town hall. It was the first time Michel had ventured to that part of the town, and he was surprised at the grandness of the buildings. It reminded him of Savannah or sections of the Garden District.

The building was large, rising three stories and spanning the full block. It was designed in a Beaux-Arts style, with a simple red brick facade, large rectangular windows, and stairs across the entire front leading up to ten concrete columns that supported a triangular pediment.

As he stepped out of his car, Michel saw Porter DeCew leaning on a cane at the top of the stairs, near the main entrance. He was dressed in a lightweight gray pinstriped suit, white shirt, and blue-and-green striped tie, and was smoking a cigar.

"Good morning, Mr. Doucette," he said as Michel and Blue walked up the steps.

"Please, call me Michel," Michel said. "I hope you don't mind that I brought Blue."

"Not at all," DeCew replied. "I hope you don't mind if I finish my cigar before we go up. I have to sneak them in when Terry's not around these days or he'll give me holy hell."

"That's fine," Michel replied with a smile. "I'd join you, but Blue doesn't like it when I smoke."

"Kids," DeCew said with a gruff laugh.

Michel turned and looked at the park. In the center was a circular white gazebo surrounded by dormant flower beds. A spoked wheel of tree-lined paths led from the gazebo to the corners and sides of the park.

"This is really beautiful," he said.

"It should be considering what Verle paid to renovate and maintain it," DeCew said.

"Really?" Michel asked.

DeCew nodded.

"It was in pretty bad shape. The town just didn't have the money for upkeep. But Verle felt it was important to have a nice common space, so..."

He trailed off.

"Do people know that?" Michel asked.

"Some probably suspect it," DeCew replied. "Verle wanted to keep it secret. He didn't want the townsfolk to think he was trying to buy them off. So the town council just said the money was donated."

"That's sad," Michel replied. "Maybe if people realized how much Verle did for the town, more of them would have shown up for his funeral."

"Maybe," DeCew replied with a slight frown. "I'm not sure people would have appreciated anything Verle did."

"I take it you didn't approve of Verle spending the money then," Michel said.

"It's not that," DeCew replied wistfully. "I suppose it was a good thing to do, but in a lot of ways it was just prolonging the inevitable. This town's on its last legs, and no matter how much you dress it up for the people who remain, that's not going to change. Your cousin was an idealist. He wanted to hold onto a way of life whose time has passed."

He dropped his cigar onto the concrete and stepped it out.

"Shall we go up to my office?" he asked.

*****

DeCew's offices were on the top floor of the building, in the former private chambers of the district judge. It was a suite of five rooms at one end of the hall. So far as Michel could tell, the rest of the offices were unoccupied.

"This shouldn't take long," DeCew said. "Please, have a seat."

He walked slowly around his desk, holding onto the edge with his right hand, and settled into a large, wing-backed leather chair.

He pushed a document across the desk toward Michel.

"This is a copy of Verle's will," he said. "It's pretty straightforward. With the exception of cash gifts for Russ Turner and Ruby Fish, and some charitable donations, the entirety of his estate goes to you."

"To me?" Michel replied with genuine surprise.

DeCew nodded.

"That includes real estate, personal property, and all financial holdings."

He pushed a single piece of paper toward Michel.

"That's a summary of his assets," he said.

Michel numbly picked up the paper and looked at it. At the bottom in bold, it read, "Net Assets: $16,876,443.45."

"Mr. DeCew," Michel started.

"Porter," DeCew corrected.

"Porter," Michel started again, "are you telling me that Verle left me almost seventeen million dollars?"

"Well, after the gifts and estate tax, and assuming there are no claims against his estate, it will be somewhere in the range of ten million dollars, plus the actual property," DeCew replied.

Michel frowned.

"You seem disappointed," DeCew said, giving Michel a curious look.

"It's not that," Michel replied. "It's just that...I mean, you and Verle were friends. I'm sure you know that he and I hadn't spoken in a long time."

DeCew nodded.

"And then suddenly I find out he's been arrested for murder," Michel continued, "and then he dies, and now this. I'm just not sure how to feel. It's all kind of overwhelming."

"That's understandable," DeCew replied.

"Are you sure about this?" Michel asked.

"Absolutely," DeCew replied with certainty. "When I started working with Verle, you were already his sole beneficiary. Since then, the only changes that were made were the additions of the gifts for Russ and Ruby."

Michel put the paper down and sat back in his chair. He suddenly craved a cigarette.

"It just seems wrong," he said. "I realize I'm his only living relative, but the money should have gone to the people who cared about him."

"So you didn't care about him?" DeCew asked dubiously.

Michel realized what he'd said and shook his head.

"No, of course I cared about him," he said. "I loved him. But I wasn't around for him. I wasn't a part of his life."

"I think you were," DeCew said. "From the way he talked about you, I'd say you were a very big part of his life. I think Verle still felt very connected to you."

Michel felt a surge of guilt.

"I don't know," he said, shaking his head. "I'm going to have to think about this."

"There's really nothing to think about," DeCew replied earnestly. "You can give it all away if you want, but it's yours. If you refuse it, the estate will just go to the state because there are no secondary beneficiaries."

Michel nodded slowly.

"And Verle did want you to have it," DeCew added.

"I know," Michel said. "It's just kind of...unexpected."

There was more he wanted to say, but realized it wasn't appropriate. DeCew was Verle's lawyer, not his own therapist. DeCew seemed to sense Michel's discomfort and waited a few seconds before continuing.

"As the executor, I'll be submitting the will for probate," DeCew said. "Sometimes that can drag on for years when you've got a bunch of folks making claims and they get into a squabble, but in this case it should move pretty quickly. I expect I'll be able to make some assets available to you in a few months, and the rest within the year."

Michel nodded. He was familiar with the probate process from executing his mother's will.

"In the meantime, the estate will continue to make tax payments, et cetera," DeCew continued, "and I'll make sure..."

"What about my father?" Michel asked suddenly.

DeCew raised his right eyebrow.

"What about him?"

"Russ told me that Verle was paying him to stay away from me," Michel replied.

"I don't know if that's the case," DeCew replied, "but Verle was giving him a place to live and paying him $1,000 per month. Based on what Russ told me about your run-in with him at the Gator's Belly yesterday, I assumed you'd want to stop the payments."

Michel thought about it for a moment, then shook his head.

"No, go ahead and pay the miserable fucker. Maybe that'll keep him away from me."

"Okay," DeCew replied, "but just so you understand, it's not a legal obligation of the estate. It would be a discretionary expense. It's possible that the probate court may decide that it's inappropriate and seek restitution to the estate."

"Meaning?"

"You may have to pay the estate back before they'll okay the distribution of assets to you. That could slow things down."

"I'm willing to risk it," Michel replied.

"May I ask why?" DeCew asked.

"I'm not sure," Michel replied honestly. "But for now, I'd like to continue it."

DeCew nodded slowly.

"Well, that's pretty much it for now," he said, "but you will need to make some choices soon on which assets you'd like to liquidate and which you'd like to retain. I'll be happy to advise you on that, but ultimately you'll have to make the decisions."

"I understand," Michel replied.

"I have to run some errands," DeCew said, "but if you have the time, you could stay and review the assets in detail and make some decisions now. That would save making copies of everything."

"Could I take the files with me?" Michel asked.

"I'm afraid not," DeCew replied. "It's a lot of paper and I can't risk anything being misplaced."

Michel looked at Blue. She was curled up on the floor in the corner of the room, sleeping in the sun.

"Sure," he said, "but would you mind if we went outside for a smoke first?"

DeCew looked at his watch and nodded.

"Terry won't be back for another hour."

*****

"I'm curious about something," Michel said.

He and DeCew were sitting on the steps of the courthouse, looking out over the park.

DeCew raised an eyebrow and nodded for him to continue.

"Russ told me that you used to be a lawyer for the oil companies."

"Well, I had a private practice, but yes, I did represent several oil and gas companies," DeCew replied.

"So how did you end up switching sides?" Michel asked.

DeCew smiled.

"I wouldn't say I switched sides. I simply retired, more or less. The truth is, I always supported conservation. I grew up in Baton Rouge, but my family had a place a few miles from here. We used to come down here in the summers and I'd fish and hunt in the bayou. I love this area. But I'm also a pragmatist, and when you practice corporate law in Louisiana, oil and gas companies are very lucrative clients."

Michel nodded.

"Did you ever represent any of your clients in cases against Verle?" he asked.

DeCew furrowed his brow.

"On a few occasions," he replied. "When he stopped renewing the leases. But I always liked Verle. He was a little eccentric, but he was smart. And he stood by his principles."

It almost sounded like an admission that DeCew hadn't always stood by his own principles, but Michel decided not to pursue it.

"So what made you decide to give it up?" he asked instead.

"Terry," DeCew replied simply. "After my wife passed, I realized that I wanted a relationship with him again. I had enough money to retire at that point, so I did."

"So you and Terry were estranged?" Michel asked, pretending that Turner hadn't already told him as much.

DeCew nodded.

"After he graduated law school and decided to become a lobbyist for the Audubon Society."

"Why?"

DeCew sighed.

"Because I was worried about him," he said. "I never had a problem with his choice philosophically, but practically it seemed shortsighted. I thought he should join the firm and practice law until he could build up a nest egg, then go follow his heart. He disagreed and I didn't react well. It was foolishness on my part. And ego."

"Ego?"

"I'd always dreamed of the two of us practicing together. I wanted to pass my legacy on to him, and hoped that someday he'd pass it on to his children."

"So Terry has children?" Michel asked, masking his surprise.

"No, not yet," DeCew replied with a hint of sadness.

Michel sensed that DeCew didn't believe there ever would be children.

"Well, at least you and Terry are working together now for a common cause," he said.

DeCew smiled.

"That's true. I guess things work out the way they're meant to happen."

Michel considered what to say next. He wanted to find out about the land trust, but didn't want to appear overly curious.

"So Ruby's convinced you're going to sell all the land in the conservation trust and get rich now that Verle is gone," he said with a casual laugh.

DeCew shook his head and smiled.

"I'm afraid Ruby is a little confused about the exact nature of the trust," he said. "Even if I wanted to sell the land, which I don't, I couldn't. And if it were sold, I wouldn't be the one getting rich from it."

"Why not?"

"Because the land still belonged to Verle," DeCew said. "He just granted a conservation easement to the trust. Essentially he gave us control of the drilling, logging, mineral and development rights, but he maintained ownership. Which means now it belongs to you."

"To me?" Michel asked reflexively.

DeCew nodded.

"It's listed on the asset sheet under real estate holdings. Of course that number just reflects the valuation for property tax purposes. If you sold it, it would be worth far more than that...if you also controlled the rights."

"Okay, now I'm confused," Michel said. "I thought Verle wanted to have the land turned into a federal wildlife preservation area."

"Is that what he told you?" DeCew asked with a small chuckle.

"Yeah, why?"

"I think Verle may have been engaging in a little revisionist history there," DeCew replied.

"Meaning?"

"Well, I was still working for the 'other side' at that point," DeCew replied, "and I can tell you we were well into negotiations with Verle to renew the leases."

"So what happened?" Michel asked.

"One day Verle showed up with a list of demands to safeguard the environment. They were good ideas, but they were going to be costly, and would have limited production. It would have been at least five years before my clients could have broken even on the investment, so we rejected them. At the time, we figured it was just a negotiating ploy. That what he really wanted was more money, and if we gave him that he'd forget about the rest."

"But he didn't?"

DeCew shook his head.

"No. When the leases ended, that was that," he said. "Essentially Verle decided that if we wouldn't play by his rules he was going to take his toys and go home."

"That's an interesting way of putting it," Michel said.

"From our perspective, that's pretty much how it looked," DeCew replied.

"But you said you always liked Verle," Michel said.

"I did," DeCew replied. "But I didn't like what he did. I thought it was naive. I respected that he knew he had a bargaining chip and tried to use it to get what he wanted, and in retrospect my clients and I underestimated the sincerity of his demands, but I thought he walked away from the table too quickly. He ended up costing a lot of people jobs and hurt the town pretty badly."

"But he did what he could to make up for that," Michel replied defensively.

"He did," DeCew agreed, "and he wanted to do more, but it just didn't work out as quickly as he'd hoped. As far as the wildlife preservation idea goes, he may have entertained it briefly, but I suspect he told you that more as a way of saving face. He thought he held a winning hand, but ended up leaving the table with nothing."

Michel couldn't imagine Verle feeling embarrassed enough to lie to him, but decided to let it go.

"You said he wanted to do more?" he asked.

"Well, for a while Verle was convinced that the Basin could be the next Amazon rainforest in terms of biomedical research," DeCew replied. "With all the plants and animals here, he figured there might be a cure for cancer or other diseases, so he tried to lure some drug companies to the area, figuring it would revitalize the town's economy."

"But it didn't happen."

"No, he never got any traction with that idea," DeCew replied. "Apparently the drug companies disagreed with him. So then he thought about opening a resort and trying to attract tourists for swamp tours and hunting and fishing, but he realized that having too many people tramping around was going to do more harm than drilling."

"I take it you weren't working with Verle at that time," Michel said.

"No," DeCew replied. "At that point Terry was still working for the Audubon Society, and I was just sitting in my rocking chair watching the world go by."

Michel knew DeCew was being facetious. He had far too much vitality to sit idly for very long.

"So how did you end up working together?" Michel asked.

"He and Terry became friends," DeCew replied. "Verle was a member of the Audubon Society, and they met at a few events and hit it off. Then a few years later, Terry and I created the Atchafalaya Preservation Trust and Verle was one of our first supporters."

"Why did Terry leave Audubon?" Michel asked.

"An organization like that has a lot of irons in the fire," DeCew explained. "They're trying to fight on a lot of fronts at the same time. Terry wanted to focus on the watershed issue in the Basin."

"So he wasn't even fighting against the oil companies?" Michel asked.

"Peripherally," DeCew replied. "Some of the drilling operations can effect the watershed, but he was focused on the larger picture."

Michel nodded.

"So then, how did Verle end up giving the trust the rights to his land?"

"That didn't happen until his bypass," DeCew replied. "He'd donated money to us, and helped out with some things, but until then he was pretty much hands-off. But when he had the bypass it scared him. He realized that if he died, the land might be sold to an oil or gas company."

"By me," Michel added.

"I don't think he thought you'd do it on purpose, but a lot of times companies like that set up trusts of their own to purchase land," DeCew replied. "It makes it a lot harder to find out who's actually doing the buying. Verle wanted to make sure the land would still be protected after he was gone, so he gave us the easement, and in exchange we elected him as a trustee so he could have a vote on how the rights were used. That's when Terry shifted his focus from the watershed to lobbying the state and federal governments for stronger drilling regulations."

"That sounds like getting paid to smack your head against a brick wall every day," Michel replied.

DeCew let out a dry chuckle.

"In most cases that's true," he replied, "but when you have a very valuable asset, it's amazing how people are suddenly willing to compromise with you. It's in their best interest to make changes to get at the resources."

"I can see why it would be in the best interests of the companies, but why the politicians?" Michel asked.

"Pretty tough to get elected down here if the energy companies aren't behind you," DeCew replied.

Michel knew better than to argue the point.

"So then the goal was to get more safety regulations, then start leasing the land again?" he asked.

"Pretty much," DeCew agreed with a slow nod.

"Doesn't that seem sort of odd for a conservation trust?" Michel asked.

DeCew studied Michel with a hard expression for a moment, and Michel wondered if he'd hit a nerve.

"There's nothing inherently evil about drilling," DeCew replied finally, his tone smoothly controlled. "At least not if it's done responsibly. And the money generated by the leases would free us up from fundraising and allow us to do more work in other areas to protect the Basin. It's a practical solution that would benefit a lot of people."

Michel realized he was right, but couldn't help but feel that the whole thing was ethically dubious. He considered saying so but stopped himself. He knew he wouldn't be saying anything that DeCew didn't already know.

Suddenly he remembered something DeCew had said earlier.

"When I first got here this morning, you said that the town was dying," he said. "But if the leases were renewed, wouldn't that change?"

DeCew shrugged.

"It would certainly bring back jobs," he said, "but that's not what I meant. I meant the way of life. You can bring back jobs and move new people into the area, but they're not going to want things the way they were. They're going to want new houses and a big grocery store and shopping malls."

"It sounds like you're not really excited by the prospect," Michel replied.

DeCew gave him an appreciative smile.

"You're a master of understatement," he said.

"So why help speed along the process?" Michel asked.

"Because my own quaint notions of how things ought to be shouldn't stand in the way of progress," DeCew replied with a hint of sadness. "Once Verle stopped renewing the leases, the die was cast. Either the town was going to disappear entirely or it was going to become something else."

He stared at the steps for a moment, then shook his head.

"Actually that's not fair," he said. "Maybe what Verle did made it happen a little quicker, but the change was inevitable, and probably even necessary. I don't have a right to try to stop it. The best I can do is try to manage it in a way that will do the least damage."

Michel wondered briefly what changes he would lament when he reached DeCew's age. He pushed the thought away.

"So you intend to continue on with the plans?" he asked.

"I think it's what's best," DeCew replied with a nod.

Then he stubbed out his cigar and looked at his watch.

"We'd better get back upstairs so I can set you up before I have to leave," he said.

Chapter 19

"It's pretty simple," DeCew said as he slid open a top drawer from the bank of walnut file cabinets that spanned one wall of the room. "Up here are all the summary documents. Basically the lists of assets and monthly value for each for the last five years."

"Five years?" Michel queried.

"That's when Verle hired me to manage things," DeCew replied.

"So you were his financial advisor, too?" Michel asked.

"More like a glorified accountant," DeCew replied with a smile. "Verle was pretty shrewd about his investments, but he had a tendency to forget to pay his bills. He had them all sent here and I made sure they got paid."

Michel nodded, though he was curious just how much control DeCew had had over Verle's money.

"Then in these drawers," DeCew continued with a sweeping gesture to indicate the other eleven drawers in the block, "are all the details. If you have any questions, you can probably find the explanations there."

Michel noticed how precise and crisp DeCew's gestures were in contrast to the slow, unsteady movement of his legs.

"I can't imagine what questions I'd have," he replied.

"Well, that's the funny thing about questions," DeCew replied. "If you knew what they were going to be, you probably wouldn't have them in the first place."

"I suppose that's true," Michel replied.

"Help yourself to coffee or whatever from the kitchen," DeCew said. "The bathroom's just down the hall on the right."

"Thanks," Michel replied.

"Terry should be back in about 45 minutes," DeCew said. "If you leave before he gets back, just make sure the door locks behind you."

"I will," Michel replied.

*****

Michel placed the file folder back into its slot and shut the heavy drawer. He'd given the summaries only a cursory look, realizing quickly that he had no practical basis for deciding which assets to keep and which to liquidate. He knew he'd have to ask DeCew for advice.

He perused the neatly typed labels inserted into the brass plates on the other drawers. The two remaining drawers on the top row, and all three on the second, were marked "Real Estate." The three on the third row were marked with the names of investment companies.

He knelt down and looked at the drawers on the bottom row. The label on the far left read, "Bank Statements, 2000–2005." He paused for a moment, feeling a twinge of guilt that he would be invading Verle's privacy.

"Sorry," he said quietly, looking up at the ceiling.

He opened the drawer and began thumbing through the green hanging folders until he found one marked "April, 2004." It was the month before his mother had died. He pulled the folder out and opened it.

In the front was a four-page statement, and nestled behind it, a thin stack of cancelled checks. Michel took them out and laid the folder on the floor.

I guess that means DeCew didn't have the authority to sign them, he thought as he leafed through the checks, noting that each had the date, the name of the payee, and the amount typed in, but had been signed by Verle.

"Electric, insurance, internet, groceries," he recited aloud in a sing-songy voice as he flipped through the checks. "Propane. Kind of ironic. Gasoline. Even more ironic."

He stopped when he got to the check he'd been looking for, made out to his mother in the amount of $3,000.00.

"That settles that question," he said.

Blue stirred on the floor and stretched, then settled back down. She'd found a new sunny spot in the corner of the conference room, though the sun had moved a few inches to her right so that now her face was in shade.

Michel flipped to the last check. It was to his father for $1,000.00. He stared at it for a few seconds, then returned it to the back of the stack and put the checks back in the folder.

"Fucker," he said.

He put the folder back in the drawer and closed it. The other two drawers on the row were unlabeled and empty.

"I guess that's that," he said, standing up and stretching.

Blue suddenly looked up expectantly. Michel was about to tell her it was time to leave, but stopped. He moved to the next bank of file cabinets and read the label on the top left drawer: "APT Income/Expenses, 2005–2006."

He looked up at the clock over the door. If DeCew had been right, Terry wouldn't be back for another half hour.

"Just a few more minutes, girl," he said.

*****

The Trust's records had been organized identically to Verle's, with the summary statements in the top left drawer and support documentation in the others. From the summaries, Michel could see that the Trust's monthly operating expenses were pretty regular. The only figures that varied were those listed under "Fundraising," "PAC Contributions," and "Lobbying," with each ranging from just under $10,000 up to $12,000 per month.

The Trust's income, on the other hand, fluctuated dramatically, from $12,600 in February to $160,000 in October. "Membership Dues" accounted for $2,500 each month, with the rest coming from "Donations."

Michel put the summaries back in the drawer and closed it, then began checking the labels on the other drawers. In the second row, he found one labeled "Donations, 2005" and opened it. The folders inside were organized by month. He pulled out the folder for October and walked over to the conference table.

The list of donors had been sorted by amount, with the first page consisting entirely of $50 and $100 donations. He turned to the second page and the amounts increased to $500. He turned to the final page. There were only five listings, each for $20,000. Three of the donations were from individuals, and the others from organizations. None of the names were familiar.

Michel picked up the sheet and walked into the central room that connected all of the other rooms in the suite. Had there been a staff, it undoubtedly would have served as the reception area. As it was, it seemed to be a cross between a storage closet and a common workspace, with supplies and boxes of older files on shelves lining both side walls, two computer stations, and a copy machine.

Michel looked down the hallway to make sure no one was coming, then quickly made a copy of the page. He folded it carefully and placed it in the inside pocket of his jacket, then walked back into the conference room, returned the original to the folder, and put the folder back into its drawer.

He continued down the rows of drawers until he found one labelled "Receipts, 2005." He opened it and randomly pulled out the folder for April.

Most of the receipts were from restaurants. Twelve were in Baton Rouge, nine in Washington, DC, and three in Alexandria, Virginia. On each, someone had written names, a few of which Michel recognized as Congressmen and Senators. The receipts from Baton Rouge were spread throughout the month, while those from Washington and Alexandria all came from a four-day period. Based on the varying amounts—from $89.00 to $783.00—it was obvious that some were for breakfast, some for lunch, and some for very expensive dinners.

"It's amazing he's so thin with all that wining and dining," Michel muttered.

He continued though the receipts: gas, parking, dry cleaning. The last was from a Marriott Hotel in Chantilly, Virginia, for $330.00 plus tax for a three-night stay.

"Well, he certainly wasn't splurging on accommodations," Michel said.

He closed the folder and returned it to the drawer, then pulled out the folder for May. The receipts were nearly identical to those from April, including many of the same restaurant and another three-day stay at the Chantilly Marriott.

"Boring," Michel sang to himself.

He replaced the folder and took out the one for June.

That's odd, he thought as he flipped through the receipts. There's nothing from Washington.

He did a quick calculation in his head. The receipts totaled under $7,000, despite the fact that the amounts listed on the summary sheet for lobbying had all been at least $10,000.

He put the folder back in the drawer and began checking the labels on the other drawers until he found one marked "Credit Card Statements, 2005." He opened it, pulled out the folder for June, and started scanning the statement.

"Well, isn't this interesting," he said, his finger stopping on a charge for $6,673.40 from the Hotel Monteleone in New Orleans.

"Seems like maybe we have ourselves..."

Suddenly Blue jumped up and looked at the door, her head cocked to the right.

Fuck, Michel thought.

He quickly folded up the statement and stuck it in the inside pocket of his jacket, then closed the folder and returned it to the drawer.

"Hello?" Terry's voice called.

"Hello," Michel called back as he quietly slid the drawer shut.

As Blue walked to the door, Michel moved back to the first bank of file cabinets and opened the top left drawer a crack.

"Hey Blue," Terry said. "What are you doing here?"

"She's with me," Michel said with forced casualness as Terry appeared in the doorway. "I had a meeting with your dad to go over Verle's estate, and then he let me to stay to review Verle's assets so I could make some decisions about what to liquidate and what to keep."

"Oh," Terry replied with mild surprise as he crouched down to rub Blue's neck. "He didn't tell me."

He seemed to be studying Michel as Michel pushed the drawer shut.

"So did you find what you were looking for?" Terry asked.

The question seemed somewhat pointed. Michel wondered if it was just his own paranoia.

"Yeah, thanks," he replied. "But I'm afraid I wasn't able to figure much out. Finance isn't my strong point."

He shrugged sheepishly.

"Well, I'm sure my father can help you out," Terry replied in a neutral tone as he stood up. "He's much more familiar with Verle's finances than I am."

"Yeah, he said he would," Michel replied.

Terry nodded slightly. Michel got the sense that Terry wasn't comfortable with him being there and wondered why.

"By the way, did he say where he was going?" Terry asked.

"Just on some errands," Michel replied.

For a second, Terry's forehead furrowed with worry.

"What's the matter?" Michel asked.

"Nothing," Terry replied diffidently.

"Are you sure?" Michel asked.

Terry seemed unsure how to react to Michel's show of concern.

"Yeah," he replied finally. "I just worry about him sometimes. I'm sure Russ told you he had a stroke?"

Michel nodded.

"I think it took a lot more out of him than he likes to let on," Terry said. "Lately he's been going on a lot of 'errands.' Last week he told me he was going on one and an hour later I saw him leaving his house."

"So what do you think is going on?" Michel asked, his curiosity piqued.

"I think he's actually going home to rest," Terry replied. "But he won't tell me because he doesn't want me to worry. I mean, let's face it, there are only so many errands you can run in a town like this, and Dad can't drive anymore."

Michel smiled, both at the joke and the fact that Terry seemed to be relaxing a little.

"I'm sure he's okay," he said reassuringly. "He seems like a pretty hearty guy to me."

"I suppose you're right," Terry replied with a sigh. "I guess I just can't help compare how he is now to how he was before the stroke. I swear, when I was growing up he never slept. He'd be in the kitchen helping my mother make breakfast when I got up in the morning, then he'd drive me to school and go to work, then he'd be home for dinner, then we'd play games or he'd help me with my homework, then when I went to bed he'd go into his office and work for a few more hours. And he never seemed to get tired. He was always just incredibly...present."

He suddenly looked embarrassed. Michel wasn't sure if it was because of his word choice or because he'd been so forthcoming with a stranger. He guessed it was the former.

"It's okay," he said with a small laugh. "I don't begrudge anyone who had a good father."

Terry gave him a sympathetic smile.

"I'm sorry," he said. "I heard about your run-in with Jack."

"I'm sure it's the talk of the town," Michel replied without any judgment. "It's okay. I thought he was dead, so it's not like it's a big loss."

Terry just nodded. It was clear that he didn't know what more to say. Michel decided to take advantage of the fact that Terry had let his guard down.

"That's a charming crew he hangs with," he said, watching Terry carefully. "Especially Donny Heath."

Terry's right eye twitched involuntarily, then his expression grew wary again. Michel realized he'd made a tactical mistake and needed to recover.

"Definitely not people I'd care to spend time with again," he said, shaking his head with exaggerated disapproval.

Terry continued to watch him carefully for a moment, then averted his eyes and shook his head, too.

"Me neither," he said, looking back at Michel. "I make it a point to stay clear of the Gator's Belly unless my father wants to go there to eat."

"Is the food any good?" Michel asked, though he didn't really care. He just wanted to keep the conversation going.

"Actually it's pretty good," Terry replied. "It's just the decor and clientele that need improvement."

Michel smiled.

"So do you ever make it down my way?" he asked casually. "We've got some of the best restaurants in the world in New Orleans."

"Not in a long time," Terry replied a little too quickly.

"Not even for work?" Michel asked. "I'd imagine that with your lobbying you'd travel all over the place."

"Not to New Orleans," Terry replied flatly. "Mostly just Baton Rouge and Washington."

"It's probably changed quite a bit since the last time you were there because of the hurricane," Michel said.

Terry nodded noncommittally.

"So is there anything else I can help you with?" he asked. "I have some work I need to do."

It distinctly sounded like an invitation for Michel to leave.

"Uh no, not that I can think of," he replied. "Just tell your father I'll give him a call about the assets."

"Okay," Terry replied.

*****

As soon as he was back in his car, Michel took out the credit card statement and punched the number for the Hotel Monteleone into his cell phone.

"Hotel Monteleone. This is Eileen. How may I help you?" a pleasant woman's voice answered after the second ring.

"Hi, Eileen," Michel replied just as pleasantly. "I'm sorry to bother you, but I'm calling from the Atchafalaya Preservation Trust. I've been reviewing our records for last year and found a charge on one of our credit cards for your hotel, but I don't have any receipts, and I'm embarrassed to say I'm not sure which of our people was down there. Is there anyway you can look that up for me?"

"Certainly, sir," Eileen replied. "Do you have the dates and the credit card number?"

Michel gave her the information.

"And your name, sir?" Eileen asked.

"Porter DeCew," Michel improvised.

"Just a moment, please, Mr. DeCew," Eileen replied.

The line was suddenly filled with a swell of dramatic music. Michel recognized it as something from "Scheherazade" by Rimsky-Korsakov.

"Thank you for holding, Mr. DeCew," Eileen's voice came back after fifteen seconds. "I have that information for you."

"Thank you," Michel replied.

"The charges were for three nights in the Tennessee Williams Suite, dinner in the Hunt Room Grill, room service, and several charges at the Carousel Bar."

"And do you have a name?" Michel asked.

"Certainly," Eileen replied. "Mr. Terry DeCew and Mr. Donald Heath."

Michel smiled to himself.

"Oh, that's right," he said, feigning embarrassment. "I forgot that my son Terry and Don were down there for the Solar Energy Conference. I'm so sorry to have bothered you."

"Not at all, Mr. DeCew," Eileen replied. "Would you like me to send you a copy of the bill?"

"No, thank you," Michel replied. "I'll ask Terry and Don first. If they don't have it, I'll call you back."

"Is there anything else I can help you with today, Mr. DeCew?" Eileen asked.

"No," Michel replied. "You've already been more than helpful."

Chapter 20

As he pulled into the front yard, Michel was surprised to see Ruby sitting on the steps of Verle's house. She immediately stood up and started shifting uncomfortably from one foot to the other while he parked the car.

"Hey, Ruby," Michel called as he got out, followed by Blue.

Blue dashed around the back of the car to Ruby.

"Hey," Ruby called back.

She crouched down and began vigorously rubbing Blue's neck while Blue licked her face.

"How's my girl?" she cooed in a hushed, girlish voice. "Have you missed me?"

Michel smiled and grabbed the bag of sandwiches he'd picked up at the diner from the back seat.

"So to what do we owe the honor?" he asked as he approached Ruby and Blue.

Ruby stood up, the discomfort returning to her posture.

"Oh, no honor," she replied with embarrassment, looking down at the ground. "I just wanted to come by and see how the dog was doing. You weren't here, so I figured I'd wait around for a while. Hope that was okay."

Michel felt a twinge of sympathy, realizing how lonely Ruby must be now that Verle was gone.

"Of course not," he replied. "I just got some lunch. Do you want to join us?"

"No, that's okay," Ruby replied. "You weren't expecting company. I don't want to be eating all your food."

"It's okay," Michel replied. "I got three sandwiches because I wasn't sure what I really wanted. There's plenty."

Ruby looked up at him for a moment and he could sense that she wanted to stay but didn't feel comfortable enough with him yet.

"Please, we'd love to have you stay," he added. "Blue's been missing you."

A small, sweet smile played briefly across Ruby's lips, then she began swaying back and forth slightly, as though the debate in her mind had turned into a physical battle that was rocking her whole body. After a few seconds, she stopped moving.

"Well, okay," she said shyly. "If you're sure it's okay."

"I'm sure," Michel assured her.

*****

"So where are you originally from?" Michel asked once they were settled at the square table adjacent to the kitchen.

Ruby held up a finger as she loudly chewed an overly large bite of her chicken salad sandwich. From the way she'd attacked it, Michel wondered when she'd last eaten, though she certainly didn't seem to be suffering from malnutrition.

Ruby swallowed and took a long swig of her beer.

"Bayou Chene," she said finally.

"My partner grew up in Butte La Rose," Michel said. "Is that anywhere near there?"

"You mean your boyfriend?" Ruby asked bluntly.

Michel was momentarily taken aback by the question.

"Uh, no," he replied. "I meant my business partner, Sassy. And actually she was my partner on the police force, as well."

Ruby nodded.

"I don't know," she said. "I never been to any place called Butte La Rose. The only places I ever been were Bayou Chene, Boston, Massachusetts, and here."

"Boston?" Michel asked with surprise. "What were you doing up there?"

Ruby took another large bite of her sandwich and made him wait for an answer.

"I went up there to the Berklee College of Music," she said finally, as though it were the most natural thing in the world. "They invited me up for an audition, but I didn't like it much."

Michel wondered if she was toying with him, delusional, or telling the truth. He was surprised she'd even heard of Berklee.

"How'd you get invited to Berklee?" he asked, deciding to play along with her story.

"I used to play the piano," Ruby replied. "I was playing at the church and one of the professors from up there was down visiting family. He heard me, and the next thing I knew they were inviting me up."

"When was this?" Michel asked, deciding she was telling the truth, or at least what she believed to be the truth.

"1974," Ruby replied. "Just after I turned eighteen. I only went because I wanted to see the city. I figured I already could play as good as I wanted. There wasn't really any reason for me to go to school for it."

Michel sat back in his chair.

"So you don't play anymore?" he asked.

"Not so much," Ruby replied matter-of-factly. "I have a piano at my place, but what with the humidity and all it's hard to keep it tuned. Verle used to have someone come out every six months or so to fix it and then I'd be able to play for a while, but it's not sounding so good right now."

"I'm sure I could have Porter DeCew arrange to have it tuned," Michel offered.

Ruby shook her head vehemently.

"No. He'd just send someone to spy on me."

"Why would he want to spy on you?" Michel asked with curious amusement.

145

"Cuz so long as I'm around, he knows he can't sell the land," Ruby replied. "He'll have his spy watch my comings and goings, and one day when I'm out, he'll lock the door on me."

Michel suddenly felt pity that Ruby was so paranoid.

"He's not going to sell the land," he assured her. "The trust doesn't even own the land. They just have the rights for it. The land belongs to me now, and I promise I'm not going to sell it. You can stay at your place as long as you want."

Ruby eyed him with distrust. Michel wasn't sure if she thought he was lying or naive.

"You sure about that?" she asked.

"I saw the documents myself," Michel replied, fudging the truth.

Ruby screwed her face up for a moment, then nodded.

"If you say so," she said.

"In fact, I was thinking that if you wanted to move into this house, it would be okay with me," Michel said.

"No, that wouldn't be right," Ruby replied. "You should live here."

"Well, I'll be going back to New Orleans soon," Michel explained.

"Oh," Ruby replied. "I thought maybe you'd change your mind about that."

"I'm afraid not," Michel replied. "My friends are all back in New Orleans. And my job."

"But you don't have to work any more," Ruby said. "I know Verle left you all his money."

Michel was mildly surprised that Verle had discussed his financial affairs with Ruby, but he nodded.

"That's true, but I still want to work."

"Suit yourself," Ruby replied with a touch of annoyance. "And I suppose you'll be taking Blue with you?"

"I'm not sure about that yet," Michel replied honestly.

Though he was becoming more attached to Blue each day,

he still wondered whether he could provide a good home for her in New Orleans.

"Well, I'd be happy to look after her, if you want," Ruby replied.

"Thanks," Michel replied. "I'll keep that in mind."

"And I can check in on the place when you're not here, too," Ruby added. "Make sure no critters move in and such."

"I'd appreciate that," Michel replied with a smile.

They were both quiet for a few moments.

"So are you done?" Ruby asked abruptly.

"Huh?" Michel replied, confused since they'd just started eating.

"Talking," Ruby clarified. "You done talking? Cuz I thought you invited me here to eat."

"Yeah, I'm done," Michel replied with a laugh.

*****

Ruby had wolfed down her lunch without another word, then said a quick thanks and left. Michel watched her walk around the corner of the house, then went back inside to get his cell phone.

"Hey," he said when Sassy answered.

"Hey. So when are you coming home?"

"Why, do you miss me?"

"No, but we do have a business to run," Sassy replied dryly.

"I'm not sure yet," Michel replied.

"But I thought you just had to meet with Verle's attorney and then you'd be leaving," Sassy replied.

"That was the original plan."

"So what happened? Problems with the will?"

"No, nothing like that," Michel replied, "but I came across something kind of interesting in the trust's records."

"Oh?"

Michel explained about the missing receipts in the file, his call to the Hotel Monteleone, and the interaction he'd seen between Donny Heath and Terry at the diner.

"So are you thinking they're somehow connected to Verle and the murder?" Sassy asked.

"I don't know," Michel replied, "but Donny works for Gulf Coast Oil."

"I imagine a lot of folks up there do," Sassy replied. "That doesn't mean there's a connection."

"True," Michel replied, "but Donny went on disability eight months ago, which coincides with when he went to New Orleans with Terry, and so far as anyone can tell, there's nothing wrong with him."

"Okay, that's a little suspicious," Sassy admitted, "but still..."

"I know it's pretty thin," Michel replied, "but I think it's worth looking into. At the very least, there's obviously something going on between Terry and Donny."

"Something sexual?" Sassy asked.

"That's the sense I got at the diner," Michel replied, "and if Terry hasn't ended up on the wrong end of a dick at some point, I'd be pretty surprised."

"And which end of a dick is the 'wrong end' exactly?" Sassy asked.

"You know what I mean," Michel replied. "And I'm not the only one who thinks so. Verle's friend Ruby called him Porter's 'sissy boy'."

"What about Donny?" Sassy asked.

"Outwardly he's your typical small town bad boy," Michel replied. "Loud talking, hard drinking, fighting, gambling, womanizing."

"Sounds like maybe he's overcompensating," Sassy replied.

"That's what I'm thinking," Michel replied. "He's definitely self-conscious. Always posturing like he's sure people are watching him. And he gives off this weird predatory vibe. Both at the diner and at the Gator's Belly, he gave me looks that just made me feel...dirty. Like I'd been violated."

"Those must have been some looks to make *you* feel dirty," Sassy replied.

"Thanks," Michel replied sarcastically.

"Hey, I'm just saying," Sassy replied. "I mean, I'm not the one who hooked up with suspects on our last two cases."

"They weren't suspects," Michel replied. "Or at least not both of them."

"Oh right, the other was just a Rastafarian gangster," Sassy replied.

"Can we please just focus on the present?" Michel asked.

"Of course," Sassy replied with exaggerated sweetness. "So what are you planning to do?"

"I'm not sure yet," Michel replied. "I guess I'll just play it by ear."

"Well, what does your buddy Russ think?" Sassy asked.

"I haven't told him," Michel replied.

"Why not?" Sassy asked. "I thought he was your shiny new best friend."

Michel smiled.

"You know you could never be replaced," he said.

"Yes, I *do* know that," Sassy replied. "But that doesn't explain why you haven't told him."

"I guess I'm not sure that I can trust him," Michel replied.

"Ooh, you think it might have been a threesome?" Sassy asked with faux lasciviousness.

"Very funny," Michel replied. "No, but he's got strong ties with Porter and Terry DeCew."

"So?"

"Well, there's more than just the issue of whether Terry and Donny are sleeping together," Michel replied. "There are some things about the trust that seem kind of peculiar to me."

"Such as?"

"Well, once Verle got hooked up with them, they shifted their focus from trying to protect the basin's watershed to lobbying for stronger drilling regulations so that they could start leasing the land again."

"What about the federal wildlife preservation idea?" Sassy asked.

"Porter DeCew told me it was a fleeting idea, if Verle ever actually considered it at all," Michel replied. "He said that Verle was trying to renegotiate the leases ten years ago, but when the oil companies balked at the safety measures he wanted, he just walked away from the negotiations."

"Hmmm, that's interesting," Sassy replied. "And he was working with the trust to try to lease the land again?"

"More or less."

"Why? Was he running out of money?"

"Hardly," Michel replied. "In fact, he gave the drilling and development rights to the trust, so he wouldn't even have profited."

"So a conservation trust was planning to lease drilling rights?" Sassy asked. "That seems kind of hypocritical."

"To say the least," Michel replied. "And according to their records, the trust also makes significant PAC contributions."

"That's not so strange," Sassy replied. "Depending on which PACs. Did you get a list?"

"No," Michel replied. "I got interrupted before I could check them out."

"Interrupted?" Sassy asked. "Are you telling me you were going through their records without permission?"

"Well, they didn't say I *couldn't* look at them," Michel replied. "I mean, DeCew left me alone in the room so I could look at Verle's finances, and I just happened to notice that the trust's files were there, as well."

"Uh huh," Sassy replied. "Just happened to notice."

From the tone of her voice, Michel knew she was shaking her head reproachfully at him.

"Anyway," she said.

"But I did get a list of their top donors," Michel replied. "I was hoping you could check them out for me. I don't have internet access up here."

He read her the list of names.

"Okay, I'll have Chance do some research," Sassy replied.

"Thanks."

"It's amazing," Sassy said.

"What's that?"

"You've only been in Bayou Proche for five days now, and you've already got a murder, Verle's death, two guys having a secret rendezvous in New Orleans, and a trust with questionable practices."

"Well, technically the murder happened before I got here," Michel replied. "But yeah, it's pretty amazing."

"I don't remember that much intrigue in small towns when I was a girl," Sassy said.

"Maybe you were just too young to notice," Michel replied with a laugh.

"Oh no," Sassy replied definitively. "I always noticed everything."

"I'll bet you did," Michel replied. "So what's going on down there? Any luck figuring out what happened with the money?"

"No," Sassy replied. "The bank swears it never happened, despite the fact that Chance showed them a printout of his computer screen with the lower balance. They say they have no records of any $10,000 payments in or out of the account in the last week."

"Well, at least the money's there now," Michel replied. "Anything else?"

"Joel will be back tomorrow," Sassy replied.

Michel felt a flutter of both anticipation and dread. He'd

been so focused on what was happening in Bayou Proche that he'd forgotten Joel was coming home.

"Anything you want me to tell him?" Sassy asked.

Michel considered it for a moment.

"Just hi, I guess," he replied finally.

"You and your silver tongue," Sassy replied.

"What do you want me to say?" Michel replied. "That I long to run my fingers through his silken locks and caress his firm young buttocks?"

"That'll work," Sassy replied with a laugh.

"Don't you dare," Michel warned, though he couldn't help laughing, too.

"Fine, have it your way," Sassy replied. "Is that it?"

"I think so," Michel replied. "Oh wait. How far is Butte La Rose from Bayou Chene?"

"About 18 miles," Sassy replied.

"You ever been there?"

"Yeah, once. That's where Pearl was born. And no more jokes about her name. Why?"

"Ruby is from Bayou Chene," Michel replied, "but when I asked her how far it was from Butte La Rose, she said she'd never heard of it. I thought that was kind of strange."

"Not really," Sassy replied. "Bayou Chene is the sort of place that makes Bayou Proche look like a big city. A lot of the folks there never get more than a few miles away."

"Did Pearl ever mention anything about a girl there who was a piano prodigy?" Michel asked.

"Not that I remember," Sassy replied, "but her family moved when she was just a girl. Are you talking about Ruby?"

"Yeah. She claims that she auditioned at the Berklee College of Music."

"And you believe her?" Sassy asked.

"I believe she believes it," Michel replied, "but that doesn't mean it's true."

"I'll give Pearl a call and see what she knows," Sassy offered.

"That would be great," Michel replied. "I'm just really curious whether it's true."

"Okay," Sassy replied. "So now tell me how much money Verle left you."

"What? I'm not going to tell you that," Michel protested.

"Oh, come on," Sassy cajoled. "Why not?"

"Because it would be unseemly," Michel replied.

"Wow, *that* much?" Sassy replied.

"What are you talking about?" Michel replied with a laugh.

"You said 'unseemly'," Sassy replied. "Only really rich people use words like 'unseemly'."

"Really?" Michel replied, then paused for dramatic effect before continuing. "Well then I guess you're going to be hearing it a lot from now on."

He hit the disconnect button and smiled at the phone with amused satisfaction.

Chapter 21

Michel sat in his car smoking the last cigarette in his pack as he watched the lunch crowd filter out of the diner. He'd been parked on the narrow side street around the corner from the police station for almost two hours. He looked at his watch impatiently, knowing that he'd have to get back to the house soon to let Blue out.

"Come on, Terry," he said to himself.

He'd decided against going to the trust's offices in case Porter DeCew was there. He wanted to talk to Terry alone.

He was about to get out of the car to stretch when Terry suddenly came into view, walking past the hardware store toward the diner. Though Terry's attention was on the contents of a folder he was carrying, Michel reflexively slouched down in his seat.

"Bingo," he said.

He waited until Terry had gone into the diner, then got out of the car.

As he walked into the diner, three older men sitting at the counter turned to look at him. They nodded slightly, then returned to their low conversation. Save for the booth by the window where a young woman was imploring her toddler to finish his hot dog, the rest of the tables were empty. Michel looked around, confused. Then he spotted the folder Terry had been carrying on the table of the back corner booth.

"Hey, hon," Darlene called from behind the counter. "Sit wherever you like."

Michel made a show of looking around the room. Most of the tables were still cluttered with dirty plates, glasses, and silverware. Then he started casually toward the corner.

Just as he reached the booth, Terry appeared in the entrance to the adjacent hallway. He took a step toward the booth, then saw Michel and faltered.

"Oh, I'm sorry," Michel said. "Are you sitting here?"

"Oh," Terry stammered. "That's okay. I can sit somewhere else."

It wasn't the invitation Michel had wanted. They both stood there awkwardly for a moment, then Darlene came up beside them.

"So what can I get you boys?" she asked.

Michel looked at Terry and raised his eyebrows as if to say "shall we?" Terry looked back it him uncomfortably for a few seconds, then shrugged. They both slid into the booth, with Terry on the side facing the front window. He nodded deferentially at Michel.

"Can I still get breakfast?" Michel asked.

"Whatever you like, hon," Darlene replied with a pleasant smile.

"A ham and cheese omelet, home fries, bacon, and coffee."

"White or wheat?"

"Wheat, please," Michel replied.

"Cheddar, okay?" Darlene asked. "I think we're out of everything else."

"That's fine," Michel replied.

"You got it, hon," Darlene replied, then looked at Terry.

"I'll just have a turkey sandwich and some coffee, please," he said in a tone that was almost apologetic.

"Okay," Darlene replied, then smiled and whirled away toward the counter.

"Late lunch, eh?" Michel asked immediately.

"Yeah," Terry replied. "I usually try to avoid the rush."

Michel imagined that he was probably trying to avoid Donny Heath.

Darlene walked backed with two cups, placed them on the table and filled them.

"It'll be a few minutes," she said rolling her eyes. "Jimmy Joe just went on a smoke break."

"That's okay," Michel replied with a reassuring smile.

He watched as she walked back behind the counter and began filling salt shakers, then turned his attention to Terry.

"So, what's going on with you and Donny Heath?" he asked.

Terry blinked his pale blue eyes, then tried to muster a confused look.

"What do you mean?"

"I saw that interaction between you two the other day," Michel replied. "I was just wondering what it was about."

Terry furrowed his nearly invisible eyebrows in concentration for a few moments, then let out what seemed intended as an easy laugh.

"Oh, that," he said. "Nothing. Donny just likes getting up in people's faces. If it hadn't been me, it would have been someone else."

Michel nodded.

"And what about when you and Donny were at the Hotel Monteleone?" he asked. "What was going on then?"

Terry's large eyes widened, and the scant color drained from his cheeks.

"What are you talking about?" he asked unconvincingly.

Michel pulled the credit card statement from his jacket and handed it to Terry.

"I came across that yesterday when I was at your office," he said.

Terry stared at the paper for a moment as though he expected it to turn into a snake and bite him. Then he quickly slipped it into the folder on the table.

"You mean you *stole* it," he said in an angry whisper.

"So call the cops," Michel replied with a shrug.

Terry glared at him.

"So again, what were you and Donny doing at the Hotel Monteleone?" Michel asked.

Terry gave him a tight-lipped frown.

"I could ask again a little louder if you like," Michel replied.

Terry suddenly sat forward.

"Why are you doing this?" he asked in an urgent, hushed voice as he looked around the room to make sure no one was watching them. "It's none of your business."

"Maybe, maybe not," Michel replied with a shrug. "But here's the way I see it. My cousin was accused of a murder I don't think he committed. You work for a trust that controls the drilling rights to his land, and you went to New Orleans for a very expensive vacation with a guy who works for a company that would love to get their hands on those rights. A guy, by the way, who's been on paid disability since your trip, despite the fact that there doesn't seem to be anything wrong with him. So you tell me why it's none of my business."

He sat back and folded his arms across his chest.

Terry stared down at the table for a long time. Michel could see his lower lip working, as though he were on the verge of tears. Finally he looked up. Though his eyes were dry, the rims were red.

"It didn't have anything to do with Verle or the trust," he said. "I swear. I would never have done anything to hurt Verle."

"Okay, so then what was it about?"

The color flushed back into Terry's cheeks, several shades darker than before.

"Sex," he whispered.

"Sex?" Michel repeated skeptically. "That's it?"

Terry nodded.

"Why go all the way to New Orleans and stay in an $1,800

a night suite just for sex?" Michel asked. "Why not a Motel 6 or behind a dumpster?"

"Because I was trying to impress him," Terry admitted with an anguished sigh.

"Why?" Michel asked, leaning forward. "Are the two of you in a relationship?"

Terry looked around nervously again.

"I wish I'd never met Donny Heath," he replied, shaking his head.

From the pained tone of his voice, Michel knew he was telling the truth.

"So then how did you end up in New Orleans?" he asked.

Terry frowned and studied the table for a moment.

"There's a truck stop off the main highway," he said. "It's a known cruising place. Guys from all of the towns around here go there."

Michel nodded. He knew there were similar spots near most small towns.

"And that's where you and Donny hooked up?" he asked.

Terry shook his head.

"I saw him there a few times," he said, "but we never talked to each other."

"Why's that?"

"It's not like we were friends," Terry said with a touch of dismay. "People don't hang out there and make small talk. They just go there looking for sex, and I wasn't Donny's type."

"What type is that?" Michel asked.

"Truckers," Terry replied. "Big burly guys. I guess he likes rough trade."

Michel was surprised that Terry was familiar with the term, but nodded.

"So then how did the two of you end up together?"

"I was coming back from Baton Rouge one night and I stopped there," Terry said. "It was raining and the place was deserted, but I decided to wait around for a while. Donny showed up while I was there."

Michel suddenly had the sense that Terry was actually excited by telling the story. While he still looked nervous, there was an intensity to the way he was talking now that hadn't been there before.

"When I saw him pull in I was going to leave, but he waved to me so I waited," Terry continued. "Then he came over and got in the car."

"But you said you didn't hook up there," Michel interrupted.

"We didn't," Terry replied. "But he said he wanted to. He said he'd wanted to for a while, but he'd been too shy."

"Shy doesn't seem like something Donny does," Michel replied.

"That's what I thought," Terry replied. "I figured it was a trick, that he was trying to lure me into the woods and then his friends would show up and steal my car or rob me."

"Hey, Jimmy Joe!" Darlene's voice cut through the room. "You tryin' to set a record for the world's longest smoke break? I've got hungry customers in here."

Michel turned his head and saw her standing in the doorway to the kitchen with her hands on her hips.

"And don't forget to wash your hands this time," she said.

There was the sound of a door slamming, then a gruff voice drifted out of the doorway.

"Hey, Darlene, if I'd wanted someone to nag me, I would have gotten married."

Darlene turned back toward the counter with a satisfied smile on her face. When she saw Michel looking at her, she gave an embarrassed shrug.

"As if anyone would have his sorry ass," she said.

Michel smiled at her, then looked back at Terry.

"So then what?" he asked.

"I told him I wasn't interested," Terry replied.

"What did he say?"

"He said okay," Terry replied, "but then he started dropping by the office late at night when I was working by myself. It went on for a few weeks. And then one night I finally gave in."

"When was that?" Michel asked.

"About a month before we went to New Orleans," Terry replied.

"So then you did have a relationship," Michel said.

"If you want to call it that," Terry replied. "He'd come by the office a few nights a week and we'd fuck."

The unexpected bluntness of the statement seemed completely out of character and took Michel by surprise.

"But you said you were trying to impress him with the suite at the Monteleone," he said. "You don't try to impress people you're just fucking like that."

Terry nodded.

"I thought it was more than that," he admitted. "I thought he really liked me. When we were together, he wasn't the way he is in public. He was gentle and kind. There was a whole other side to him."

Michel had met enough men like that to know it was possible, though he questioned whether Donny had had an ulterior motive.

"I already had the trip to New Orleans scheduled," Terry continued, "so I asked him if he wanted to go. I figured it would be a chance for us to really spend some time together."

"And you decided to go all out," Michel said.

Terry nodded.

"I don't know what I was thinking," he said. "I thought I was in love, and I guess I was hoping that he'd fall in love with me, too."

It seemed hopelessly naive to Michel, but he sensed that Terry hadn't had much experience with relationships.

"So how did you go from a romantic getaway to the scene here the other day?" he asked.

Terry looked down and the flush returned to his cheeks.

"A few days later he called me and said he wanted to meet," he said. "He came by the office that night and showed me photos he'd taken on his cell phone. He said he wanted $50,000 or he'd show them to Carolyn and my father."

Michel sat back again and exhaled loudly.

"You didn't give it to him, did you?" he asked.

"Of course not," Terry replied. "I don't have that sort of money. The only way I could get it would be to steal from the trust, and I was already feeling guilty about the money I'd spent in New Orleans."

"So what did you do?" Michel asked.

"I told Carolyn and my father what happened," Terry replied.

Michel realized he'd underestimated Terry. Most people would have caved in and paid the money in similar circumstances. He admired Terry's willingness to take responsibility for his actions and accept the consequences.

"My father insisted we tell Verle since I'd paid for the trip with money from the trust," Terry continued, "I offered to resign, but Verle and my father both voted against it."

It didn't surprise Michel that Verle had shown compassion, though he was slightly surprised about Porter DeCew, despite the fact that Terry was his son.

"I've been paying the money back since," Terry said.

"Did you tell Russ?" Michel asked.

Terry shook his head.

"I wanted to prosecute, but my father talked me out of it," he said. "He didn't think Carolyn would be able to handle the public embarrassment."

Michel wondered if Porter had been more worried about the embarrassment to Carolyn or himself.

"I'm sorry," he said gently. "And I'm sorry that you had to tell me about it. But under the circumstances..."

"I understand," Terry replied.

Michel suddenly wondered if Terry had any close friends he'd been able to talk with about what had happened. Although he realized it was probably inappropriate, he felt an urge to give Terry that chance now.

"So how are you doing?" he asked.

Terry stared at him uncomprehendingly for a second.

"What do you mean?" he asked.

"I mean are you okay?" Michel replied.

Terry's expression changed first to confusion, then to suspicion. It was clear that he wasn't used to people inquiring about his feelings.

"I'm okay, I guess. Why?" he asked cautiously.

Michel gave him a gentle smile.

"This isn't part of the interrogation," he said. "I'm just concerned. If you don't want to talk about it, that's okay."

Terry studied him intently for a few seconds, then he sighed deeply and sank back against the red leather banquette. His usual anxious energy seemed to be draining from his body.

"I don't know," he said finally. "I cheated on my wife. I got played like some stupid school girl. I had to admit to the only people I care about that I like cock. How would you feel?"

"Embarrassed, angry," Michel replied sympathetically.

"That pretty well sums it up," Terry replied.

"Probably resentful," Michel added.

Terry seemed to flinch slightly at the word. He looked down at the table, then took a long sip of his coffee.

"Probably," he said finally, looking back at Michel with a closed expression that suggested he was either unwilling or unable to discuss it any further.

"How have things been with Carolyn since?" Michel asked.

Terry seemed to consider his answer carefully.

"I think she always knew I had those tendencies," he said, "Our marriage was never about passion. It was about companionship and trust. I'm sure she feels betrayed."

"You don't know?" Michel asked with surprise.

"She won't talk about it," Terry replied.

Michel nodded.

"Do you think she can get past it?" he asked.

"In her way," Terry replied. "She's always been emotionally fragile. When things upset her, she tends to pretend they never happened. That's how she copes. I imagine that eventually she'll be able to pretend this never happened, too, and things will go on like before."

"And you're okay with that?" Michel asked.

"Why wouldn't I be?" Terry asked.

"Well, your sexuality is part of who you are," Michel replied. "Do you really think you can just go back to pretending you're not attracted to men?"

"I love my wife," Terry replied indignantly.

"I'm not saying you don't," Michel replied carefully. "But pretending you don't like men isn't going to make those feelings go away. In fact, from what I've seen, it usually makes things worse. People who repress their feelings usually end up acting out in dangerous ways."

"I never said I wouldn't acknowledge my feelings," Terry replied curtly. "I said Carolyn wouldn't."

Michel gave him a curious look. It had sounded like an admission that Terry intended to go on having sex with men behind his wife's back.

"You boys okay over there?" Darlene called suddenly. "Your food should be ready in a minute or two. You need any more coffee?"

"We're fine for the moment, thanks," Michel called back.

"Okay, just let me know if you need anything," Darlene replied, then walked into the kitchen.

Michel looked back at Terry. He was sitting rigidly upright, his eyes nervously fixed on the door.

"What's wrong?" Michel asked.

"It's him," Terry whispered back, barely moving his lips.

"Donny?"

Terry nodded almost imperceptibly.

"So what?" Michel replied. "He doesn't know what we're talking about. Or at least he won't if you relax."

"Hey, darlin'," Donny's voice cut through the room, much louder than necessary.

"What do you want?" Darlene asked with amused aggravation as she walked out of the kitchen.

"I just wanted to see my baby," Donny purred back. "I missed you when I woke up."

"You just woke up?" Darlene replied. "That's disgusting. You need to be getting your lazy ass out of bed and looking for a job."

"I have a job," Donny replied.

"You won't if they find out there's nothing wrong with you," Darlene shot back. "At least not physically."

Then she began giggling. Michel turned his head and saw Donny hugging her and nuzzling his scruffy chin against her neck. He was wearing what looked like the same loose jeans from a few days before, scuffed brown cowboy boots, and a wrinkled ribbed gray tank top. Michel felt a surge of pity for Darlene that she'd obviously succumbed to Donny's dubious charms again.

"Eww, you stink," Darlene said, playfully pushing Donny away from her. "Couldn't you at least have taken a shower before you came in here? You're gonna make my customers sick."

"Not any sicker than the food," Donny replied.

He turned his head to make sure he had an audience and saw Michel watching him. His smile widened a little, then froze when he noticed Terry, too. Michel thought he saw a momentary flash of worry in Donny's eyes, then Donny quickly looked back at Darlene.

"How about a cup of coffee, darlin'?" he asked in a more subdued voice.

"Sure, I'd love one," Darlene replied.

"Don't sass me before I've had my coffee," Donny replied with a sudden irritation that made Darlene take a step back.

"I'm sorry, honey," she said. "Let me just go pick up an order, and then I'll get you your coffee."

The way she hurried back into the kitchen made it clear she'd been on Donny's bad side a few times too many.

Donny watched her go, then stood by himself for a moment, looking at the floor. Michel could see him calculating what to do next. As he began to turn toward their table, Michel turned back to Terry and gave him a steadying look.

"So who's your friend, Terry?" Donny asked as he ambled up to the table.

Terry looked down with a tight expression.

"Michel Doucette," he said.

"Oh, that's right, Black Jack's son," Donny replied. "I saw you at the Gator's Belly the other day. That was quite a touching family reunion."

Donny pressed his thighs against the edge of the table and pushed his hips forward. Michel fought the urge to stick his fork into Donny's crotch. Instead he smiled calmly.

"Donny, now don't be bothering the customers or Jimmy Joe's gonna kick you out of here," Darlene said as she came up behind him carrying two plates.

She bumped him out of the way with her left hip.

"I wasn't bothering anyone," Donny said. "Just being friendly."

As Darlene placed the plates on the table, Terry suddenly stood up.

"I'm sorry, Darlene," he said, "but can I get that to go? I should probably get back to the office."

Darlene's sunny expression faltered for a moment, then she shrugged and picked his plate back up.

"Sure thing, hon," she said, then walked back to the counter while Terry shuffled sideways out of the booth.

"Well then, I guess there's a seat for me now," Donny said with a big smile. "I'll be seeing you, Terry."

He clapped Terry hard on the left shoulder. Terry winced and looked at Michel. It seemed to be a pleading look. Michel nodded slightly to him.

"So, how do you like it here in Bayou Proche?" Donny asked as he slid backwards into the booth.

He pushed his back up against the wall and crossed his legs, his boots resting on the side edge of the banquette, then locked his hands behind his head and flexed his biceps. He reminded Michel of a cat preening in a sunny window.

"It's okay," Michel replied. "I've been worse places."

"I can't imagine that," Donny replied, then finished the remainder of Terry's coffee in one gulp.

"Darlin', when you have a chance," he said, holding up the cup toward Darlene who was giving Terry his change.

"Be right there," she replied quickly.

"So you ever been down to New Orleans?" Michel asked.

"Oh sure, lots of times," Donny replied with an attempt at a worldly nod. "Me and my friends go down a few times a year to the titty bars on Bourbon Street."

He stopped as Darlene approached.

"Thanks, baby," he said with an overly sweet smile after she'd filled his cup.

"I'm surprised you'd be interested in that," Michel replied as soon as Darlene was back behind the counter.

"And why's that?" Donny replied too sharply, his torso suddenly tensing.

Michel couldn't help but smile. He decided he'd like to play poker with Donny sometime.

"Well, I figured you'd be able to get all the titty you want around here," he replied.

Donny studied him for a few seconds, then smiled back. He cut a quick look to make sure that Darlene wasn't watching, then lowered his hands and cupped his chest tightly.

"Well, there's small town titty," he said, nodding in Darlene's direction, "then there's big city titty, if you know what I mean."

To illustrate his obvious point, he pulled his hands away from his chest and flexed his fingers as though squeezing large grapefruits, then gave Michel a lewd smile. Michel felt a swell of contempt.

"Why don't you just leave her alone?" he said.

Donny's smile faded and he blinked.

"Who?"

"Darlene," Michel said. "Why don't you just leave her alone? She doesn't need you fucking up her life again."

Donny slid his feet off the banquette and turned his body to face Michel, his elbows resting on the edge of the table and his fists held up loosely in front of his chest.

"What do you know about it?" he asked challengingly.

"I know a born loser when I see one," Michel replied coldly.

Donny started to stand, but Michel shook his head.

"You get up, and I'm going to slam your head down on that table so hard your grandma's going to feel it," he said.

Michel knew that if it came down to a physical confrontation, there was every chance he'd be the one getting his head slammed, but hoped it wouldn't come to that if he could convince Donny otherwise. Donny hesitated uncertainly, then settled back onto the banquette.

"Good boy," Michel said as though talking to a dog.

"The only reason I don't kick your ass right now is because

I don't want Darlene gettin' fired," Donny said in a low growl, his eyes narrowing to slits.

"Yeah, you wouldn't want to have to start paying rent or supporting the baby, would you?" Michel replied.

Donny was breathing hard now, but seemed under control for the moment. Michel just hoped that he wouldn't unleash his anger later on Darlene.

"We both know you're going to cheat on her again," Michel said, adopting a reasonable tone. "If you really care about her at all, why put her through it?"

Donny stared back at him with an unyielding expression.

"Is your ego really that fragile?" Michel asked.

"My ego is just fine," Donny replied deliberately. "I love Darlene."

"Enough to keep your dick in your pants?" Michel asked.

Donny sat back and a sudden smirk crept across his lips.

"Is that what this is about?" he asked. "You're worried that if I'm with Darlene, you won't have a shot? Don't worry. I'd be happy to throw you a little on the side. There's more than enough to go around."

Michel was taken completely off-guard, but kept his face neutral. He knew Donny was trying to put him on the defensive.

"I'm sure Darlene would be interested to hear that," he said.

"Go ahead and tell her," Donny replied with a shrug. "You think she's going to believe you?"

Michel knew he was right. Even if Darlene suspected the truth, she'd never be able to admit it to herself. Still, he wanted to wipe the smug expression off Donny's face.

"She might not believe me," he said pointedly, "but she might believe someone else."

Michel saw the flicker of fear in Donny's eyes again and realized he'd made a mistake. He'd made an implicit promise to protect Terry's confidence.

"I'll bet if I showed your picture around the gay bars back home, it wouldn't be too hard to find someone who remembers you sucking their dick," he said, trying to recover.

Donny studied him for a few seconds, then seemed to relax. He put his hands behind his head and flexed again.

"Yeah, good luck with that," he said with another smirk.

Michel felt the tension in his back ease. Donny had apparently bought the misdirection.

"You can get up now," he said.

Donny looked at him with confusion.

"We're done," Michel said, nodding toward the door.

Donny sat forward. Michel could see that he didn't like being dismissed and was trying to think of a way to leave under his own terms.

"Well, if you change your mind..."

"I won't," Michel interrupted him abruptly.

Donny smiled confidently. "That's what they all say. But eventually they all change their minds."

He stood up and sauntered across the room toward Darlene. Michel took a deep breath and exhaled slowly. He didn't doubt what Donny had said for a moment.

*****

"Hey Cyrus," Michel said as he walked up to the counter of the corner market. "How's it going?"

"Can't complain, and you probably wouldn't want to hear it if I did," Cyrus replied. "Missed you yesterday."

"Yeah, I got tied up with legal stuff," Michel replied.

Cyrus nodded knowingly.

"So what are you smoking today?"

"Actually I think I'm going to skip the smokes," Michel replied. "Blue doesn't like them, so I was thinking maybe I'd try to do without for a day."

"Smart dog," Cyrus replied. "So then what can I get you?"

"I'm almost out of food," Michel replied. "Got anything good for dinner?"

Cyrus smiled and nodded emphatically.

"I've got a nice porterhouse out back," he said. "I ordered it for Miss Evans, but she's not feeling well. I was going to eat it myself, but I'd rather sell it."

"Are you sure?"

"Can't keep the store open if I eat all the merchandise," Cyrus replied. "There's fresh vegetables over there. I'll go get it."

While Cyrus shuffled to the back of the store, Michel perused the produce. He grabbed a potato, a head of lettuce, a tomato, and an ear of corn.

"There's a nice big bone in this one for the dog," Cyrus said as he shuffled back to the front of the store carrying a small package wrapped in white paper.

"Is that okay?" Michel asked, walking up to the counter.

"Oh sure," Cyrus replied. "Steak, lamb, pork. Those are all fine. Just don't give her any chicken bones. They'll splinter and she might choke on 'em."

Michel realized just how little he knew about having a dog and thought again about what he was going to do with Blue when it was time to go back home.

"Thanks for the information," he said.

"No problem," Cyrus replied. "And I won't even charge you for it."

He chuckled to himself while he rang up the total.

"That'll be $18.50," he said. "Sorry 'bout that, but the steak *was* a special order."

Michel smiled, knowing that he would have paid more than that just for the steak at the market near his house. He opened his wallet and frowned.

"Do you take credit cards?" he asked sheepishly. "I've only got ten dollars."

"Nope," Cyrus replied, "but I can put it on account. Just pay up before you leave town."

Michel nodded.

"Thanks. I appreciate that."

"No problem," Cyrus replied. "At the Corner Market, customer service is our number one priority."

From the way he began chuckling to himself again as he put the groceries into a brown paper bag, Michel imagined it was a slogan that the old man had heard on a commercial or read in the newspaper and had been waiting a while to use.

"I'll let you know how the steak is," Michel said as he picked up the bag.

"You do that," Cyrus replied. "And if you want me to order anything else in for you, just let me know."

"I will," Michel replied with a warm smile.

As he stepped onto the sidewalk, his phone began to ring. He pulled it out of his pocket and saw Sassy's number.

"Hey," he answered.

"Hey," Sassy replied. "What are you up to?"

"Well, let's see. I found out that Terry and Donny had a little fling last year, then after they went to New Orleans, Donny tried to blackmail Terry for $50,000 so Terry told his wife, his father, and Verle about it. Then Donny propositioned me while I was having lunch. Then I went grocery shopping."

"Wow, busy day," Sassy replied. "You'll have to tell me all about it later."

"Why later?"

"Because I'm about to get my hair done."

"Your hair?" Michel replied. "Are you actually doing any work while I'm away?"

"You mean while you're away not doing any work?" Sassy shot back.

"I'm doing work," Michel replied with mock indignation.

"Not that's putting money in *my* pockets," Sassy replied.

"Anyway, I just wanted to see what you're doing tonight."

"Probably sitting on the porch and staring into space, just like last night and the night before," Michel replied. "Why?"

"I spoke to Pearl," Sassy replied. "She's going to be in Baton Rouge and wants you to meet her for dinner."

Michel looked down at the bag in his arm. He knew he'd feel guilty if he went into the store the next day and had to lie to Cyrus about eating it, but the idea of meeting Pearl was too intriguing to pass up.

"Okay," he said. "I need to get some clothes anyway and I'm not going to find anything around here. I can drive up early and do a little shopping before we meet."

"Good," Sassy replied. "Meet her at 7 at a place called The Roux House on 3rd Street. She said it's about a block from the Hilton Baton Rouge Capitol Center."

"Okay, I'm sure I can find it," Michel replied. "But what does she look like?"

"About my height, a few shades lighter, whip thin, and I'm sure she'll be wearing something colorful," Sassy replied. "But don't worry, I'm sure she'll recognize you from your picture."

"When did you show her my picture?" Michel asked.

"I didn't," Sassy replied. "I sent her some pictures from the party I had two years ago and you happened to be in some of them. She wanted to know who the gay-looking guy was."

"She did not," Michel protested. "That's such a lie."

"Okay, don't let it swell your big old head, but she wanted to know who the cute guy was," Sassy replied.

"Of course she did," Michel replied with a pleased smile. "By the way, did you ask her about Ruby?"

"Uh huh. She can tell you all about it," Sassy replied. "That way you'll have something to talk about."

"Oh, don't worry. We'll have plenty to talk about," Michel replied. "You know I'm going to be asking her all about what you were like when you were a little girl, don't you?

"You can ask all you want," Sassy replied, "but I already warned her not to tell you anything or I'd disown her."

"It won't matter once I turn on the charm," Michel replied.

"Charm?" Sassy replied. "What charm is that?"

"Oh, don't you worry," Michel replied with exaggerated suaveness. "I have *plenty* of charm."

"Really?" Sassy replied, then paused for dramatic effect. "Then I guess Verle must have left you that, too."

Then she hung up.

"Very funny," Michel said when he heard the click.

He turned toward the police station and saw Russ Turner standing there watching him.

"Oh, hey Russ," Michel said with an embarrassed smile.

"Hey Michel," Turner replied. "Everything okay?"

"Yeah, Sassy's just being funny," Michel replied. "Listen, I'm glad you're here. I have a favor to ask."

"Shoot."

"I have to go to Baton Rouge to have dinner with Sassy's cousin, Pearl. Any chance you and Corey could look after Blue? The last time I left her with Ruby she kept running back to the house looking for me."

"Sure," Turner replied. "What time?"

"About 4:30."

"Okay. Just drop her at the station on your way."

"Thanks, I appreciate it," Michel replied. "I'm not sure what time I'll be back, but if it's late, can she stay for the night?"

"No problem."

"Great," Michel replied.

Chapter 22

Michel arrived at The Roux House promptly at 7 PM, after spending an hour and a half at the Mall of Louisiana. He was wearing one of the two pairs of jeans he'd bought and a lightweight, pale yellow v-neck sweater. It had been an uncharacteristic purchase given his usual palette of blacks, grays, and browns, but had seemed appropriate given Sassy's comment that Pearl would probably be wearing something bright.

He scanned the sea of white faces in the narrow, brick-walled room. There appeared to be an equal mix of men and women in business attire, and college students.

Suddenly the crowd seemed to part, and Michel saw a woman moving purposefully toward him. Unlike the elderly country aunt he'd been expecting, however, this woman was strikingly beautiful. She was dressed in a bright floral knee-length wrap dress that was cinched tightly at the waist to accentuate her slim frame. Her straight white hair was cut in a stylish bob that she'd combed back and tucked behind her ears. Although Michel guessed she was close to sixty, her skin was smooth and glowing.

Michel suddenly felt underdressed and exceedingly drab, though he suspected he would have felt the latter even if he'd been wearing the same dress. Even from a distance, the woman radiated a vibrant energy that filled the space around her.

"Pearl?" Michel asked, raising his eyebrows questioningly as she neared.

"Michel," Pearl replied as though she were seeing an old friend for the first time in years. "It's so nice to finally meet you."

Though she had only a soft accent, Michel noticed that her voice had the distinctive Creole rhythmic cadence.

"You, too," Michel said, holding out his right hand.

Pearl stopped and looked at his hand for a moment, then raised her left eyebrow and shook her head disapprovingly.

"No, we're family," she said, pushing past his hand and enveloping him in a warm embrace, "and family don't do handshakes."

Michel smiled and hugged her back. He decided he already liked her.

"I hope you don't mind," Pearl said as she stepped back, "but I asked for a table on the patio. It's a little quieter out there."

"That's fine," Michel replied.

*****

"Can I get you something to drink?" the waitress asked once they'd been seated along the back wall of the patio and she'd recited the specials.

"A Jack on the rocks," Pearl replied.

"Same," Michel added.

"Great, I'll give you a few moments to look at the menu," the waitress replied.

"You know, you don't have to keep up with me," Pearl said as the waitress walked away. "There's not too many who can."

Michel smiled. He was sure that Pearl didn't weigh more than 110 pounds. He imagined she'd be tipsy after two drinks.

"That's my usual," he replied. "So do you come here often?"

"Whenever I'm in town," Pearl replied, "though usually a little later so I can listen to the music."

Michel looked around at the other diners. Most appeared to be in their early twenties, yet Pearl seemed perfectly at home. Michel guessed she felt at home anywhere.

"So what brings you to Baton Rouge?" he asked.

"I'm a jewelry designer," Pearl replied, holding out her wrists so Michel could see the delicate jeweled silver hoops that dangled around them. "I come up here about once a month to drop off orders at a few boutiques. Sassy didn't tell you?"

"You know Sassy," Michel replied with a smile. "She keeps a lot to herself."

"She tells me the same about you," Pearl replied.

Michel was surprised that Sassy had talked with Pearl about him, and wondered what else she'd said.

"I suppose," he replied with a noncommittal shrug. "Sassy wears your jewelry, doesn't she?"

"She better," Pearl replied. "I've given her some of my best pieces."

"I recognize the style," Michel replied. "They're beautiful."

"Thank you," Pearl replied with genuine appreciation.

Michel reflexively reached for the inside left pocket of the jacket he wasn't wearing, then stopped.

"You wouldn't happen to have a cigarette, would you?" he asked.

Pearl shook her head. "No, I limit myself to three vices."

"Three?"

"Drinking, shopping, and marrying."

Michel laughed.

"Marrying? How many times have you been married?"

"I'm between my fifth and six right now," Pearl replied.

"Wow," Michel replied.

"The first three died, the last two just didn't work out," Pearl replied matter-of-factly, then she sighed dramatically. "I guess I'm just a traditional girl. I like having a man to look after, even if most of them don't deserve it."

Michel imagined that there wasn't much else about Pearl that was traditional.

"And what about you?" she asked, tilting her head and gazing at him quizzically.

"What?" Michel replied. "Do I like having a man to look after?"

Pearl gave a slight shrug, as if to say, "If that's what you want to talk about." Michel furrowed his brow and looked down at his hands for a second.

"That's a good question," he said finally, looking back up at Pearl. "I don't know. I've never really had a man to look after. At least not for very long."

"But Sassy told me there was a young man," Pearl replied.

Michel nodded.

"Joel."

"Yes, that's the one," Pearl replied. "What happened with Joel?"

To his own surprise, Michel didn't find the question intrusive. Though he was generally reluctant to share information about his personal life with strangers, he felt oddly comfortable with Pearl.

"That's kind of a long story," he replied.

"I've got all night," Pearl replied with a warm smile.

Michel studied her for a moment, then nodded.

"Okay," he said, "but first let's order dinner."

*****

"So what are you going to tell him?" Pearl asked after Michel had filled her in on his history with Joel.

"I don't know," Michel replied.

"Why not?" Pearl asked. "Seems pretty clear to me that you love him."

"I do," Michel replied, "but it's complicated. I'm worried

that I can't really give him what he wants, or that I'll change my mind and end up hurting him even more."

Pearl fixed him with an expression that was a combination of perplexity and annoyance.

"It's only complicated because you make it complicated," she said. "Your problem is that you want a guarantee before you're willing to take a chance. And I hate to tell you this, but there are never any guarantees."

Michel started to respond, but Pearl held up her right hand.

"In each of my marriages, there were times when it was pure joy and times when I wished I'd had a shotgun," she continued, her accent becoming more pronounced as she gained steam, "but I wouldn't have passed up a minute of any of them. If you really love someone, there's a point where you just have to have faith and take your chances. If it doesn't work out, then it doesn't work out, and you both move on. So stop trying to control the situation before it even happens. That's just being a fool."

Michel sank back against his chair. He felt like a grade schooler who'd just been scolded by his teacher.

"I'm sorry," he said without thinking. "Wow. How come Sassy never talks to me like that? I mean, she calls me on my bullshit, but never quite like that."

"That's because Sassy doesn't know men the way I do," Pearl replied. "She thinks you all are smart enough to figure things out on your own. I know better. The best thing you can do for a man is tell him where to go, when to be there, and what to do when he gets there. You can't just leave them there all stupid trying to figure things out for themselves."

Michel suspected she was being only partly facetious.

"Thanks," he said.

"You're welcome," Pearl replied. "Now where's that pretty little waitress? I need another drink."

Michel caught the waitress' eye and pointed down at their

glasses. She smiled back and nodded. Michel decided it would be his last or he'd have to get a hotel room for the night.

"Okay," he said. "Now that you've fixed my problem, it's time to get to the good stuff. What was Sassy like as a girl?"

"Oh, she warned me to not to tell you anything," Pearl replied quickly, waving her hands dismissively.

Michel gave her his best doe-eyed look.

"But you're going to anyway, aren't you?" he asked.

Pearl looked at him reproachfully for a few seconds, then broke into a smile.

"Of course," she said. "As soon as I get my cocktail."

*****

"So, I'm sure you already know the story about how she got her name," Pearl began after she took a sip of her drink.

Michel nodded.

"So what would you like to know?" Pearl asked.

"Did she have many friends?" Michel asked.

"That's a good question," Pearl replied, frowning thoughtfully. "Butte La Rose is a small town, so she certainly knew everyone, but I don't imagine she considered too many of them her friends. Least not the ones her own age. She always gravitated toward the adults, especially the ones who'd left and come back. I think she wanted to pick their brains about what was out there in the rest of the world."

"Do you think she was unhappy living there?" Michel asked.

"I'm not sure that Sassy ever *did* live there," Pearl replied with a laugh. "At least not mentally. I think she already had a movie in her head about what her life was going to be, and she spent a lot of time watching it."

"How do you mean?" Michel replied.

"Sometimes she'd just be sitting out in the yard with a book," Pearl replied, "but she wouldn't actually be looking at the pages. She'd be staring off into the distance, like she was looking at something else. I always thought of it as her looking at her future."

"Do you think she was lonely?" Michel asked.

"I don't think so," Pearl replied. "As I said, she was friendly with a lot of the adults, and she was very close with her folks and our grandmother. I just think she was always making her plans."

She paused for a moment, then began laughing to herself.

"Back when we were kids, we'd all get together every summer for a family reunion," she said, "and we'd always put together little plays that we'd perform for the adults after supper. Just stories we'd make up. Usually about swamp monsters and such. The rest of us would all be fighting over who was going get the biggest parts, but not Sassy."

"Because she was too shy?" Michel asked.

"No, because she was too bossy," Pearl replied with a joyful laugh. "She always wanted to be the director. She'd be telling us all what to say and what to do. And God help you if you made a mistake."

"So she was a little tyrant?" Michel asked.

"I'm five years older than she is, and I was afraid of her until I was about twenty," Pearl replied. "If you were gonna be in her play, you were going to do it her way."

"I've never seen that side of her," Michel replied. "She can be bossy, but never uncompromising."

"That's because she respects you," Pearl replied. "I'm not sure she respected any of us, at least as far as our dramatic talents went. And I have to admit, we were pretty awful."

She smiled and shook her head wistfully, as though looking at a cherished photo.

"But she also had a bit of the devil in her," she added. "Oh Lord, when she had a mind to, she could be as funny as you wanna be."

"She still can," Michel replied.

"Oh, no," Pearl replied, shaking her head. "Now she's just witty. Back then she was fall out funny."

"What do you mean?" Michel asked.

"We had an Uncle Cobb," Pearl replied. "He was our mothers' brother. Heart of gold, but simple as the day is long. And he was a schemer. Always had a plan for how he was gonna do this or gonna do that to make it rich. Big talker, but didn't have the common sense to get out of his own way. You know what I mean?"

Michel nodded.

"So one day when I was twelve or thirteen, the adults decided they were all going to go to the movies and left us kids alone," Pearl continued. "I was watching after the little ones because I was the oldest, and I wondering where Sassy had gotten off to. All of a sudden there was a knock at the door. Back in those days we weren't afraid to open the door the way folks are now, so I opened it up, and there's Sassy, dressed in a pair of overalls with pillows stuffed down in them, a straw hat, and a cigar stuffed in her mouth. She gives me a big smile and I can see she's blacked out about half her teeth so she looks just like Uncle Cobb."

She began laughing at the memory.

"She comes strutting into the room, and starts waving her cigar around and saying that she's just had an idea. That's what she kept saying: 'I just had an idea!' Just like that."

She was laughing harder now, and the diners at other tables were staring at her. Some were beginning to laugh, too.

"And then she spun some nonsense about teaching goats how to rollerskate...so she could open up a drive-in restaurant," she managed haltingly through gasps for air, "and have them deliver the food to the cars...and how she could make a fortune ...because she could pay them...with hay!"

Then she burst into helpless, near-hysterical laughter.

181

Everyone around them was laughing hard, too. Finally, after a full minute, she took a few deep breaths and was able to calm herself down.

"And she just kept going," she said, "and the stories kept getting bigger until we were all laughing so hard that a few of the little ones wet themselves."

She stopped for a second to wipe the tears from her eyes.

"Oh Lord, she was funny."

Michel was laughing, too, though more at Pearl's storytelling than the actual story. He was struck by the sharp contrast between her polished look and her raw exuberance.

"It's hard to reconcile that with the image of the shy little girl I've always had," he said.

Pearl waved her hand dismissively at him.

"She was usually quiet, but I don't know that she was ever actually what I'd call shy," she replied, then sighed the last of the laughter away. "I think she just took her time getting to know people. She'd watch for a while first to make sure it wasn't going to be a waste of time."

Michel nodded. He could relate to that.

"I think our grandmother just took it as shyness because she didn't understand what was going on in Sassy's head," Pearl said. "When you live each day the way she did, the way most people there did, just taking what came along as it came, it's hard to understand someone who dreams and plans the way Sassy did. Sassy might as well have been an alien."

"Did people treat her that way?" Michel asked, bothered by the thought that Sassy had been ostracized because of her intelligence and ambition.

"Oh, no," Pearl replied reassuringly. "People liked Sassy. I don't think they understood her, but they liked her. She was very special. Always the first to help other people out when they needed it, and very kind."

Michel knew that those parts of Sassy hadn't changed.

"I have to admit I was a little surprised when she decided to become a policeman, though," Pearl said.

"Why's that?" Michel asked. "The police help people."

"That's true," Pearl replied, "but I was always sure she'd be a doctor. No offense, but I thought she was too intelligent to be a cop."

Michel laughed.

"None taken," he said, "but I think you'd be surprised at how many intelligent people go into law enforcement. There are a lot who aren't so bright, too, but most of them are pretty sharp. Maybe not Sassy sharp, but sharp."

"Well, I suppose you don't seem like too much of a half-wit," Pearl replied with a sardonic smile, "except maybe when it comes to men."

"Thanks," Michel replied laughing, "and for what it's worth, you actually come off as quite bright yourself...for a coonass Cajun."

Pearl sat back and fixed him with a cold stare.

"Oh, you're just lucky I see my food coming," she said, narrowing her eyes comically, "because I've killed husbands for less than that."

*****

An hour later, after he'd paid the check, Michel looked at his watch. It was almost 9:30.

"I'm sorry, Pearl, but I'd better get going," he said. "I've got to drive back. Do you want me to walk you to your hotel?"

"Oh, no," Pearl replied. "I think I'll stay a while longer and listen to the music. Maybe my next husband will ask me to dance."

"You think he's here?" Michel asked.

"You never know," Pearl replied.

They both stood.

"Thanks so much for having dinner with me," Michel said. "I'm glad I got to meet you."

He gave Pearl a tight hug and kissed her on the right cheek.

"You're welcome," she replied with a pleased smile. "I hope you and Sassy and I can all get together some time soon."

"I'd like that," Michel replied.

He started to turn away, then stopped.

"Oh shit, I almost forgot," he said. "I didn't ask you about Ruby."

Pearl nodded.

"I remember Ruby," she said. "Pretty little thing in her way, but a little peculiar. Very quiet and shy."

"And she played piano?" Michel asked.

"Oh yes," Pearl replied emphatically. "You ever see anyone speak in tongues?"

Michel nodded.

"It was like that," Pearl said. "When she sat down at that piano, it was like she went into a trance, and the music just flowed from her fingertips. I'm not sure she even knew she was doing it. She couldn't have been more than four or five when we moved away, and she was already playing at the church every Sunday."

Michel nodded. Both the age difference and the description of Ruby as being kind of peculiar sounded right, and he could easily imagine the Ruby he knew going into a trance and playing piano.

"Do you know what happened to her?" he asked.

Pearl shook her head.

"I'm afraid not," she said. "Once we moved I lost contact with people back there. With her talent, I imagine she could have gone anywhere, though I'm not sure she was cut out for life outside the bayou. As I said, she was a little strange."

"That hasn't changed," Michel replied. "Anyway, thanks again. And good luck finding that husband."

*****

As he walked back to his car, Michel took his phone out of the right pocket of his jeans and called Russ Turner.

"Hey, Michel," Turner answered.

"Hey Russ. Listen, I'm just leaving now. Would it be all right if I picked up Blue in the morning?"

"Oh sure," Turner replied. "She and Corey were out playing ball for about an hour after dinner. They both looking pretty pooped right now. I'm sure she'll be okay."

Michel felt a twinge of jealousy and made a mental note to look for a ball at the house.

"Okay," he said. "Should I pick her up at your house or the station?"

"Either way," Turner replied. "If you don't make it to the house before I leave, then I'll just bring her in with me."

"Sounds good," Michel replied. "Good night."

"Good night."

Chapter 23

The house was dark when Michel pulled into the drive.

"Shit," he said, peering into the bushes nearest the car.

Though he felt fairly confident there weren't any alligators around, he still felt nervous about the other creatures living in the swamp, and suddenly wished Blue were with him.

He reached into the back seat to grab his shopping bags, then opened the door and stepped out. He paused and watched for any movement, then quickly crossed the yard to the front porch, his heart pumping a little faster than normal.

I'm such a pussy, he thought as he walked up the steps. He unlocked the door and stepped inside, then closed the door and let out a sigh of relief.

He felt the wall for the light switch and flicked it. Nothing happened.

"Fuck," he mumbled, hoping it was just a burned out bulb.

His phone began to ring and he pulled it out of his pocket. Russ Turner's number was on the display. He opened the phone and hit the answer button. In the dim light of the screen, he saw something move to his right. Then everything went black.

*****

"What if he's dead?" a voice asked.

"He's not dead," another voice replied.

Not again, Michel thought, feeling the too familiar dull ache in the back of his skull as he regained consciousness.

"How can you tell? You hit him pretty hard," the first voice said.

"I didn't hit him that hard, and I can tell because he's breathing."

Michel recognized the voice. It was Donny Heath.

"But maybe he hit his head when he fell," the first voice replied nervously. "I don't think he's breathing."

"Me neither," said a third voice. "I think he hit his head."

"Would you two shut the fuck up," Donny replied with obvious frustration. "He didn't hit his head and he's not dead."

"So then why isn't he awake? He ought to be awake by now. It's been a long time."

"It's only been a few minutes," Donny replied. "Sweet Jesus, you're like two nervous old hens."

The pain in Michel's head was getting worse, but he forced himself to concentrate on what he was hearing.

"So what are we supposed to do?" the third voice asked.

"Just scare him," Donny replied.

"Why?"

"Because he's a fag."

"So?"

"What, are you turning queer on me?" Donny asked coldly.

"No," the third voice protested, "but it doesn't matter to me if he's a fag."

"Me neither," the first voice added. "And why does he have to be naked? We're not gonna put anything inside him or anything, are we?"

Michel was becoming more aware of sensation. He could feel a slight warm breeze on the front of his body, roughness against his back, and numbness in his arms and shoulders.

"No, we're not going to put anything inside him," Donny replied in a mocking voice. "But people feel more vulnerable when they're naked. Plus it's easier to threaten to cut off someone's balls that way."

"But we're not really gonna do it, right?" the first voice asked.

"Would you two please shut the fuck up," Donny said angrily, his voice getting nearer to Michel. "I swear you're both useless."

"I'm not useless," the first voice protested weakly. "I just don't see why we're doing this."

Michel felt a spray of cold liquid on his face.

"Wake up, faggot," Donny said, obviously trying to disguise his voice by making it lower and exaggerating his accent.

Michel made a show of coming back to consciousness, rolling his head from side to side and moaning slightly. He hoped he wasn't overselling it.

He opened his eyes slowly and looked around as though confused. Donny was standing directly in front of him. The other two men were standing at the edge of the clearing, roughly twelve feet back. All three were wearing burlap sacks with eyeholes cut out of them on their heads. Donny was holding a large hunting knife in his right hand and a beer can in his left, and the man on the right was nervously cradling a double-barreled shotgun.

Michel looked down and saw four loops of thick rope across his chest and stomach. He looked back up at the three men and smiled.

"Nice hoods. Did you make those yourselves?" he asked, then winced as genuine pain throbbed in his head.

He guessed that Donny wanted to humiliate him by making him grovel, and was determined not to give Donny the satisfaction. He'd heard enough to know that he wasn't in any real danger.

"We don't like your kind around here," the man with the shotgun offered weakly.

"What kind is that?" Michel asked.

"Faggots," the other man replied.

188

It was clear from their tones that neither had much heart for the charade.

"So you're going to kill me because I'm a fag?" Michel asked skeptically. "So much for southern hospitality."

Donny dropped the beer can and took a sudden step forward. He jabbed his knife into Michel's right thigh. It wasn't a deep puncture, but it was dangerously close to the femoral artery. Michel gritted his teeth and took a sharp breath.

"Shut the fuck up," Donny growled, his beer-soaked breath seeping through the burlap and washing over Michel's face. Then he took a few steps back.

Michel felt suddenly uneasy. Clearly Donny was drunk, and apparently far more committed to scaring him than he'd let on to the others.

"Jesus!" the man with the gun shouted when he saw the blood dripping down Michel's leg. "What the hell did you do?"

Donny turned to face him.

"You shut the fuck up, too," he shouted angrily.

He turned back to face Michel and Michel could hear him breathing hard.

"You made me do that," Donny said in a tone that was both wounded and pathetic at the same time.

Michel wondered how many times Darlene had heard those same words in that same tone.

"Come on, man," the man with the gun said. "Let's just get out of here."

"Yeah, let's just go," the other man pleaded.

It was clear they realized the situation was getting out of control and Donny needed to be talked down. Michel guessed it wasn't the first time they'd had to do it.

"No," Donny said with sudden intensity, completely abandoning any attempt to disguise his voice. "I can't."

There was an unexpected tone of fear in his voice that caught Michel's ear. He wondered if Donny had realized he was in over his head but was afraid to back down, or if there was something else going on entirely.

Michel quickly tried to assess his options. If Donny really just wanted to humiliate him, then the prudent thing to do would be to play scared and promise to leave town, but he questioned his ability to play scared convincingly.

"Look," he said in a reasonable tone, "you don't need to do this. I'm going to be leaving in a few days anyway."

"See, he's going to be leaving anyway," the man with the gun said optimistically. "We can just go on home."

Donny stared at Michel for a few seconds without responding. Michel could see that he was breathing more calmly now.

"Please," Michel said, deciding to give Donny some small level of satisfaction.

Donny began chuckling, then he moved closer until his face was only an inch from Michel's.

"Don't worry, sweetheart," he purred in a low voice, "I'm not gonna kill you. I'm just going to take some souvenirs."

He ran his left hand slowly up the inside of Michel's right thigh and cupped Michel's testicles hard.

The fact that Donny had gone back to the planned script gave Michel some hope, but he wasn't certain that it was just a bluff anymore. He decided to change tactics.

"You know," he said in steady voice, "this isn't the first time someone's tied me up and threatened to cut off part of my body. I still have all my parts, but the last two guys are dead, and they were a hell of a lot tougher than you are."

Even as he said it, he realized how absurd it sounded given his present situation, but to his surprise Donny immediately let go of him and took a step back.

"What the fuck?" the man with the gun exclaimed.

Michel felt something rub against his right calf and flinched. He looked down and saw Blue. The fur along her spine was raised into a ridge and her tail was up. She stepped in front of him and growled. Donny backed away another three steps.

"Shit, that's Verle's dog," the man on the left said. "She hates me."

"Don't be a dumbass," the man with the gun replied. "You got on a hood. She doesn't know who you are."

Suddenly Blue looked at the first man and let out another low growl. She advanced another two steps as Donny slowly backed away.

"Like hell she doesn't," the first man said nervously.

"Shoot her," Donny said.

He had almost reached the others.

"I can't shoot a dog," the man with the gun replied.

"Then give it to me," Donny replied.

He started to turn.

"I wouldn't do that if I were you," Michel said. "She may be small, but she's strong, and she's a lot faster than you are. I bet she'll have you down before you can get your hand halfway to that gun."

He prayed that Donny wouldn't put it to the test. He didn't want Blue to get hurt.

Donny stood motionless for a second, seemingly trying to decide whether to risk it or not.

"And if she doesn't, I'll put a bullet in your head," a voice said from behind Michel.

Michel saw the barrel of a rifle appear next to his left shoulder, then Russ Turner stepped into view.

"All right," Turner said calmly. "Everyone just relax."

"Spread out," Donny said, obviously not ready to give up just yet.

The man with the gun took a step to his left. He had the barrels of the gun pointed vaguely in Turner's direction. Blue growled and took a step toward him.

"No, no, no," Turner said aiming his rifle at the man.

The man stopped. Michel could see that the shotgun was visibly shaking in his hands.

"As far as I'm concerned, no crime has been committed yet," Turner said. "You can all just walk away from here."

Though it was an obvious lie, Michel realized he was trying to diffuse the situation. The mix of nerves, guns, and an agitated Catahoula was too volatile to control.

"You can keep the gun," Turner said, "but I want you to empty out the shells. And any you've got in your pockets, too."

"He's lying," Donny growled, though Michel noticed he was trying to disguise his voice again.

"I give you my word," Turner said reassuringly. "Just empty the gun and you can go."

The man with the gun hesitated for moment, then lowered the shotgun and cracked the barrels way from the stock. He removed both shells and tossed them on the ground a few feet in front of him.

"That's all I've got, Sheriff," he said. "I swear."

"Okay," Turner said. "Now you can all go."

He waved the barrel of his rifle toward the woods on his left. The three men stood there for a few seconds, then broke and ran into the dense forest.

"Stay, Blue," Turner said.

She watched the men go for a few seconds, then walked back toward Michel and sat down.

"Why didn't you arrest them?" Michel asked.

"I didn't have to," Turner replied quietly. "I know where they live."

"So then you know that was Donny Heath?" Michel asked, surprised.

Turner nodded and propped his rifle against the side of the tree next to Michel. He pulled a hunting knife from a sheath on his belt and walked around to the back of the tree.

"How?" Michel asked.

He felt his arms suddenly come free and grimaced at the pain shooting through his shoulders.

"Terry called me," Turner replied as he reappeared. "He said that Donny paid him a visit at the office about an hour ago. Wanted to know what the two of you were talking about at the diner today. He roughed Terry up a little."

"Is he okay?

"Just some cuts and bruises," Turner said as he cut the rope around Michel's chest. "He was worried Donny might come after you. I tried to call you, but I didn't get an answer."

Michel closed his eyes and tried to remember what had happened before he awoke in the woods.

"That's right," he said, looking at Turner. "I got your call right after I got into the house. The lights weren't working, but when I answered the phone I saw something move. Then I woke up here."

He rubbed the back of his head. There was a lump the size of a quarter of an egg.

"So how'd you find me?" he asked.

"Blue found you," Turner replied. "We drove out to the house, and as soon as I let her out of the car she took off into the woods."

"So where are we?" Michel asked.

"About two hundred yards from the house," Turner replied. "We should probably get back there in case Donny changes his mind and comes back. Then you can explain what the fuck is going on."

Although his voice was controlled, Michel could tell Turner was angry.

"Okay," he replied.

He looked down at the ground and saw the shredded remains of his clothes.

"Fuck," he said. "I just bought those."

Chapter 23

"So what's this all about?" Turner asked, settling into the chair opposite Michel. "What were you and Terry talking about?"

"He didn't tell you?" Michel asked.

He adjusted the ice pack on the back of his head and settled against the couch.

"There wasn't time," Turner replied.

Michel looked down at the table for a moment. He didn't want to betray Terry's secret, but realized he didn't have a choice.

"Terry and Donny had a sexual relationship," he said finally. "Last year. I found out about it while I was going through the trust's records. There was a charge for a suite at the Hotel Monteleone in New Orleans. I called to check on it and found out the room was registered to both Terry and Donny."

"So that explains the tension between them," Turner said.

"Partly," Michel replied. "After the trip, Donny tried to blackmail Terry. He said he wanted $50,000 or he'd show incriminating photos to Terry's wife and Porter."

"Jesus. What did Terry do?"

"He told Carolyn and Porter the truth," Michel replied.

"Wow, that took some balls," Turner said admiringly.

Michel nodded.

"So then Donny was trying to scare you away so you wouldn't tell anyone?" Turner asked.

"I guess so," Michel replied. "At the time I thought he was

just trying to get back at me for some things I said at the diner today, but I didn't know he'd paid Terry a visit at that point."

"What did you say?" Turner asked.

"Basically I called him a loser, told him to leave Darlene alone, and I threatened to slam his head into the table."

"Oh, is that all?" Turner replied with a laugh. "I can see why that might have upset him."

"But obviously there was more to it than that," Michel replied.

He stared at the floor for a moment, then nodded.

"Now the whole thing makes more sense."

"What do you mean?" Turner asked.

"The way it all went down," Michel replied. "I didn't get the sense that anything had been planned out. I was awake for a few minutes before they knew it, and heard them talking. It was clear Donny's buddies didn't even know why they were there."

"Which means they're probably not going to be much help."

"Probably not," Michel agreed. "Donny must have just panicked after Terry told him I knew about their relationship."

"Or about the blackmail," Turner added.

Michel raised his eyebrows.

"What makes you say that?"

"Having sex with Terry would just be an embarrassment," Turner replied. "Blackmail is a crime."

"But Terry decided not to file charges," Michel replied.

"The DA could still prosecute," Turner replied.

Michel shook his head. "But I don't think Donny would know that."

"Probably not," Turner agreed, "but there's got to be something more than just fear you'd expose his relationship with Terry. Think about it. If that's all it was, then he came up with a pretty stupid plan."

195

"How do you mean?"

"You two just had a run in today, so it was pretty likely you were going to figure out it was him under that hood. Suppose you'd decided to say something about him and Terry in front of his buddies?"

"That's true," Michel replied, "but he was pretty drunk. I don't think he was thinking too straight, so to speak."

"Donny thinks plenty straight when he's drunk," Turner replied, "but not when he's scared."

Michel considered it for a moment.

"Maybe you're right," he said. "Maybe there is something more going on."

Turner nodded.

"So what now?" Michel asked.

"I figure I'll give Donny an hour to get home, and then go pick him up."

Michel nodded, then looked down at the floor for a moment.

"Listen, Russ," he said finally, looking up. "Thanks for saving me."

"That's my job."

"I know, but still," Michel replied. "And I'm sorry I didn't say anything to you before."

"Why didn't you?" Turner replied.

"Because I didn't think it was anything," Michel replied with a shrug. "Terry and Donny having a fling isn't exactly police business."

"But blackmail is," Turner replied seriously.

"I know," Michel replied, "but I figured I owed it to Terry not to say anything."

Turner pursed his lips and nodded.

"I understand that," he said "And I'm sure I would have done the same thing in your position, but you obviously thought something was going on before you found out about

Terry and Donny or you wouldn't have been snooping through the trust's records. Why didn't you tell me about that?"

"I didn't plan to snoop," Michel replied sincerely. "Porter left me alone to go through Verle's stuff, and I happened to notice the files for the trust. I was just curious. If I thought something was going on, I would have told you."

"You're sure about that?" Turner replied, cocking his left eyebrow skeptically.

"Yeah, I'm sure," Michel replied.

It was a lie, but he didn't want to hurt Turner by admitting he wasn't sure that he could trust him.

Turner studied him for a moment, then nodded.

"Okay," he said. "By the way, that was some pretty brave talk I heard when I got there."

Michel looked at him curiously for a second, then laughed.

"Oh, that," he said. "Well, it really wasn't the first time I've been tied up and threatened with dismemberment."

"Really?" Turner replied.

"You remember the old guy I told you about who knocked me out?" Michel asked.

Turner nodded.

"Afterward he tied me up and threatened to cut my thumb off," Michel said.

Turner shook his head with disbelief.

"How is it that I've been a cop for almost as long as you've been alive and I've never once been knocked out, tied up, or had anyone threaten to cut off a piece of me, but it's happened to you twice in the last few weeks?"

"Just unlucky, I guess," Michel replied sheepishly.

Turner let out a small laugh. "Okay," he said, pushing himself up from the chair. "Are you going to be all right here, or do you want to stay at my place tonight?"

"I'll be all right here," Michel replied. "I've got Blue to protect me."

When she heard her name, Blue jumped up from the floor and walked over to Michel. She began nuzzling her face against his leg. He reached down and scratched the sides of her face.

"Yes, you'll protect Uncle Michel's goodies, won't you, darling?" he said.

Turner rolled his eyes.

"All the same, do you have a gun?" he asked.

"It's locked in the truck of my car."

"Then I'll leave you that," Turner replied, pointing at his rifle leaning just inside the doorframe. "Just in case."

"Thanks," Michel replied.

"How about we meet at the station tomorrow morning around nine?" Turner asked. "You can give me a statement and then we can have some breakfast."

"Okay," Michel replied.

"Anything you need before I leave?" Turner asked.

"You wouldn't happen to have a cigarette, would you?" Michel asked.

Turner smiled and shook his head.

"Sorry, my friend. I'm afraid you're just going to have to tough it out tonight."

*****

After Turner left, Michel checked the dressing on his leg to make sure there was no fresh blood, then hobbled into the kitchen and poured two inches of Jack Daniels into a glass and added some ice. As he walked back into the living room, he noticed a small, rectangular, rosewood box nestled behind a stack of magazines on the table next to the couch. He picked it and opened it. Inside was a single cigarette.

"Thank you, God...or Verle," he said, looking up.

He put the cigarette behind his right ear, grabbed his lighter and cell phone, and headed toward the front door.

"Come on, Blue," he encouraged.

She raised her head briefly, then lowered it back onto the floor and closed her eyes.

"Okay, but if I get killed by a raccoon it's your fault," Michel said.

He opened the door, picked up the shotgun, and stepped out onto the porch. He was wearing only boxer shorts, and the cooling air felt good against his skin.

He took his usual chair and hit the speed dial button.

"I didn't wake you, did I?" he asked when Sassy answered.

"Hell no. I was waiting up to find out how your date with Pearl went."

"Well, you know me," Michel replied. "Any night that ends with me tied naked to a tree is a good night."

"Excuse me," Sassy replied.

"I got kidnapped by Donny Heath and two of his buddies," Michel said. "They were waiting for me at the house when I got back from Baton Rouge."

"Are you okay?" Sassy asked with alarm.

"Yeah. Donny threatened to castrate me, and I got a little stab wound in the thigh, but I'm all right. Blue and Russ rescued me."

"Jesus. What the hell happened?" Sassy exclaimed.

Michel lit the cigarette and proceeded to fill her in on the details.

"So clearly Donny wants you out of town," Sassy said when he'd finished.

"Yeah, so now the question is why."

They were both quiet for a few seconds.

"And you're sure you're okay?" Sassy asked finally.

"Yeah," Michel replied. "It got a little scary there for a while, but I've been in worse situations."

"You and me both," Sassy replied. "Still, you be careful."

"I promise," Michel replied, smiling at Sassy's concern.

"Okay," Sassy replied. "Now tell me all about your dinner with Pearl."

"It was great," Michel replied. "She's quite a woman. Why haven't you invited her down to New Orleans for a visit?"

"I invite her all the time, but she's always too busy getting married or divorced," Sassy replied.

"Yeah, she told me about that," Michel said with a laugh. "In fact, when I left she said she was hoping that husband number six might ask her to dance tonight."

"Oh Lord," Sassy replied. "So what did you two talk about?"

Though she was obviously trying to keep her tone conversational, Michel could detect an undertone of suspicion.

"Oh, this and that," he replied breezily.

"Do *not* test my patience," Sassy replied. "It's way too late for that."

"Don't worry, we didn't talk about you," Michel reassured her. "Pearl told me that was off limits."

"So then what *did* you talk about?" Sassy asked, sounding more relaxed."

"Her jewelry, Ruby, being a cop," Michel replied. "But mostly we talked about relationships."

"About you and Joel?" Sassy asked.

"Uh huh. She gave me some advice."

"I'll bet she did," Sassy replied with a laugh.

"No, it was good," Michel replied. "I don't know if I'm capable of following it, but it was good."

"Good. And that's it?" Sassy asked.

"Yeah, pretty much," Michel replied. "But you know what I was thinking?"

"What?"

"Maybe when I get back, we can put on a play at the office. Chance and I can be the actors and you can be the director. What do you think?"

There was a long pause and Michel smiled, imagining the scowl on Sassy's face.

"I think the next time I see Pearl I'm gonna cut her," Sassy replied. "What else did she tell you?'

"Nothing," Michel replied innocently. "I swear to God... Uncle Cobb."

Then he hung up.

Chapter 24

Michel arrived at the station a few minutes before 9 AM. Russ Turner was waiting at his desk.

"So did he tell you anything?" Michel asked.

"I couldn't find him," Turner replied. "I stopped by Darlene's first and she said she hadn't seen him since he left the diner. Then I went by his place. It looks like he packed up in a hurry and left."

"Any idea where he might go?"

"He's got some family, but none he's close with so far as I know," Turner replied. "I notified the State Police and they put out an ABP on his truck, but I suspect he's just holed up somewhere in the area trying to figure out what to do next."

"Did you talk to his friends?"

"No, I decided not to," Turner replied. "I figured Donny might call them and it'd be better if he didn't know we were looking for him."

"Good thinking," Michel replied. "But what about Darlene? Aren't you afraid he'll call her?"

"I'm sure he will," Turner replied, "but I don't think she'll tell him anything. Darlene and I had a nice long talk last night, and I'm pretty sure she's finally done with Donny for good."

"You didn't tell her about him and Terry, did you?" Michel asked.

"No," Turner replied. "That's Terry's business. I just asked her what she wanted for herself and the baby, and gave her some fatherly advice."

"I'm glad," Michel replied. "I hope it sticks."

Turner nodded. "Me, too. So in the meantime I guess we wait and see if Donny shows up somewhere."

Michel thought about it for a moment.

"Not necessarily," he said.

"Meaning?"

"Do you know if he has a computer?"

"There was one of those router boxes at his house, but no computer," Turner replied.

"Good. That means he probably has it with him," Michel said.

"So?"

"So we may be able to use it to flush him out."

"How?"

"Well, if I were living around here and I wanted to hook up with guys on the down low, I'd use the internet," Michel replied.

Turner stared at him blankly.

"Welcome to the twenty-first century, Russ," Michel said with a smile. "There are whole websites devoted to meeting guys for sex."

He walked to the other desk and sat down.

"Do you have a department credit card?" he asked.

"For what?"

"We're going to need to set up an account."

Michel began typing on the keyboard, then hit the enter button. A collage of burly shirtless men standing in front of an eighteen-wheeler appeared on the screen.

"What in the name of hell is that?" Turner asked, walking up behind him.

"It's a site for guys interested in truckers," Michel said. "Terry told me that Donny had a taste for rough trucker types. Hopefully he's got a profile on here. Otherwise there are about a dozen other sites we'll have to check. So do you have a card?"

"You want me to use my official credit card to sign up for *that*?" Turner asked skeptically.

"It's official business," Michel replied.

Turner thought about for a moment, then took out his wallet and handed Michel the card.

"Fine," he said, "but this better work, because I'm not looking forward to explaining to the town council why I was signing up for gay sex sites."

Michel began typing rapidly.

"Okay, we are now officially DieselDaddy18," he said after a minute.

"Why eighteen?" Turner asked.

"Because one through seventeen were already taken," Michel replied. "Now we just need to find some suitable bait."

He began typing again. A column of photos appeared on the left side of the screen, with statistics and text to their right. Michel scrolled down the page.

"This one looks good," he said, as he moved the cursor over a photo of a muscular man with a shaved head and heavy beard.

"What are you doing?" Turner asked.

"Just borrowing a photo for our profile," Michel replied as he dragged the image to the computer's desktop.

"That doesn't seem right," Turner replied, shaking his head.

"If you don't like that, you're probably going to hate the rest," Michel replied distractedly as he began typing in a profile.

After a few minutes he sat back and hit the enter button.

"It'll take a few minutes for our profile to show up, and Donny's probably still sleeping anyway," he said. "What do you say we go get some breakfast?"

*****

After breakfast, Michel had gone back to the house to get Blue, then returned to the station to give Turner his statement about the previous night. For the three hours since, he'd been sitting at the computer, ignoring chat requests from old men.

"So you ever think you could live in a place like this?" Turner asked suddenly.

Michel swiveled in his chair to face him.

"I'm not sure," he said. "I like it here, but I've lived my entire life in the city and I've gotten pretty used to it."

Turner nodded.

"And I imagine it would be tough living in a place that doesn't have any sort of gay community."

"New Orleans definitely has a lot of gay people," Michel replied, "but I don't know that I'd call it a *community*. At least not most of the time."

"What do you mean?" Turner asked.

"To me, community suggests cohesiveness and unity," Michel replied. "I don't see a lot of either."

"It always looks like everyone's pretty unified when I see the parades and protests on the news," Turner replied.

"That's because at parades and protests everyone has a common cause," Michel replied. "The rest of the time it's just a bunch of people who all happen to be gay. And a lot of them are only too willing to shit on each other."

"How so?"

"If you're too feminine, someone's going to shit on you. If you're too butch, someone else is going to shit on you. And if you're transgendered or a drag queen, a lot of people are going to shit on you. And not just in New Orleans."

"That surprises me," Turner replied. "I'd think that everyone would get along being as how you're all gay."

"Do all black people get along?" Michel asked.

"Hell no!" Turner replied with an emphatic laugh.

"Exactly," Michel said. "But if you watched tapes of the Civil Rights marches, you'd think you all get along just fine. Black, gay, whatever, people are all the same. We come together when we need to, and the rest of the time we're just looking for someone else to shit on. Sometimes I think we don't need anyone else trying to hold us back because we do a good enough job of that on our own."

"That sounds pretty cynical," Turner replied.

"I prefer to think of it as realistic," Michel replied.

Turner gave a small laugh.

"Sounds like you've given this a lot of thought."

"Some," Michel replied.

"You have a lot of close friends who are black?" Turner asked.

"Just one," Michel replied. "My partner, Sassy."

"Your partner is a black woman named 'Sassy'?" Turner asked, wincing. "That's just wrong."

"I know," Michel replied with an appreciative laugh, "but she's not like that at all. She's actually one of the most grounded and elegant people I've ever met. Not elegant in terms of being fancy, but she's got true grace. Her real name's Alexandra, but her grandmother nicknamed her Sassy as sort of a joke because she was such a serious girl. It just stuck."

Turner nodded.

"She's actually from around these parts," Michel continued. "Butte La Rose."

"I know a few people from around there," Turner replied. "What's her last name?"

"Jones."

"I'll have to ask around."

"Do that," Michel joked, "and let me know what you find out, because she won't tell me *anything* about her past."

"Smart woman," Turner replied. "So is she gay, too?"

"No," Michel replied emphatically. "She was married once upon a time. Not that that necessarily means anything, but no, she's definitely straight."

"And she never remarried?" Turner asked.

"No, the first marriage didn't work out so well," Michel replied. "I think that kind of soured her on the institution. She's been single for as long as I've known her. At least so far as she's told me."

Though he felt slightly guilty discussing Sassy's personal life with a relative stranger, Michel realized that he was oddly comfortable talking with Turner.

"Maybe she just needs to find the right man," Turner replied.

"Maybe," Michel agreed without much conviction.

"Does she have any kids?" Turner asked.

Michel considered how to respond. He decided it would be a betrayal to share the details about the child Sassy had lost.

"Just me," he said.

Turner sensed it was a sensitive subject and decided to move onto something else.

"So back when you were a cop, did the other cops know you were gay?" he asked.

"I didn't think so," Michel replied with a laugh, "but when I decided to out myself, it turned out my Captain already knew."

"So there were no repercussions, professionally speaking?"

"Well, I was booted from the force about seven months later," Michel replied, "but my sexual preference didn't have anything to do with it."

Turner nodded but didn't push for a further explanation.

"Do you go out to gay bars much?" he asked instead.

"Sometimes," Michel replied, "but that's been a relatively recent thing. I pretty much avoided the whole scene until a few years ago."

"Why's that?" Turner asked.

"Partly professional concerns, partly personal, but mostly because from the outside it didn't seem like something I wanted to be a part of," Michel replied. "I thought that all the guys there were trying to conform to some idealized version of gayness that I didn't fit."

"And now?"

"Now I realize there's a place for everyone," Michel replied. "There are guys like me, guys like Terry, guys like you, even guys like Ruby."

They both laughed.

"So then you feel comfortable now?" Turner asked.

Michel nodded.

"Yeah. There's a sense of camaraderie that I like, even if I prefer to mostly stay on the edges and just watch."

"That sounds like a kind of community if you ask me," Turner replied.

"I suppose, in a sense," Michel replied thoughtfully.

They were interrupted by a sudden ping from the computer. Michel turned to the screen and saw a chat request from someone with the screen name "TruckerSucker."

"That's subtle," he said.

He clicked on the link next to the name and brought up the profile. There was a photo of a man's torso and thighs. He was wearing only a leather thong, harness, and dog collar.

"Does that look like Donny to you?" Michel asked rhetorically as Turner came up beside him.

"Sure does," Turner replied.

Michel gave him a curious look.

"The tattoo," Turner said quickly, pointing at a black and orange bobcat on the man's right thigh. "That's our high school mascot. The seniors on the football team get them every year."

"He's twenty-six," Michel said.

"That sounds right," Turner replied, "but that could also be about a dozen other guys who graduated in that class."

"Well, he's got two locked pictures," Michel said. "I'm guessing one is his face and one is his dick. Let's see if I can get him to open them."

"Why do I get the feeling you've done this before?" Turner asked.

"Just for professional reasons," Michel replied with a smirk. "Okay, you should probably go sit over there now. I don't think you're going to want to be a part of this."

He nodded his head toward the other desk.

"I can handle it," Turner protested.

"I'd like to see you speared on the end of my...," Michel recited aloud as he began typing.

"Okay, you know what?" Turner interrupted immediately. "I'm going to go sit over there."

Michel smiled and continued typing.

*****

"Is there a local motel that caters to truckers?" Michel asked a few minutes later.

"The Super 8 on Route 10 outside of Port Allen is probably the closest," Turner replied. "Why?"

"Can you call and see if they have a room available?" Michel asked.

Turner nodded and picked up the phone.

Michel returned his attention to the screen. Donny had just unlocked the other two photos. The first was of him with his arm around Darlene, though her face had been blacked out. The other was a shot of him sitting on the open tailgate of a truck, drinking a beer in the nude. I wonder who took that, Michel thought as he studied Donny's body.

"They've got two rooms," Turner said a few seconds later, holding his left hand over the receiver. "You want me to book one?"

"Yeah," Michel replied without looking at him. "And I'll need the room number."

"Are you absolutely sure it's him?" Turner asked pointedly.

"I'm sure," Michel replied. "He unlocked the other photos."

"Is one really his dick?" Turner asked.

Michel nodded.

"Among other things."

"Then I'll take your word it's him," Turner replied.

*****

"Well, we've got a date," Michel declared fives minutes later, swiveling his chair toward Turner.

"Great, let's go," Turner replied, standing up.

"It's not until nine," Michel replied.

"Why so late?"

"Donny said he couldn't make it until then," Michel replied. "He probably wants to wait until dark before he comes out of hiding."

Turner nodded.

"We should probably get there an hour early in case he decides to stake the place out."

"Agreed," Michel replied. "We're also going to have to borrow a truck."

"A truck?"

"To park in front of the room," Michel replied.

"You told him there'd be a truck in front of the room?" Turner deadpanned.

"He asked," Michel replied defensively.

"Did you tell him what kind of truck?"

"No. I told him his questions were starting to piss me off."

Turner shook his head.

"Fine, we'll borrow a truck," he said. "I've got a friend who runs a garage in Port Allen. I'm sure he can arrange it."

He looked at his watch.

"So then we've got about six and a half hours to kill. What are you going to do?"

"I figured Blue and I would go home, maybe go for a long walk," Michel replied. "I feel like I haven't been able to pay much attention to her the last few days."

"All right, just be careful out there," Turner replied. "You want to come over for dinner?"

"No, thanks," Michel replied. "I still have that steak I got from Cyrus. I'm going to feel guilty if I don't eat it before I see him again."

Turner nodded.

"Okay, then why don't you bring Blue by the house around 7:30 and we'll go from there."

"Sounds good," Michel replied as he stood up. "Oh, and do you have a camera?"

m

Chapter 25

Michel stood in the bathroom doorway at the back of the room, while Russ Turner sat in a chair near the door in the front. With the curtains drawn, the room was nearly black.

"I was thinking about something while Blue and I were out walking this afternoon," Michel whispered.

"What's that?"

"I can't figure out why she seems to like having me around."

Turner chuckled quietly.

"Probably because you know how to operate a can opener."

"Seriously," Michel replied. "It really doesn't make any sense if you think about it. In most ways, she's actually superior to me. She's stronger, she's faster, she can hunt, and she can defend herself much better, especially in the swamp."

"True," Turner replied.

"And yet she seems to like having me there, and even lets me be the leader," Michel said.

"It's been bred into them over the centuries," Turner replied. "They crave affirmation from us, so they're willing to let us take control, though sometimes you have to put them on their backs when they're puppies to establish dominance."

"Exactly," Michel said. "Which got me thinking about Donny."

"Come again."

"Donny's like a dog looking for someone to put him on his back and prove that they're dominant."

"So the whole harness and collar thing," Turner said.

"Well, those are just props in his fantasy. The thing that seems to get him off is submission," Michel replied.

"Why?"

"I think because deep down he feels like he's a fake," Michel replied. "He's built up this whole swaggering macho persona to mask it, but it's all an act. I think that's why he goes for the burly trucker types. In his mind, they represent the masculine ideal, and that's who he needs to put him in his place."

"That's kind of fucked up," Turner replied.

"But not that uncommon," Michel replied. "A lot of overtly dominant people secretly long to be someone's bitch."

Turner chuckled quietly.

"So do you think it's a conditioned response?" he asked. "Like maybe he was molested by a trucker when he was a kid?"

"Oh God, I hope not," Michel replied quickly. "I was just thinking he was a kinky fucker and maybe we could use it to our advantage."

"How?"

"Well, what would you think about leaving me alone with him for a little while?"

"Why?" Turner replied.

"Because I think I've already started to get to him," Michel replied. "I think that's why he stabbed me last night. He panicked because he was afraid he was losing control of the situation, and he couldn't let that happen in front of his pals."

"But you think one-on-one would be different?"

"Yeah," Michel replied. "I think that Donny's intrigued by me. He sees me as a challenge. That's what that shit he pulled at the Gator's Belly was all about. Basically he was pissing on my leg to see how I'd react."

"I think he does that a lot," Turner replied.

They were both silent for a few moments.

"I don't know," Turner said finally. "This is police business, and you're not a cop anymore."

"But we're not here to arrest him," Michel replied. "We're just here to find out what he's trying to hide, right?"

"I'm not sure about that yet," Turner replied. "Depends on what he has to say."

He was quiet for a few more seconds, then sighed.

"Let's play it by ear," he said. "If it looks like you've got things under control, then I'll leave you alone. Until then you can take the lead."

"Okay," Michel replied.

There was a single knock on the door, followed a second later by three more in quick succession. Michel turned on the digital camera and raised it, covering the green light on the top with his left index finger.

"It's show time," he whispered. "You ready?"

He could hear Turner getting out of his chair.

"Ready," Turner whispered back.

"Come in!" Michel barked in a deep, gruff voice, then stepped back where the light from the door wouldn't reach him.

The door opened. Through the viewfinder, Michel could see Donny standing in the doorway, silhouetted by the lights from the gas station across the street. Donny stepped into the room and closed the door.

"You know what to do," Michel growled.

"Yes, sir," Donny replied eagerly.

Michel heard two thumps, then the soft rustling of fabric.

"I'm ready, sir," Donny said a few seconds later.

"Now," Michel said.

Turner flicked the switch next to the door and the overhead light came on. Donny stood in the middle of the room wearing the same thong, harness, and dog collar he'd been wearing in his profile photo. His clothes and boots were on the floor in front of him.

"Smile," Michel said as he stepped into the room and fired off three quick shots with the camera.

A look of shock came over Donny's face. He stared at Michel for a second, then turned and bolted for the door. Turner was already blocking his way, but Donny didn't stop. He lowered his head and drove it into Turner's chest, knocking him backwards into the doorframe. As Turner bounced back, Donny brought his knee up hard into Turner's groin, then threw him sideways into the chair where he'd been sitting a few moments earlier. The chair tumbled over, taking Turner with it.

Donny had the door halfway open when Michel caught the chain leash hanging from the back of his dog collar and yanked it hard. Donny's neck snapped back and he let out a choking rasp. Michel kicked the door shut with his left foot, then grabbed the harness in the middle of Donny's back and threw Donny face down on the bed. As Donny scrambled onto his back, Michel held up the camera and took another four pictures.

"Oh, those will be nice for your Christmas card," he said.

Donny slowly pushed himself up. Michel took a step to his left, blocking the door. Out of the corner of his eye, he could see that Turner was on his feet, but leaning against the wall and struggling to catch his breath.

"It's okay," Michel said. "I got it."

Donny suddenly lunged and threw a looping right hand toward Michel's head. Michel grabbed Donny's wrist with his left hand and stepped into Donny's body, driving his right elbow hard into Donny's solar plexus. Donny dropped to his knees and let out a pained gasp.

"That's for stabbing me," Michel said.

He looked at Turner.

"You all right?"

Turner took an unsteady step and grimaced.

"Yeah. Just had the wind knocked out of me."

He took another step, then stopped and pressed his hands against his lower abdomen.

"He's all yours," he said, shaking his head. "I'm going to get some ice."

Michel looked down at Donny and saw a flicker of fear in his eyes.

"What?" Donny stammered, his head spinning toward Turner. "You can't leave me here with him. You're the cop."

From his tone, it was clear he didn't like what was happening.

"Sorry, not my jurisdiction," Turner said.

He walked slowly to the door, then looked back at Michel. "I'll be outside if you need me."

Michel waited until the door was closed, then sat on the dresser directly in front of Donny. He made a show of looking Donny up and down, then smiled.

"Nice outfit," he said. "Has Darlene seen that one?"

"What the fuck is this?" Donny asked, his face red and contorted with a mixture of pain and anger.

"Well, since we couldn't come to you, we figured we'd get you to come to us," Michel replied.

"This is kidnapping," Donny protested.

"Yeah, well I guess you'd know about that," Michel replied lightly and smiled again.

He paused and stared at Donny without expression. Donny met his gaze for a few seconds, then looked down at the floor.

"So I guess we're finally going to find out who's the top dog," Michel said calmly.

"What the fuck are you talking about?" Donny mumbled.

Though his voice was still angry, his posture had lost its aggressiveness. His shoulders were slumped forward and his hands dangled loosely at his sides.

"Isn't that what all the circling and sniffing has been about?" Michel asked. "To find out who was going to fuck who?"

Donny continued staring down without responding.

"So let's talk about last night," Michel said.

"I don't have to talk to you," Donny replied without conviction. "You're not a cop."

Michel stood up and took off his belt. He held the buckle in his right hand and flipped the other end onto the floor between Donny's knees.

"I know you're not too bright," he said, "so let me spell it out for you. This isn't police business."

He walked to Donny's right side, dragging the tip of the belt up Donny's body and over his right shoulder.

"Get down on your hands and knees," he said.

"What?" Donny replied nervously.

"I said get down on your hands and knees," Michel barked back. "Now!"

Donny hesitated a half second, then lowered his hands onto the floor.

"That's better," Michel said. "Now you're showing me your ass like a good bitch."

It was a line he'd remembered from a porn movie, though now that he'd actually said it, he felt silly.

"Now tell me about last night," he said.

"What about it?" Donny replied.

"Why'd you kidnap me?" Michel asked.

"I don't know what you're talking about," Donny replied. "I was with Darlene all night."

"Sheriff Turner went to Darlene's last night," Michel replied patiently. "You weren't there. Besides, I was awake for a few minutes before you threw that beer in my face. I heard you talking, and I heard one of your pals say your name."

Donny stared hard at the carpet. It was clear he was trying to remember whether that was true.

"So what if it was me?" he said finally. "Go ahead and arrest me."

"I'm not interested in having you arrested," Michel replied. "I just want to know why you want me out of town. And don't tell me it's because you don't like fags. We both know that's not true."

Donny just continued staring silently at the floor.

Michel suddenly realized that he'd miscalculated how easy it would be to break Donny. He'd assumed that Donny would automatically assume a submissive role, but he'd forgotten the key component of Donny's sexual fantasies: he wanted to be forced to submit. Michel thought about their online exchange and tried to get back into the mind-set of DieselDaddy18.

"So what's it like?" he asked.

"What's what like?" Donny replied sullenly.

"Pretending to be the macho stud when all you really want is for some big hairy trucker to use you as his fuck toy."

Donny didn't respond, but Michel saw his body stiffen slightly.

"Is that what you want now?" Michel continued, stepping closer. "You want me to bend you over the dresser, handcuff you, and fuck you? While Russ listens outside the door?"

"No," Donny replied in a shaky voice.

"I'll bet your cock would tell me different," Michel replied.

He made a quick move as though he were going to reach under Donny, and Donny flinched.

Michel knelt down and checked the pockets of Donny's jeans.

"So then what are these for?" he asked, pulling out a pair of handcuffs and a ball gag and tossing them on the floor in front of Donny.

"You told me to bring those," Donny replied weakly.

"No," Michel corrected coldly as he stood up. "You asked to bring them, and you begged me to use them on you. Didn't you?"

Donny nodded.

"What did you say?" Michel asked sharply.

"I said, yes sir!" Donny replied.

His face was red and he sounded on the verge of tears now.

"Imagine what your friends would think if they knew what a sick, pathetic faggot you are," Michel said, shaking his head.

Donny's shoulders began to tremble and he let out a small wet gasp.

"Okay, now let's try this again," Michel said. "Why did you want me out of town?"

"Because I was afraid you'd tell people about me and Terry," Donny replied, his voice breaking.

"Bullshit," Michel replied. "You were afraid I was going to find out about something else. What?"

Donny's arms suddenly collapsed and his face dropped to the carpet. He covered it with his hands.

"I can't tell you," he replied, then his body began shaking.

Michel watched him for a moment and felt an unexpected swell of pity. He decided he'd pushed far enough.

"Look, Donny," he said as he knelt down, "I already know about you and Terry. I know about the blackmail. I know about your fantasies. I..."

He stopped and settled back onto his heels.

"It *is* the blackmail, isn't it?" he said, as much to himself as Donny. "Russ was right. It wasn't your idea, was it?"

"I can't tell you," Donny replied miserably.

Michel put his right hand on Donny's back.

"Who was it, Donny?" he asked. "Just tell me the truth, and I promise it's going to be all right. If you're worried, I'm sure Russ can arrange to put you into protective custody."

Donny's body continued to shake and Michel stroked the back of his head soothingly.

"All right," Donny said finally. "I'll tell you."

He took a few deep breaths and straightened up, wiping his eyes with the back of his right hand. Then he lowered his hand and looked at Michel. His eyes were dry. He winked and drove his right elbow into Michel's temple.

*****

When Michel opened his eyes, he could see Donny standing at the foot of the bed, already dressed. He looked at Michel and smiled.

"Wow, you must have a really thick skull," he said. "You don't stay out for very long."

From the ache in his jaw and the bright red ball protruding from below his nose, Michel knew he couldn't respond. He looked up and saw his hands had been cuffed to the headboard.

"Maybe someday we'll have a little more time to see how the rest of this scene would play out," Donny said, raising his eyebrows suggestively, "but right now I've got to go."

He walked to the head of the bed, leaned down, and slowly licked the side of Michel's face.

"I guess now we know who's the top dog and who's the bitch," he said with a laugh. "See you later, darlin'."

He walked into the bathroom and slid open the window, then turned back to Michel.

"By the way, thanks for trying to help me out," he said with a giggle. "That was really touching."

Then his body grew rigid and began to twitch. He staggered forward a half step and slumped to the floor.

Michel saw Russ Turner through the open window, holding a Taser in his right hand.

"What happened?" Turner asked with exasperation.

I got metaphorically fucked, Michel thought bitterly.

Chapter 26

"You are really pissing me off," Turner said. "My balls hurt, I'm tired, and I want to get back home to my boy."

"So arrest me," Donny replied casually.

He was seated in a chair in the middle of the motel room, each wrist handcuffed to one of its back legs.

"Is that what you want?" Turner shot back angrily. "You want me to arrest you? Fine, I'll arrest you. And then I'll give a nice interview to the local paper about how exactly we got you to come here. Hell, we even have pictures for them to print."

The defiance in Donny's eyes faltered, but his expression remained unyielding.

Michel tried to stand, but a wave of dizziness forced him back onto the edge of the bed. He moved the bag of ice from his right temple to the back of his neck.

"Look, Donny," he said, "we already have a pretty good idea what happened. Someone from Gulf Coast bribed you to blackmail Terry. That's how you got paid disability. Just give us a name."

Donny looked at Michel and Michel could see him calculating his next move.

"I want immunity and protection," he said finally.

"Immunity from what and protection from whom?" Turner asked with exasperation.

"From whatever and whoever," Donny replied.

Michel gave Turner a questioning look.

"Fine," Turner said. "I'll talk to the DA."

"I want it in writing first," Donny replied quickly.

Before Michel even registered that he'd moved, Turner had grabbed Donny's hair and yanked his head back over the back of the chair.

"Stop fucking with me, boy!" he yelled. "You're not in a position to negotiate. Now give me a name!"

Donny's whole body pulled back as though it were trying to dissolve into the chair to escape from Turner's fury.

"Larry Midland!" Donny cried.

"Who's Larry Midland?" Turner asked, twisting Donny's head to the side.

"He's the vice president of operations at Gulf Coast," Donny blurted out, gasping in pain. "He's the one who wanted me to blackmail Terry."

Turner let go and Donny's head bounced forward.

"Why?" Michel asked.

"I don't know," Donny replied, rolling his neck from side to side and wincing.

"How'd you meet this Larry Midland?" Turner asked.

"He came to the plant for an inspection," Donny replied. "I saw him looking at me, so later on when he was alone I introduced myself. He asked me if I wanted to have dinner with him at his hotel, so I did."

"Did you have sex with him?" Michel asked.

"Yeah," Donny replied.

"And how did Terry's name come up?" Michel asked.

"It was after, while we were lying in bed," Donny replied. "He was asking me where I met guys in the area and I told him about the truck stop. He asked me if I'd ever seen Terry there."

"So obviously he already had suspicions about Terry," Turner said to Michel.

"Wouldn't you?" Donny asked.

"So then what?" Michel asked.

"About a week later he called me up and said he was coming

222

back to town. We hooked up again, and afterward he told me he wanted me to do him a favor. He said he'd give me $5,000 if I could get pictures of me and Terry having sex."

"Did he tell you why he wanted them?" Turner asked.

"No, and I didnt ask him," Donny replied. "I just wanted the money."

Michel believed that was true.

"So how did it go from that to blackmail?" he asked.

"I wasn't able to get the pictures until Terry and I went to New Orleans," Donny replied. "I got Terry drunk, and then after he passed out I took them and emailed them to Midland."

"Then what?" Turner asked.

"He called me and said he was coming to town again and wanted to get together," Donny replied. "That's when he told me he wanted me to tell Terry about pictures and say that I'd show them to his wife and father if he didn't pay me $50,000 within twenty four hours."

"He didn't want to give Terry a chance to get a loan," Michel said to Turner. "He was trying to force him to steal it from the trust."

Turner nodded.

"And he offered to put you on paid disability if you did it?" Michel asked.

Donny nodded. "For a year, but only if Terry paid."

Michel exchanged curious looks with Turner.

"So then how come you're still on disability?" he asked. "The blackmail didn't work."

Donny gave a crooked smile. "Well, *that* blackmail didn't work," he said with some of his usual bravado.

"You blackmailed Midland, too?" Michel asked.

"Hey, I was the one taking all the risk and there was no guarantee I was going to get paid," Donny replied with exaggerated innocence. "I just wanted some protection in case things didn't go right."

"He's married?" Michel asked.

Donny nodded.

"What did you use to blackmail him?" Turner asked.

"Pictures," Donny replied. "Same as Terry. I figured if Larry thought pictures would work on Donny, then they'd probably work on him, too. So I just waited until he was asleep, then click, click, click."

Michel felt a grudging admiration for Donny's devious instinct for self-preservation.

"You still have them?" he asked.

"Why, you want to see my dick?" Donny asked with a lewd smile.

Turner took a menacing step forward and the smile immediately disappeared.

"No, I gave them to Larry," Donny said quickly.

"Bullshit," Michel replied. "You're not stupid enough to give away all your insurance."

"I swear to God," Donny said with a hint of desperation. "I didn't have a choice. Larry just showed up at my place. I was afraid to put the pictures on my computer in case Darlene saw them, so I just had them on a memory card. He took it."

Michel decided that it sounded plausible. The fact that Donny had been able to keep his extracurricular trucker activities from Darlene for so long suggested he could be careful, and Midland had probably decided to pay an unexpected visit when he'd realized Donny couldn't be trusted. It even made sense that Midland would have honored their agreement anyway. Even without the photos, Donny could have made his life miserable if he'd started making accusations.

"Do you have any proof that he asked you to blackmail Terry?" Turner asked. "Any emails or letters?"

"No, we always talked about it in person, and he paid me the $5,000 in cash," Donny replied.

"Maybe we can bluff him about the photos," Turner said.

"Maybe," Michel agreed. "So are we done here?"

"I think so," Turner replied.

He unlocked the handcuffs, put one pair in the case on his belt, and dropped the other into Donny's lap.

Donny looked from Turner to Michel and back again with a mixture of confusion and distrust.

"You're free to go," Turner clarified in response to the unspoken question.

"But what about my protection?" Donny asked, his voice noticeably higher than usual.

"From what?" Turner replied. "So long as you keep your mouth shut, you won't need any for now. Midland doesn't know you talked to us. No one does."

"But he'll figure it out when you talk to him," Donny protested.

"*If* we talk to him," Turner corrected. "And if we do, we'll make arrangements to protect you then."

"So what am I supposed to do now?" Donny asked.

"Well, if I were you I'd go home, take off my little bondage costume, and lay very low for a few days," Michel replied.

He and Turner walked to the door. Michel opened it and stepped into the parking lot. Turner started to follow, then stopped and turned back.

"Oh, and one more thing," he said. "Stay the fuck away from Darlene. If I find out you're sniffing around her again, I'll charge you with battery against Terry and throw your ass in jail."

*****

"That was a very illuminating evening in many ways," Turner said as he drove them back to Bayou Proche. "'You want me to bend you over the dresser, handcuff you, and fuck you?' Is that standard interrogation technique down there in New Orleans?"

Michel gave an embarrassed smile.

"You heard that, huh? He wasn't cooperating, so I figured I'd evoke a little DieselDaddy18 to encourage him."

Turner smiled and nodded.

"So I'm thinking we should talk with Terry before we do anything else," Michel said.

"We?" Turner asked, raising his eyebrows.

"Come on," Michel replied. "You can't keep me out of it now. You wouldn't even know about any of this if I hadn't gotten myself kidnapped."

"Well, I suppose that's true," Turner replied, chuckling. "But promise me you won't do anything without checking with me first. Okay?"

"Okay," Michel replied.

He stared out the window for a while, watching the dark fields roll past.

"I didn't want to say anything in front of Donny," he said finally, "but Midland's name sounds familiar."

"You think you've met him?"

"Doubtful. Those oil industry boys aren't exactly my crowd."

"Maybe in a bar?" Turner asked.

Michel didn't respond. He closed his eyes and tried to stop concentrating in hopes it would come to him. He wished he had a cigarette. A minute later he began to snore quietly.

*****

Michel awoke when the car came to a stop in Russ Turner's driveway. He opened his eyes and looked around with confusion. He tried to focus his eyes on Turner and blinked a few times.

"Sorry about that," he said. "Guess I dozed off for a minute."

226

"Try fifteen," Turner replied.

"I guess I just...."

Michel stopped and his eyes suddenly cleared.

"Holy shit, I think I know," he said.

He pulled out his phone and speed dialed Sassy.

"What do you want?" she answered.

"That's charming," Michel replied.

"Maybe I'd be more charming if you stopped hanging up on me."

"I'm sorry," Michel replied. "I just have a quick question for you. Was there a Larry or Lawrence Midland on the list of donors I faxed you?"

"Hold on," Sassy replied with an impatient sigh.

Michel heard a loud clunk, then footsteps. Nina Simone's "My Baby Just Cares for Me" was playing in the background. Then he heard what sounded like a man's voice, followed by Sassy laughing. He looked at his watch. It was 10:22 PM. The footsteps came back toward the phone.

"Yeah," Sassy said. "He was one of the big spenders. Twenty grand."

"Did I catch you at a bad time?" Michel asked.

"What?" Sassy replied.

"I thought I heard a man's voice. Do you have a date over?"

"It was probably just the TV," Sassy replied too quickly.

"Why would you have the TV on and music playing at the same time?" Michel asked.

"Why would you be asking me questions that are none of your business?" Sassy retorted curtly. "Do you want to know about Lawrence Midland or not?"

"Yeah, I'm sorry," Michel replied.

"According to Chance's notes, he's a VP at Gulf Coast Oil. In fact, all of the top donors were associated with Gulf Coast. The other two guys are also VPs, and the two organizations are charitable trusts set up by Gulf. Why, what's this all about?"

"Russ and I just questioned Donny Heath. He said that Midland paid him to blackmail Terry DeCew."

"That's interesting. Any idea why?"

"Donny didn't know."

"And you believe him?" Sassy asked.

"Yeah," Michel replied. "I don't think Midland would have told him anything. Donny's not exactly a reliable ally."

"Does Donny have any proof?" Sassy asked.

"No," Michel replied. "Midland was careful. There's no physical evidence connecting them."

"Except for some naked pictures," Turner said.

"Who was that?" Sassy asked.

"Russ."

"He's there right now?"

"Uh huh."

"Put him on," Sassy said. "I want to talk to him."

Michel put his hand over the receiver and looked at Russ.

"She wants to talk to you."

"Me? About what?"

"I don't know."

Russ gave a confused look but took the phone.

"Hello?"

There were a few seconds of silence.

"Well, we plan to talk to Terry in the morning," Turner said, followed by another brief pause, then, "Yes, depending on what Terry says."

Turner listened quietly for a full half minute, then looked at Michel.

"I wouldn't say that," he said, then began to laugh.

He nodded several times.

"Oh, don't worry, I won't," he said. "Yeah, it was great talking to you, too."

He handed the phone back to Michel. Michel looked at Turner curiously for a moment, then put the phone to his ear.

"Hello?"

He heard a loud click as the line went dead.

"What was that all about?" he asked.

"She just wanted to make sure I had a handle on what to do next," Turner replied matter-of-factly. "Seems like a smart woman. Maybe a bit bossy, though."

"And that was it?" Michel asked skeptically.

"Yeah, why?"

"Then why did you look at me and say, 'I wouldn't say that?'"

Turner's eyebrows knitted together and he tilted his head to the side as though deep in concentration.

"Hmmm, I don't recall," he said.

Michel sat back and folded his arms across his chest.

"Fine," he said. "See if I help you next time you take a knee to the balls."

Turner laughed.

"So Sassy told me that Midland donated $20,000 to the preservation trust," he said. "Care to discuss theories about what's going on?"

Michel played at being offended for a few more seconds, then shook his head.

"I think we should wait until we talk to Terry," he said. "Maybe Midland has a personal grudge against him. Maybe they had a relationship in the past."

"Okay," Turner agreed. "I'll call him now and ask him to come by the station tomorrow morning around ten."

They both opened their car doors and stepped out.

"You know, Russ," Michel said, "I've got to tell you, despite the fact that you were obviously justified, I was a little hurt by your lack of confidence in me tonight."

"Lack of confidence?" Turner replied, confused.

"Not trusting that I could handle Donny," Michel clarified. "Staking out the back of the motel."

Turner laughed.

"That wasn't a lack of confidence. I went out back to take a piss, and suddenly the window opened. I figured you had it all under control after the way you took him down with that elbow."

"Yeah, that was pretty good, wasn't it?" Michel replied, clearly pleased with himself.

"Don't get too cocky," Turner replied. "You still ended up handcuffed to the bed."

Chapter 27

Terry DeCew arrived at the station promptly at ten. His right eye was swollen and red, and he had a cut in the center of his lower lip. Michel noticed that he looked paler and more anxious than usual.

"Hey Terry, how are you doing?" he asked.

"I've been better," Terry replied with a pronounced chilliness. "Where's Russ?"

"He'll be right back," Michel replied. "He's just using the restroom."

Terry nodded indifferently and took the chair in front of Turner's desk, twelve feet from Michel. The distance seemed deliberate, and Michel wondered if Terry blamed him for what had happened to him.

"Thanks for calling Russ the other night," he said. "You may have saved my life. Or at least my testicles."

Terry shrugged.

"I'm sure you would have done the same."

Michel thought he detected a hint of sarcasm in the remark.

"Look, Terry, I'm sorry about what happened," he said. "I swear I didn't say anything to Donny."

"Well obviously you didn't have to," Terry replied petulantly. "I guess being the genius he is, he just figured it out on his own."

Michel wasn't sure how to respond.

"Do you ever think about the consequences of your actions for other people?" Terry continued. "I get it. Verle was accused of murder and you don't think he did it. Fine. You wanted to check out the trust's records. Fine. You wanted to talk to me about what I was doing in New Orleans with Donny. Fine."

With each "fine," his voice grew louder and his tone more agitated.

"But why couldn't you have just called me on the phone or asked to meet with me privately? Why did you have to ambush me in the diner where everyone in fucking town goes?"

Michel sat back, startled by Terry's venom. He hadn't imagined he was capable of it.

"Yeah, I made a mistake," Terry said, his voice rising higher, "but I admitted it and I suffered the consequences. And now, just when Carolyn and I are starting to get past it, you come along and dredge it all up again and reopen the wounds. How many times do I have to pay for the same fucking mistake?"

Michel knew there was nothing he could say. Everything Terry had said was true, if skewed to make his intent seem malicious.

Suddenly Russ Turner walked into the room. When he saw the angry look on Terry's face, he stopped.

"Am I interrupting something?" he asked.

"We're done," Terry replied with finality. "Why did you want to see me?"

Turner gave Michel a questioning look. Michel gave a slight warning shake of his head, as if to say "just let it go." Turner frowned for a second, then walked to his desk and sat down.

"We talked to Donny last night," he said, watching Terry carefully. "He told us that he was paid to blackmail you by a man named Larry Midland. He's a vice president at Gulf Oil Company, and one of the trust's big donors. You know him?"

Terry sat forward suddenly.

"Larry Midland?" he replied incredulously. "Of course I know him. He's one of my father's oldest friends. Why would Larry want to blackmail me?"

"We're not sure," Turner replied. "We were hoping you could help us figure that out."

Terry sat back hard, as though he'd been pushed.

"That doesn't make any sense," he said. "I've known Larry most of my life. There's never been any problems between us."

"Was there ever anything else between you?" Michel asked.

Terry looked at him with bewilderment.

"You mean something sexual?"

Michel nodded.

"No, of course not," Terry replied, as though the thought sickened him. "He's like an uncle."

He looked down at the desk and shook his head.

"It's got to be a mistake," he said. "Donny must have been lying."

"Maybe," Turner replied without conviction. "But why would he choose to pin it on Midland?"

"I don't know," Terry replied agitatedly. "Why don't you ask him? Where is he?"

"Probably hiding out in some dive motel," Turner replied.

"Wait, you didn't arrest him?" Terry asked.

Turner shook his head.

"Why not?" Terry asked with disbelief.

"Because if we did, Midland would know we'd questioned him," Turner replied.

"This is un-fucking-believable," Terry said.

Turner looked at Michel and raised his eyebrows. Michel stood up and walked to the front of Turner's desk. He sat down a foot from Terry.

"I know this is all a big shock," he said in a calming tone, "and maybe you're right. Maybe Donny did lie. But can you think of any reason why Midland might have wanted to blackmail you?"

Terry looked up at him. The anger in his eyes was gone, replaced by confusion and helplessness.

"No," he said in a small voice. "It just doesn't make any sense."

He stared down at the floor and took several quick, shallow breaths, as though fighting to hold back tears.

"Why would Midland have donated $20,000 to the trust?" Michel asked. "It seems kind of odd for an executive at an oil company."

Terry didn't respond for a moment. He seemed lost in his own thoughts.

"It's good PR," he replied finally, looking up. "A lot of them do it. And most oil companies have charitable arms that support environmental groups."

Michel nodded.

"All of the trust's top donors last year were from Gulf Coast," Michel replied. "Any reason?"

Terry gave him a quizzical look.

"They were?"

"You didn't know? Michel asked.

Terry shook his head slowly.

"I don't really get involved with the fundraising," he said. "My father handles that because he has the connections. Maybe we should call him."

"I think we should hold off on talking to Porter about any of this for now," Turner said quickly. "Given his health issues, I don't think we should worry him until we're sure what's happening. As you said, Donny may have been lying."

Terry studied him for a moment, then nodded.

"You're probably right," he said.

He looked down again for a moment, then from Turner to Michel.

"Why is this happening to me?" he asked.

"I don't know, Terry," Michel replied, "but we're going to find out."

*****

"You care to share theories on what's going on?" Turner asked as soon as Terry had left.

"I'm not sure if I do," Michel replied, "because I don't think you're going to like what I'm thinking."

"You're thinking Porter's involved."

"Yeah, but that's not the part I think you're not going to like."

"You think the blackmail and Dolores Hagen's murder are connected," Turner replied.

Michel looked at him with surprise.

"Yeah, how'd you know?"

"Because I'm thinking the same thing," Turner replied.

"Okay, so what's *your* theory?" Michel asked.

"Well, there's no question that Gulf Coast Oil wants those leases," Turner said. "That's pretty clear. And I don't think there was much chance they'd have been able to get them with Verle and Terry on the trust's board, so I think they were trying to get one or both of them out of the way."

"I agree," Michel replied.

"What I can't figure out, though, is why Midland didn't just use the photos to force Terry to vote in GCO's favor? Seems like that would have been much easier. All they needed were Terry's and Porter's votes."

"True," Michel replied, "but that would have put Midland and GCO in a much more vulnerable position. If Terry had gone to the Attorney General, they would have been screwed."

Turner nodded.

"So instead he gets Donny to do his dirty work, Terry's forced to steal the $50,000 from the trust, and Verle and Porter have to remove him from the board."

"Exactly," Michel replied.

"So then are you thinking that framing Verle was always

235

part of the plan, or did they come up with that when Terry didn't take the bait?"

"I don't know," Michel replied. "I guess we'll have to find out whether Porter has the right to make final decisions in the case of a deadlocked vote. And then the other big question is whether Porter's been a willing participant or a pawn."

"A pawn? What makes you say that?" Turner asked.

"Well, Porter wouldn't benefit personally from leasing the rights. The money would go to the trust."

"Officially. But, that doesn't mean he couldn't be compensated on the side."

"Again, that's risky. You can be sure that if the trust leased that land to GCO, there'd be a lot of scrutiny by the AG. I'm thinking maybe Porter didn't have a choice."

"So Midland has something on Porter, too?" Turner asked.

Michel shrugged.

"He worked for the bad guys for a long time. I'd be willing to bet that not everything he did was on the up-and-up."

"That's probably true," Turner replied.

He looked down at his desk and frowned.

"What's the matter?" Michel asked.

"I can't see Porter going along with blackmailing Terry or framing Verle if it's just a case of Midland having something on him," Turner replied. "I think he'd take the hit before he'd throw either of them under the bus."

"Which would mean he's been a willing participant."

Turner sighed.

"I don't see how else it makes sense."

"I'm sorry," Michel said. "I know he's your friend."

"Apparently not a very good one," Turner said.

They were both quiet for a few moments.

"I think I'll call Otis Lewdet," Turner said finally.

"Before we have any proof?" Michel replied, surprised.

"Just to find out if they've got anything else on Dolores

Hagen's murder," Turner replied. "We're basing our whole theory on the assumption that Verle was innocent. I want to make sure we have some justification for that before we talk to Midland."

Michel nodded.

"Okay, call me if you find out anything."

"Don't worry," Turner replied. "I will."

Chapter 28

"Hey," Michel said when Sassy answered.

"Hey," Sassy replied. "So what do you need from me now?"

Michel smiled.

"Nothing. I just called to say hello."

"Oh," Sassy replied with mild surprise. "So what's been going on?"

"Russ and I met with Terry this morning," Michel replied. "We told him about Midland. Turns out Midland and Porter DeCew are old friends. Terry said Midland's been like an uncle to him."

"So then he has no idea why Midland would want to blackmail him?"

"No."

"Do you think Donny was lying?" Sassy asked.

"No. We think that Midland and Porter were working together. They were trying to get Terry to take the $50,000 from the trust so that Porter would have an excuse to remove him from the board."

"So that Porter could award the leases to Gulf Coast?"

"Seems like it," Michel replied.

"You think he'd do that to his own son?" Sassy asked incredulously.

"I wouldn't have," Michel replied, "but it's the only thing that makes sense."

"And what about Verle?" Sassy asked. "You think they set him up, too?"

"Yeah."

"I'm sorry," Sassy said.

"Thanks," Michel replied.

"So is Russ planning on bringing Midland in?" Sassy asked.

"He wants to talk to the State Police captain in charge of the Hagen investigation first," Michel replied. "See if they found any physical evidence linking Verle to the murder. We're basing everything on the assumption that Verle was innocent. If they found more evidence, then we're going to have to rethink that theory before we talk to Midland."

"That makes sense," Sassy replied.

She paused for a moment before continuing.

"Are you all right?" she asked. "You sound kind of subdued."

"Yeah, I'm fine," Michel replied. "It's just sad. How could someone try to ruin two people's lives like that? All for money."

"You were a cop long enough to know that people have done far worse for money," Sassy replied.

"I know, but Terry is family, and Verle was Porter's friend."

"Since when do family and friends get a free pass?" Sassy asked.

"I suppose you're right," Michel replied

There was a long silence.

"Are you sure you're all right?" Sassy asked finally.

"Yeah," Michel replied. "I'm just feeling a little bit...contemplative.

"About?"

"I miss you," Michel replied. "And I miss Joel, and being home. Hell, I even miss Chance a little. But at the same time, I'm going to miss being here when I leave."

"You can always go back to visit," Sassy said. "I mean, you're going to have a house there now, after all."

"I know, but it'll be different. I sort of feel like when I leave, I'll be leaving Verle behind, if that makes any sense."

"You won't be leaving him," Sassy replied. "You'll always have him in your memories. You know that."

"But I feel like when this is all over, a whole chapter of my life will be over, too," Michel replied. "Verle was the last of my family. And I don't know if I'll be able to come back here."

"Because it'll be too painful?"

Michel didn't respond, but Sassy could hear him take a deep breath.

"That's just part of life," she said. "If you cut yourself off from the things that hurt, you cut yourself off from the good things, too. It's like when you were a kid. You stopped going to visit Verle and your aunt and uncle because it hurt too much when you left. But think about all of the good times you missed out on because of that. You can't live your life trying to avoid pain."

Michel looked at Blue, curled up on the floor by his feet, and felt tears well up in his eyes.

"I've got to go," he said.

"No," Sassy replied. "We're not done talking."

"But..."

"But nothing," Sassy interrupted. "This is one of those times you're just going to have to deal with the pain. I'm not going to let you avoid it. Now talk to me."

Michel couldn't help but smile. He wiped his eyes and took a steadying breath.

"I don't want to leave Blue behind," he said finally.

"Is that what this is all about?" Sassy asked. "You're going to miss a dog?"

Michel laughed.

"Essentially," he replied.

He thought about saying more, explaining that Blue represented his last connection to Verle and that he felt like he owed it to Verle to look after her, but he realized the simple truth was that he'd grown very attached to her.

"So then bring her back with you," Sassy said.

"I can't," Michel replied. "It wouldn't be fair to her. She wouldn't be happy living in the city. She needs space to run around."

"She needs love, food, and a safe place to live," Sassy replied. "That's what she needs. And if you're really worried about space, then use some of that money Verle left you and buy a new house with a big yard."

"I hadn't thought about that," Michel admitted.

"Of course you hadn't," Sassy replied reproachfully.

"What's that supposed to mean?" Michel replied.

Sassy sighed. "Everytime you're faced with a challenge in your personal life, you start out by thinking about all the reasons that something *can't* happen. What you should be doing is thinking about how you can *make* it happen. You need to develop a more positive attitude. You can change your life any time you want, you know."

Michel suddenly flashed back on his dinner in Baton Rouge.

"Were you talking to Pearl?" he asked suspiciously.

"No. Why would I want to talk to her after she was putting all my business out in the street?"

"You're just expressing your opinions a little more stridently than usual," Michel replied.

"Stridently? Are you calling me a bitch?"

Michel laughed. He suddenly felt much better.

"No, I'm not calling you a bitch," he said. "And thank you. You're right. I can change my life."

"You're welcome," Sassy replied. "And I can change my life, too. Especially if you give me some of Verle's money."

"Oh gee, I've got to go," Michel replied with exaggerated breeziness. "Blue needs to go for a walk. Be right there, honey."

"Oh sure, now you're going to be using your dog as an excuse to avoid things. Some people never change. I swear..."

Michel hung up on her. He waited ten seconds, then hit the redial.

"You are not even a little cute," Sassy answered with obvious irritation.

"I just wanted to say thank you," Michel said.

"Well, you're welcome," Sassy replied, her tone softening.

"I really appreciate it," Michel said.

"Fine. Don't go getting all touchy-feely on me," Sassy replied sardonically.

"Don't worry, I won't," Michel replied. "So, have you seen Joel yet?"

"Yeah, he stopped by the office this morning."

"How was he?"

"Anxious to see you, but otherwise fine."

Michel smiled.

"Well, if you see him again, tell him I'll be home soon."

Chapter 28

Michel padded out onto the porch and sat on the top step. He unwrapped the dressing on his thigh. The inch-long gash had scabbed over and appeared to be healing well.

Blue walked up beside him and dropped down, sprawling onto her side.

"There's that belly," Michel said, running his fingers through the light gray hair that covered her pink stomach.

He took a sip of coffee, then breathed deeply and let it out, sighing with contentment. Suddenly he realized that something was missing: something that had been a part of his mornings for as long as he could remember. He took another deep breath and let it out.

"I'm not coughing up crap," he said with amazement.

He realized he felt good, better than he could remember feeling first thing in the morning for years.

"Shit, maybe there's something to this no-smoking thing after all," he said.

Blue stared at him blankly for a moment, then closed her eyes and rolled onto her back. Michel rubbed her stomach more vigorously and she let out a low groan. Michel smiled.

Suddenly his cell phone began to ring inside the house.

"Sorry," he said as he pushed himself up. "I'll be right back."

He walked into the living room and picked up his phone from the coffee table. Russ Turner's number was on the display. It was 6:30 AM.

"Hey," Michel answered.

"Did I wake you?" Turner asked.

"No, Blue and I were just sitting on the porch having coffee."

"You gave her coffee?" Turner asked.

"Well, no," Michel replied. "I was having coffee. She was just getting her belly scratched."

"Okay, just checking," Turner replied. "I know you haven't had a dog before."

"So what's up?" Michel asked.

"I spoke to Lewdet last night," Turner replied. "Pretty interesting."

"How so?"

"They haven't found any evidence that Verle was in Dolores Hagen's car or that she was in Verle's truck."

"That *is* interesting," Michel replied.

"Lewdet also said that Hagen had several small gouges on the back of her neck, but they didn't find any of her skin under Verle's fingernails."

"So then he really didn't kill her," Michel replied excitedly.

"That's the way it looks," Turner replied.

"Why didn't Lewdet call you before?" Michel asked.

"He just got the results yesterday," Turner replied. "Since Verle was already dead, they didn't fast-track the tests."

"So did you tell him about Midland?" Michel asked.

"No way," Turner replied. "Our theory is still a lot of conjecture. I've got my reputation to protect."

Michel smiled.

"So does this mean we're going to talk to Midland?"

"I'll call his office at nine and make an appointment."

"You don't want to just show up and surprise him?"

"And sit in a waiting room all day while he pretends to be in meetings?" Turner replied. "No, thanks. If we're going all the way to Baton Rouge, I want to make sure we see him."

"I suppose you're right," Michel replied. "I'm sure he'll be surprised enough when he finds out why we're there."

Chapter 28

"I was expecting something a little more like Dr. No's lair," Michel whispered, looking around at the warm wood paneling and overstuffed pale green chairs in the reception area outside Larry Midland's office.

"That's probably in the basement," Turner whispered back with a quiet chuckle. "This is just for show."

The pretty brunette behind the desk looked up at them and smiled pleasantly.

"Are you sure I can't get you anything?" she asked.

"No thanks. We're fine," Michel replied, though he wondered if cigarettes were included in the offering.

The phone on the receptionist's desk buzzed.

"Yes, Mr. Midland," she replied into her headset. "I'll bring them right in."

Michel looked at his watch. It was exactly 1 PM. Well, the guy's prompt if nothing else, he thought.

Larry Midland greeted them just inside the door of his office. Unlike the slick, manicured politician Michel had been expecting, he was small and slump-shouldered, with thinning brown hair and tired eyes that peered out from behind round wire-framed glasses. He looked more like an overworked accountant than a vice president of a major oil company.

"Sheriff Turner," Midland said, extending his right hand. "I'm Lawrence Midland."

"Mr. Midland," Turner replied as they shook hands. "Thank you for seeing us."

He turned and indicated Michel.

"This is Michel Doucette."

"Mr. Doucette," Midland said as he shook Michel's hand. "Please come in, gentlemen. Did Deena offer you anything to drink?"

"Yes, thank you," Turner replied.

Midland ushered them to a cluster of chairs matching those in the reception area.

"So what can I do for you, gentlemen?" he asked solicitously as soon as they were all seated.

"Do you know a man by the name of Donny Heath?" Turner asked.

Midland's eyes narrowed as though he were searching his memory, then shrugged.

"Not that I remember, but I meet a lot of people as part of my job. Why?"

"Are you sure?" Michel asked. "Because he swears he knows you. Intimately."

Midland sat back slowly in his chair, but his expression remained neutral.

"I see," he said. "And my friendship with Mr. Heath is police business why?"

There was a sudden steeliness in his tone that took Michel by surprise. He suspected Midland was a lot tougher than he appeared.

"Donny claims that you hired him to blackmail Terry DeCew," Turner replied.

Midland's expression still didn't change.

"And why would I want to do that?" he asked. "I've known Terry since he was a boy. His father is one of my oldest friends."

It was obvious from Midland's calm demeanor that he wasn't going to break down and confess any time soon. Michel decided to deviate from the approach he and Turner had discussed.

"We know that," he replied before Turner could respond, "which is why the whole thing struck us as so unlikely. Can you think of any reason why Donny would want to make trouble for you like that?"

Midland studied him carefully, then nodded gravely.

"Unfortunately, my relationship with Donny ended rather badly," he said.

"How so?" Michel asked.

"I trust I can count on your discretion?" Midland replied, looking from Michel to Turner.

They both nodded. Midland looked down at his hands and sighed deeply.

"Donny and I were involved for a short time," he said. "He developed feelings for me, and wanted me to leave my wife for him. Obviously I couldn't do that, so I ended the relationship. He was upset."

"So you think he's trying to get back at you?" Turner asked.

"Apparently," Midland replied. "I can't think of any other reason why he'd tell you that."

Michel nodded sympathetically for a moment, then leaned forward in his chair.

"It's odd, though, that if he wanted to get back at you, he wouldn't just send the photos he took to your wife," he said.

The left corner of Midland's mouth twitched slightly, but his expression remained calm. "Photos?" he said.

"Maybe you haven't noticed," Michel said, "but Donny doesn't have a lot of integrity. You didn't really think that he didn't back up those files, did you?"

Midland's gaze hardened, though he still didn't look concerned. He seemed more intrigued to see where things were heading.

"But don't worry," Michel said. "Donny no longer has them. He turned them over to us when we threatened to arrest him for blackmailing Terry."

"We?" Midland replied. "Don't you mean Sheriff Turner. If I'm not mistaken, you're no longer a policeman, Mr. Doucette."

Michel smiled. Midland had clearly prepared for their meeting.

"So let's just cut to the chase," Midland said. "Why are you here? If you had any evidence, you would have already had me arrested. And note I said, 'had me arrested,' since this clearly isn't your jurisdiction."

His direct manner suggested that they were conducting a business negotiation.

"Okay," Michel replied, deciding to lay their cards on the table. "We think you were trying to get Terry and Verle removed from the board of the trust so that Porter DeCew could award you the leases on Verle's land."

For the first time, uncertainty clouded Midland's face.

"Verle? What does Verle have to do with any of this?" he asked.

"We think you framed him for Dolores Hagen's murder," Michel replied.

Midland sat up and tented his fingers below his chin. He pursed his lips and stared into the middle distance for a few moments.

"I can see why you might believe there's a connection," he said finally, sounding very deliberate in his choice of words, "but you'll have to trust me that there isn't."

"Trust you? Just like that?" Michel replied incredulously.

"I'm afraid I can't say more than that," Midland replied. "It wouldn't be my place."

"Perhaps you'd feel more talkative at the station." Turner replied.

"Again, this isn't your jurisdiction, Sheriff," Midland replied somewhat dismissively. " And Dolores Hagen's murder is a State Police matter."

"That's true," Michel replied, trying to maintain his

patience, "but I'm sure they'd be very interested in talking with you if we told them what we suspect."

"Perhaps," Midland replied indifferently. "The problem is that you're putting me in a very difficult position."

"Difficult?" Michel replied, his voice rising angrily. "Fuck difficult, Mr. Midland. My cousin is dead and he was accused of a murder I know he didn't commit. I want to know the truth."

Midland regarded him evenly for a few seconds, then nodded.

"I respect your loyalty to your cousin," he said, "but you're asking me to betray a confidence, and that's something I take very seriously. Before I say anything else, I want an assurance."

"An assurance? You want to bargain with us?" Michel asked.

"No. I'm just asking for a favor."

Michel started to get up to leave, but Turner stopped him.

"What kind of favor?" Turner asked.

"I want you to make Donny Heath go away."

"Away?"

"I want him out of my life," Midland replied. "Make whatever threats you have to, but convince him it's in his best interest to never contact me again."

"Are you willing to honor the remaining terms of your agreement with him?" Turner asked.

Midland gave a small smile.

"We have a letter from a qualified physician stating that Mr. Heath is unable to work as a result of injuries sustained on the job," he replied. "Until we receive a letter to the contrary, his disability payments will continue. I believe his next examination is scheduled for four months from now."

"Okay," Turner replied. "Anything else?"

"That's it," Midland replied.

"You're not asking for immunity from prosecution?" Michel asked with surprise.

"There won't be any prosecution," Midland replied confidently.

"And how can you be so sure of that?" Turner asked.

"Because I'm certain that there's nothing connecting me to Donny Heath. No letters, no emails, no personal phone records. Not even the photos you claim to have."

Michel sat back and took a deep breath, fighting the urge to jump up and smack Midland.

"If you're so certain, then why would you tell us anything?" Turner asked skeptically.

"Because I don't believe that Verle was guilty either," Midland replied, "and I think you have the right to prove that. But so long as you're convinced I framed him, that's not going to happen."

"Excuse me if I have a hard time buying your sudden altruism," Michel replied sarcastically, "but..."

"It's not altruism," Midland shot back immediately. "It's a matter of pragmatism. You're accusing me of having a woman murdered just so I could get the leases to Verle's land. Those kinds of accusations are very bad for business."

He closed his eyes for a moment as though collecting his thoughts, then looked at Michel soberly.

"Think about it for a moment," he said. "Why would I want to frame Verle? There was nothing to be gained from it. Terry didn't give in to your hypothetical blackmail plot, and so long as he remains on the board, there'd be no point in putting Verle in jail."

"Unless Porter has the right to override a tie," Michel said.

"Which he doesn't," Midland replied with certainty. "The bylaws of the trust are very clear. No agreements can be entered into without the approval of the majority of the trustees. It's a matter of public record."

Michel sank back into his chair. Assuming that he was telling the truth about the trust's bylaws, everything Midland had said made sense. Murdering Dolores Hagen and framing Verle would have been high-risk maneuvers with no return. Michel felt a sudden sense of hopelessness.

"Look, Mr. Doucette," Midland said, his tone softening. "I can't tell you exactly what happened. As I said before, it would be a betrayal of a confidence. But I can tell you that you're looking in the wrong direction. You're assuming what happened was about business."

Michel stared at him for a moment.

"So then you're saying it was personal?"

Midland shrugged noncommittally.

"Certainly not on my part," he said, "but maybe you should be looking closer to home."

Michel looked at him with confusion, wondering if he meant New Orleans. He suddenly remembered the emails between Verle and Severin Marchand.

"Or perhaps I should say *nearer*," Midland clarified, seeming to read the reason for Michel's confusion.

Michel looked at Turner and smiled. Turner gave him a questioning look, but Michel turned back to Midland.

"Thank you, Mr. Midland," he said. "We appreciate your help. And we'll certainly do what we can to take care of your problem with Donny."

*****

"Okay, what did I just miss?" Turner asked as soon as they were outside Midland's office.

"I take it you didn't study French," Michel replied.

"No. Spanish and Latin. Why?"

"And you've been living in Bayou Proche for almost twenty years, and never wondered what the name meant?" Michel asked.

252

"I assumed it was named after some guy named Proche," Turner replied defensively.

Michel smiled.

"It means Near Bayou," he said.

Turner stopped walking.

"So he's saying Porter is behind it all?" he asked.

"That's the way I took it," Michel replied.

"Then I guess it's time we had a talk with him," Turner said with a hint of resignation.

"But I think we should wait and talk to him at home," Michel said.

"Why?"

"I think we should give him a chance to talk in private. I have a feeling that things aren't at all what we've been thinking."

"What makes you say that?" Turner asked.

"What Midland said about not wanting to betray a confidence, and it not being his place to tell us what was happening," Michel replied. "That sounds like something more than trying to protect a co-conspirator."

"It was pretty specific language," Turner agreed. "How about we meet at the station at 7 PM? We can walk to Porter's house from there."

"Sounds like a plan," Michel replied.

Chapter 29

Michel had nearly dozed off when Blue suddenly growled. He opened his eyes and saw her standing a few feet away, looking at the door. Her tail was up and her body rigid.

"What's the matter, girl?" Michel asked.

He heard a car door close and jumped up from the couch. Through the living room window, he could see the battered front of a dark green GTO.

"Shit, now what?" he said under his breath.

There were heavy footsteps on the stairs and Blue growled again. Michel moved closer to the window and peered around the edge of the curtain. Black Jack Doucette was standing on the porch, smoothing his hair with both hands.

Michel walked to the door and opened it before Black Jack could knock.

"What do you want?" he asked. "Your check? Don't worry, you'll get it. Same as always."

A momentary flash of anger lit his father's eyes, then it was gone.

"I was hoping we could talk," he said.

"Yeah, because that went so well last time," Michel replied.

"I'm sorry about that," Black Jack replied. "I get mean when I drink."

"Well then I guess I won't offer you a cocktail," Michel replied.

He turned and walked to the couch, leaving Black Jack standing in the doorway.

"So talk," Michel said as he sat down.

Black Jack took a few cautious steps inside. Blue growled once, but settled on the floor.

"Mind if I sit down?" Black Jack asked.

"Suit yourself," Michel replied with a shrug.

Black Jack lowered himself stiffly into the chair closest to the door, leaning heavily on its the thick wood arms for support. He settled back and let out a deep sigh.

"The old back locks up on me from time to time," he said.

"Must be all that hard work you've done over the years," Michel replied dryly.

Black Jack let out a small laugh.

"You aren't going to make this easy on me, are you?"

"No, I'm not," Michel replied.

Black Jack nodded resignedly.

"I don't blame you for hating me," he said.

"I don't hate you," Michel replied flatly. "I don't feel anything about you."

It was a lie, but the truth was too complicated to explain, and he didn't feel inclined to share it with his father anyway.

"Okay," Black Jack replied.

He looked down at his scuffed black cowboy boots for a moment, then back at Michel. Michel noticed that his eyes were clear, and his skin appeared less sallow than it had at the Gator's Belly.

"I was sorry to hear about your momma's passing," Black Jack said. "She was a good woman."

"Apparently not good enough," Michel replied.

Black Jack's eyes narrowed and he leaned forward slightly.

"Don't ever say that," he said in a warning tone.

Michel sat back involuntarily. He realized he'd just been reprimanded by his father for the first time in his life. It gave him an odd sensation.

"So then why did you leave?" he asked.

Black Jack looked down again.

"It's complicated," he said.

"Gee, why did I know you were going to say that?" Michel asked sarcastically. "You know what? I've been waiting thirty-three years to hear this. Figure out how to explain it."

Black Jack took a deep breath and looked up at Michel.

"I realized that I'd never be able to make her happy," he said simply.

"Oh, but leaving her alone with a kid to support did?" Michel asked.

Black Jack suddenly came forward in his chair.

"Are you going to keep flapping your lips or are you going to give me a chance to talk?" he asked angrily.

Despite his own anger, Michel realized that his father was right.

"I'm sorry," he said. "Go ahead."

The anger slowly drained from Black Jack's face. He reached into the breast pocket of his black button-down shirt and pulled out a pack of Lucky Strikes.

"Okay if I smoke?" he asked.

"Out on the porch," Michel replied.

*****

Michel leaned against the wall to the left of the door, while Black Jack stood at the top of the steps. He took out a cigarette, then held the pack out to Michel. Michel fought the impulse to take one.

"No, thanks," he said.

"Damn things'll kill you anyway," Black Jack said as he slipped the pack back into his pocket.

He lit his cigarette and took several long drags.

"I imagine your momma told you some stories about me," he said finally.

"Actually no," Michel replied. "In fact, she didn't talk about you at all. But Verle told me some stories."

Michel thought he saw hurt in his father's eyes, but Black Jack just nodded.

"I left home when I was young," he said. "Went off to sow my wild oats for a few years, then moved to New Orleans. That's where I met Vera and started courting her."

"Courting?" Michel asked, amused by the quaintness of the expression.

"Oh yeah," Black Jack replied, nodding his head emphatically. "Your momma required some courting, for sure. She wasn't the type to have her head turned by some smooth talker, handsome as I was. I had to work hard. Took me two weeks to get her to go out on a date, another month before I got my first kiss, and a year before she agreed to marry me."

"Why her?" Michel asked. "Verle said you were a real ladies' man. What made her so special that you were willing to put in all that effort? From what I've heard, perseverance was never one of your strong suits."

"I suppose that's true," Black Jack admitted, "and it's also true I never had any trouble with the ladies, but I fell in love with Vera. And that was the first time."

"The first time?" Michel replied skeptically.

"As God is my witness, and I am a God-fearing man," Black Jack replied with theatrical fervor, holding up his right hand as though swearing an oath. "I was with plenty of women before that, of course, but Vera was the first one I ever loved."

"So what happened?" Michel asked.

"The sadness," Black Jack replied.

He studied Michel for a moment, then nodded.

"I can see by the look in your eyes, you know what I'm talking about," he said.

"I know," Michel replied quietly.

"I guess it was always there," Black Jack said, "but I was too dumb and in love to recognize it, and when I finally did, I was naive or egotistical enough to think I could make it go away. I thought that if I loved her harder and bought her a big house, and gave her a baby, it would finally stop and she'd be happy. That's what I wanted more than anything in the world. To see her happy."

Michel felt his throat tighten and took a deep breath.

"So that's what I tried to do," Black Jack continued. "When we found out she was pregnant, I brought her up to meet your Uncle Lee and Aunt Betty. I still had a twenty-five percent stake in the company at that point and I sold it to Lee so I could buy the house and put some money away."

"So *you* bought her the house?" Michel replied.

Black Jack nodded.

"I even put it in her name so she'd know she had the security, though I've wondered many times since if I didn't do it because I already knew I'd be leaving, but just hadn't admitted it to myself yet."

"But if you loved her that much, how could you leave?" Michel asked.

He almost added, "*I* didn't," but stopped himself. He wasn't ready to reveal too much about his own feelings about his mother yet.

"Frustration. Hurt, I guess," Black Jack replied. "You have to understand, up until that point in my life, everything had come easy. Anything I'd wanted, any*one* I'd wanted, I'd been able to get. But Vera was different. Hell, maybe that's what drew me to her in the first place. I figured if I could get her to love me, it would mean I was special. I suppose that's a pretty selfish thing to say, but that's what I felt."

Michel nodded.

"But after you were born," Black Jack continued, "I realized I was never going to be able to make her happy, and it started to eat away at me. That's the downside of pride, I guess."

"Pride?" Michel asked.

"Maybe you'll understand this, maybe you won't. I don't know you well enough to say," Black Jack said, "but the way I was raised, a man was supposed to be able to take care of things. That's what you did. When I realized I couldn't even make my own wife happy, it hurt my pride. I felt that if I were any kind of man, I should at least be able to do that. Does that make any sense?"

"Yeah, I suppose it..." Michel suddenly stopped and cocked his head to the side, as though listening to distant voices.

Black Jack gave him a curious look.

"You said *after* I was born," Michel said.

Black Jack nodded slowly, warily.

"But you left *before* I was born," Michel replied, though his voice suddenly lacked conviction.

Black Jack stared at him blankly for a moment, then his eyes darkened.

"That's what she told you, is it?" he asked, the question sounding more like a challenge.

Michel gave an uncertain nod. He could see his father's body stiffen, and the flush of anger rising in his cheeks. Then suddenly the storm clouds passed, and Black Jack slumped back against the railing.

"I suppose she had her reasons," he said with a deep sigh, "but let me ask you a question. If I'd left before you were born, why would she have given you my name?"

Michel felt the hairs on the back of his neck prick up. It was a question that had never occurred to him.

"Maybe she thought you'd come back," he offered weakly, though he already knew that his father was telling the truth.

Black Jack shook his head sadly. Michel studied him for a moment, then dropped his gaze to the dusty floorboards. He suddenly felt both embarrassed and ashamed. His willingness to accept his mother's story as a child had been acceptable, but why had he never thought to question it as an adult? He'd wanted to believe that his father had a reason for leaving. He'd wanted an excuse to forgive him. Yet he'd never even tried to find one. Had he been afraid to find out the truth? Afraid that his secret fear would be confirmed, and he'd find that he was the reason his father had left?-

He wondered how much more of what his mother had told him had been a lie, and felt a swell of anger building in the pit of his stomach.

"I wouldn't be too hard on Vera," Black Jack said, as though reading his thoughts. "Maybe she didn't tell you the whole truth, but she told you enough of it. I don't suppose it really matters much when I left."

"Of course it does," Michel replied in a tight voice.

"No, it doesn't," Black Jack replied firmly. "The fact is, I left. I guess I really wasn't much of a man after all. If I had been, I would have stuck it out. But I couldn't. It was like there was a big empty pit inside of Vera, and no matter how much I tried, it was never going to be filled. I guess I finally got scared it was going to swallow me up, too."

They were both quiet for a long moment, then Michel sighed wearily. His anger had subsided, leaving him drained, but he needed to know more.

"Was she happy when I was born?" he asked.

Black Jack saw the fear and hope in his eyes and smiled warmly. "That was the only time I ever saw her feel true joy."

Then his expression turned serious.

"But a week or so later, I started to see the sadness again," he said. "And that's when I knew I had to go."

"Did she ever tell you why she felt sad?" Michel asked.

"I tried to talk to her about it," Black Jack replied, "but she either didn't understand, or pretended she didn't. She got angry. She said I was accusing her of not loving you. She made it real clear I was welcome to leave any time I wanted."

"She kicked you out?" Michel replied.

"No," Black Jack replied. "I left of my own accord, but I knew she wasn't going to lose any sleep over it."

Michel looked down at the porch again. His pulse began racing as he realized it was time to ask the question he'd waited his entire life to ask. He took a few calming breaths.

"But what about me?" he asked finally, trying to control his voice. "I understand why you couldn't stay with her, but why did you leave me, too?"

Black Jack stared at Michel for a few moments before responding.

"I thought you deserved better as a father," he said finally.

"That's not good enough," Michel shot back. "You never even tried."

His eyes began to well up with tears.

"The day you were born was the happiest day of my life," Black Jack said. "You have to believe that. And when I saw how happy your momma was, I figured it was all going to be different from then on. 'Course I was wrong."

"But you didn't have to abandon me, too," Michel replied, his voice breaking. "You could have called, or written, or sent me fucking birthday cards with five-dollar bills stuck in them."

He realized he sounded like a whining child, but he didn't care. The emotions he'd bottled up for so long were all boiling to the surface.

"I was afraid to," Black Jack replied, fighting to control his own voice. "Or maybe I was just too embarrassed."

"But you're my father," Michel replied, his voice rising into a near scream. "You...owed it to me."

Black Jack looked down and shook his head sadly.

"No," he said. "You never had a father. You have my blood, but I was never your father. I was never a father to any of my children."

"What?" Michel replied, stunned. "You have more children?"

Black Jack shrugged.

"Maybe," he said. "I never stuck around to find out."

Whatever sympathy Michel had felt was gone instantly. All he could feel was overwhelming anger. He took a few steps toward his father. Black Jack stood up and squared his shoulders.

"You want to take a poke at me?" he asked with surprise. "Will that help you feel..."

Michel felt the knuckles of his right hand suddenly connect with Black Jack's jaw. Black Jack's knees buckled and he fell back against the railing post. He staggered to his feet unsteadily and rubbed his jaw with his left hand.

"Shit, I'm so sorry," Michel said, shocked by his own action. "I didn't mean to...it just happened."

He reached out to steady Black Jack, but Black Jack pushed his hand away.

"Don't touch me," he said in a low growl.

His face conveyed a mixture of anger and wounded dignity.

"Don't touch me," he repeated, straightening himself up.

He threw his cigarette down on the porch and crushed it out with his boot.

"I came here to explain myself," he said in a hurt tone. "That was all. I didn't deserve that."

He turned and walked quickly down the steps, his whole body rigid.

"Wait," Michel said weakly. "I'm sorry."

He watched helplessly as Black Jack got into his car, gunned the engine, and spun the car around, spraying the base of the porch with dirt and gravel.

Suddenly he felt Blue pressing up against his left leg and looked down. She seemed to be looking back at him with sympathy.

"I fucked up," he said.

Chapter 30

"So what's the matter with you?" Russ Turner asked as he and Michel walked through the dark, silent town green toward Porter DeCew's house.

"What do you mean?" Michel asked half-heartedly.

"You haven't said more than two words since you got to the station," Turner replied.

"Sorry," Michel said. "I'm just a little distracted. Black Jack stopped by the house today and we had another run-in."

"What did he do this time?" Turner asked.

"It wasn't him," Michel replied. "I lost my temper and hit him."

Turner stopped.

"Did he deserve it?"

"Well, in the big picture, yeah probably," Michel replied with a dry laugh, "but not today."

"What did he want?"

"Just to explain why he left."

"Explain or make excuses?" Turner asked.

"Explain," Michel replied.

"Do you want to talk about it?" Turner asked.

"Not really," Michel replied. "I need to think about it for a while."

"Well, do you want to wait until tomorrow to do this?" Turner asked.

"No," Michel replied. "Let's get it over with. It'll give me one less thing to think about."

*****

Porter DeCew opened the door as soon as Michel rang the bell. He was dressed in blue-and-white-striped cotton pajamas, well-worn brown leather slippers, and a pale blue flannel robe.

"I thought I might be seeing you," he said. "Larry called me and told me you'd stopped by his office. Come on in."

Michel noticed that his eyes had lost their usual intensity, and he looked tired.

"I hope it's not too late," Turner said.

"No, I just finished dinner," DeCew replied.

He lead them into a handsome, wood-paneled library to the left of the entry hall.

"Can I get you a drink?" he asked as he walked up to a set of crystal decanters on a shelf along the side wall.

"No, thanks," Turner replied.

"You sure?" DeCew asked. "You don't need to keep your wits about you. I promise I won't try to make a run for it."

Turner smiled. "Yeah, I'm sure."

"Michel?"

"Jack Daniels?" Michel asked.

"Good man," DeCew replied.

He poured an inch of Jack into two tumblers, and gave one to Michel with a slightly trembling hand.

"Please, have a seat," he said, nodding toward a red leather couch in the center of the room.

He settled into a matching chair by the front window and took a sip of his drink.

"I don't think this will take too long," he said. "Larry already filled me in on what you discussed."

"He told us that what happened had nothing to do with the trust," Michel said. "He said it was personal."

DeCew nodded.

"So you were trying to hurt Terry?" Michel asked.

264

"I wasn't trying to hurt him," DeCew replied. "I was trying to help him. I was hoping to break up his marriage."

"Excuse me?" Turner asked.

"I was trying to set him free," DeCew clarified.

Michel and Turner exchanged confused looks.

"I'm sorry, but you've already lost me," Michel said. "How would blackmailing Terry break up his marriage? And why would you want to?"

DeCew took another sip from his drink, then took a cigar and lighter out of his robe pocket.

"I know my son, Michel," he said. "I knew he didn't have that kind of money, and I knew that he'd never steal it from the trust. I assumed his only option would be to ask me for it."

"Okay, I'm with you so far," Michel replied.

"And, of course, I would have given it to him," DeCew continued, "but I would have insisted that he tell Carolyn what happened first. As it turned out, he did that on his own."

"So you were hoping that when Carolyn found out, she'd divorce Terry?" Turner asked.

"Exactly," DeCew replied.

He put the cigar in his mouth and lit it.

"But why?" Michel asked.

"Because Terry deserves a chance to be happy," DeCew replied. "But so long as he stays in that sham marriage, he never will be."

"Because he's gay," Michel said.

"Because he's gay, and because Carolyn will continue to drain the life out of him if he stays."

"That's pretty dramatic, don't you think?" Michel asked.

"Dramatic?" DeCew replied with a harsh laugh. "You didn't know Terry when he was younger. He was confident, vibrant. And over the years I've watched Carolyn chip away at that. He's a shell of what he used to be."

"If that's true, why does he stay with her?" Michel asked.

"Guilt," DeCew replied emphatically. "He believes Carolyn is emotionally fragile because that's what she's convinced him. He's afraid that if he leaves her, she'll fall apart. Maybe kill herself. But she's not fragile. She's manipulative."

Michel thought back to Verle's funeral. Carolyn DeCew's expression of sympathy had been note-perfect despite the lack of emotion on her face. What DeCew had said seemed plausible.

"Have you talked to Terry about it?" he asked.

"I've tried, but he denies it," DeCew replied, shaking his head sadly. "He says that Carolyn is different in private. That she's warm and caring."

"Isn't that possible?" Turner asked.

"I've made my living out of being able to read people," DeCew replied, shaking his head, "and I've seen the way Terry has changed. There's no warmth and caring in Carolyn. Just insecurity and vindictiveness. That's why she still hasn't divorced Terry. Now she has the opportunity to punish him for something legitimate instead of imaginary transgressions."

"But if Terry's been her whipping boy for years, why did you just try to do something about it recently?" Michel asked.

"My stroke," DeCew replied simply. "It made me realize that I might not have much more time left, and that if I was ever going to help Terry, I'd have to do something drastic."

"How did Midland get involved?" Turner asked.

"Larry was aware of my feelings about the marriage," DeCew replied. "He was someone I could talk to because I knew he was sympathetic."

"Because he's in the same situation?" Michel asked.

"Not exactly," DeCew replied. "He and his wife actually have a very loving relationship. They're very close. But he's told me many times over the years that if he could do it all over again, he'd do things differently."

"So who came up with the actual idea?" Turner asked.

"It began by accident," DeCew replied. "When Larry met Donny Heath and asked him about Terry."

He took another sip of his drink.

"When I found out what he'd been doing, it scared me," he continued. "I realized how dangerous it was for Terry. He could have been killed by some stranger at a rest stop. And I also realized how vulnerable it made him."

"To blackmail," Michel said.

DeCew nodded.

"I just wanted to protect him," he said, "and give him a chance at happiness."

He took a meditative puff on his cigar.

"And I don't regret it either," he said after a moment. "I just wish that it had worked."

"Are you planning to tell Terry?" Michel asked.

"I already did," DeCew replied. "As soon as I got off the phone with Larry."

"And?" Turner asked.

"It went about as you'd expect," DeCew replied.

He took another long puff on his cigar and blew the smoke out, watching the cloud swirl in front of him.

"I'm sorry," Michel said. "I feel like a lot of this is my fault. If I hadn't been searching for conspiracies, Terry would never have found out."

"You were just trying to protect Verle's legacy," DeCew replied. "I understand that. Though I do wish you'd come to me when you found out about the Hotel Monteleone."

"Would you like me to try talking with him?" Michel offered. "I feel like I owe him an apology, too, anyway."

"I don't know that it'll do any good," DeCew replied, "but you can try. I imagine he's probably still at the office. He spends most of his time there since Carolyn found out about Donny."

"I'll give it a shot," Michel replied.

"You want me to go with you?" Turner asked.

"No, thanks. I think this calls for a homo-to-homo chat," Michel replied. "I'm afraid you're playing for the wrong team."

Turner smiled and nodded.

"Then if you don't mind, Porter, I think I'll have that drink now," he said.

Chapter 30

The third floor of the old courthouse was dark except for the light coming from the half-open door at the end of the hallway. As Michel pushed the door fully open, he could see Terry sitting at one of the desks in the reception area. He was staring at the floor, a half-empty pint bottle of Dewars in front of him.

"Terry?" Michel said gently.

Terry looked up. His eyes were unfocused for a moment, then cleared.

"What the fuck do you want?" he asked coldly.

"To talk," Michel replied.

"I have nothing to talk to you about," Terry replied flatly. "Leave me alone."

Michel took a step into the room.

"Terry, I'm really sorry about what happened," he said. "I didn't mean to create more problems for you."

Terry stared at him uncomprehendingly for a few seconds, then laughed. It was a dark, pained laugh.

"Don't worry, it wasn't your fault," he said. "Play with fire and you get burned."

From his slow, deliberate speech and the slight wobble of his head, it was obvious he was far drunker than he should have been on a half pint of Scotch. Michel looked around and saw another empty pint bottle on the floor next to the desk.

"I think maybe you should take it easy on the Scotch," he said carefully.

"Fuck you," Terry replied, then lifted the bottle on his desk and took a long swig.

He put the bottle down hard, then opened the desk drawer and took out a pack of Marlboros. He felt his pockets, then began rummaging through the papers on the top of the desk.

"I have a light," Michel said.

He walked to the desk and took out his lighter. He flicked it and held it out while Terry tried to steady the cigarette long enough to get it lit.

"Thanks," Terry said finally, sitting back and holding the cigarette awkwardly between his index and middle fingers.

"I didn't know you smoke," Michel said.

"I don't," Terry said, then took a long drag and blew the smoke at Michel. He giggled and closed his eyes for a second.

"You know, my father is wrong," he said suddenly, his eyes snapping open. "I'm not the victim. Carolyn is the victim, because she trusted me and believed in me, and I betrayed her."

"But your marriage is built on a lie," Michel replied.

"There's no lie," Terry said, looking at Michel with exaggerated contempt. "Carolyn knows I'm gay. She's always known I'm gay."

"What?"

"I said she's always known I'm gay," Terry replied. "Pay attention."

"But if she knew you were gay, why did she marry you?" Michel asked.

"To save me," Terry replied dramatically.

"From what?"

"Myself," Terry replied.

Then he closed his eyes again and took another drag of his cigarette. He snaked his head slowly from side to side as he exhaled, as though listening to a silent rhythm.

"You know, I was in love once," he said without opening his eyes. "With a man. For almost a year."

270

"What happened?" Michel asked.

"One night I was supposed to meet him at a bar in Atlanta," Terry replied in a dreamy voice. "He got there early, and on his way in some rednecks grabbed him and beat him to death with a crowbar."

He opened his eyes and smiled. Michel was stunned into momentary silence.

"I'm sorry," he managed finally.

"Why? You didn't do it," Terry replied. "Did you?"

He stared at Michel expectantly, as though waiting for a genuine response.

"Of course not," Michel replied.

"I didn't think so," Terry replied.

He took another drag from his cigarette.

"That's when I came here and met Carolyn," he said through a plume of smoke. "I figured it would be safe here, but no place is really safe. At least not when you don't really want it to be."

"What does that mean?" Michel asked.

Terry sat forward suddenly.

"It means you can find danger any place you want it," he said, punctuating each word by poking the air with his cigarette. "And I found plenty of it."

He sat back again, took a swig of Scotch, and smiled lecherously. Michel felt as though he were watching a nervous breakdown in progress.

"But Carolyn tried to save me," Terry said, nodding. "She became my friend. Yes, she did. She's a good woman. She offered me comfort and love, and I decided that maybe passion wasn't so important after all, so I asked her to marry me. I figured that would keep me safe."

"But it didn't," Michel replied.

"Of course not," Terry replied with a casual shake of the head. "We want what we want."

His eyes suddenly became serious, and he stared at Michel for a moment.

"I hate her," he said finally.

"What? Why?" Michel asked, confused.

"Because she's so fucking forgiving," Terry replied, spitting out each word. "It's pathetic. What more do I have to do to her? Her and my father and Verle. So fucking forgiving."

"Because they love you," Michel replied.

"If they loved me, they'd leave me alone," Terry said.

He took a final drag on his cigarette, then stubbed it out on the top of the desk.

"So what's it like?" he asked.

"What?" Michel replied. "Being openly gay?"

"No. Being happy about it," Terry replied.

"You're not happy about being gay?"

"Why would I be happy about it?" Terry replied disdainfully. "It's a sickness."

Again Michel was momentarily shocked into silence. Terry studied him as though he were an exhibit in a museum, then laughed.

"My father says he wants me to be happy," he said. "If he really wants me to be happy, he should buy me a fucking gun."

"You really think killing yourself is the solution?" Michel asked. "Think about the pain you'll cause your father and Carolyn."

Terry cocked his head and regarded Michel curiously.

"Why would I kill myself?" he asked. "I'd kill Carolyn."

Then he burst into near-hysterical laughter.

Michel put his hands in the center of the desk and leaned in close to Terry.

"Terry, if I find out you so much as touch her, I swear I'll kill you myself," he said.

Terry's laughter died immediately and he wilted back into his chair.

"I was just kidding," he said with a childish pout.

*****

Michel walked out of the old courthouse, the cigarette he'd taken from Terry's pack already pressed between his lips. He took out his lighter.

"You sure you want to do that?" Russ Turner asked.

Michel jumped nervously. He turned and saw Turner leaning against the wall to the left of the door.

"Seems like I haven't seen you smoke in a few days," Turner said.

Michel took the cigarette out of his mouth and stared at it for a moment, then threw it on the stairs.

"That's littering, you know," Turner said, pushing himself off the wall.

"So write me a ticket," Michel replied.

"I take it things didn't go so well," Turner said.

"I think it's time for me to go home," Michel replied. "You've got some sick, twisted people in this town."

"Terry?" Turner replied with surprise.

"You have no idea."

"Worse than Donny?"

"Oh please," Michel replied with a weary laugh. "They're like night and...earlier in the night."

Chapter 31

Michel finally got up just before 5 AM, after lying awake most of the night. Once he'd made the decision to go back to New Orleans, his mind had been crowded with the details of what he needed to do before he left: packing; cleaning out the refrigerator; bringing in the porch furniture; turning off the water; closing up the house; saying goodbye to Ruby, Cyrus, and Russ; meeting with Porter DeCew He realized he also needed to see his father again, but decided he'd do that last.

"You ready to go to your new home today?" he asked when Blue walked into the bedroom.

She just stared at him with her tongue hanging out the right side of her mouth.

"It won't be that bad," Michel said. "I promise. You can hunt rats in the back yard."

He stood up and stretched. He felt even better than he had the previous morning, despite his lack of sleep.

"What do you say we get some coffee, take a shower, and then go visit Ruby?" Michel asked.

Blue's tail began to wag, then she ran out of the room.

"Not yet," Michel called after her. "I said we had to have coffee and take a shower first."

*****

As Michel walked around the final bend in the path, he saw a rusted white pickup parked in front of Ruby's cabin.

Shit, he thought.

He looked around, hoping Ruby would be somewhere in the yard.

"What do you think?" he asked Blue. "Should we risk it? I really don't want to have to come back later."

Blue looked at him for a few seconds, then started toward the cabin.

"I guess that's a yes," Michel said.

He walked to the front door and knocked twice. A few seconds later the door flew open. Rudy was standing in the doorway, cradling her shotgun.

"Oh, it's you," she said, then looked over Michel's shoulder as if making sure he was alone.

"I'm sorry, is this a bad time?" Michel asked.

"Why would it be a bad time?" Ruby replied, eyeing him suspiciously. "You think I'm up to somethin' I shouldn't be?"

"No," Michel replied quickly, "but I saw the truck and figured you had company."

Ruby gave him a challenging look.

"Why? You think I can't drive?" she asked. "You think Verle had to drive me everywhere?"

"No, it's just that I've never seen it before," Michel replied defensively.

"Well it's been here," Ruby replied. "I just usually keep it up closer to the road so it doesn't make the yard look messy."

Michel fought the urge to laugh given that Ruby's yard was just a cleared patch of dirt.

"So you come to say goodbye?" Ruby asked.

"Yeah."

"That's what I figured," Ruby said, nodding. "Come on in."

She stepped away from the door and waited impatiently for Michel and Blue to walk in, then immediately closed the door.

Michel stood in the near-darkness, waiting for his eyes to adjust. The only light in the room filtered in around the sides of the drawn shades on three windows. He was struck by the rich, musty smell of the air. It reminded him of an old library.

Finally his eyes began to adjust and he could make out the basic shapes in the room: a single bed along the back wall, an upholstered chair and side table holding a lamp in the left front corner, and an upright piano along the right wall between two doorways. In the back right corner were two stacks of boxes that looked to be in the process of collapsing toward the bed, and filling the rest of the available floor space were dozens of small piles of books.

"So'd you prove Verle was innocent?" Ruby asked.

"Huh?" Michel replied, turning to see her staring at him expectantly.

"That's what you stayed up here for, wasn't it?" she asked. "I figured if you were leaving, it meant you'd proved it."

Michel felt a pang of guilt. He hadn't been able to prove Verle's innocence, but knew it was time to go anyway.

"I thought I had, but I was wrong," he said. "I'm afraid the State Police will have to handle it now."

Ruby nodded, but Michel thought he saw a hint of disapproval in her eyes.

"So you all packed up?" she asked.

"Yeah, I didn't bring all that much with me when I came up," Michel replied. "I didn't think I'd be here this long."

Ruby nodded.

"You clean out the ice box?" she asked. "You wouldn't want to leave anything in there. Next time you come up, it wouldn't smell too good."

"It's on my list," Michel replied.

"Okay," Ruby said. "Like I said before, I'll check on the place from time to time. Make sure nothing happens to it."

"Are you sure you don't want to move in there?" Michel asked, looking around. "There's a lot more room."

"No," Ruby replied firmly. "I've got all my stuff here, and I know where everything is. No sense in having to organize it all over again."

Again Michel had to fight the urge to laugh.

"So then you'll be taking the dog?" Ruby asked abruptly.

"Yeah, I'm sorry," Michel replied. "I've gotten pretty attached to her."

"No need to be sorry," Ruby said. "Just look after her."

She squatted down.

"Come here, sweetheart," she said in a sweet, girlish voice.

Blue walked over and pushed the top of her head against Ruby's left knee. Ruby began scratching her under the chin with her left hand while stroking the top of Blue's head with her right.

"I'm going to miss you, girl," she said. "Yes I will. You gonna miss me?"

Blue leaned harder into Ruby's knee.

"You be a good girl and come back to visit me soon. Okay?"

She kissed Blue gently on the side of her face, then slowly stood up. Michel could see that she was trying hard not to show any emotion.

"Well, then I guess that's it," she said, thrusting her right hand out.

Michel looked at it for a moment. He wanted to give Ruby a hug, but from her rigid posture it was obvious it would be unwelcome. Finally he reached out and took her hand.

"Thanks for looking after Blue for me," he said. "Hopefully we'll be back up to visit before too long."

"That'd be nice," Ruby replied, and for a split second Michel thought he saw a break in her stoic expression.

Then it was gone. She let go of Michel's hand and opened the door.

"You have a nice trip," she said without emotion.

*****

277

"That was oddly unsatisfying," Michel said to Blue as they started back down the trail. "I thought that Ruby and I had kind of a connection going on."

Chapter 32

"Is it okay if Blue comes in?" Michel asked.

"I don't imagine the health department'll be stopping by any time soon," Cyrus replied dryly.

"Come on, girl," Michel said, holding the door open.

Blue took a few cautious steps inside the store and began furiously sniffing the air. Then she looked at Michel, turned around, and hurried back outside.

"Come on, Blue," Michel cajoled.

Blue looked back over her right shoulder at him, then sat down on the sidewalk.

"I expect she'll be okay out there," Cyrus said. "You can leave the door open if you want."

"Thanks," Michel replied.

He propped the door open with the rock that was obviously intended for that purpose, and walked up to the counter.

"I'm not sure what that was all about," he said.

"Dogs are naturally cautious about unfamiliar things and places," Cyrus said. "Sometimes they just smell something that doesn't strike them as right."

"I hope she doesn't smell anything like that at my house," Michel replied.

"You going back to New Orleans?" Cyrus asked with a disappointed look.

"Yeah," Michel replied. "It's time, but I wanted to stop in and say goodbye. And also to thank you for the porterhouse. Blue and I both enjoyed it."

"I'm glad to hear that," Cyrus replied. "Especially since Miss Evans gave me holy hell when she showed up looking for it that afternoon and found out I'd sold it. I swear that woman's getting more senile every day. Claimed she never called and told me she was sick."

"Sorry about that," Michel replied.

"No need to be," Cyrus replied with a chuckle. "She ordered two more just so she could punish me."

He reached under the counter.

"Well, if you're leaving, then I guess I have a going-away present for you, though you're going to have to pay for it."

He pulled up a bright yellow carton of American Spirit Lights and placed it on the counter.

"These the right ones?" he asked, arching his eyebrows.

Michel managed a smile.

"Those are right ones," he said.

"So you want a pack?" Cyrus asked, obviously very pleased with himself.

Michel didn't have the heart to disappoint him.

"Tell you what," he said. "Since I have a feeling you're not going to sell too many of those to anyone else, I'll take the whole carton."

"I was kind of hoping you'd say that," Cyrus replied, pumping his bony fist once.

He opened the cash register and took out a pile of receipts.

"Let's see," he said as he started thumbing through them. "Oh yeah, here we go. Looks like $48.00. 'Course that's the wholesale price."

He peered at Michel over the top of his glasses with basset hound eyes. It took Michel a few seconds to realize that the old man was waiting for him to make an offer.

"Oh, well back home those would run me $6.50 a pack," he said. "So how about we say $6.00 each? That way I save a little, and you make a little profit."

"I suppose that'll be okay," Cyrus replied with a hint of disappointment, then a mirthful sparkle lit his eyes and he shrugged. "I probably would have been willing to split the difference with you, but it's your money."

Michel gave a comic scowl, but pulled out his wallet.

"You're lucky I remembered to stop at the bank," he said.

He counted out three $20 bills.

"And how much did I owe you for the other day?"

"$18.50," Cyrus replied without hesitation.

Michel realized the old man was a lot sharper than he let on. He suspected that checking the cigarette receipt had just been for show, part of Cyrus' doddering-old-man act to lull customers before he gouged them. He decided that playing poker with Cyrus would be a mistake.

He handed Cyrus another twenty.

"And don't think I'm not going to count my change," he said.

Cyrus smiled as he handed Michel the change, then he turned his crooked hand sideways.

"It was a pleasure to meet you, Michel," he said.

"Thank you. You, too, Cyrus," Michel said as he shook the old man's hand. "And hopefully I'll see you again soon."

"I'm not planning to go anywhere," Cyrus replied, "so I expect you will."

*****

Michel looked down the block toward the police station. Russ Turner's car wasn't there.

"Then I guess we'll go see Porter," he said to Blue.

He started walking in the other direction, hoping that Terry wouldn't be in the office.

Chapter 33

"So what exactly did you say to Terry last night?" Porter DeCew asked as Michel and Blue walked into his office.

"Why?"

"Because Carolyn called me first thing this morning. She said that Terry got home last night and asked her for a divorce."

"Lucky her," Michel replied.

DeCew gave him a surprised look.

"I don't want to go into it," Michel said, "but I think you misjudged Carolyn. It wasn't her making Terry miserable."

DeCew frowned.

"I have to admit I was surprised by how she sounded on the phone," he said. "She seemed genuinely heartbroken, and concerned for Terry. She said Terry was planning to move out, and asked if he could stay with me so I could look after him."

Michel nodded.

"That doesn't surprise me," he said. "From what Terry said, she really loves him. But I think it'll be better for both of them if they divorce."

DeCew studied Michel for a moment.

"It sounds like I need to talk to Terry," he said finally.

"I'm not sure he's ready for that yet," Michel replied. "He said a lot of things last night while he was drunk that I don't think he'd have said otherwise. He's pretty conflicted. I actually think it might be better for him to talk to a professional."

"A pyschiatrist?"

"Or a psychologist," Michel replied. "I don't think he needs

282

any drugs. Just someone objective to talk to who can help him deal with some issues."

DeCew nodded.

"Whatever will help," he said. "So what can I do for you?"

"I wanted to talk to you about Verle's estate. I'd like you to continue handling whatever bills come in."

"Okay," DeCew replied. "What about his assets?"

"I'm fine with whatever you recommend," Michel replied. "I'd like to keep the house, and Ruby's place, and wherever my father is living. Beyond that, whatever you think is best."

"I'll put together a proposal and we can go over it tomorrow," DeCew said.

"You'll have to send it to me," Michel replied. "I'm heading back to New Orleans tonight."

"Oh," DeCew replied. "I didn't realize you were leaving so soon."

"I just decided last night," Michel replied. "Now that I know there was no conspiracy to frame Verle, there's really no reason to stay. It's up to the State Police now."

"I'm sure they'll figure it out," DeCew replied reassuringly.

"I hope so," Michel replied.

He held out his hand to DeCew.

"So I guess I'll be talking to you soon," he said, "and I hope everything works out with Terry."

"Thank you," DeCew replied. "It was nice to finally meet Verle's famous cousin."

"Thanks," Michel replied with a small laugh.

"One last thing before you go," DeCew said. "How would you feel about being on the Board? The trust's bylaws state that we're supposed to have at least three trustees. I think it would make sense if you were the third since you own the land."

"You should probably get back to me after you run that idea by Terry, but yeah, I'd be willing," Michel replied. "I think that would be nice."

*****

Michel tossed the carton of cigarettes onto the back seat and took out his cell phone. He punched in Russ Turner's number.

"Hey, where are you?" he asked when Turner answered.

"Car accident out on Bayou Road," Turner replied. "It's almost cleaned up now, so I should be back to town in about a half hour. Why, what's up?"

"I'm going to be heading back to New Orleans," Michel replied. "I wanted to say goodbye."

"So you weren't kidding last night when you said it was time to get out of town," Turner replied.

"Not even a little," Michel replied. "I'd like to say goodbye to Corey, too. Would it be okay if I came by the house around five? Blue and I can just leave from there."

"Sure. You want to stay for dinner?"

"Thanks, but I'd like to get back early. I'm going to have to stop at the market when we get home."

"Okay. Then I'll see you around 5."

"Oh, one more thing," Michel said. "Where does my father live?"

Chapter 34

The five cabins were located at the end of a short dirt road. As he stepped out of his car, Michel could see the Gator's Belly about a hundred yards down a narrow path that ran through the trees to the right. Well, isn't that convenient, he thought.

Black Jack's car was parked in front of the middle cabin. Michel walked to the door and rapped on the wood frame of the screen door. A few seconds later, Black Jack appeared. He was wearing a baggy, ribbed white tank top and black jeans with the top button undone. When he saw Michel, his eyes narrowed and his expression grew cold.

"What do you want?" he growled. "You here to punch out an old man again?"

"I'm sorry," Michel replied. "You were right. You didn't deserve that. I just want to talk."

Black Jack gave him a wary look, but then pushed open the screen door and stepped aside, gesturing for Michel to come in.

The first thing Michel noticed was the overwhelming smell of stale cigarette smoke. The second thing he noticed was that the small room was surprisingly neat and clean.

"So did it make you feel any better?" Black Jack asked.

"Huh?"

"Punching me. Did it make you feel any better?"

Michel thought about it for a moment.

"Actually, I think it did," he replied.

"Good, but you don't need to feel any better again, okay?" Black Jack replied with a sly smile.

285

Michel remembered what his mother had said about his father having his charms. He decided she was right.

"I really am sorry," he said. "It was just that when you said you have other children you'd abandoned, it kind of pushed me over the edge."

"There are no other children," Black Jack said. "I just said that. I thought that maybe you wouldn't feel so bad if you thought you weren't the only one I'd run out on."

"That's kind of perverse," Michel replied.

Black Jack nodded.

"And obviously stupid," he added, rubbing his jaw. "So what more did you want to talk about?"

Michel considered it for a moment. He didn't want to rehash Black Jack's reasons for leaving.

"I understand why you left," he said. "I know what you mean about the sadness, and I can see why it was hard for you. And I guess I also think that you deserved a chance at being happy. But I don't understand how you could just walk away from your child. From me."

Black Jack looked down at the floor, then frowned.

"Like I said before, I was scared and embarrassed," he said.

"It was cowardly," Michel replied.

"It was," Black Jack replied, looking up, "but I knew I couldn't stay in New Orleans. Every time I saw you or your momma, it would have reminded me that I'd failed. So I figured I'd just run away from it all."

"Did it work?" Michel asked.

"No," Black Jack replied. "When I left, something inside me just sort of broke. The fact that I left made me feel like more of a failure, and everything just kept feeding into everything else. It took a long time before I felt like myself again, and by that point, so many years had gone past that I was afraid to see you."

"But you could have written or called," Michel replied. "Just something so I'd know that I still had a father."

"I visited Lee from time to time," Black Jack replied. "He told me about your visits to the farm. It sounded like you were happy. I figured you didn't need me anymore."

Michel thought about saying that the only times he *had* been truly happy were at the farm, but decided against it.

"Where did you go?" he asked instead.

"Europe mostly."

"Why Europe?"

"Because it was far away from New Orleans, and because there were a lot of rich women there," Black Jack replied.

"You were a gigolo?" Michel asked with disbelief.

"I was a companion," Black Jack corrected. "A companion for women whose husbands had a lot of money but too little time for their wives. I gave them the attention their husbands didn't."

"That's kind of ironic, don't you think?" Michel asked.

"I suppose," Black Jack replied, "but maybe it was fitting. Maybe it was some sort of karmic retribution. I couldn't make my own wife happy, so I was sentenced to a life making the wives of other men happy."

Michel nodded. He realized his father was a lot more intelligent and introspective than he'd seemed.

"Did you enjoy it?" he asked.

"For a while," Black Jack replied wistfully. "I met some nice ladies, got to go places, and do things I'd never imagined. But eventually it just became another job. Then my looks started to go and I couldn't meet the rich ones anymore, so I came here."

They were both quiet for a few moments.

"Russ Turner said the rumor is that you blackmailed Verle into letting you live here, and that he was paying you to stay away from me," Michel said finally. "Is that true?"

"That was just a story I told to make myself look like a big man at the bar," Black Jack replied, looking down. "I didn't want anyone knowing that Verle was taking care of me out of

287

pity. Verle never tried to keep me away from you. In fact, he offered to invite you up here."

Good old Verle, Michel thought.

"If I hadn't come up to you at the Gator's Belly, would you have tried to find me while I was in town?" he asked.

Black Jack nodded.

"Just to see how you turned out. But I don't know as I would have talked to you."

"Why not?"

"You think I wanted you to see me like this?" Black Jack asked. "A broken-down old drunk living on handouts from family? I'd rather you just thought I was dead."

They were both quiet again, then Black Jack looked at his watch.

"I need to take my pills," he said. "Nothing serious. Just to keep everything running regular. You want something to drink?"

"No, thanks," Michel replied.

He watched his father go into the tiny kitchen, fill a glass from the dish drainer, and take his medication. He suddenly realized that his father's stomach was more pronounced than it had appeared before, and that he was moving more easily.

"Can I ask you a personal question?" Michel asked.

"You mean what we've been talking about isn't personal?" Black Jack replied with a wry smile.

"Different kind of personal," Michel replied.

Black Jack studied him for a second, then nodded.

"Go ahead."

"Do you usually wear a girdle?" Michel asked.

"It's not a girdle," Black Jack replied quickly. "It's a back support."

"Then why is it you walk so much better without it?" Michel asked.

Black Jack opened his mouth to reply, then stopped and let out a self-deprecating laugh.

"That's just our little secret, okay?" he said.

"Okay," Michel agreed, "but is it really worth walking like Frankenstein just so people don't know you have a gut?"

"Probably not," Black Jack replied, "but at this point, my looks are all I have going for me."

He gave Michel an ironic smile. Michel smiled back, then looked around the room.

"I have to admit, this place is a lot nicer than I'd expected," he said. "I was picturing sort of a tenement full of crackheads."

"Thanks," Black Jack replied with mock offense.

"Aside from the obvious proximity to the Gator's Belly, though, it's kind of remote," Michel said. "Does anyone else live out here?"

"Chappy, the bartender at the Gator, and Lou and Frenchie, the cooks," Black Jack replied.

"I guess that makes sense," Michel said.

"And it wasn't always remote," Black Jack said. "There used to be a trading post out here, down along the bayou next to the old Gator's Belly. When the bayou got too shallow for the bigger boats, it got turned into a hunting lodge and they built the cabins."

"What happened to the lodge?" Michel asked.

"It got washed away in the same storm that took the old Gator's Belly," Black Jack replied.

"Hmmm," Michel replied. "Seems like kind of a random place for Verle to buy, though."

"Not really," Black Jack replied. "He already owned the Gator. Made sense to have a place for the help to live. He let them live here for free."

"What?" Michel said. "I didn't see the Gator's Belly listed in his assets."

"And you wouldn't," Black Jack replied. "At least not directly. It's owned through a holding company."

"How long did he own it?" Michel asked.

"Since Lee died," Black Jack replied. "It's been in the family since 1882."

"Are you serious?" Michel asked incredulously.

"Your great grandfather bought it just after he started the logging company," Black Jack explained. "He figured that if there were going to be a bunch of hungry, thirsty loggers out here, he might as well be the one to feed them and get them liquored up. But he didn't want anyone to know it was him, so he created the holding company."

"Why didn't he want people to know?"

"Cause then they'd realize he was paying them at the end of every day and taking the money right back out of their pockets every night."

"So he really was kind of a carpetbagger, wasn't he?" Michel asked.

"Well, we always preferred to think of him as a shrewd businessman," Black Jack replied dryly.

"Wow, so I own a bar," Michel said excitedly. "How cool is that? But why didn't Russ or Porter mention that to me?"

"Russ probably doesn't know," Black Jack replied. "Not too many people do. Not even the folks who work there. It's always been sort of a family secret. Verle decided to keep it that way because he figured people would stop going if they knew he owned it."

Michel felt a stab of sadness.

"It's too bad people didn't know how much Verle did for them," he said.

Black Jack nodded.

"But that's the way he wanted it," he said. "He didn't want people thinking he was trying to buy them."

Michel suddenly wished he could stay and talk more with his father. He realized there was a lot about his family he'd never known. He took a deep breath and let it out.

"I'm heading back to New Orleans tonight," he said.

"I'm sorry to hear that," Black Jack said. "I was hoping maybe we could spend some more time together. Get to know each other a little."

"I'm gay," Michel said abruptly.

Like the punch, it had been completely unexpected, but this time he felt his own knees buckle a little.

Black Jack stared at him without expression for a moment, then nodded his head.

"That's okay," he said. "I've known quite a few gay people over the years. I don't have a problem with that. Did your momma know?"

"I never told her, but she knew," Michel replied. "I found out reading a letter she wrote to Verle."

"I don't imagine she had a problem with it," Black Jack replied. "In fact she always seemed to be drawn to gay people."

"Really?" Michel asked.

Black Jack nodded.

"I remember there was one who lived not too far from the house," he said, "though I don't know if technically you'd have called him gay since he dressed as a lady."

"Lady Chanel?" Michel asked.

"That's the one," Black Jack said with a nod. "Lady Chanel. He still around?"

"No," Michel replied sadly.

"That too bad," Black Jack replied with what seemed like genuine sadness. "He and your momma were kind of close. In fact, your momma used to always say that he was the most elegant woman she'd ever met. I kept reminding her that he wasn't a real lady, but Vera insisted that he was more of a lady than anyone she'd ever known. I always thought that was kind of funny, but I suppose it could have been true."

Michel smiled.

"Yes, it was."

"So do you dress up like that?" Black Jack asked.

"Never," Michel replied with a laugh.

"You got a fella waiting for you back home?"

"Yeah, I guess I do," Michel replied.

"You guess?"

Michel shrugged noncommittally.

"Seems to me you either do or you don't," Black Jack replied.

Michel almost said, "It's complicated," but stopped himself, realizing the irony of the situation.

"He's waiting for me," he said instead, "but I'm not sure I can make him happy."

"Does he carry the sadness?" Black Jack asked.

Michel shook his head. "Not even a little."

"Then I think you'll do all right," Black Jack replied.

He held out his hand to Michel. Michel shook his head. He took a step forward and put his arms around his father's shoulders. Black Jack hesitated for a few seconds, then wrapped his arms around Michel's back and embraced him tightly.

"I'm sorry," he said.

"I know," Michel said, struggling to control his emotions, "but don't get me started. I don't like crying in front of other people."

He felt his father's body shaking, and heard him take a deep breath.

"Me neither," Black Jack said, his voice breaking.

They held each for almost a minute, then let go and each took a step back.

"All right, that went pretty well," Michel said with a sigh.

"Yeah, it did," Black Jack replied, wiping his eyes. "So can I call you sometime?"

"Yeah," Michel replied.

He took out his wallet and handed his father a card.

"The cell phone is the best way to reach me."

"Okay," Black Jack replied.

They walked to the door.

"I'll be in touch," Black Jack said. "I promise."

"You better," Michel replied, "because now I know where you live."

He stepped out into the late afternoon sun. A familiar feeling came over him. It was the same feeling he'd had as a child when he'd had to leave the farm. This time, however, he knew he wanted to come back.

He walked to the car and took out his keys, then looked back at his father.

"By the way, you ever find any of Verle's buried treasure?" Black Jack asked from the doorway.

"What are you talking about?" Michel replied with a disbelieving laugh.

"Oh, it's just some nonsense around town," Black Jack replied with an amused smile. "People think that Verle was some kind of survivalist living out there by himself. Some of the locals said they saw him digging holes in the yard at night, and rumor got around that he was burying money out there."

"Did anyone ever try looking for it?" Michel asked.

"Doubtful," Black Jack replied. "People were afraid of Verle. They stayed clear of his place. But maybe now that it's going to be empty, some of them might start snooping around. I could check in on it from time to time if you like."

"Actually Ruby said she'd keep an eye on it, so..." Michel suddenly stopped and stared hard at the ground.

"What's the matter?" Black Jack asked with concern.

"I need you to do me a favor," Michel said quickly.

"What?"

"I need you to look after your niece for a little while."

"My what?"

"Blue," Michel said.

He opened the door and Blue jumped out. She looked at Black Jack curiously. Black Jack looked back at her nervously.

"I don't know," he said.

"Don't worry, she won't hurt you," Michel replied. "Just don't smoke around her."

"But she makes me nervous, and I always smoke when I'm nervous," Black Jack

"Deal with it," Michel replied. "Please."

Black Jack looked at Blue suspiciously for a few moments, then nodded.

"All right," he said. "I guess it'll be all right. Just don't be too long."

"Thank you," Michel said.

He knelt down and scratched Blue behind the ears.

"I'll be back soon," he said. "You be a good girl, and don't eat your great uncle."

*****

Michel got in the car and dialed Russ Turner's number.

"Change of plans," he said.

Chapter 35

"Why did Verle have to build his house so far from the road?" Turner whispered. "I'm afraid I'm going to trip over a rock and bust my head open."

"I'm afraid something's going to jump out and rip my face off," Michel whispered back.

The roof of the house appeared through the trees, glowing in the moonlight.

"What if you're wrong?" Turner asked.

"Then I guess we're going to sit and wait for no one all night long," Michel replied.

They walked another twenty feet, staying in the shadows along the right edge of the driveway, then Michel stopped. Turner almost stumbled into him from behind.

"You hear that?" Michel asked.

"What?" Turner asked.

"It sounded like a shovel hitting a rock to me," Michel replied.

They listened for a few seconds, then started toward the house again.

They were almost to the yard when Turner put his hand on Michel's back to stop him.

"I can hear it now," he whispered. "That's definitely digging."

Suddenly a beam of light illuminated the trees along the left side of the house. It bounced up and down for a few seconds, then disappeared.

"How do you want to do this?" Michel asked, turning to face Turner. "You want me to circle around behind the house?"

Turner shook his head.

"Too much deadfall back there. They'd be able to hear the branches cracking in town. I say we stick together. You cover and I'll cuff."

"Okay," Michel replied.

As they approached the corner of the house, the sound of digging grew louder and they could see a faint glow across the ground. They pressed their backs up against the house and drew their guns. Turner waved Michel forward and they both stepped around the corner.

Ruby was standing fifteen feet away, with her back to them. An old camping lamp rested on the ground to her right, its beam pointed down at the hole she was digging. There were three holes behind her, each with a dirt-caked mason jar next to it. Turner nodded to his right. Michel looked and saw a metal detector and shotgun resting against the side of the house.

"All right, Ruby," Turner called out. "Drop the shovel and turn around slowly."

Ruby froze with the shovel in mid-descent.

"You aren't going to shoot me now, are you, Sheriff Turner?" she asked.

"Not unless I have to," Turner replied firmly. "Now drop the shovel and turn around."

Ruby's hands came down slowly until the point of the shovel's blade rested on the ground, then she let go of the handle and the shovel fell to her left.

"Now turn around slowly," Turner said.

Ruby lifted her hands out to her sides and slowly turned.

"That's good," Turner said. "Now step away from the hole."

Ruby stared at him calmly, then took three steps forward.

"That's good right there," Turner said, holding up his left hand. "Now lock your hands together on top of your head."

"Whatever you say, Sheriff," Ruby replied.

Michel realized there was something different about her voice. It was harder, and the accent had changed.

"You have her?" Turner asked, looking quickly at Michel.

Michel pulled back the slide on his Smith & Wesson, then sighted it on Ruby's chest.

"I've got her," he said.

Turner holstered his gun and took the handcuffs from their belt case. He approached Rudy, staying a few feet to her right. Ruby watched him without turning her head, then looked at Michel.

"You ever shot anyone before, sissy boy?" she asked with a smirk.

Michel felt suddenly apprehensive.

"Shut the fuck up, you crazy bitch," he replied.

Ruby laughed in response. It was a deeper, throatier laugh than usual, and it made Michel even more anxious.

Turner circled behind Ruby. He reached up and cuffed her left hand, then brought it down behind her back. Suddenly Ruby stepped into him hard and threw her head back, hitting him in the chin. Turner stumbled backward with a grunt, his right foot falling into the hole behind him. Ruby was on him in a split second, knocking him to the ground and pinning his arms with her knees. She grabbed the shovel and lifted it above her head like a spear.

"Stop!" Michel yelled. "I swear to God I'll shoot you."

Ruby stopped with the blade of the shovel poised high above Turner's face. She twisted her head to look at Michel and smiled, then turned away and drove the shovel down.

Michel fired two shots into Ruby's upper back. The impact knocked her forward and the shovel's blade dug into the ground a foot above Turner's head. Turner rolled quickly to his right, throwing Ruby onto her back, then scrambled to his feet.

"Jesus fuck!" he said, trying to catch his breath.

Michel ran up beside him and pointed his gun at Ruby. She was conscious, still holding the handle of the shovel in her left hand. Michel kicked it away.

"Are you all right?" he asked Turner.

"Barely," Turner replied.

He looked down at Ruby. She coughed twice and blood began spilling from the sides of her mouth. She made what seemed like an attempt at a smile, then closed her eyes.

"As much as I'd like to let her die," Turner said, "we'd better call an ambulance."

Chapter 35

The lights in the cabin were on when Michel pulled up just after midnight. He walked to the screen door and looked in. Black Jack was asleep on the couch, with Blue lying between his legs, her head resting on his right thigh. When she saw Michel, she lifted her head and started sweeping the couch with her tail.

Michel let himself in.

"Were you a good girl?" he whispered as he crossed the room.

He scratch the top of Blue's head and her tail began moving more quickly.

"I'm sure you were," Michel said.

He leaned over and kissed her on the nose, then gently touched his father on the shoulder.

"Jack," he said softly. "Wake up."

Black Jack opened his eyes with a start and looked around in confusion for a moment. Then he looked up and saw Michel, then down at Blue.

"There's my girl," he said with a smile.

Blue's tail began wagging even more vigorously.

"So how did this happen?" Michel asked, gesturing at the two of them.

"Oh, I gave her a piece of chicken, and the next thing I knew, she was on her back wanting to get her belly rubbed," Black Jack replied.

Michel looked down at Blue.

"You gave up the belly for a piece of chicken?" he chided. "You tramp."

299

"Don't be calling my granddaughter a tramp," Black Jack said, sitting up.

"Granddaughter?" Michel asked. "Since when did she become your granddaughter?"

"She's yours now, isn't she?" Black Jack replied. "You're my son, so that makes her my granddaughter."

Michel thought about it.

"Yeah, I suppose it does," he said.

"So where did you go to in such a hurry?" Black Jack asked. "I was starting to think it was just a trick to leave me with the dog."

Several pointed replies popped into Michel's head, but he decided not to voice any of them.

"Russ Turner arrested Ruby for Dolores Hagen's murder," Michel replied.

"I can't say as that surprises me," Black Jack replied. "There was always something not right about that woman. But why'd you have to run off so suddenly?"

"It was what you said about the treasure," Michel replied. "I'd originally thought that Verle was framed by someone from Gulf Coast Oil so that they could get the leases to drill on his land, but I was wrong. I was still sure Verle was innocent, but I couldn't figure out why anyone else would frame him."

"So she was just trying to get him out of the way to look for the treasure?" Black Jack asked.

Michel nodded.

"We found her digging. In fact, she'd already dug up three mason jars. Three thousand dollars."

"So Verle actually *was* burying money?" Black Jack replied with disbelief.

"Apparently."

"She in jail now?"

"The hospital," Michel replied. "She tried to cut off Russ' head with a shovel, so I shot her. Twice."

Black Jack gave him an impressed look, then frowned.

"Just doesn't make any sense that she'd do that," he said. "Verle would have given her the money if she'd asked."

"I know," Michel replied. "She's in surgery now. Russ will question her when she wakes up."

Black Jack pulled his legs out from around Blue and swung them over the edge of the couch. He twisted his body from side to side and grimaced slightly.

"I have to admit it feels a little better without the girdle on," he said. "So you still planning to drive back to New Orleans tonight?"

"No, but we'll probably get an early start in the morning."

"Then I guess this is goodbye," Black Jack said, pushing himself up to his feet.

"Yeah," Michel replied, "but I was thinking, how would you feel about moving into Verle's house? It would help me out if there was someone there looking after it."

Black Jack considered it for a few seconds before slowly shaking his head.

"I appreciate it," he said, "but I think I'm better off here near the Gator. If I was out at Verle's, I'd have to start cooking for myself. Plus I've got my friends to look after me. When I didn't show up tonight, Frenchie came looking for me to make sure I wasn't dead."

Michel nodded.

"Well, if you change your mind or need anything else, you've got my number," he said.

They walked to the door.

"I'm thinking maybe just a handshake this time," Michel said. "I'm too tired to get emotional now."

"Me, too," Black Jack replied.

They shook hands, then Black Jack squatted down. Blue walked up to him.

"You take care of your daddy, okay?" Black Jack said.

Blue lowered her head while he scratched her ears for a few seconds, then took a step back and shook her whole body as if trying to throw off the affection.

"I guess that's my cue," Michel said.

"I guess so," Black Jack replied, standing up slowly.

He pushed open the screen door, then looked at Michel.

"You know," he said, "I suspect that if I'd stuck around, I would have turned out a better man, but I'm not sure you would have benefitted much. Seems like you turned out pretty good."

Chapter 35

Michel heard a loud engine rumble into the yard and looked out the window as a white Ford F150 pulled to a stop. It looked like a newer version of Ruby's truck, though not without some dents and rust. Blue jumped up and ran out onto the porch. Michel followed.

"Good morning," Russ Turner called as he stepped out of the truck. "I brought you a present."

"You shouldn't have," Michel replied. "I don't have a thing to wear with it."

The passenger door opened and Corey got out. Blue immediately ran down the stairs and began jumping from side to side in front of him, growling playfully.

"The real present's in the back," Turner said. "But the State Police don't need the truck anymore either."

He walked to the back of the truck and opened the tailgate.

"Verle's computer?" Michel asked, looking at the large brown box marked EVIDENCE, with Verle's name beneath.

"Figured you might want it," Turner replied.

"Thanks," Michel said. "I guess I'll just leave it out here for now. I'm getting ready to pack the car."

Turner nodded, then turned to Corey.

"Corey, why don't you and Blue play out here while I talk with Mr. Doucette," he said.

"Okay," Corey replied. "Come on, Blue."

He pulled a tennis ball from his pocket and threw it up the driveway. Blue dashed after it.

"So how's Ruby?" Michel asked as soon as he and Turner were inside.

"Alive and well and living in Boston," Turner replied.

"Huh?"

"She's a pianist with the Boston Symphony Orchestra."

"Okay," Michel said, shaking his head in confusion, "so who was that you arrested last night?"

"Her name is Eileen Quinn, born in Brockton, Massachusetts, on October 12, 1955. Pretty sad case actually. She was molested by her stepfather when she was five, then bounced around in the foster care system until she was fourteen. Oh, and she's been wanted for killing her husband for eleven years."

"Holy shit," Michel replied.

Turner nodded.

"You have any coffee?"

"Yeah, sure," Michel replied.

He walked into the kitchen and took a mug from the cupboard.

"Quinn's mother remarried when Quinn was fourteen," Turner continued, "so she moved in with them. The new stepfather had a piano, and it turned out that Quinn had talent. She got a scholarship to Berklee in 1974, in the same class with the real Ruby Fish."

"Were they friends?" Michel asked as he handed Turner the coffee.

"More like rivals, at least on Quinn's part," Turner replied. "The real Ruby told the police up in Boston that Quinn seemed to have it out for her. She was always antagonizing her by stealing her sheet music, and called her Ruby Clampett, the Berklee Hillbilly."

"That's sweet," Michel said.

"Anyway, Quinn had a nervous breakdown during her sophomore year and dropped out," Turner replied. "She was institutionalized for a few months, and they diagnosed her as a borderline schizophrenic. She started taking medication and they released her."

"I take it that it didn't work," Michel replied sarcastically.

"It did for quite a while," Turner replied. "She got a job playing with an orchestra in Cambridge, met a rich real estate developer, and got married."

"So what happened?"

"Nine years later, she started going off the deep end again. According to her mother and the husband's friends and family, she began talking about imaginary children, and became paranoid that the husband was planning to leave her. He convinced her to go in for an evaluation, and she was given stronger meds. She seemed to be fine again for a while, but two months later, their housekeeper found the husband stabbed to death. Quinn was gone, along with $120,000 in cash that he kept in a safe."

"So then she came down here and assumed Ruby Fish's identity," Michel said.

"Basically. And it was a perfect situation for her. She didn't need an ID, she didn't have to open a bank account, she paid cash for everything. If she'd moved any place more connected to the grid, she probably couldn't have gotten away with it."

"You never ran a check on her?" Michel asked.

Turner gave him an embarrassed look.

"Well, I never actually arrested her," he said. "When there was trouble, I'd just show up and take her home."

Michel frowned, but didn't say anything.

"I'm sorry," Turner said.

Michel looked down for a moment. He knew there'd been no reason to suspect that Ruby was anyone other than who she'd claimed.

"Did you have a chance to question her?" he asked.

Turner nodded.

"She was actually pretty talkative once they put her on the morphine drip."

"So why did she do it?" Michel asked. "Why didn't she just ask Verle for the money."

"She was convinced that Verle was planning to leave her."

"Leave her? But they weren't a couple."

"In Ruby's mind...I mean, Quinn's mind...they were," Turner replied. "She said they'd been married for ten years, but lived in separate houses for tax purposes. But she said that Verle told her he'd met someone else and was planning to move to New Orleans."

"New Orleans?" Michel replied. "You think that was just part of her fantasy?"

"I don't know," Turner replied. "She said she checked his email and found out that he'd been writing to someone named Severin in New Orleans."

"Severin Marchand," Michel said.

"You know him?" Turner asked.

"Yeah, casually. He was a client," Michel replied. "When we visited Verle in jail, he told me that Severin was the one feeding him information about me."

"So is this Severin Marchand gay?"

"Very. Why?"

"Quinn said that Verle was leaving her for a man," Turner said.

"Verle wasn't gay," Michel replied. "Was he?"

"Not that I ever knew," Turner replied. "Then again, I didn't know about Donny and his truck driver fetish either."

Michel thought about for a few moments, then shook his head.

"I don't buy it," he said. "First of all, I don't think Verle was gay. And second of all, Marchand wouldn't have been interested in him even if he was."

"Why not?"

"Marchand is into twinks."

"Twinks?"

"Cute skinny young guys," Michel replied. "Verle definitely wasn't that."

"You could check it out on Verle's computer," Turner said.

"Believe me, I will," Michel replied. "I've been wanting to see those emails since Verle told me about them. I'll let you know what I find out."

Turner nodded.

"So I don't get why Quinn killed Dolores Hagen and tried to frame Verle," Michel asked. "That's a big jump from being paranoid that he's going to leave."

"Quinn said that Verle had been hiring hookers online for a long time," Turner replied. "She said she allowed it because they weren't intimate, but once she found out he was planning to leave her, she decided to punish him. She figured she could use his hooker habit against him."

"You think she was telling the truth about the hookers?"

"No," Turner replied. "The Staties said he never even looked at porn on his computer. There was only one visit to an escort site, and that was the one Hagen was on."

"How is it that Verle never saw the emails between Quinn and Hagen?" Michel asked.

"Quinn set up a separate email account. Verle probably never knew it was there."

Michel studied his coffee for a moment.

"When we met, you said you didn't think Ruby was really that crazy. That some of it was an act," he said. "You think she's acting now?"

"That's a good question," Turner replied. "I mean she was legitimately diagnosed as schizophrenic, but the timing of the crime seems pretty calculated. The troopers found just a little over $1,000 at her place. She was almost out of money."

"And she started digging up those jars as soon as she

thought I was gone," Michel added. "That doesn't seem too crazy to me."

"I guess that's going to be up to a jury to decide," Turner replied. "Either way, she's not going to be getting out for a long time. The DA in Massachusetts wants her to stand trial up there first, then she'll have to come back down here to be tried for Hagen's murder. That'll take at least a few years. I suspect she'll spend the rest of her life either behind bars or in an institution."

"I hope so," Michel replied. "So that's it, then."

"Seems like," Turner agreed.

"Then I guess this is goodbye," Michel said.

"Not quite," Turner replied. "You think you could give us a ride back to town?"

Michel nodded, then thought about it for a second.

"Actually, why don't you just keep the truck?" he said. "Corey's going to start driving pretty soon."

"Oh no," Turner replied, shaking his head emphatically. "I don't want him driving around in that. He'll be out racing around on the back roads. Besides, it's a standard. Thanks, but no thanks."

"Oh come on," Michel cajoled. "He'd love it."

"I'm sure he would," Turner replied with a laugh, "but I want him in something sensible...like your little Honda."

"I'm not giving you my car," Michel replied with a laugh.

"And I wasn't asking," Turner replied.

"Still..." Michel said.

He walked to the window and looked out at the truck.

"It probably wouldn't even fit in my driveway," he said more to himself than Turner.

"But it has that nifty gun rack," Turner teased.

"Just what I need in the city," Michel replied.

He looked at the truck for a few seconds more, then turned back to Turner.

"You know what? Why *don't* you take the Honda?"

"No, that's crazy," Turner protested. "I don't need it. Corey won't even be driving for another year."

"Consider it a favor to me," Michel replied. "It'll save me having to drive you home. You can just hold onto it for me. Then when Corey's ready to drive, we can work something out if you want it."

Turner shrugged.

"Okay, if that's what you really want."

Michel studied at him for a moment.

"Wait a second, did you just hustle me?" he asked. "Were you trying to get my car all along?"

"Of course not," Turner replied with mock indignation. "But I ended up with it anyway."

"Seems to me that someone's been taking lessons from Cyrus," Michel said.

Turner just smiled in reply.

"So what's next for you?" he asked.

"I'm not sure," Michel replied.

"I'm guessing you don't need to work anymore, if you don't want to," Turner said.

"I suppose not," Michel said, "but I can't see myself spending my days cultivating orchids and lunching with the ladies. I think I need to work."

"So back to Jones and Doucette Investigations?"

"I don't know," Michel replied. "I was thinking that maybe it's time for me to go back to being a cop."

Turner gave him a surprised look.

"Is that even an option?"

Michel nodded.

"After Katrina, a lot of cops quit," he replied. "A few weeks ago, our old captain offered us our jobs back."

"You think Sassy would do it?" Turner asked.

"She didn't seem too interested at the time," Michel replied, "but who knows?"

"Well, if it happens, I think NOPD will be lucky to have you," Turner said.

"Thanks," Michel said. "Thanks for everything. It was a pleasure working with you, Russ."

"Thank you," Turner replied "You, too. Though I have to admit I'm glad you're leaving so things can go back to normal."

"Thanks a lot," Michel replied.

"Hey, no offense," Turner replied, "but until you showed up, I'd only been hit by one suspect in almost thirty years, and no one had ever tried to cut off my head with a shovel."

Michel smiled.

"Yeah, I suppose I am kind of a magnet for that type of shit," he said.

Chapter 36

Blue poked her head around the corner of the doorway and began quickly sniffing the air.

"Oh fuck!" Chance yelled when he saw her, reflexively sliding back in his chair.

"What?" Sassy asked, looking up from her desk.

She followed Chance's nervous gaze. Blue took a few steps into the room and yawned loudly.

"Oh my God, aren't you the sweetest thing?" Sassy said.

She got up and walked into the center of the room, then squatted down. Blue's tail began to wag as she walked shyly over to Sassy and sniffed her hand. Then she nestled her head into Sassy's chest and Sassy began scratching her neck.

Michel stepped around the corner.

"Hey, when did you get back?" Sassy asked with a wide, warm smile.

"About two hours ago," Michel replied, "but I had to run some errands. It didnt occur to me until we got to the house that Blue didn't even have a collar or leash. She saw Mrs. Bell walking her little puffball, Bonnie, and almost jumped out the window to go after it."

"Oh oh," Sassy said.

"I don't think they'll be friends," Michel said dryly.

"What's with the wolf?" Chance asked. "Did you befriend it in the swamp? Are you like 'Prances with Wolves' now?"

"Do you want to be like 'Unemployed with No Job'?" Michel replied narrowing his eyes. "Nice to see you, too."

Sassy gave Blue another few scratches, then stood up. Michel immediately walked over and wrapped his arms around her.

"Ummm, what's this all about?" Sassy asked, holding her arms rigidly at her sides with her left cheek pressed against Michel's chest.

"Nothing," Michel replied. "I just missed you. Is it wrong to show affection to the people I love?"

Sassy relaxed a little and put her hands around Michel's waist for a few seconds. Then Michel let go of her and took a step back, smiling.

"That wasn't so bad, was it?" he asked.

Sassy shrugged noncommittally.

"Well don't be trying to hug on me," Chance said.

"Don't worry," Michel replied. "I said the people I love."

Then he smiled and walked over to Chance.

"Come on, give me a hug," he said opening his arms.

Chance stayed in his chair for a few moments, then sighed and stood up, looking like a child being forced to kiss an aunt with a hairy mole on her cheek.

"Welcome back," he said, rolling his eyes as Michel hugged him. "I just hope whatever's gotten into you wears off soon."

"Thank you," Michel said as he let him go.

Chance walked to the corner of his desk and knelt down, holding his right hand out toward Blue. She took a few steps forward, then stopped and let out a low growl.

"Whoa," Chance replied, jerking his hand back and jumping to his feet.

"Guess she's a pretty good judge of character," Sassy said.

"Don't take it personally," Michel said. "Have you had a smoke recently?"

Chance nodded.

"Yeah, she's not a big fan of cigarettes," Michel said.

"Then she must love being around you," Chance replied.

"Actually, I haven't had one in a few days," Michel replied.

"Seriously?" Sassy asked.

Michel shrugged and nodded.

"You quit just like that?"

"Well, I have to admit it was a lot easier while I was still in Bayou Proche," Michel said. "It wasn't my normal life, so I didn't have the usual smoking cues. Since I got back within the city limits, though, it's all I've been able to think about. But so far, so good."

"What a good girl you are," Sassy said in a high-pitched coo, waving Blue back over to her. "You got Daddy to quit smoking."

"Uh, baby voice," Michel said.

Sassy gave him a withering look.

"Was I talking to you?"

"Sorry," Michel replied, putting his hands up defensively.

"No, I wasn't talking to him, was I?" Sassy said, leaning close so Blue could lick her face. "This is just girl talk. Don't know why these men have to be getting all in our business."

She rubbed the sides of Blue's face for a minute, then Blue pulled away and sauntered to a patch of sun by the window. She lay down with a grunt.

"She doesn't like too much affection." Michel said.

"Like father like daughter," Sassy said.

"Hey, who's the one who got all uptight when I gave her a hug?" Michel countered.

Sassy gave him a sour smile.

"So the fact that you're back must mean you figured out what was going on," she said. "Did you prove that Gulf Oil tried to blackmail Terry?"

"Nope, because it was his father," Michel replied.

"His father?"

"Long story. I'll tell you later," Michel replied. "But I did manage to prove that Verle was framed."

"By who?" Sassy asked.

"Ruby," Michel replied. "Well, actually a woman named Eileen Quinn who was pretending to be Ruby."

"Okay, you've got a lot to tell me," Sassy replied.

"And I will," Michel replied, "but not right now. Right now I'm going to take Blue for a walk in Armstrong Park, then I'm taking the rest of the day off."

"Because you've been working so hard," Chance interjected.

"I have been working hard," Michel replied. "I just haven't been getting paid for it."

"Well, I wouldn't take her to Armstrong, if I were you," Chance replied. "Last night I heard some guy at the Bourbon Pub say his dog got bitten by a fire ant over there. Said it was really painful."

"Fire ants?" Michel replied. "Shit, I figured I wouldn't have to worry about killer wildlife once we got out of Bayou Proche. Okay, so maybe we'll just go for a walk around the Marigny instead. Try to get her acclimated to city life."

"And what about Joel?" Sassy asked.

Michel nodded.

"I'm going to invite him over tonight."

"And do you know what you're going to say?"

"Yup, but you're just going to have to wait to find out," Michel replied.

Sassy scowled at him in reply.

"So anything here I need to know about?" Michel asked.

"Nothing urgent," Sassy replied. "It can wait until tomorrow."

"No more disappearing money?" Michel asked.

"No. And it turns out the money never really disappeared," Sassy replied. "It just got transferred from our checking to our reserve account temporarily for some reason."

"For some reason?" Michel replied, looking at Chance pointedly.

"Hey, it wasn't me," Chance replied. "The bank did it. They just won't admit it."

"Uh huh," Michel replied doubtfully.

He turned to Blue.

"You ready to go for a walk?" he asked.

Blue jumped up and began jittering excitedly.

"You want to come with?" Michel asked Sassy.

"I think I'll pass," Sassy replied. "Auntie Sassy does not pick up poop."

Michel gave her a curious look.

"You mean I'm supposed to pick it up?" he said with a squeamish grimace. "No wonder the neighbors gave me such dirty looks."

*****

Michel got into the truck and hit the speed dial for Joel's number on his cell phone.

"Hey, it's me," he said after the voice mail message finished. "I was hoping you could come over to the house tonight around seven. There's someone I want you to meet. If you don't reach me, just leave me a message letting me know if you can make it."

Chapter 37

When the doorbell rang a few minutes after 7 PM, Blue jumped up from the floor and scurried into the bedroom. Michel got up from the couch and walked to the bedroom door.

"It's okay, *Nell*," he joked in a soothing voice. "It's called a doorbell. That's what we use around here instead of knocking."

He looked around curiously, then noticed Blue's tail protruding from under the drapes to the left of the windows. It thumped twice, but Blue remained in hiding. Michel smiled and continued down the hall, feeling a flutter of anticipation.

"Hey," he said as he opened the door.

"Hey," Joel replied with a nervous smile.

He looked more rested than he had the last time Michel had seen him, and his hair was cut very short. It made him look older, but in a good way. Michel fought the urge to grab him and kiss him.

"Come on in," he said instead.

"So whose truck is that?" Joel asked, looking around.

"Mine," Michel replied.

"Oh, I thought maybe it belonged to whoever you wanted me to meet."

"No, she can't drive," Michel replied with a small laugh.

Joel gave him a curious look.

"So did you get rid of the Honda?" he asked.

"No, I just left it in Bayou Proche," Michel replied. "That was Verle's truck."

"I was really sorry to hear about him," Joel replied.

"Thanks," Michel replied. "How's your grandfather?"

"Much better," Joel replied. "He's still moving a little slowly but otherwise..."

He stopped suddenly, and his eyes darted over Michel's right shoulder.

"Holy shit," he said.

Michel turned and saw Blue standing in the bedroom doorway.

"That's Blue," Michel said. "She was Verle's, too."

He stepped aside.

"Come on, Blue," he encouraged. "Come meet Joel."

Joel got down on his knees and held out his right hand. Blue came forward slowly, her ears back and her head low. When she reached Joel's hand, she sniffed it carefully, then gave it a small lick.

"Hey girl," Joel said. "Pleased to meet you."

Blue sat and held up her left paw. Joel laughed and shook it.

"Does she do other tricks?" he asked.

"Not that I've seen," Michel replied, "but she's pretty handy when someone's got a knife on you."

Joel's eyebrows raised in alarm.

"I'll tell you all about it later," Michel replied with a reassuring smile.

Joel looked back at Blue.

"So are you going to let me pet you?" he asked, edging forward.

Blue turned her head away, but stayed sitting. Joel began scratching the white star on her chest.

"She's really soft," he said. "So is this who you wanted me to meet?"

"That's her," Michel replied.

"I thought maybe you'd found a husband," Joel replied with exaggerated relief.

317

"Just a daughter," Michel replied. "You want something to drink?"

"Sure," Joel replied.

He pushed himself up onto his feet. Blue stood up, too.

"What would you like?" Michel asked.

"That depends," Joel replied.

"On?"

"On whether this is going to be a good conversation or a bad conversation."

"Well, you won't really know that until we have it, right?" Michel replied.

"Good point," Joel replied quickly.

From his tone, it was obvious he was anxious.

"Then I guess I'll have a beer," he said.

"You got it," Michel replied.

He walked into the kitchen. Joel and Blue followed him to the door. Michel grabbed a Dos Equis from the refrigerator, uncapped it, and handed it to Joel.

"You're not having anything?" Joel asked.

"I've already got a drink in the living room," Michel replied.

They walked down the hallway, Blue staying by Joel's side, then sat on the edge of the couch, facing one another. Blue lay down near Joel's feet.

"So, I've decided I don't want to give it another try," Michel said immediately, looking Joel in the eyes.

Joel took a quick sip of his beer and swallowed hard.

"I understand," he said.

He swallowed again and his lower lip quivered slightly.

"No, you don't," Michel said. "I mean I don't want to just try. That's not good enough. Try is like, 'I'm going to try to be a better person.' It sucks. If we're going to do this, then let's just do it. If it doesn't work out, then it doesn't work out. But let's commit to it."

Joel stared at him open-mouthed for a second.

"First of all," he said finally, "you're an asshole for fucking with me like that. Second of all, are you serious?"

"First of all, I'm sorry," Michel said, "and second of all, yes, I'm serious."

"So what does that mean exactly?" Joel asked.

"I hope that means you and me together, forsaking all others, forever and ever, Amen," Michel replied. "But for starters, I want us to live together, although if you want to wait until after the move that's fine."

"You're moving?" Joel asked.

"Blue needs a place with a bigger yard," Michel replied. "In Bayou Proche she had free reign to go wherever she wanted. I think she's going to go crazy here. Or drive me crazy."

"Wow," Joel said. "You need to go away more often. It's like a whole new you."

"Are you saying there was something wrong with the old me?" Michel asked, cocking his head to one side and raising his right eyebrow.

"No, not at all," Joel replied with a laugh. "I love the old you. But this is pretty amazing. It's really exciting."

"So is that a yes?" Michel asked.

"Of course it's a yes," Joel replied.

"Good," Michel replied. "I was afraid that maybe you'd come to your senses while you were in Natchez and change your mind about me."

"Not a chance," Joel replied. "So is this the part where we kiss?"

"I hope so," Michel replied.

He leaned forward, then stopped and looked down at Blue. She was staring up at them, her tongue hanging from the left side of her mouth.

"Close your eyes," Michel said. "You're too young to see this."

Chapter 38

"So, where's Joel?" Sassy asked.

"Probably picking out china patterns," Michel replied with a warm laugh.

"He's pretty excited, huh?"

"That's an understatement."

"And you?" Sassy asked, raising her eyebrows expectantly.

Michel took a sip of his drink and thought about it.

"I'm very happy and contented," he said finally.

"Are you sure you're really Michel Doucette?" Sassy asked. "Not some pod person who got sent back in his place?"

Michel gave her an appreciative smile.

"Yeah, I'm sure."

"So how are things working out with Blue?" Sassy asked.

"Not bad," Michel said. "Mrs. Bell has stopped talking to me since Blue tried to turn Bonnie into a chew toy, but otherwise okay. She gets along with most of the other dogs in the neighborhood, and she made a few friends at Cabrini Playground this morning."

"That's good," Sassy said.

"Yeah, though I'm looking forward to having a bigger yard for her to play in," Michel said. "Walks are painful. She stops to sniff every five feet. Apparently there are a lot of really interesting scents around here."

"And you probably don't want to know what they are," Sassy said, shaking her head.

"I'm sure of that," Michel replied.

"You know, you're still going to have to walk her, right?" Sassy asked.

"Yeah," Michel replied with a sigh, "but I'm hoping we can get it down to three times a day. Right now she wants to go out every hour."

"Well, the exercise is probably good for both of you," Sassy said.

"I suppose," Michel replied unenthusiastically.

"So have you found any places you want to look at?" Sassy asked.

"Not yet," Michel replied. "Porter DeCew said it would be at least six months before I got any money from Verle's estate. I figure there's no reason to start looking until then."

Sassy nodded and took a sip of her white wine.

"You had a pretty eventful week," she said. "Losing a cousin, gaining a father, dog, and husband, unraveling a mystery, and solving a crime."

"Not to mention meeting your cousin Pearl," Michel added.

"Let's not go there," Sassy replied, narrowing her eyes in warning.

"Fine," Michel replied. "But she's a lovely woman. And very informative."

Sassy scowled comically.

"So what are you going to do for a follow-up?" she asked.

"Actually, I wanted to talk with you about that," Michel replied.

"Oh oh. That sounds like trouble," Sassy replied, sitting up straighter. "Am I going to like this?"

Michel shrugged. "Probably not."

"Then I'm going to need some more wine," Sassy said.

"Could you get me a refill while you're at it?" Michel asked, holding up his glass.

Sassy stared at him with a deadpan expression.

"Do I look like your maid?" she asked. "This is your house, and I'm your guest. I was expecting you to get up and get me more wine."

"Oh, sorry," Michel replied sheepishly, standing up.

"Just because you're rich now doesn't mean that you can just be ordering us regular folks around," Sassy said.

"I said I was sorry," Michel replied. "Geez, you poor people are so touchy."

"I didn't say I was poor," Sassy replied. "I said I was regular."

Michel grabbed Sassy's glass and walked into the house. Blue was lying in the hallway, a few feet from the front door. It had become her regular spot whenever Joel left the house.

"Why don't you come outside?" Michel asked. "It's nice out. Maybe a rat will run across the top of the wall."

Blue raised her head to look at him, then dropped it with a groan.

"Joel's okay," Michel said. "I promise."

He walked into the kitchen and poured Sassy's wine, then freshened his own drink and went back out on the patio.

"Here you go, madame," he said, handing her the glass with a slight bow.

"Enough with your nonsense," Sassy said. "Sit your ass down and tell me what's going on."

Michel gave her a faux pout, then sat.

"I've been thinking about taking DeRoche up on his offer and rejoining the force," he said.

"Oh Lord," Sassy said. "And why would you want to do that?"

"To help people," Michel replied. "I mean, isn't that why we became cops in the first place?"

"We're helping people now," Sassy replied.

"But only people who can afford to pay," Michel countered. "There are a lot of people who need help who can't pay."

Sassy sighed.

"Did that Russ Turner put this in your head?" she asked.

"No," Michel replied defensively, "but while I was working with him, I realized that I missed being a real cop."

Sassy studied him for a moment.

"Look, Michel," she said. "You've got a good thing going right now. You've got Joel, you've got Blue. In a few months you're going to have money and a new house. Why do you want to fuck it up by being a cop again?"

"Was it really that bad?" Michel asked.

"Are you forgetting about the hours?" Sassy asked with disbelief. "Do you really want to go back to getting calls in the middle of the night, and working 24/7 for weeks on end? Not to mention getting shot at."

"Well, it's not like that hasn't happened since we left the force," Michel replied.

They were both quiet for a few seconds. Sassy took a long sip of wine.

"You can do what you want to," she said finally, "but don't expect me to join you. I'm done being a cop. I like my life the way it is now."

"Come on," Michel said. "You can't tell me you don't miss it. Even a little?"

"I loved being a cop," Sassy replied. "I was proud of what I did. But no, I don't miss it. Not even a little."

Michel suspected she was being less than honest, but decided not to push it.

"Just do me a favor and wait before you make a decision," Sassy said. "Wait until you get the money and buy the house, and you and Joel have settled in. Who knows, maybe you'll like it so much that you won't want to be a cop anymore. Maybe you'll just want to go shopping and hang out in bars like Severin Marchand."

"Oh shit, I almost forgot," Michel said. "I read the emails."

"Between Verle and Marchand?" Sassy asked.

Michel nodded.

"And?"

"And they were kind of creepy," Michel replied.

"Creepy how?"

"Well, they started off innocuously enough, but over time Marchand started pumping Verle for information on me. For every one thing he told Verle, he'd ask two or three questions."

"About what?" Sassy asked.

"My family," Michel replied. "He seemed pretty curious about family history, relatives, and especially my parents and my childhood."

"That's odd," Sassy replied. "Why would he want to know about that? Especially since you didn't know him until a few weeks ago."

"Gossip, probably," Michel replied. "That kind of dirt is like gold to a bitchy queen."

"Did Verle tell him anything?"

"He was pretty vague about the details," Michel replied, "though he did tell him my father was still alive. I'm sure Marchand had a grand old time telling his cronies that tidbit."

"And you're sure it actually *was* Marchand?" Sassy asked.

Michel nodded.

"The email address is SeverinIV@yahoo.com, he said he lived on Royal but had a family estate in the Garden District, and he made all sorts of references to having a lot of money. It had to be Marchand."

"Hmmm," Sassy said with a concerned frown. "And what about the romance? Was there really something going on between them?"

"Not that I could see," Michel replied. "They certainly weren't making any plans to get together."

"So Ruby imagined that," Sassy said.

"Or Verle had the hots for some other guy in New Orleans."

"Are you going to call Marchand?" Sassy asked.

Michel shook his head.

"No. I don't have any burning desire to talk with him, but if I run into him, I'll tell him Verle's dead."

Sassy nodded, then they were both quiet again for a few moments. Finally Michel leaned forward in his chair.

"All right," he said. "I'll wait."

"Thank you," Sassy replied.

"But if I still want to do it, will you reconsider?" Michel asked, giving Sassy his best imploring puppy dog eyes.

Sassy stared down at the flagstones for a moment, then looked up and nodded slightly.

"Yeah," she said with a sigh. "I'll think about it."

Available Spring 2012
from

RECKONING

A New Michel Doucette
& Sassy Jones Novel

DAVID LENNON

Chapter 1

As he drifted toward consciousness, Michel Doucette realized he was having trouble breathing. A heavy weight pressed down on his chest. He took a deep breath, held it for a few seconds, then exhaled loudly.

"Good morning, Blue," he said without opening his eyes.

He heard a sound like the beating of huge butterfly wings and felt the mattress vibrate. He knew the dog's tail was beating out a quick cadence somewhere near his feet. He opened his eyes and stared into the light brown and yellow speckled eyes only a few inches away. As always, the dog's expression looked slightly anxious, as though she'd been afraid he might not wake up.

"How are you?" he asked gently. "Did you have a good sleep?"

The dog responded by jabbing her nose against his and darting her tongue quickly into his right nostril, then pulled her head back and continued staring at him.

"Thanks," Michel replied with a combination of mock revulsion and genuine affection. "I'll take that as a yes,"

He pulled his right arm from under the blanket and began rubbing the scruff on the left side of the dog's neck. She responded as she always did—by turning her head away from him as though she didn't welcome his affection, while at the same time pressing into his hand more heavily.

"Okay, Greta Garbo," he said after a minute. "I suppose you want to go outside?"

Blue responded by increasing the rhythm of her tail, which now thumped loudly against the comforter.

"Well, I can't get up with you lying on me," Michel replied.

The dog gave him another quick lick on the nose, then jumped up excitedly and bounded from the bed toward the door. She paused for a moment and looked back at him expectantly.

"I'm coming," Michel said, rolling his eyes. "Why didn't you just have Joel let you out if you're in such a hurry?"

"Because you open the door so much better than I do," Joel's voice called from down the hall. "Besides, it's about time you got your lazy ass out of bed."

Michel smiled and threw back the comforter.

"Give me a second," he said to Blue. "I have to take care of some business."

He pushed himself up and shuffled into the bathroom, straightening the waistband of his boxer shorts as he went and wondering for the thousandth time how they got so twisted while he slept. He closed the bathroom door and stood in front of the toilet. He could hear Blue pacing in the bedroom while he emptied his bladder, her nails lightly clicking on the cypress floor.

"Okay, okay," he said as he shook off and flushed the toilet. "I'm coming."

As soon as he opened the bathroom door, Blue bolted from the bedroom and down the hall. Michel followed her at a more leisurely pace.

"Good morning, sunshine," Joel said with a faux sincere, morning-TV-anchor smile.

He was standing in the entrance to the kitchen, dressed only in a pair of low slung, baggy gray sweatpants, and holding out a mug of coffee.

"Morning," Michel replied with exaggerated grumpiness, despite the fact that seeing Joel made him want to smile.

He took the coffee and gave Joel a light kiss.

"What time is it, anyway?" he asked.

"Almost eight," Joel replied.

"What time did you get up?" Michel asked as he headed for the back of the house.

Blue was standing inside the French doors, her body taut with excitement. Michel opened the far left door and she charged outside.

"About six," Joel replied as he came up behind Michel.

"Why so early on a Saturday?" Michel asked.

"I wanted to go for a run before it got too hot," Joel replied.

"That explains that stink," Michel said with an impish smirk as he walked out to the patio.

"Very funny," Joel replied. "I already showered. You're probably smelling yourself."

Michel made a show of lifting both arms and sniffing.

"Not me," he said, shaking his head. "I smell like sunshine and lollipops, just like always."

He dropped down into one of the wrought iron chairs and immediately felt the craving for a cigarette. It had been six months since his last one, and while he didn't think about smoking most of the time, he still longed for a cigarette with his first cup of coffee every morning. He took a deep breath to remind himself how much better he'd felt since he quit.

Blue finished patrolling the walled perimeter of the garden and settled down in front of the center fountain.

"Good girl," Michel said. "Did you scare away all those dangerous killer squirrels?"

Blue looked at him and seemed to smile proudly, then lowered her head between her front paws and blew out a loud sigh that stirred the dust in front of her nose.

Michel felt a surge of affection and smiled. It continually amazed him how much his life had changed in the six months since his cousin Verle had died. At the time he'd been living alone, his relationship with Joel had been stuck in a seemingly perpetual state of limbo, his professional life was in transition after leaving the New Orleans Police Department, he thought he'd lost his last living relative, and at best he could have said that he wasn't unhappy with his life.

Since then, everything had changed. Since then, he'd been on a roll: he'd become a "father" to Blue, Verle's dog; his relationship with Joel was thriving; the private investigation firm he'd started with his former police partner and best friend, Sassy, was turning a profit; he'd met his father and begun building a tenuous relationship with him; and he'd inherited a substantial fortune. Most importantly, though, he felt happy and contented. Still, even at his happiest moments, like now, he couldn't help but worry that the other shoe was about to drop.

Maybe the other shoe will just be that I'll become a fat, boring, middle aged man, he thought.

"So what do you want to do today?" Joel asked.

Michel looked at him and raised his eyebrows mischievously.

"Guess," he replied.

"Gee, would it have anything to do with real estate?" Joel replied sarcastically.

Michel had been on an obsessive quest to find a new house with a larger yard since Blue had come to live with him.

"Ding, ding, ding," Michel replied in a sharp, nasal voice like a cartoon carnival barker. "We have a winner, folks."

Joel gave him a deadpan look.

"And apparently a great big loser, too," he said.

Michel gave a self-satisfied smile.

"You really want to look at houses again?" Joel asked with a slight note of protest. "We have to have seen every house in New Orleans by now."

He was leaving the next morning for a three-day seminar on antisocial personality disorder in Orlando, and didn't relish the idea of spending the day house hunting.

"Not quite," Michel replied. "There's one more. Though technically it's not really a house. I swear it'll only take an hour."

Joel gave a resigned sigh.

"This is a sickness, you know," he said, shaking his head tolerantly. "You really need to get some help."

"Well, that'll give you something to talk about at the seminar," Michel replied.

*****

"So what do you think?" Michel asked.

The overly solicitous realtor had just stepped outside to take a call.

"It's kind of...gothic, don't you think?" Joel replied doubtfully.

"Of course it's gothic," Michel replied. "It was a church. But just picture it without the bench-thingies and the stained glass windows."

"You can't get rid of the windows," Joel protested.

"Why not?"

"Because they're probably historic," Joel replied.

"So we can donate them to a museum," Michel replied. "And we can get rid of the big cross, though Jesus does look kind of sexy..."

"You're just not right," Joel said, shaking his head.

"...And we could have a big living room over here," Michel continued excitedly, "with a pool table over there. Then we could put the dining room back there on the left and the kitchen on the right, and we could build a half wall and put our bedroom up there."

"On the alter?" Joel replied with disbelief.

Michel shrugged innocently.

"What?"

"You want to put our bedroom on the alter?" Joel replied.

"The place where we'll be having sex? On the alter? Where they performed marriages and baptisms and funerals?"

"So?" Michel replied.

"So that's sacrilegious," Joel replied.

"Not any more it isn't," Michel replied. "The whole place has been desanctified, or whatever you call it."

Joel just stared at him in reply.

"Okay, fine," Michel replied, turning around. "Then we can put our bedroom up there where the band played."

"The choir loft," Joel interjected.

"The *choir loft*," Michel corrected himself, "and we could put the dining room up on the alter since that would go with the whole 'this is my body, eat it, this is my blood, drink it' thing. Then we could turn the priests' dressing room into a guest room."

"It's called a vestry," Joel replied.

"Okay, alter boy," Michel replied. "So what do you think?"

"I think it would be a lot of work to make it seem like a home," Joel replied.

"But it could be fun," Michel countered, "and we could work on it together. You've got a month before school starts again."

Joel had started at Tulane University the previous fall, pursuing a degree in criminal psychology, but had been forced to miss the spring semester to help care for his grandfather back home in Natchez, MS. He was starting classes again in September.

He shook his head slowly.

"I don't know."

"The location is great," Michel replied, not ready to give up his sales pitch yet, "and it's got a huge yard that's already walled in for Blue. Plus we could dig up the parking area and put in a pool."

Joel's eyes lit up a little but he kept his expression neutral.

"And you're sure that yard isn't an old graveyard?" he asked. "I can just imagine Blue coming to the door with someone's arm in her mouth."

"I'm sure," Michel replied, laughing.

Joel looked around at the bare stone walls and up at the high vaulted ceiling. He had to admit it really was quite striking, though he couldn't imagine how they were ever going to make the space seem intimate.

"I think before you make an offer you should bring in a contractor to find out how much everything would cost," he said.

"Fine," Michel replied. "I can do it while you're in Orlando. And I was thinking about asking Ray to draw up some plans."

Ray Nassir was an architect who had been dating Joel's best friend, Chance, for the past seven months.

"I wouldn't mention that to Chance just now," Joel replied.

"Why not?"

"He just dumped Ray's ass. Apparently Ray didn't consider things to be quite as monogamous as Chance did."

Michel frowned. Although his relationship with Chance had been somewhat contentious in the beginning, and still had a fair amount of competitive antagonism, he actually liked Chance quite a bit.

"That sucks," he said, "though I wasn't actually planning to mention it to Chance anyway."

Joel gave him a look that was both curious and suspicious.

"And why's that?" he asked.

Michel averted his eyes for a moment, then looked up sheepishly.

"Well, because I think that maybe he was planning to buy this place and convert it to apartments," he replied in a small voice.

In addition to managing the office and finances for Michel and Sassy, Chance had used money he'd inherited from his grandfather to start a property development company that specialized in renovating old buildings for affordable housing.

"Michel!" Joel exclaimed.

"I don't know that he was definitely planning it," Michel replied defensively. "I just happened to notice the listing on his desk while he was at lunch yesterday."

Joel shook his head and gave Michel a chastening look.

"You need to talk to him," he said.

Michel looked at the ground for a moment, then nodded reluctantly.

"Fine," he said. "I'll call him this afternoon."

Joel had to fight the urge to laugh at Michel's sullen expression. He looked like a kid who'd just been told he had to tell the cranky neighbor that he'd broken his window.

"Okay, you can wait until Monday," Joel said. "I suppose he's already got enough to be pissed off about right now."

"Thanks," Michel replied without enthusiasm.

"By the way," Joel said, "I hope you don't mind, but I made plans with Chance tonight. I figured he needed a girls' night out."

"No, that's fine," Michel said. "Maybe I'll call Sassy and see if she wants to play."

Made in the USA
Lexington, KY
30 October 2011